Australian ESCAPE

ESCAPE
COLLECTION

April 2017

May 2017

June 2017

July 2017

August 2017

September 2017

Australian
ESCAPE

Ally
BLAKE *Amy*
ANDREWS *Michelle*
DOUGLAS

MILLS & BOON

Published in Great Britain 2017
By Mills & Boon, an imprint of HarperCollins*Publishers*
1 London Bridge Street, London, SE1 9GF

AUSTRALIAN ESCAPE © 2017 Harlequin Books S.A.

Her Hottest Summer Yet © 2014 Ally Blake
The Heat of the Night © 2014 Amy Andrews
Road Trip with the Eligible Bachelor © 2014 Michelle Douglas

ISBN: 978-0-263-93103-7

09-0717

Our policy is to use papers that are natural, renewable and recyclable products and made from wood grown in sustainable forests.
The logging and manufacturing processes conform to the legal environmental regulations of the country of origin.

Printed and bound in Spain
by CPI, Barcelona

HER HOTTEST
SUMMER YET

ALLY BLAKE

In her previous life Australian author **Ally Blake** was at times a cheerleader, a maths tutor, a dental assistant and a shop assistant. In this life she is a bestselling, multi-award-winning novelist who has been published in over twenty languages with more than two million books sold worldwide.

She married her gorgeous husband in Las Vegas – no Elvis in sight, though Tony Curtis did put in a special appearance – and now Ally and her family, including three rambunctious toddlers, share a property in the leafy western suburbs of Brisbane, with kookaburras, cockatoos, rainbow lorikeets and the occasional creepy-crawly. When not writing, she makes coffees that never get drunk, eats too many M&Ms, attempts yoga, devours *The West Wing* reruns, reads every spare minute she can and barracks ardently for the Collingwood Magpies footy team.

You can find out more at her website, www.allyblake.com

CHAPTER ONE

AVERY SHAW BARELY noticed the salty breeze whipping pale blonde hair across her face and fluttering the diaphanous layers of her dress against her legs. She was blissfully deep in a whirlpool of warm, hazy, happy memories as she stood on the sandy footpath and beamed up at the facade of the Tropicana Nights Resort.

She lifted a hand to shield her eyes from the shimmering Australian summer sun, and breathed the place in. It was bigger than she remembered, and more striking. Like some great white colonial palace, uprooted out of another era and transplanted to the pretty beach strip that was Crescent Cove. The garden now teetered on the wild side, and its facade was more than a little shabby around the edges. But ten years did that to a place.

Things changed. She was hardly the naive sixteen-year-old with the knobbly knees she'd been the summer she was last there. Back when all that mattered was friends, and fun, and—

A loud whoosh and rattle behind her tugged Avery back to the present. She glanced down the curving sidewalk to see a group of skinny brown-skinned boys in board shorts hurtling across the road on their skateboards before running down the beach and straight into the sparkling blue water of the Pacific.

And sometimes, she thought with a pleasant tightening in her lungs, *things don't change much at all*.

Lungs full to bursting with the taste of salt and sea and expectation, Avery and her Vuitton luggage set bumped merrily up the wide front steps and into the lobby. Huge faux marble columns held up the two-storey ceiling. Below sat cushy lounge chairs, colossal rugs, and potted palms dotted a floor made of the most beautiful swirling mosaic tiles in a million sandy tones. And by the archway leading to the restaurant beyond sat an old-fashioned noticeboard shouting out: Two-For-One Main Courses at the Capricorn Café For Any Guests Sporting an Eye Patch!

She laughed, the sound bouncing about in the empty space. For the lobby was empty, which for a beach resort at the height of summer seemed odd. But everyone was probably at the pool. Or having siestas in their rooms. And considering the hustle and bustle Avery had left behind in Manhattan, it was a relief.

Deeper inside the colossal entrance, reception loomed by way of a long sandstone desk with waves carved into the side. Behind said desk stood a young woman with deep red hair pulled back into a long sleek ponytail, her name tag sporting the Tropicana Nights logo slightly askew on the jacket of the faded yellow and blue Hawaiian print dress, which might well have been worn in the seventies.

"Ahoy, there!" sing-songed the woman—whose name tag read Isis—front teeth overlapping endearingly. Then, seeing Avery's gaze light upon the stuffed parrot wiggling on her shoulder, Isis gave the thing a scratch under the chin. "It's Pirates and Parrots theme at the resort this week."

"Of course it is," Avery said, the eye patch now making more sense. "I'm Avery Shaw. Claudia Davis is expecting me."

"Yo ho ho, and a bottle of rum… The American!"

"That I am!" The girl's pep was infectious, jet lag or no.

"Claude has been beside herself all morning, making me check the Qantas website hourly to make sure you arrived safe and sound."

"That's my girl," Avery said, feeling better and better about her last-minute decision to fly across the world, to the only person in her world who'd understand why.

Tap-tap-tap went Isis's long aqua fingernails on the keyboard. "Now, Claude could be…anywhere. Things have been slightly crazy around here since her parents choofed off."

Choofed off? Maybe that was Aussie for *retired*. Crazy or not, when Avery had first called Claude to say she was coming, Claude had sounded giddy that the management of the resort her family had owned for the past twenty years was finally up to her. She had ideas! Brilliant ones! People were going to flock as they hadn't flocked in years!

Glancing back at the still-empty lobby, Avery figured the *flocking* was still in the planning. "Shall I wait?"

"*No* ho ho," said Isis, back to tapping at the keyboard, "you'll be waiting till next millennium. Get thee to thy room. Goodies await. I'll get one of the crew to show you the way."

Avery glanced over her shoulder, her mind going instantly to the stream of messages her friends had sent when they'd heard she was heading to Australia, most of which were vividly imagined snippets of advice on how best to lure a hot, musclebound young porter "down under."

The kid ambling her way *was* young—couldn't have been a day over seventeen. But with his bright red hair and galaxy of freckles, hunching over his lurid yellow and blue shirt and wearing a floppy black pirate hat that had seen better days, he probably wasn't what they'd had in mind.

"Cyrus," Isis said, an impressive warning note creeping into her voice.

Cyrus looked up, his flapping sandshoes coming to a slow halt. Then he grinned, the overlapping teeth putting it beyond doubt that he and Isis were related.

"This is Miss Shaw," warned Isis. "Claudia's friend."

"Thanks, Cyrus," Avery said, heaving her luggage onto the golden trolley by the desk since Cyrus was too busy staring to seem to remember how.

"Impshi," Isis growled. "Kindly escort Miss Shaw to the Tiki Suite."

Avery's bags wobbled precariously as Cyrus finally grabbed the high bar of the trolley and began loping off towards the rear of the lobby.

"You're the New Yorker," he said.

Jogging to catch up, Avery said, "I'm the New Yorker."

"So how do *you* know Claude anyway? She never goes *anywhere*," said Cyrus, stopping short and throwing out an arm that nearly got her around the neck. She realised belatedly he was letting a couple of women with matching silver hair and eye-popping orange sarongs squeeze past.

Avery ducked under Cyrus's arm. "Claude has been all over the place, and I know because I went with her. The best trips were Italy…Morocco… One particular night in the Maldives was particularly memorable. We first met when my family holidayed here about ten years back."

Not *about* ten years. *Exactly.* Nearly to the day. There'd be no forgetting that these next few weeks. No matter how far from home she was.

"Now, come on Cyrus," Avery said, shaking off the sudden weight upon her chest. She looped a hand through the crook of Cyrus's bony elbow and dragged him in the direction of her suite. "Take me to my room."

Kid nearly tripped over his size thirteens.

One wrong turn and a generous tip later the Tiki Suite was all hers, and Avery was alone in the blissful cool of

the soft, worn, white-on-white decor where indeed goodies did await: a basket of warm-skinned peaches, plums
and nectarines, a box of divine chocolate, and a huge bottle of pink bubbly.

But first Avery kicked off her shoes and moved to the
French doors, where the scent of sea air and the lemon trees
that bordered the wall of her private courtyard filled her
senses. She lifted her face to the sun to find it hotter than
back home, crisper somehow.

It was the same suite in which her family had stayed
a decade before. Her mother had kicked up a fuss when
they'd discovered the place was less glamorous than she'd
envisaged, but by that stage Avery had already met Claude
and begged to stay. For once her dear dad had put his foot
down, and Avery had gone on to have a magical, memorable, lazy, hazy summer.

The last simple, wonderful, innocent summer of her life.

The last before her parents' divorce.

The divorce her mother was about to celebrate with a
Divorced a Decade party, in fact; capitals intended.

Avery glanced over her shoulder at the tote she'd left
on the bed, and tickles of perspiration burst over her skin.

She had to call home, let her mother know she'd arrived.
Even though she knew she'd barely get in a hello before
she was force fed every new detail of the big bash colour
theme—*blood*-red—guest lists—exclusive yet extensive—
and all-male live entertainment—no, *no*, NO!

Avery sent a text.

I'm here! Sun is shining. Beach looks splendiferous. I'll call
once jet lag wears off. Prepare yourself for stories of back-
yard tattoos, pub crawls, killer spiders the size of a studio
apartment, and naked midnight beach sprints. Happy to
hear the same from you. Ave xXx

Then, switching off her phone, she threw it to the bed. Then shoved a pillow over the top.

Knowing she couldn't be trusted to sit in the room and wait for Claude without turning her phone back on, Avery changed into a swimsuit, lathered suncreen over every exposed inch, grabbed a beach towel, and headed out to marvel at the Pacific.

As she padded through the resort, smiling at each and every one of Claude's—yes, Claude's!—pink-faced guests, Avery thought about how her decision to come back had been purely reactive, a panic-driven emotional hiccup when her mother had broached the idea of the Divorced a Decade party for the very first time.

But now she was here, the swirl of warm memories seeping under her skin, she wondered why it had never occurred to her sooner to come back. To come full circle.

Because that's how it felt. Like over the next few weeks she'd not only hang with her bestie—or nab herself a willing cabana boy to help get the kinks out—but maybe even be able to work her way back to how things had been here before her family had flown back to Manhattan and everything had fallen apart. To find the hopeful girl she'd once been before her life had become an endless series of gymnastic spins from one parent to the other and back again. Cartwheels to get her absent father's attention. Cheerleading her way through her mother's wild moods.

She'd never felt quite as safe, as secure, as *content* since that summer.

The summer of her first beer.

Her first beach bonfire.

Her first crush…

Avery's feet came to a squeaking halt.

In fact, wasn't *he*—the object of said crush—in Crescent Cove, right now?

Claude had mentioned him. Okay, so she'd bitched and

moaned; that he was *only* in the cove till he and Claudia sorted out what they were going to do with the resort now that their respective parents had retired and left the two of them in charge. But that was about *Claude's* history with the guy, not Avery's.

Her history was nice. And at that moment *he* was there. And *she* was there. It would be nice to look him up. And compared to the supercharged emotional tornado that was her family life in New York, this summer Avery could really do with some *nice*.

Jonah North pushed his arms through the rippling water, the ocean cool sliding over the heat-baked skin of his back and shoulders, his feet trailing lazily through the water behind him.

Once he hit a sweet spot—calm, warm, a good distance from the sand—he pressed himself to sitting, legs either side of his board. He ran two hands over his face, shook the water from his hair, and took in the view.

The town of Crescent Cove was nestled behind a double row of palm trees that fringed the curved beach that gave the place its name. Through the gaps were flashes of pastel—huge resorts, holiday accommodation, locally run shops, as well as scattered homes of locals yet to sell out. Above him only sky, behind and below the endless blue of the Pacific. Paradise.

It was late in the morning for a paddle—there'd been no question of carving out enough time to head down the coast where coral didn't hamper actual surf. Who was he kidding? There was never any time. Which, for a lobsterman's son, whose sea legs had come in before his land legs, was near sacrilege.

But he was here now.

Jonah closed his eyes, tilted his face to the sun, soaked in its life force. No sound to be heard bar the heave of his slowing breaths, the gentle lap of water against his thighs, a scream—

His eyes snapped open, his last breath trapped in his lungs. His ears strained. His gaze sweeping the gentle rolling water between himself and the sand, searching for—

There. A keening. Not a gull. Not music drifting on the breeze from one of the resort hotels. Distress. Human distress.

Muscles seized, every sense on red alert, he waited. His vision now locked into an arc from where he'd heard the cry. Imagining the reason. Stinger? No, the beach was protected by a stinger net this time of year so it'd be tough luck if they'd been hit.

And then he saw it.

A hand.

His rare moment of quietude at a fast and furious end, Jonah was flat on his belly, arms heaving the ocean out of his way before he took his next breath.

With each swell he glanced up the beach to see if anyone else was about. But the yellow and red flags marking out the patch of beach patrolled by lifesavers were farther away, this part cleared of life bar a furry blot of brown and white dog patiently awaiting his return.

Jonah kept his eyes on the spot, recalculating distance and tidal currents with every stroke. He'd practically been born on the water, reading her as natural to him as breathing. But the ocean was as cruel as she was restorative, and if she decided not to give up, there wasn't much even the most sea-savvy person could do. He knew.

As for the owner of the hand? *Tourist.* Not a single doubt in his mind.

The adrenalin thundering through him spiked when sunlight glinted off skin close enough to grab. Within seconds he was dragging a woman from the water.

Her hair was so long it trailed behind her like a curtain

of silk, so pale it blended with the sandy backdrop behind. Her skin so fair he found himself squinting at the sun reflecting off her long limbs. And she was lathered in so much damn sunscreen she was as slippery as a fish and he could barely get a grip.

And that was before she began to fight back. "No!" she spluttered.

"Hell, woman," Jonah gritted out. "I'm trying to rescue you, which will not be possible unless you stop struggling."

The woman stopped wriggling long enough to shoot him a flat stare. "I'm an excellent swimmer," she croaked. "I swam conference for Bryn Mawr."

Not just a tourist, Jonah thought, her cultured American accent clipping him about the ears. *From the whole other side of the world.*

"Could have fooled me," he muttered. "Unless that's what passes for the Australian Crawl stateside these days."

The stare became a glare. And her eyes… A wicked green, they were, only one was marred with a whopping great splotch of brown.

And while *he* stared at the anomaly, her hand slipped. Lucky she had the smarts to grab the pointy end of his board, leaving him to clench his thighs for all he was worth.

"Honey," he growled, by then near the end of his limited patience, "I understand that you're embarrassed. But would you rather be humbled or dead?"

Her strange eyes flinted at the *Honey*, not that he gave a damn. All he cared was that she gave a short nod. The sooner he dumped her back on the sand and got on with his day, the better. And if a dose of reality was necessary to get it done, then so be it.

"Good. Now, hoick yourself up on three." When her teeth clamped down on her bottom lip to suppress a grimace, and her fair skin came over paler again, he knew there'd be no hoicking. "Cramp?"

Her next grimace was as good as a yes.

Damn. No more finessing. In for a penny, Jonah locked his legs around the board, hooked his elbows under her arms, and heaved.

She landed awkwardly in a mass of gangly limbs and sea water. Only Jonah's experience and strength kept them from ending up ass up, lungs full of sea water, as he slid her onto his lap, throwing her arms around his neck where she gripped like a limpet. He grabbed her by the waist and held her still as the waves they'd created settled to a gentle rock.

Jonah wondered at what point she would become aware that she was straddling him, groin to groin, skin sliding against him all slippery and salty. Because after a few long moments it was just about all he could think about. Especially when with another grimace she hooked an arm over his shoulder, the other cradling the back of his head, and stretched her leg sideways, flexing her foot, easing out the cramp, her eyes fluttering closed as her expression eased into bliss.

He ought to have cleared his throat, or shifted her into a less compromising position, but with those odd eyes closed to him he got a proper look. Neat nose, long curling lashes stuck together with sea water, mouth like a kiss waiting to happen. If he had to have his paddle disturbed, might as well be by a nice-looking woman…

Tourist, he reminded himself.

And as much as the tourist dollar was his life's blood, and that of the entire cove, he knew that with all the Hawaiian shirts and Havana shorts they packed, it didn't leave much room for common sense.

And those were just the uncomplicated ones. The ones who were happy to come, and happy to go home. Lanky

Yankee here—a city girl with clear dibs on herself—had *complication* written all over.

"You all right?" Jonah asked.

She nodded. Her eyes flicked open, and switched between his and finally she realised she was curled around him like seaweed.

Light sparked in the green depths, the brown splodge strangely unmoved. Then, with a quick swallow, she slid her gaze down his bare chest to where they were joined at the hip. Lower. She breathed in quick, rolling as if to separate only to send a shard of heat right through him as she hit a sweet spot with impressive precision.

"May I—?" she asked, rolling again as if to disentangle.

Gritting his teeth, Jonah grunted in response. Having a woman be seaweed on him wasn't necessarily a bad thing. But out here? With a tourist on the verge of cramp? Besides which she was a bossy little thing. Skin and bone. Burn to a crisp if he didn't get her indoors. Not his type at all.

"This is nice and all," he said, boredom lacing his voice, "but any chance we could get a move on?"

"*Nice?* You clearly need to get out more."

She had him there.

With that she got to it, lifting a leg, the edge of a foot scraping a line across his bare belly, hooking a hair or two on the way, before her toes hit the board, mere millimetres from doing him serious damage. He shifted an inch into safe territory and breathed out. And finally they were both facing front.

Not better, he realised as The Tourist leant forward to grip the edges of his surfboard, leaving nowhere for him to put his hands without fear of getting slapped.

Especially when, in place of swimmers, the woman was bound in something that looked like a big-girl version of those lacy things his Gran used to insist on placing on every table top—all pale string, and cut-out holes, the stuff lifted and separated every time she moved, every time she breathed.

"Did you lose part of your swimmers?"

With a start she looked down, only to breathe out in relief. "No. I'm decent."

"You sure about that?"

The look she shot him over her shoulder was forbearing, the storm swirling in her odd eyes making itself felt south of the border.

"Then I suggest we get moving."

With one last pitying stare that told him she had decided he was about as high on the evolutionary scale as, say, *kelp*, she turned front.

Jonah gave himself a moment to breathe. He'd been on the receiving end of that look before. Funny that the original looker had been an urbanite too, though not from so far away as this piece of work, making him wonder if it was a class they gave at Posh Girls' Schools—*How to Make a Man Feel Lower Than Dirt*.

Only it hadn't worked on him then, and didn't now. They bred them too tough out here. Just made him want to get this over with as soon as humanly possible.

"Lie down," he growled, then settled himself alongside her.

"No way!" she said, wriggling as he trapped her beneath his weight. The woman might look like skin and bone but under him she felt plenty female. She also had a mean right elbow.

"Settle," Jonah demanded. "Or we'll both go under. And this time you can look after your own damn self."

She flicked him a glance, those eyes thunderous, those lips pursed like a promise. A promise he had no intention of honouring.

"Now," he drawled, "are you going to be a good girl and

let me get you safe back to shore, or are you determined to become a statistic?"

After a moment, her accented voice came to him as a hum he felt right through his chest. "Humility or death?"

He felt the smile yank at the corner of his mouth a second too late to stop it. Hers flashed unexpected, like sunshine on a cloudy day.

"Honey," he drawled, "you're not in Kansas any more."

One eyebrow lifted, and her eyes went to his mouth and stayed a beat before they once again looked him in the eye. "New York, actually. I'm from New York. Where there are simply not enough men with your effortless charm."

Sass. Bedraggled and pale and now shaking a little from shock and she was sassing him. Couldn't help but respect her for that. Which was why the time had come to offload her for good.

Jonah held on tight and kicked, making a beeline for the beach.

He did his best to ignore the warmth of the woman beneath him, her creamy back with its crazy mass of string masquerading as a swimsuit.

As soon as they were near enough, he let his feet drop to the sand and pushed the board into the shallows.

She slid off in a gaggle of limbs. He made to help, but she pulled her arm away. Didn't like help this one. Not *his* at any rate.

Hull stood at their approach, shook the sand from his speckled fur, then sat. Not too close. He was as wary of strangers as Jonah was. Smart animal.

Jonah took note and moved his hand away. "Stick to the resort pool, next time. Full-time lifeguards. Do you need me to walk you back to the Tropicana?" Probably best to check in with Claudia, make sure she knew she had a knucklehead staying at her resort.

"How on earth do you know where I'm staying?" asked said knucklehead.

He flicked a dark glance at the Tropicana Nights logo on the towel she'd wrapped tight about her.

"Right," she said, her cheeks pinkening. "Of course. Sorry. I didn't mean to suggest—"

"Yeah, you did."

A deep breath lifted her chest and her odd eyes with it so that she looked up at him from beneath long lashes clumped together like stars. "You're right, I did." A shrug, unexpectedly self-deprecating. Then, "But I can walk myself. Thanks, though, for the other. I really am a good swimmer, but I... Thanks. I guess."

"You're welcome." Then, "I guess."

That smile flickered for a moment, the one that made the woman's face look all warm and welcoming and new. Then all of a sudden she came over green, her wicked gaze became deeply tangled in his, she said, "Luke?" and passed out.

Jonah caught her: bunched towel, gangly limbs, and all.

He lowered himself—and her with him—to the sand, and felt for a pulse at her neck to find it strong and even. She'd be fine. A mix of heatstroke and too much ocean swallowed. No matter what she said about how good a swimmer she was, she was clearly no gym junkie. Even as dead weight she was light as a feather in his arms. All soft, warm skin too. And that mouth, parted, breathing gently. Beckoning.

He slapped her. On the cheek. Lightly.

Then not so lightly.

But she just lay there, angelic and unconscious. Nicer that way, in fact.

Luke, she'd said. He knew a Luke. Was good mates with one. But they didn't look a thing alike. Jonah's hair was darker, curlier. His eyes were grey, Luke's were...buggered if he knew. And while Luke had split Crescent Cove the first chance he had—coming home only when he had no choice—nothing bar the entire cove sinking into the sea would shift Jonah. Not again.

Literally, it seemed, as he tried to ignore the soft heat of the woman in his arms.

Clearly the universe was trying to tell him something. He'd learned to listen when that happened. *Storm's a coming: head to shore. A woman gets it in her head to leave you: never follow. Dinner at the seafood place manned by the local Dreadlock Army: avoid the oysters.*

What the hell he was meant to learn from sitting on a beach with an unconscious American in his arms, he had no idea.

Avery's head hurt. A big red whumping kind of hurt that meant she didn't want to open her eyes.

"That's the way, kid," a voice rumbled into her subconscious. A deep voice. Rough. Male.

For a second, she just lay there, hopeful that when she opened her eyes it would be to find herself lying on a sun lounge, a big buff cabana boy leaning over her holding a tray with piña coladas and coconut oil, his dark curls a halo in the sun…

"Come on, honey. You can do it."

Honey? Australian accent. It all came back to her.

Jet lag. Scorching heat. A quick dip in the ocean to wake up. Then from nowhere, cramp. Fear gripping her lungs as she struggled to keep her head above water. A hand gripping her wrist: strong, brown, safe. And then eyes, formidable grey eyes. Anything but safe.

Letting out a long slow breath to quell the wooziness rising in her belly, Avery opened her eyes.

"Atta girl," said the voice and this time there was a face to go with it. A deeply masculine face—strong jaw covered in stubble a long way past a shadow, lines fanning from the corners of grey eyes shaded by dark brows and thick lashes, a nose with a kink as if it had met with foul play.

Not a cabana boy, then. Not a boy at all. As his quick-silver eyes roved over her, Avery's stomach experienced a very grown-up quiver. It clearly didn't care that the guy was also frowning at her as if she were something that had washed up from the depths of the sea.

So who was he, then?

Luke? The name rang in her head like an echo, and her heart rate quickened to match. Could *this* be him?

But no. Strong as the urge was to have her teenage crush grow up into *this*, he was too big, too rugged. And she'd had enough updates about Claude's family friend over the years to know Luke had lived in London for a while now. Worked in advertising. If *this* guy worked in an office she'd eat her luggage.

And as for *nice*? The sensations tumbling through her belly felt anything but. They felt ragged, brusque, hot and pulsey. And oddly snarky, which she could only put down to the recent oxygen deficit.

On that note, she thought, trying to lift herself to sitting. But her head swam and her stomach right along with it.

Before she had the chance to alter the situation, the guy barked, "Lie down, will you? Last thing I need is for you to throw up on me as well."

While the idea of lying down a bit longer appealed, that wasn't how she rolled. She'd been looking after herself, and everyone else in her life, since she was sixteen.

"I think I'm about done here," she said.

"Can I get somebody for you?" he asked. "Someone from the resort? Luke?"

Her eyes shot to his. So he wasn't Luke, but he knew him? How did he know *she* knew him…? Oh, my God. Just before she'd passed out, she'd called Luke's name.

Heat and humiliation wrapped around her, Avery untwisted herself from Not-Luke's arms to land on the towel. She scrambled to her feet, jumbled everything into a big ball and on legs of jelly she backed away.

"I'm fine. I'll be fine." She pushed the straggly lumps of hair from her face. "Thanks again. And sorry for ruining your swim. Surf. Whatever."

The brooding stranger stood—sand pale against the brown of his knees, muscles in his arms bunching as he wrapped a hand around the edge of the surfboard he'd wedged into the sand. "I'm a big boy. I'll live."

Yes, you are, a saucy little voice cooed inside her head. But not particularly *nice*. And that was the thing. She'd had some kind of epiphany before she'd gone for a swim, hadn't she? Something about needing some sweet, simple, wholesome, *niceness* in her life compared with the horror her mother was gleefully planning on the other side of the world.

"Take care, little mermaid," he said, taking a step back, right into a slice of golden sunlight that caught his curls, and cut across his big bronzed bare chest.

"You too!" she sing-songed, her inveterate Pollyannaness having finally fought its way back to the surface. "And it's Avery. Avery Shaw."

"Good to know," he said. Then he smiled. And it was something special—kind of crooked and sexy and fabulous. Though Avery felt a subversive moment of disappointment when it didn't reach his eyes. Those crinkles held such promise.

Then he turned and walked away, his surfboard hooked under one arm, his bare feet slapping on the footpath. And from nowhere a huge dog joined him—shaggy and mottled with deep liquid eyes that glanced back at her a moment before turning back into the sun.

Definitely not Luke. Luke Hargreaves had been taller,

his hair lighter, his eyes a gentle brown. And that long-ago summer before her whole world had fallen apart he'd made her feel safe. To this day Avery could sense the approach of conflict as tingles all over her skin, the way some people felt a storm coming in their bad knees, and Mr Muscles back there made her feel as if she'd come out in hives.

She blinked when she realised she was staring, then, turning away, trudged up the beach towards the road, the resort, a good long sensible lie-down.

"Avery!"

She glanced up and saw a brilliantly familiar blonde waving madly her way from the doorway of the Tropicana: navy skirt, blinding blue and yellow Hawaiian shirt, old-fashioned clipboard an extension of her arm. *Claudia.* Oh, now *there* was a sight for sore eyes, and a bruised ego and—

Avery's feet stopped working, right in the middle of the street. For there, standing behind Claudia and a little to the left, thumb swishing distractedly over a smartphone, was Luke Hargreaves—tall, lean, handsome in a clean-shaven city-boy kind of way, in a suit she could pin as Armani from twenty feet away. If that wasn't enough, compared to the mountain of growly man flesh she'd left back there on the beach, not a *single* skin prickle was felt.

With relief Pollyanna tap danced gleefully inside her head as Avery broke out in a sunny smile.

CHAPTER TWO

A CAR HONKED long and loud and Avery came to. Heat landed in her cheeks as she and her still wobbly legs made their way across the road.

She wished her entrance could have been more elegant, but since in the past half an hour she'd near drowned, passed out, woken up looking into the eyes of a testosterone-fuelled surfer who made her skin itch, she had to settle for still standing.

Avery walked up the grassy bank to the front path of the resort where Claudia near ploughed her down with a mass of hugging arms and kisses and relieved laughter. When Avery was finally able to disentangle herself she pulled back, laughing. Compared with the stylishly subdued Mr Hargreaves, Claudia with her bright blue eyes and wild shirt was like sunshine and fairy floss.

"What happened to you?" asked Claudia. No hellos, no *how was your flight*. The best kind of friendship, it always picked up just where it left off.

"Just been out for a refreshing ocean dip!"

Avery shot a telling glance at Luke. Claudia crossed her arms and steadfastly ignored the man at her back. Avery raised an eyebrow. Claudia curled her lip.

They might have lived on different continents their whole lives but with Skype, email, and several overseas trips together, their shorthand was well entrenched.

Finally Claudia cocked her head at the man and with a brief flare of her nostrils said, "Luke, you remember Avery Shaw."

Luke looked up at the sound of his name. Avery held her breath. Luke just blinked.

Rolling her eyes, Claudia turned on him. "My *friend* Avery. The Shaws stayed at the resort ten odd years ago."

Still nothing.

"They booked out the Tiki Suite for an entire summer."

"Right," he said, a flare of recognition *finally* dawning in his seriously lovely brown eyes. "The Americans."

Claudia clearly wasn't moved by it. Something he'd said, or the way he said it, had Claudia bristling. And Claudia wasn't a bristler by nature; she was as bubbly as they came.

Avery didn't have a problem with him seeming rather… serious. Serious was better than hives, any day. And like the worrying of a jagged tooth her mind skipped back to the scratch of the other man's leg hairs on her inner thighs. To the hard heat of his hands gripping her waist, calloused fingers spanning her belly, big thumbs digging uncomfortably into her hips. Those cool grey eyes looking right through her, as if if he could he would have wished her well away…

She shook herself back to the much more pleasant present where Claude snuggled up to her with love. Waiting till she had Luke's distracted attention, she brought out the big guns—a smile that had cost her parents as much as a small car. "Nice seeing you again, Luke. Hopefully we'll bump into one another again. Catch up on old times."

He blinked again, as if he thought that was what they'd just done. But it was early days. She had time. To do what, she was as yet undecided, but the seeds were there.

"I'm off duty as of this second, Luke," Claude said, not even deigning to look his way. "We'll talk about that *other stuff* later."

"Soon," he said, an edge to his voice.

Claude waved a dismissive hand over her shoulder, offloaded Avery of half her gear as they headed up the stairs into the resort.

"Are you sure?" Avery said. "You must be so busy right now, and I don't want to get in the way. I can help! Whatever you need. I have skills. And they are at your disposal."

"Relax, *Polly*," Claude said, using the nickname she'd given Avery for when she got herself in a positivity loop. "*You* are never in my way."

"Fine, *Julie*," Avery shot back. Claude's nickname had sprung from an odd fascination with *The Love Boat* that Avery had never understood. Though when Claude instantly perked up as a seniors tour group from the UK emerged from behind a pylon—amazingly remembering everybody by name—it couldn't have been more apt.

Cyrus—who'd been leaning on the desk staring out at nothing—straightened so quickly his pirate hat flopped into his eyes.

Claudia frowned at Cyrus, who moved off at quite a pace. "Welcome to Crescent Cove," she said to Avery, "where heat addles the hormones."

"Is that in the town charter?" Avery asked, grinning. "Did I read it on the sign driving in?"

"Unfortunately not. Do you think it would work? As a marketing ploy?" Claude looked more hopeful than the idea merited.

Avery, whose business was public relations and thus who was paid to create goodwill, gave Claude's arm a squeeze. "It couldn't hurt."

They reached the Tiki Suite and Claudia dumped Avery's stuff on a white cane chair in the corner, oblivious to the bucketload of sand raining onto the floor. "Now, refreshing dip, my sweet patooty. What happened to you out there?"

"You should see the other guy," Avery muttered before landing face down on the bed.

Claudia landed next to her face up. Then after a beat she turned on her side, head resting in her upturned palm as she loomed over Avery, eyebrows doing a merry dance. "What other guy?"

Avery scrunched up her face. Then rolled onto her back and stared up at the ceiling. "My leg cramped, and a guy on a surfboard dragged me out of the ocean. I'd have been fine, though. I am a very good swimmer."

Claudia landed on her back and laughed herself silly. "I've been locked inside with Luke all morning, forced to listen to him yabber on about figures and columns and hard decisions and I missed it! Who was the *guy*?"

Avery opened her mouth to give his name, then realised he hadn't given it. *Barbarian.* "I have no clue."

Claude flapped a hand in the sky. "I know everybody. What did he look like?"

Avery tried a shrug, but truth was she could probably describe every crinkle around those deep grey eyes. But knowing she would not be allowed to sleep, till Claudia knew all, she said, "Big. Tanned. Dark curly hair. Your basic beefcake nightmare."

Claudia paused for so long Avery glanced her way. Only to wish she hadn't. For the smile in her friend's eyes did not bode well for her hope that this conversation might be at an end.

"Grey surfboard with a big palm tree on it? Magnificent wolf dog at his heels?"

Damn. "That's the one."

Claude's smile stretched into an all-out grin. "You, my sweet, had the pleasure of meeting Jonah North. That's one supreme example of Australian manhood. And he rescued you? Like, actually pulled you out of the ocean? With his bare hands? What was that like?"

Avery slapped her hands over her face to hide the rising pink as her skin kicked into full-on memory mode at the feeling of those bare hands. "It was mortifying. He called me *honey*. Men only do that when they can't be bothered knowing your name."

"Huh. And yet I can't even remember the last time a guy called me honey. Raoul always called me Sugar Puff."

"Raoul?"

"The dance instructor I was seeing. Once upon a million years ago."

"Well, Sugar Puff is sweet. Toothache inducing, maybe, but sweet."

Truth was Avery usually loved an endearment. They always felt like an arrow to the part of her that had switched to maximum voltage the day her parents had told her they were getting divorced. *Like me! Love me! Don't ever leave me!*

Maybe the fact that she'd responded unfavourably to the barbarian meant she'd grown. "Either way, the guy rubbed me the wrong way."

"I know many a woman who'd give their bikini bottoms to have Jonah North rub them any which way."

"Are you one of them?"

Claude blinked, then laughed so hard she fell back on the bed with a thump.

"That's a no?"

Claude just laughed harder.

"What's so funny?" *Honestly.* Because even while it had been mortifying, it had been one of the more blatantly sensual experiences of her recent memory: the twitch of his muscles as she'd slid her foot across his flat belly, the scrape of longing she'd felt when she'd realised he was holding his breath. Talk about addled.

Claudia brought herself back under control, then shrugged. "Aside from the fact that Jonah really learned how to pull off 'curmudgeonly' the past few years? He's a born and bred local, like me. You know what it's like when you know a guy forever?"

"Sure. Pretty much everyone in my social circle will end up with someone they've known forever."

Claudia's eyes widened. "That's…"

"Neat?"

"I was going to say 'demoralising,' but neat works too."

"It's the Park Avenue way. Dynastic. Families know one another. Finances secured. Much like if you and Luke ended up together. It would keep the resort all in the family."

Claudia flinched, and shook her head. "No. Don't even… But that's *my* point. Anyway, I don't want to talk about Luke. I don't like him very much at the moment."

"I have no idea why. He's grown into quite the dish. And he seems perfectly nice." There was that word again. It had sounded quite wonderful before, all poignant and time-gone-by lovely. This time it fell kind of flat. But that was just semantics. She'd find another word.

In the meanwhile Claude shot her a look that said she'd quite like to lock the man up and throw away the key, but not before she'd lathered him in pollen and set a pack of bees on him. She might look like rainbows and sunshine, but there were clever, cunning, dark places inside Claude. Places she tapped into if those she loved were under threat. While Avery had shut her touchy tendencies away in a box with a big fat lock, oh, about ten years ago, in fact.

"Well, then," said Avery, finding her smile, "how do you feel about my getting to know him a little better while I'm here?"

"Jonah? Perfect! He used to be such a cool guy, so chilled. But he's been so damn broody nowadays. Laughs at my jokes only three times out of ten. Go shake him up, for all our sakes."

"Actually..." Avery said, then cleared her throat. "I meant Luke."

Claude's eyes snapped wide, then settled back to near normal. "Hargreaves?"

"*Yes*, Hargreaves."

Claude thought about this a moment. A few moments. Long enough Avery began to wonder if Claude's irritation with the man was the flipside of something quite the other. In which case she'd back-pedal like crazy!

Claude put her mind to rest when she said, "You do realise he has a stick up his backside? Like, permanently?"

"So says you." Avery laughed. "I thought he seemed perfectly—"

"*Nice?* Okay, then. You have my blessing. Shake that tree if it floats your boat. Just don't get hurt. By the stick. Up his—"

"Yes, thank you. I get it."

"In fact have at them both if you so desire. *Neither* Jonah Broody North or Luke Bloody Hargreaves are my type, that's for sure."

Avery swallowed down the tangled flash of heat at thought of one and focused on the soothing warmth that settled in her belly at thought of the other. "So what *is* your type these days, Miss Claudia?"

Claude's hand came to rest on her chest as she stared at the ceiling. "A man who in thirty years still looks at me the way my dad looks at my mum. Who looks at me one day and says, 'You've worked hard enough, hon, let's go buy a campervan and travel the country.' Who looks at me like I'm his moon and stars. Hokey, right?"

Avery stared up at the ceiling too, noticing a watermark, dismissing it. "So hokey. And while you're at it, could you find me one of those too, please?"

"We here at the Tropicana Nights always aim to please. Now," Claude said, pulling herself to sitting and reaching for the phone, "time to tell me why you are really here. Because I know you too well to know an impromptu month off had nothing to do with it."

Then she held up a finger as someone answered on the other end. And while Claudia ordered dinner, a massage, and a jug of something called a Flaming Flamingo, Avery wondered quite where to start.

Claude knew the background.

That after the divorce Avery rarely saw her dad. Mostly at monthly lunches she organised. And thank goodness they honestly both loved baseball, or those meetings would be quiet affairs. Go Yanks!

As for dear old Mom, she'd turned on Avery's father with such constant and unceasing venom when he'd left it had been made pretty clear to Avery that once on her mother's bad side there was no coming back.

In order to retain any semblance of the family she had left, what could Avery do but become the perfect Park Avenue daughter?

Until the moment her mother had announced her grand plans for her Divorced a Decade party. And Avery—being such a great party planner—*of course* was to be in charge of the entire thing! After a decade of smiling and achieving and navigating the balance between her less-than-accommodating parents, Miss Park Avenue Perfect had finally snapped.

"*You* snapped?" Claude asked as Avery hit that point of the story, her voice a reverent hush. "What did Caroline say when you told her *no*?"

Okay, so this was where it kind of got messy. Where Avery's memory of the event was skewed. By how hard she'd worked to retain a relationship with her distant dad. And how readily her mother had expected she'd be delighted to help out.

"I didn't exactly say…that. Not in so many words."

"Avery," Claude growled.

Avery scrunched her eyes shut tight and admitted, "I told her I couldn't help her because I was taking a sabbatical."

"A sabbatical. And she believed you?"

"When she saw the mock-up I quickly slapped together of my flight details she did. Then I just had to go ahead and call you and actually book the flights. And let all my clients know I was on extended leave from work and couldn't take any new jobs. And close up my apartment and turn off my electric and water and have my mail diverted for a couple months. And voilà!"

"Voilà!" Claude repeated. "Good God, hon! One of these days you're going to have to learn to say the word *no*!"

Avery pish-poshed, even though she and Claude had had the same argument a dozen times over the years.

"Starting now," said Claude. "Repeat after me—*No*."

"No," Avery shot back.

"Good girl. Now practise. Ten times in the morning. Ten times before bed."

Avery nodded, promised and wondered why she hadn't brought up the fact that she hadn't had a problem saying "no" to Jonah North. And that saying "no" to *him* had felt good. Really good. So she had the ability. Buried somewhere deep down inside perhaps, but the instinct was there when she really meant it.

But Claude was right. She should have told her mother "no." Well, considering there were more venomous snakes in the world's top ten here than any other place on earth, if she was ever going to toughen up, this was the place.

The Charter North Reef Cruiser was on its way to Green Island. In the engine room everything looked shipshape, so Jonah headed up the companionway to the top deck.

The crew ought to have been used to him turning up on a skip unannounced; he did it all the time. There was no point having a fleet of boats with his name on them if they weren't up to his standards. Besides, his father had been a boatman before him and he knew an extra pair of hands was always welcome.

But the moment he entered the air-conditioned salon, the staff scattered. He caught the eye of one—a new girl, by the starched collar of her Charter North polo shirt, who wasn't as quick off the mark as the others. With a belated squeak she leapt into action, polishing the silver handrails with the edge of her sand-coloured shorts. Odd. But industrious.

So he walked the aisles. The passenger list was pretty much as per usual—marine biologists researching the reef, Green Island staffers, a group of girls who looked as if they'd closed one of the resort bars the night before, a toddler with a brown paper bag under his chin.

His gaze caught on a crew of skinny brown boys, skateboards tucked on their laps, eyes looking out of the window as if urging the island nearer. Part of the Dreadlock Army who lived in these parts, kids who survived on sea water and fresh air. A lifetime ago he'd been one of them.

Fast forward and this day he'd been awake since five. Gone for a five-kilometre run. Driven the half-hour to Charter North HQ in Port Douglas. Checked emails, read the new safety procedures manual he'd paid a small fortune to set up, negotiated the purchase of a new pleasure cruiser he had his eye on in Florida. No time for sticking a toe in the ocean, much less taking it on.

As the captain began his spiel over the speaker system about the adventures available once they hit the island, Jonah slid his sunglasses in place and headed aft.

A few customers had staked out prime positions in the

open air, laughing as they were hit with ocean spray. He didn't blame them. It was a hell of a day to be outside.

When they said Queensland was beautiful one day and perfect the next, they were talking about Crescent Cove. The Coral Sea was invariably warm, a slight southerly bringing about a gentle swell. The sky was a dome of blinding blue with only a smattering of soft white streaks far away on the horizon. And soon they'd hit the edge of the Great Barrier Reef, one of the natural wonders of the world.

He was a lucky man to have been born here. Luckier still to remain. He breathed deep of the sky and salt and sun. He didn't need surf. All he needed was never to take the place for granted again.

He nodded to the staff keeping watch on deck and made to head back inside when someone caught his eye. Not just any someone, it was his waterlogged mermaid herself.

She lifted a hand to shield her eyes and turned her gaze to Crescent Cove. She had nice hands. Fine. Her nails were the colour of her dress—a long flame-orange thing flapping against her legs—and her hair was twisted up into a complicated series of knots atop her head making her look as if she were about to step out onto the French Riviera not a small island on the edge of the Pacific.

Jonah glanced at his own hands knowing they'd be less than fine. Burly brown with many a war wound, and motor oil under his chipped nails. He rubbed his fingers across his rough chin. How long since he'd shaved? Three days? Four?

He shoved his hands deep into the pockets of his long shorts, his forehead pinching. What did he care about all that?

Unfortunately, in the time he'd spent *caring*, she'd turned to face him, all elegant stance and plaintive eyes.

Caught out, his breath found itself caught somewhere

in the region of his gut.And then her eyes narrowed. As if he'd done anything to her other than save her ass.

Then the boat hit a swell, the bow lifting and crashing to the water with a thud.

Squeals of excitement ricocheted through the cabin. But, facing him, his mermaid had no purchase. She lost balance, knocked a hip against the side of the boat, and began to topple—

From there everything happened in slow motion— Jonah's leap over a bench, his canvas shoes landing on the slippery deck then sliding him towards her. He reached for her hand, grabbed, caught, and dragged her back to safety and into his arms.

Her hands fisted into his shirt, the scrape of nails through cotton hooked his chest hair, pulling a couple right from the roots. At the sharp tug of pain, he sucked in a breath. And her eyes lifted swiftly to his. Those odd mismatched eyes. Seriously stunning in such an otherwise quiet face.

"Seriously?" he growled. "I'm going to start thinking these moments are all for my benefit."

She gave him a shove. Strength in those lean arms. "Seriously?" she shot back. Then heaved up a hunk of her skirt, flapped it at him accusingly and shot him a look that said that if she had the superpower, she'd have set him on fire. "All that I know is that thanks to you, I'm soaked!"

"Stick around here, princess, and chances are you're gonna get wet."

She opened her mouth…but nothing came out. Instead high spots of pink burned into her cheeks creating hollows beneath her elegant cheekbones, pursing those kissable lips, and bringing wild glints to those eyes. Not such a quiet face after all. "Maybe next time you decide to go all He-Man, try not to rip the victim's arm from its socket."

She rubbed her arm as if to prove as much, only bringing his attention to the fact that her skin was covered in goosebumps. With the temp edging into the high thirties, that was some feat. Only one other reason Jonah knew for a woman to go goosey when locked in a man's arms...

Testing his theory, Jonah leaned an inch her way, caught the intake of breath, the widening of her eyes, the fresh pink staining her cheeks. Seemed Miss Yankee Doodle Dandy here wasn't as unaffected by him as she was making out.

She swallowed and shoved, with less oomph this time. "Oh, go peddle your He-Man act to someone else for a change."

"No one else seems to need it." The fact that nobody else had ever brought out the urge he kept to himself.

Yeah, he'd heard the chatter since he'd come home; heard himself called hell-bent, a lone wolf. But the truth was even before that, as a kid with all the freedom in the world, he'd known he could count the people he could truly depend upon on one hand. He was glad of that instinct now. Less chance he'd make the mistake of counting on the wrong someone again.

And yet, with this one, it took someone else to wrench him away.

"Mr North?"

Jonah turned to find one of his staff standing in the doorway, wringing his hands, swallowing hard, as if his head might be bitten off for disturbing the boss.

"Sir," said the kid, "we have a Code Green."

"Right." Awesome. He'd asked the crew before they'd taken off to grab him in the event of any major incidents so that he could watch any of the new policies and procedures in action. Code Green was otherwise known as Puke Patrol.

"I'll be there in a sec."

The kid disappeared so fast into the salon he practically

evaporated. Leaving Jonah to turn back to Avery, whose eyes were locked onto his chest.

"Twenty minutes till touchdown, Avery," he said.

She blinked, looked up, then pinked some more. He'd never much been one for girls who blushed, but it suited her. Took the edge off her sharp tongue. Heaven help the guy who fell for one before he was witness to the other.

"You might want to get out of the sun. Get something to drink. Complimentary sunscreen's inside. Whatever you do, get something between you and the big blue. One of these days I won't be around to save you."

Not intending to stick around to see how that went down, Jonah slipped inside.

It was a little under twenty minutes before Green Island came into view: a sliver of land on the horizon that grew into a small atoll of forest-green with a long crooked jetty poking out into the ocean. The cruiser slipped through the reef to park and the passengers staggered off; some clutching snorkels ready for a close encounter with tropical fish, others planning to head straight to a bar.

Jonah caught a flash of orange out of the corner of his eye and turned to find Avery now with a huge sunhat covering her face. Lifting her long dress, she stepped onto the gangplank, her shoe caught and she tripped. Jonah near pulled a muscle in an effort not to grab her. Chin tilted a mite higher, she walked steadily along the jetty, where all sorts of adventures awaited.

Adventures…and dangers. Things happened to tourists all the time—swimming too far, diving too deep, getting knocked off by ingenious spouses.

"Avery!" he called.

She turned, surprise lighting her features. "Yes, Jonah?"

She knew his name. A thick slide of satisfaction washed through him—then he remembered the Code Green. *Down boy.* "Take care."

She blinked, those odd eyes widening, then softening in a way that made him want to howl at the moon.

Hence the reason he added, "Don't get eaten."

The next look she shot him might as well have said, *Bite me*. But when she realised they had an audience, she found a sweet-as-pie smile, and said, "Oh, *don't* get eaten. Thanks for the advice. I'll keep it in mind."

And he found himself laughing out loud.

With a frown and twitch of her mouth, she disappeared into the crowd.

Leaving Jonah to use the respite to remind himself that despite the lush mouth, and the bewitching eyes and the rich vein of sexual attraction she'd unearthed, he didn't much *like* her.

Because he'd known a woman like her once before.

He hadn't realised *why* Rach had stood out to him like bonfire on a cloudy night from the first moment he'd seen *her* until it was too late. Turned out it was because despite her attestations that a sea change was exactly what she needed she'd never left the city behind enough to really fit in. Too late by the time he'd seen it to stop her leaving. Too late to convince himself not to follow. Until he'd woken up in Sydney, cut off, miserable, realising what he'd given up for her, and that he'd lost her anyway.

Returning to Crescent Cove after that whole disaster had been hard. Returning to find *he* no longer quite fitted in the place he'd been born had been harder still. He'd had to remake his life, and to do that remake himself. As if the cove had needed a sacrifice in order to take him back, in order to make sure he'd never take her for granted again.

So no, for however long Avery Shaw flitted about the periphery of his life she'd mean no more, or less, to him than a pebble in his shoe.

Because this time his eyes were wide-open and staying that way. This time he wouldn't so much as blink.

CHAPTER THREE

JONAH WASN'T LOOKING for Avery, not entirely.

He found her anyway, on the beach. Her big hat, so wet it flopped onto her shoulders. Half in, half out of a wetsuit that flapped dejectedly against her legs as she jumped around slapping at her skin as if fighting off a swarm of bees.

Jonah picked up his pace to a jog.

"Avery," he called when near enough, "what the hell's wrong now?"

She didn't even look up, just kept on wriggling, giving him flashes of bare stomach through a silver one-piece with great swathes of Lycra cut away leaving the edges to caress a hip, to brush the underside of a breast, keeping Jonah locked into a loop of double takes.

"I'm stung!" she cried, jogging him out of his daze. "Something got me. A box jellyfish. Or a blue bottle. Or a stone fish. I read about them on the flight over. One of them got me. I sting. *Everywhere.*"

"Bottles don't come this far north, the suit protects from jellies, and the flippers from stone fish."

Avery jumped from flippered foot to flippered foot as if something terrible was about to explode from out of the sand at her feet. "Then what's wrong with me?"

Jonah made a mental note to have a talk with Claudia. She always had some crazy theme going on at her resort, with games and the like—surely she could keep the woman indoors and out of his sight.

But until then he had to make sure she wasn't actually hurt. Meaning he had to run hands down her arms, ignoring as best he could the new tension knotting hard and fast inside him.

He spun her around to check behind, wrapping the fall of hair about his hand to lift it off her neck, doing his all to avoid the mental images *that* brought forth. He swept his gaze over the skin the swimsuit revealed round back. Then grabbed her by the chin and tilted so he could see her face under the ridiculous hat. Her very pink face.

"Hell, woman," he growled, snapping his hand away. "You're sunburnt."

Her mismatched eyes widened. "Don't be ridiculous."

He took off the hat to make sure, and with a squeak her hand swept to her hair. Jonah rolled his eyes and slapped the hat back on her head. "Did you bring anything for sunburn?" *Sunscreen perhaps?*

He glanced at her silver bag to find its contents already upended and covered in a million grains of white sand. Clearly she'd been looking in the hopes of a remedy herself. *A remedy for stone fish*, he reminded himself, biting back a smile.

"Don't you dare laugh at me!"

Only made him smile all the more. "Don't tell me you were All Conference in Sun Protection at Brown Mare too?"

"Bryn Mawr," she bit out. And, whoa, was that a flicker of a smile from her? The one that lit her up brighter than the sun?

Jonah looked away, tilting his chin towards the jetty. "There's aloe vera on the boat. It'll soothe it at the very least. At least until the great peel sets in."

"I don't peel."

"You will peel, princess. Great ugly strips of dead skin sloughing away."

Muttering under her breath, she shoved all her bits and pieces back into her bag—including, he noted, a dog-eared novel, a bottle of fancy sparkling water, and, yep, sunscreen.

He plucked the sunscreen from her fingers and read the label. "American," he muttered under his breath.

"Excuse me!" she shot back, no muttering there.

"Your SPF levels are not the same as ours. With your skin you can't get away with this rubbish."

"What's wrong with my skin?" she asked, arms wide, giving him prime view of her perfectly lovely skin. And neat straight shoulders, lean waist, hips that flared just right. As for her backside, he remembered with great clarity as she bent over on his board...

Jonah closed his eyes a moment and sent out a blanket curse to whatever he'd done to piss off karma enough to send him Avery Shaw.

"I'm well aware I'm not all golden bronzed like the likes of you," she said, "which is why I bought a bottle from home. *Ours* are stronger."

"Wrong way around, sweetheart," Jonah drawled. "Aussies do it better."

She coughed and spluttered. That was better than having her eyes rove over his *golden-bronzed* self while standing there all pink, and pretty, and half-naked.

Then, feeling more than a little sorry for herself, she slowly went back to refilling her bag, now with far less gusto. Her drooping hat dripped ocean water down her pink skin, she had a scratch on her arm that could do with some antiseptic and a couple of toes had clearly come out badly in a fight with some coral before she'd remembered her flippers.

Suddenly she threw the bag on the sand, slammed her

hands onto her hips and looked him right in the eye. "In New York we have cab drivers who don't know the meaning of the words *health code*. Rats the size of opossums. Steam that oozes from the subways that could knock you out with its stench. I live in a place it takes street smarts to survive. But this place? Holy Jeter!"

After a sob, she began to laugh. And laugh and laugh. It hit the edge of hysteria, but thankfully it never slipped quite that far.

Jonah ran a hand up the back of his neck and looked out at the edge of the jetty visible around the corner of the beach where his boat and the bright blue sea awaited. Basic, elemental pleasures. Enduring... Then glanced back at the tourist whose safety had clearly, for whatever reason, been placed in his hands.

Whatever problems he had with her kind, there was no denying the woman was trying. Enough that something slipped inside him, just a fraction, just enough to give her a break.

"Come on, princess," he said, holding out a hand. "Let's get you a drink."

She glanced at his sand-covered hand and her nose crinkled. "I don't need a drink."

Knowing it was only a matter of time before he regretted it, Jonah took a moment to brush the sand from his hand before holding it out again. It looked so dark near her skin. Big and rough near all that softness. "Well, I do," he said, his voice gruff. "And I'm not about to resort to drinking alone."

Avery watched him from beneath her lashes. Then, taking her bag in one hand and the arms of her wetsuit in the other, she flapped her way back up the beach, leaving him to catch up. "So long as drink doesn't mean beer. Because I don't do beer."

Jonah watched her walk away, flinching every third step

in fear of having unearthed some other Great Australian Wildlife intent on taking her down. Shaking his head, he dug his hands into the pockets of his shorts and did what he'd promised himself he'd never do again—follow a city girl anywhere. "Pity, princess, you really are missing out on one of the great experiences of an Australian summer."

She cut him a look—straight, sure, street smart indeed— and said, "I'll live."

And for the first time since he'd met the woman Jonah believed she just might.

When her straw slurped against the bottom of the coconut shell, dragging in the last drops of rum, coconut milk, and something she couldn't put her finger on, Avery pushed the thing away and looked up with a blissful sigh to find that the fabulous outdoor bar that Jonah had escorted her to some time earlier was empty.

Jonah North of Charter North. About halfway through the cocktail she'd put two and two together and figured the boat was his. She was clever that way, she thought, fluffing up her nearly dry hair, the happy waves in her head making it feel nice. She liked feeling nice.

Now what about Jonah? Big, gruff, handsome, bossy Jonah. Oh, yeah, he'd left her a few minutes ago to go and do…something. She looked around, shielding her eyes against the streak of bright orange cloud lighting up the dark blue horizon. Oops. Since when had the sun begun to set?

She found her phone in her bag and checked the time. Holy Jeter, she'd missed the boat! With a groan she let her head fall into her hands.

She knew the guy had only taken her for a drink because he'd got it into his thick He-Man head that she'd perish without supervision, but now the cad had damn well left her on an island in the middle of the Pacific, with night falling, and nowhere—

"Everything okay?" a familiar deep voice asked.

Avery peeled one eye open and looked through the gaps between her fingers to find Jonah standing by the table, his hands in the pockets of his khaki shorts, his white Charter North shirt flapping against the rises and falls of his chest in the evening breeze, the sunlight pouring over his deeply browned skin.

The guy might be wholly annoying in an I Told You So kind of way, but there was no denying he was Gorgeous— capital G intended. What with that handsome brown face all covered in stubble. And those shoulders—so big, so broad. Those tight dark curls that made a girl want to reach out and touch. And the chest she'd had her hands all over when he'd pulled her out of the ocean, all muscle and golden skin and more dark curling hair. In fact there was plenty about him that made a girl want to touch…

But not her, she reminded herself, sinking her hands down onto the chair so that she could sit on them before they did anything stupid.

If anybody was going to get the benefit of her touch on this trip, it would be that unsuspecting cabana boy—and, boy, did that sound seedy all of a sudden. So maybe not. Maybe, ah, Luke! Yes, dashing, debonair, dishy Luke Hargreaves. *There you go, that was way better than* nice—

"You okay there, Avery?"

"Hmm? Sorry? What?"

Jonah's laugh was a deep low *huh-huh-huh* that she felt in the backs of her knees.

"How many of those have you had?" he asked.

"Just one, thank you very much." A big one. "I'm fine."

"You say that a lot. That you're *fine*."

She did? Funny, she could hear it too, like an eerie echo inside her head. *I'm fine! All good! Don't worry about me!*

Now what can I do to make you *feel better? Cheer-cheer, rah-rah-rah!*

"I say it because I am." *Mostly.* "And I am. Fine. Just too much sun. And those cocktails have quite a kick, don't they? And—" she pointed one way, and then turned and pointed the other, not quite sure which direction was which "—I do believe I'm meant to be on a boat heading back to the mainland right about now."

Jonah pulled out a chair and straddled the thing, like he needed extra room between his legs to accommodate…you know. Avery blinked fast at the direction of her thoughts, before lifting her eyes quick smart to his, only to connect with all that quicksilver. Cool and hot all at once. As if he knew exactly where her eyes and thoughts had just been.

She swallowed. Hard. Tasted rum and coconut and… whatever the other thing was. The deadly wicked other thing that seemed to have made her rather tipsy.

"Avery."

"Yes, Jonah."

The quicksilver shifted, glints lighting the depths. "Our boat left about the time you started filling me in on why you came to the cove."

Avery swallowed, wondering just how much rum she'd imbibed. She'd told him? What exactly? How she'd been a big chicken and fled New York so as to avoid her mother's mortifying divorce anniversary party?

"To catch up with Claudia," Jonah reminded her when she'd looked at him blankly for quite some time.

"Right! Of course. For *Claude*. We're friends, you know? Have been a *lo-o-ong* time."

No laugh this time, but a smile. An honest-to-goodness smile that made his eyes glow and his eye crinkles deepen. Sheesh; the man didn't need to have a sexy smile to go along with the sexy laugh and all the other sexy bits. But there it was. Talk about a potent cocktail.

"I've secured a room at a local resort, the Tea Tree—"

"Wow. It was decent of you to buy me a drink—" *a kicker of a cocktail* "—in order to ease the sunburn—" *embarrassment* "—and all, but a room's rather presumptuous, don't you think?"

A few more glints joined the rest and his next smile came with a flash of white teeth. The rare and beautiful sight made her girl parts uncurl like a cat in the sun.

"Avery," he said, and she kind of wished he'd called her princess, or honey, because her name in that drawl from that mouth was as good as ten minutes of concentrated foreplay. "The room is for you. Just you. Alone."

"Oh," she said. Then several moments too late, "Of course. I knew that. I just— How do you even know that I could pay? I might be broke. Or tight with the purse strings. Or—"

"We're more than a tourist town. The cove is a real community. All I had to do was drop Claude's name and it was comped."

"Really?" Oh, how lovely! They loved Claude enough to look after *her*? Oh, she loved this resort already. Belatedly she wondered why they wouldn't simply comp it for *him*. Probably because Jonah North was a big scary bear. Or maybe he wasn't big on favours. *She* certainly owed him a few.

"I also let Claudia know I'd make sure you got home safe and sound tomorrow."

Avery's eyes shot back to his. A drink. A room. A ride. Maybe he wasn't such a jackass after all. Huh. Did that mean she had to try harder to be nice to him now too? Saying "no" had actually been fun, like being outside her own skin rather than curled up tight inside…

He pushed back his chair and held out his hand to her, and not for the first time. And not for the first time, she baulked.

She glanced up into his eyes to find him watching her, impatience edging at the corner of his mouth. Not wanting to start an international incident, she placed her hand in his to find it warm—as she'd expected—and strong—as she'd imagined—and roughly calloused—which sent a sharp shot of awareness right down her arm.

"Sorry," she said in a rush of breath as he tugged her to her feet, "my manners seem to fly right out the window where you're concerned. I can't seem to figure out why."

His pale grey eyes now shadows in the falling light, he said, "Can't you?"

Avery's belly clenched at the intensity of his gaze, and her heart beat so hard she could hear it behind her ears.

Such a simple question, with such a simple answer: she could.

She was obnoxious when he was around because he flummoxed her. He made her feel as if she had to keep her emotional dukes up, permanently, lest he find a way in and knock her out.

And if the past few days far away from the drama of her real life had told her anything, it was that she sorely needed a break. A return to simpler times. Like the summer when the most important thing that had ever happened to her had been a smile from the dreamy brown-eyed boy across the other side of the beach bonfire.

"The thing is," she said, regretting opening her mouth even as the words poured out, "I'm currently…thinking about… seeing someone."

"Someone?" he asked, everything in him suddenly seeming very still.

"Well, a man, to be more specific."

Jonah looked about the bar where an islander was putting chairs onto the tables so he could sweep the floor. He hooked a thumb in the guy's direction.

"No!" said Avery, grabbing his thumb and pulling it

down by his side. It brought her within inches of his chest, so that she could feel the steady rise and fall of his breaths, the heat of his skin, could count his individual eyelashes, all one million of the gorgeous things. She let go. Backed away. Breathed. "Someone *else*. Someone I met here years ago. Someone I'm hoping to…*reconnect* with."

"So then you're *not* here to help out Claudia." His words were tinged with such depths of boredom she wondered how she'd even come to think it was any of his business in the first place.

"Of course I am." Avery lifted her chin. And she was. Or at least she would be. But since their big girlie talk, she hadn't been able to pin her friend down long enough for a coffee, much less a conversation. *Go play tourist!* Claude would say on the fly. *Swim, drink cocktails, take a boat to Green Island.* Look how that turned out.

"You city girls," said Jonah, his voice dropping into a by now familiar growl. "Can't relax. Can't do one thing at a time. Can't settle your damn selves for love or money."

"That's a pretty broad brush."

"Am I wrong?"

Well…no. Back home "busy-busy" or "can't seem to get anything done" was akin to "fine, thanks."

"Yeah," he said, ducking his head as he ran a hand up the back of his neck and through those glorious curls. "That's what I thought. Come on, princess, let's get you checked in."

He jerked his chin in the direction of the exit, and this time he didn't hold out a hand.

Feeling strangely bereft, Avery collected her sandy, sodden gear and followed in her wet clothes and bare feet as at some point she'd lost her shoes. Beneath the shadows of the palm trees that grew everywhere in this part of the world, up the neat paths nearly empty of tourists now most had headed off the island.

And her mind whirled back to how that mortifying conversation had begun.

Can't you? he'd asked, when she'd admitted not knowing why she pushed his buttons. But then why did he insist on pushing hers? Maybe, just maybe, she rubbed him the wrong way too. That very particular kind of wrong way that felt so right.

At that moment Jonah looked back, and she offered up her most innocuous smile.

"All okay?"

"Fine, thanks. You?"

The edge of his mouth twitched, but there was no smile. No evidence he thought she was hot stuff too. He merely lifted a big arm towards a small building with a thatched roof—the Tea Tree Resort and Spa—and they headed inside into blissful air-conditioned luxury.

Once she'd got her key and thanked the guy at Reception profusely for the room, promising him payment, free PR services, a night in a hotel in New York if he was ever in town—all of which he rejected with a grin—she headed in the direction of her bungalow.

The clearing of a male throat brought her up short, and she turned to find Jonah leaning against the wall.

"You're not staying here?" she asked, and the guy's jaw twitched so hard she worried he'd break a tooth. "I mean in another room?"

"I have a place on the island."

"Oh." She waited for more. A description would have been nice. A little shanty hidden from view in the mangroves on the far side of the island? A towel on the sand, nothing between him and the stars? But no, he just stood there, in the only patch of shadow in the entire bright space.

"Think you'll be okay here?" he asked, his voice rough

around the edges, and yet on closer inspection…not so much. Much like the man himself.

"You tell me. You're the one who seems to think I can't walk out the door without facing certain death."

"I'll make you a deal," he said, his expression cool, those eyes of his quiet, giving nothing away. "If you're still alive in the morning, I'll change my tune."

"Till the morning, then," Avery said, taking a step outside the force field the guy wore like a second skin. "Now I'm going to take a long cold shower."

His gaze hardened on hers, and she felt herself come over pink, and fast.

"For the sunburn."

At her flat response, his mouth kicked into a smile, giving her another hint of those neat white teeth. A flash of those eye crinkles. A flood of sensation curled deep into her belly.

"Good night, Jonah."

He breathed in deep, breathed out slow. "Sleep tight," he said, then walked away.

Yeah right, Avery thought, watching the front doorway through which he'd left long after he was gone.

When she got to her room it was to find a fruit basket, a bottle of wine, and a big fat tub of aloe vera with a Post-it note slapped on top that read, "For the American who now knows Aussies do it better."

CHAPTER FOUR

AVERY WOKE TO an insistent buzzing. Groaning, she scrunched one eye open to find herself in a strange room. A strange bed. Peering through narrowed eyes, she saw the pillow beside her was undisturbed. That was something, at least.

She let her senses stretch a mite and slowly the day before came back to her... Green Island. Jonah. Sunburn. Jonah. Cocktail. Jonah. And lusting. Oodles of coconut-scented lusting. *And Jonah.*

And she rolled over to bury her face in a pillow.

When the buzzing started up again, she realised it was the hotel phone. She smacked her hand around the bedside table till she found it. "Hello?" Her voice sounded as if she'd swallowed a bucket of sand.

The laughter that followed needed no introduction.

"Don't. Please. It hurts."

"I don't doubt it," Jonah rumbled, his voice even deeper through the phone. "How long till you can be ready to leave?"

"A week?"

She felt the smile. Felt it slink across her skin and settle in her belly. "Half an hour."

"I'll meet you in Reception in forty-five minutes. And don't forget the sunscreen. Australian. Factor thirty. Buy some from the resort shop."

"Where are we going?"

"Home," he said, then hung up.

Avery heaved herself upright and squinted against the sunshine pouring through the curtain-free windows. The scent of sea air was fresh and sharp, the swoosh of the water nearby like a lullaby. It was a fantasy, with—thanks to rum—glimpses of hell. But it sure wasn't home.

Home was blaring horns and sidewalks teeming with life, not all of it human. City lights so bright you could barely see the stars. It was keeping your handbag close and your frenemies closer. It was freezing in New York right now. And heading into night. The storefronts filled with the first hints at hopeful spring fashion even while the locals scurried by in scarves and boots and coats to keep out the chill.

As soon as she turned on her phone it beeped. Her mother had sent a message at some point, as if she could sense her beloved daughter was about to have less than positive thoughts.

Hello, my darling! I hope you are having a fabulous time. When you get a moment could you please send me Freddy Horgendaas's number as I have had a most brilliant idea. I miss you more than you can know. xXx

Freddy was a *most brilliant* cake-maker, famous for his wildly risqué creations. Avery pressed finger and thumb into her eye sockets, glad anew she wouldn't be there when her mother revealed a cake in the shape of her father's private parts with a whopping great knife stuck right in the centre.

She sent the number with the heading 'Freddy Deets' knowing the lack of a complete sentence would make her mother twitch. It wasn't a *no*. More like passive aggression. But for her it was definitely a move in the right direction.

Forty minutes later—showered and changed into the still-damp bikini she'd found on the bathroom floor—

she made a quick stop to the resort gift shop where she picked up an oversized It's Easy Being Green! T-shirt, a fisherman's hat, and flip-flops to replace the shoes she'd somehow lost along the way, and slathered herself in *Australian* sunscreen and handed her key in to the day staff at Reception.

The girls behind the desk chattered about the shock of Claudia's and Luke's parents suddenly heading off into the middle of nowhere, and asked how Claudia was coping. Avery said her friend was coping just great, all the while thinking *shock* and *coping* were pretty loaded words. Making a deal with herself to pin Claude down asap, Avery still knew the moment Jonah had arrived, for she might as well have turned invisible to the two women behind the desk.

"Hi, Jonah!" the girls sing-songed.

"Morning, ladies," he said from behind her, his deep Australian drawl hooking into that place behind Avery's belly button it always seemed to catch. Then to Avery, "Ready to go?"

And the girls' eyes turned to her in amazement and envy.

Avery shook her head infinitesimally—*I get the lust, believe me, but don't panic, he's not the guy for me.*

Then she turned, all that denial ringing in her head as it got a load of the man who'd arrived to take her away.

It shouldn't have been a surprise that Jonah was *still* unshaven, and yet the sight of all that manly stubble first thing in the morning did the strangest things to her constitution. As did the warm brown of his skin against the navy blue shirt, and the strong calves beneath his long shorts, and the crystal-clear grey eyes.

"Shall we?" he asked.

We shall, she thought.

"Bye, Jonah!" the girls called.

Avery, who was by then five steps ahead of Jonah, rolled her eyes.

When they hit sunlight, she stopped, not knowing which way to go.

"What time's the boat?"

"No boat today. Not for us anyway." And then his hand strayed to her lower back, burning like a brand as he guided her along the path, leaving nothing between his searing touch but the cotton of her T-shirt and her still-damp swimmers.

"This way," he said, guiding her with the slightest pressure as he eased her through a gate marked Private then down a sandy path beneath the shade of a small forest, and back out into the sunshine where a jetty poked out into the blinding blue sea. And perched on a big square at the end—

"A helicopter?" A pretty one too, with the Charter North logo emblazed across the side.

"It was brought here this morning on a charter. They don't need it back till four. Quickest way off the island."

"No, thanks," she said, crossing her arms across her chest, "I'll wait for the boat."

"You sure?" he asked, his eyes dropping to where her crossed arms had created a little faux cleavage. Her next breath in was difficult. "It'll be a good eight hours from now, the sea rocking you back and forth, all that noise from a bunch of very tired kids after a long hot day at the beach—"

Avery held up a hand to shush him as she swallowed down the heave of anticipatory post-cocktail seasickness rising up in her stomach. "Yes, thank you. I get your point. So where's our pilot?"

At the twist of his smile, she knew.

Before she could object, Jonah's hands were at her waist, shoving her forward. Her self-preservation instincts actually propelled her away from his touch and towards the contraption as if it were the lesser danger.

When he hoisted her up, she scrambled into her seat with less grace than she'd have liked. And then suddenly he was there, his silhouette blocking out the sun, the scent of him—soap and sea and so much man—sliding inside her senses, the back of his knuckles scraping the T-shirt across her belly…

Oh, he was plugging her in.

"That feels good," she said. Then, cheeks going from sunburned to scorched in half a second flat, added, "The *belt* feels good. Fine. Nice and tight." *Nice and tight?*

A muscle in Jonah's cheek twitched, then without another word he passed her a set of headphones, slid some over his dark curls, flipped some dials, chatted to a flight-control tower, and soon they were off, with Avery's stomach trailing about ten feet below.

It didn't help that Jonah seemed content to simply fly, sunlight slanting across the strong planes of his face, his big thighs spread out over his seat.

Three minutes into the flight Avery nearly whooped with relief when she found a subject that didn't carry some unintentional double entendre. She waved a hand Jonah's way.

He tapped her headphones. *Right.*

"I hope you found someone to look after your dog," she said, her voice tinny in her ears. "I was thinking about it before I fell asleep last night. I mean, since it was my fault you couldn't go home to him last night."

"Hull'll be fine."

Hull. It suited the huge wolfish beast. Like something a Viking might call his best friend.

Then Jonah added, "But he's not my dog."

"Oh. But I thought… Claude said—"

"He's not my dog."

Okay, then.

An age later Jonah's voice came to her, deep and echoey through the headphones. "Want to know what I was thinking about when I finally fell asleep?"

Yes... But she was meant to be getting better at saying no. And this seemed like a really good chance to practise. "No," she lied, her voice flat even as her heart rate shot through the roof.

He shot her a look. Grey eyes hooded, lazy with heat. And the smile that curved at his mouth was predatory. "I'm going to tell you anyway."

Oh, hell.

"I wondered how long it will be before I have to throw myself between you and a drop bear."

Avery wasn't fast enough to hide the smile that tugged at her mouth. Or slow enough not to notice that his gaze dropped to her mouth and stayed. "I may be a tourist, Jonah, but I'm not an idiot. There's no such thing as a drop bear."

His eyes—thankfully—slid back to hers. "Claudia tipped you off, eh?"

"She is fabulous that way."

At mention of her friend another option occurred to her! Sitting up straighter, she turned in her seat as much as she could, ignoring the zing that travelled up her leg as her knee brushed against his.

"Speaking of Claudia," she said. *Here goes.* "She thinks you're hot."

A rise of an eyebrow showed his surprise. "Really?" And for a moment she thought she had him. Then he had to go and ask, "What do *you* think?"

Her stomach clenched as if taking a direct hit. "That's irrelevant."

"Not to me."

"Why do you even care?"

His next look was flat, intent, no holds barred. "If you don't know that yet, Ms Shaw, then I'm afraid that fancy education of yours was a complete waste."

She tried to blink. To think. To come up with some fabulous retort that would send him yelping back into his man cave. But the pull of those eyes, that face, that voice, basking in the wholly masculine scent of him filling the tiny cabin, she couldn't come up with a pronoun, much less an entire sentence.

And the longer the silence built, the less chance she had of getting herself off the hook.

It took for him to break eye contact—when a gust of wind picked them up and rocked them about—for her to drag her eyes away.

With skill and haste, he slipped them above the air stream and into calmer air space. While her stomach still felt as if it were tripping and falling. All because of a little innocent flirting.

Only it didn't feel innocent. It *felt* like Jonah was staking a claim.

But he scared the bejesus out of her. Not *him* so much; the swiftness of her attraction to him. It was fierce. And kind of wild. And she was the woman who calmed the waters. Not the kind who ever went chasing storms.

Even while she knew she was about to admit she understood exactly what Jonah meant, she said, "I told you— I'm interested in someone else." *Considering becoming interested, anyway.*

Then, as if it just didn't matter, he said, "You didn't answer my question."

"Because it's a ridiculous question!"

"You brought it up."

So she had. How had this suddenly gone so wrong?

Avery risked a glance to find Jonah's eyes back on her mouth. His jaw was tight, his breaths slow and deep. And his deep grey eyes made their way back to hers.

"Good Lord, Jonah, first the girls at the hotel were all swoony over you—"

"You noticed?" The smile was back. And a sheen of perspiration prickled all over her skin.

She held up a hand to block his face from sight. "Then Claude mentions in passing that she thinks you're a 'supreme example of Australian manhood—'"

His laughter at *that* echoed through the tiny space till her toes curled. But still she forged on.

"You really need *me* to be in the line-up too? Are you really that egotistical?"

"No, Avery. I'm really that interested. I want to hear you admit you're as attracted to me as I think you are," he said, and not for a second did he take his eyes from hers.

If she hadn't been strapped up like a Thanksgiving turkey she'd have been on him like cranberry sauce. But she was, and she couldn't. And the conversation had become such a hot mess, Avery wished she could go back in time. Perhaps to the very beginning when all that mattered in life was sleep, food, and a safe place in which to hide from pesky dinosaurs.

"You want to know what I *want*?" she asked, proud of the fact that her voice wasn't quavering all over the place. "What I want is for you to keep your eyes on the sky! No matter what you think of my survival skills, I have no intention of dying today."

She waited, all air stuck in her lungs, for him to say something like *I'd rather keep my eyes on you*. But he merely smiled. As if he knew that she was a big fat liar. Deep down in the dark places inside her that she avoided at all costs. The place where Pollyanna had been born: always positive, not a bother, things would get better, they would! No wonder she worked in PR.

When Jonah's smile only grew, she muttered, "Oh, shut up."

"I didn't say a thing."

"Well, stop *thinking*. It doesn't suit you."

The smile turned into a laugh—*huh-huh-huh*. Then,

easy as you please, he shifted eyes front and left her alone
for the rest of the flight.

Disappointment and temptation rode her in equal measure, so much so she clenched her fists and let herself have
a good internal scream. Because she didn't need this, feeling all breathless and weightless with all the hot flushes
and the like. Avery wasn't looking for sparks. Sparks were
incendiary. Their sole purpose was to start fires. And fire
burned.

She couldn't have been more relieved when the helicopter finally came to rest on a helipad at the end of a
jetty belonging to one of the bigger resorts just north of
Crescent Cove.

Even better when she saw Claudia waving as if Avery
had been rescued from some deserted island.

And, bless his shiny black shoes, there was Luke, leaning against the Tropicana Nights shuttle bus in the car park
at the far end of the jetty. Tall, and handsome, with half
an eye on his phone.

Hull was there too. The beast sat apart, upright on a
cluster of rocks in the shadow of a tilting palm tree at the
end of the jetty. Not Jonah's dog? Maybe somebody should
tell the dog that.

Avery managed to get herself unstrapped without help.
But getting down was another matter.

Strong hands at her waist, Jonah dropped her to the
ground. She didn't dare breathe as all that hard muscle and
sun-drenched skin imprinted itself upon her and good. The
second her feet hit terra firma, she peeled herself away.

"Here's hoping that's the last time you feel the need to
come to my salvation."

Jonah didn't second that thought. In fact, even as he
stood there, like some big hot, muscly statue, the look in
his eyes told her he wasn't on the same page at all. With a
shake of her head, she turned and walked away.

"Avery," he called.

She scrunched her eyes tight a second, held her breath. And when she looked back, she saw he was holding out her missing shoes.

Meaning at some point after he'd dropped her at the Tea Tree he must have gone looking for them. Which was actually…really…nice.

She walked to him, hating every second of it. And when she slid her fingers into the straps, her fingers brushed his. And there was the spark. Hard, fast, debilitating.

Their eyes met. One corner of his sexy mouth lifted. *Deny that*, he said without saying anything at all. And her heart thumped so hard against her ribs she dared not look down in case it was leaving a mark.

"Aaaaaveryyyy!" Claudia's voice carried on the air.

Jonah's eyes followed the sound, and lit up with an easygoing smile, one not fuelled with sex appeal and intent. When his eyes once again found hers, he caught her staring. And the next smile was all sex, all intent, all for her.

"Don't say it," she said, walking backwards, using her dangly sandals as a shield. "Don't even think it. The end."

And then she turned, looped her arm through Claudia's and swung her away from the crazy-making guy at her back.

"You okay?" Claude asked. "You looked all flushed."

"Sunburn," Avery deadpanned. Then bumped shoulders with her friend. "Now did you guys *really* drive out here just to get me?"

"Of course we did. When Jonah rang to say you'd nearly been eaten by a giant squid I had to find out the real story!"

"Funny man," she mumbled, "that friend of yours."

"Seems he's becoming quite the friend of *yours*. I've never been on his chopper before. Not once."

Avery turned back to find Jonah leaning on his helicopter watching her. The big wolf dog now sitting at his heels was watching her too.

"What is with the dog anyway?" she asked, distracting Claudia. "Jonah says it's not his."

"And yet there they are, their own private little wolf pack. It's kind of romantic really, in a tragic, Heathcliffian loner-type way."

"Except instead of cold, wet, English moors he wanders a sunny Aussie beach?"

"Exactly."

"Not quite so tragic, then."

Claude grinned. "If you're going to wander anywhere the rest of your days, might as well be here."

Avery opened her mouth to ask if there'd been a "Catherine" to send him wandering the moors/beach in the first place. Then snapped it shut tight. Jonah North was none of her business. Hopefully she could get through the rest of her holiday without tripping over the guy or she'd go back home even more tightly wound than when she left.

They neared the end of the jetty and Avery looked up and saw Luke watching them from his position at the shuttle bus. She stood straighter, smiled big, and lifted her hand in a cheery wave.

Luke shot her a nod. A smile. Just looking at him she knew he'd know his way around a wine cellar. That he knew a Windsor knot from a Prince Albert. He'd slip into any dinner party with her friends back home as if he were born there. And yet she could still feel Jonah behind her, even at twenty paces away.

"Thanks for the offer of a lift," she said to Claude, backing away, "but I think I'll walk back. Stretch my legs. Lunch later? Just you and me?"

"Lunch would be great."

Avery gave Claude a big hug, then wiggled her fisherman's hat tighter on her head, the strap of her bag digging into the sunburn on her shoulder, and headed off.

* * *

Hull padding along warm and strong beside him, Jonah ambled down the jetty towards Luke.

While he waited for his old mate to finish up his phone call, Jonah's eyes slid to the retreating back of the crazy-making blonde in the oversized green T-shirt that stopped just short of her backside. And he brooded.

With Claude the woman was like some kind of puppy dog, all floppy and happy and bright. Waving to Luke she'd practically preened. While with *him* she was a flinty little thing, all snappy and sharp. It was as if she didn't know who she was. Or that she felt a need to be different things to different people. And *then* there was all that talk of her 'reconnecting' with some other guy... And Jonah was a man who appreciated good faith above all. And yet there was no denying her physical response any time he came near. Or, for that matter, his. It had been a while since he'd felt that kind of spark. Real, instant, fiery. And like a fish-hook in the gut, it wasn't letting go. Every touch, every look, every time he caught her staring at him with those stunning odd eyes it dug deeper.

He should have known better. He *did* know better. Seemed his hormones didn't give a flying hoot. They wanted what they wanted. And they wanted restless little tourist Avery Shaw.

Rach had been a tourist too. Even while she'd *insisted* she wanted to be more. Even when her actions hadn't backed it up, even when she'd never really tried to fit in.

Not that he'd let himself see it. He'd been too caught up in the fantasy of a girl like her seeing something worthy in a drifter like him.

When *she'd* had enough of playing tourist and moved back to Sydney, he'd followed. She'd let him, probably for no stronger reason than that it felt good to be chased. While Jonah had given up everything, leaving his home, his friends, his way of life, selling his father's boat, getting a job on the docks as if water were water. Unable to admit he was wrong...

When he'd had run out of money and finally admitted to himself that it was all a farce, she was happily ensconced in her old life, while his was in tatters.

Lesson learned.

His biggest mistake had been thinking something was more than what it was.

Meaning he had to decide what this was, and soon. A spark. Attraction. A deep burn. Nothing more. So long as he owned it, he could use it. Enjoy it. Till it burned itself out.

Yeeeah, mind made up between one breath and the next. Next time he saw Avery Shaw it was game on.

As for her mysterious 'reconnect'? If it wasn't all some story she'd made up and the guy hadn't manned up by now, fool had missed his chance.

"Jonah, my man," Luke called, jerking Jonah from his reverie.

Jonah moved in and gave his old friend a man hug.

"Funny," said Luke, "riding in the resort van got me to thinking about that summer I used to hitch rides in your Kombi, driving as far as it took to find the best surf of the day."

"Ah, the surf. I remember it well."

"And the girls."

"That too," Jonah added, laughing. They'd spent long summers surfing and laughing and living and loving with no thought of the future. Of how things might ever be different.

Look at them both now. Luke, in his suit and tie, phone glued to his palm, a touch of London in his accent. Jonah the owner of a fleet of boats, a helicopter, more. Successful, single...satisfied.

"Found any wave time since you've been back?" Jonah

asked. If he had it'd be more than Jonah had seen in a long time.

Luke bent down to give Hull a quick scoff about the ears, which Hull took with good grace. "Nah," he said, frowning. "Not likely to either."

Maybe not completely satisfied, then.

"Aww, young Claude have you wrapped around her little finger, does she?"

Luke straightened slowly and slid his hands into his pockets, his gaze skidding to their sunny little friend at the end of the jetty. "Let's just say it's taking longer than I might have hoped for us to…set the tone of our new business relationship."

Jonah laughed. Luke had been one of the big reasons he'd even been able to carve a new life for himself in the cove after Rach. He owed him more than money could repay. But not enough he'd take on Claudia Davis. He patted his friend on the back and said, "Good luck there."

"And good luck there," Luke said, the tone of his voice shifting. Jonah followed the shift in Luke's eyeline to find him watching Avery shuffle off into the distance, her thongs catching at the soft sand, her ridiculously inappropriate city-girl shoes dangling from one hand—the shoes he'd spent an hour the night before combing the moonlit beach to track down.

"Cute," Luke added, both men watching till she disappeared into a copse of palms.

Jonah admitted, "She is that."

"She was here once before, you know," said Luke. "Ten odd years ago. With her family. Odd couple, I remember—father quiet, mother loud, dripping money. And Avery? Skinny little thing. Shy. Overly well-bred. Had a crush on me too, if memory serves. Big eyes following me up and down the beach. If I'd known then she'd turn out like that…"

Jonah missed whatever Luke said next as blood roared between his ears and a grave weight settled in his gut, as if he'd swallowed a load of concrete.

Luke.

Avery planned to 'reconnect' with Luke.

The way she'd bounced on her toes as she'd waved to the guy just now, fixing her hair, smiling from ear to ear, the sunshine smile and all. Hell, she'd called out Luke's name that day on the beach, hadn't she?

The concrete in Jonah's gut now turning his limbs to dead weights, he turned to face his old friend to find Luke's gaze was on the water now, following the line of white foam far out to sea. Avery clearly not on his mind. As the guy hadn't a single clue.

Hull whimpered at his side. Jonah sank a hand into the dog's fur before Hull lifted his big snout and pressed it into Jonah's palm, leaving a trail of slobber Jonah wiped back into his fur.

It had been Luke who'd put up the money to buy back his father's boat when Jonah had come back home to the cove with his tail between his legs, calling it 'back pay of petrol money' from the times he'd hitched rides in that old Kombi. From there Jonah had worked day and night, fixing the thing up, accepting reef charters to earn enough money to buy the next boat, and the next, and the next. Becoming a grown-up, forging a future, one intricately tied to the cove, his home.

He'd paid Luke back within a year. But he *owed* him more than money could ever repay.

Which was precisely why, even while the words tasted like battery acid on the back of his tongue, he said, "You should ask her out."

"Who?" Luke's phone rang, then, frowning, he strolled away, investing everything into the call. Leaving Jonah to throw out his arms in surrender.

Which was when Claudia stormed up. "No getting through to him now." Then, shaking her head, she turned to Jonah with a smile. "Now that you've brought my girl home safe, what's the plan?"

"Work," Jonah said. "Haircut, maybe."

"Don't you dare! Your curls are gorgeous."

Jonah glanced down at the petite bundle of energy at his side. A woman who was as much a part of the landscape as he was. A local. Someone who'd stick around. "Your little friend told me you think I'm hot."

"She did not!"

Jonah smiled back.

Claudia gaped at him a moment before she burst out laughing. "Of course I think you're hot. The entire region of females thinks you're hot. Anyone else simply hasn't met you yet." She squeezed his biceps, gave a little a shiver, and then went back to walking congenially at his side.

And *that* was why he'd never gone there with her. Because while Claudia was cute as a button, and local, and available, there'd never been that spark. That all-out, wham-bam, knock-the-wind-from-your-sails spark that he knew was out there for the having.

He knew because he'd felt it.

Twice.

The first woman who'd made him feel that way had made him believe it was real, until the day she woke up and decided it wasn't.

The other one had convinced herself she wanted to 're-connect' with his best mate.

To think, his week had started with such high hopes.

CHAPTER FIVE

FEELING BETTER ABOUT the world after having just signed a lucrative contract to keep his newest luxury yacht on call for clients of the Hawaiian Punch Hotel, Jonah set off through the outdoor Punch Bowl Bistro, Hull meeting him at the door and padding along beside him.

He'd nearly hit the path between resorts when Hull whimpered, ran around in front of him, and nudged his hand with his nose.

"What's up, boy?" Jonah asked, right at the moment he realised it wasn't a what, it was a *who*.

For there at a table sat Avery Shaw.

It had been days since he'd set eyes on her. After the Luke revelation, he'd figured total avoidance was the safest bet.

Now as he watched her sit at the table doing nothing more seductive than swirl a straw round and round in a pink drink the staunched heat clawed its way through his gut like some creature kept hungry way too long, settling with a discomforting ache in his groin.

Before he even felt his feet move Jonah was threading his way towards her.

Hull got to her first, curling around the base of her table and lying down as if he was expected.

"Hey!" Avery said, her face lighting up with surprised laughter. With sunshine.

Then he saw the moment she knew what Hull's sudden appearance meant. Her head whipped up, her eyes locking onto his, lit by an instant and wild flicker of heat, before she tilted her chin as if to say, *I refuse to admit my cheeks are flushed because of you.*

Yeah, honey, he thought, *right back at ya.*

Then her eyes slid past him, to the empty doorway leading inside the hotel. And all sunshine fled to leave way for sad Bambi. What scrape had she gotten herself into now?

His vision expanded to notice her knife and fork were untouched. The bread basket mere crumbs.

And he knew.

Luke. She'd made plans to have lunch with Luke. And for whatever reason, the goose had clearly failed to show.

That was the moment Jonah should have walked away. Considering how much he owed Luke, how long a friendship they'd enjoyed, and the fact that being anywhere near Avery made him feel like a rubber band stretched at its limit, it was the only honourable option.

And yet he dragged out a chair and—blocking Ms Shaw's view of the front door—sat down.

Luke not carving out time for a surf during his first time in the cove for years was one thing. But not knowing when a gorgeous woman wanted to get to know him better? Unforgivable.

And she was gorgeous. Her pale hair clipped neatly away from her face in some kind of fancy braid, eyes soft and sooty, lips slicked glossy pink, ropes of tiny beads draping over a black-and-white dress that made her look like a million bucks. If he ever needed a reminder she was not from here, that whatever spark was between them had *no* future...

Then she had to go and say, "Oh, you're *staying*?"

And that was it. He was hunkered in. His voice was

one notch above a growl as he said, "Nice to see you too, Miss Shaw."

She pointed over his shoulder. "I'm actually—"

"Thrilled to see me?"

She swallowed, clearly undecided as to whether to admit why she was there alone. In the end she kept her mouth shut.

"Saw you sitting here all alone and figured it was the gentlemanly thing to rescue you from your lonesomeness," he said, casually perusing the menu he already knew by heart. He put the menu down, and settled back in his chair, sliding a leg under the table, navigating Hull's big body. Only to find himself knocking shoes with Avery. Her high-heel-clad foot slipped away.

"Really?"

"Hand to heart," he said, action matching words.

Her eyes flickered to his hand, across his chest, over his shoulders, to his hair, pausing longest of all on his mouth, before skimming back to his eyes. And while he knew it was not smart, was *traitorous* even, he enjoyed every second of it.

"Is your dog even allowed in here?" she said, pointing under the table.

He lifted a shoulder, let it fall. "Not my dog."

She leaned forward a little then. Her mouth kicked into a half-smile.

"Well, whoever's dog he is," that mouth said, "he's sitting on my foot. And my toes are now officially numb. He's enormous."

"Huge," said Jonah, lifting his eyes to hers to find them darkened, determined, as if making some kind of connection between man and beast. Enough that he had to fight the urge to adjust himself.

Wrapping her lips around her straw in a way that was

entirely unfair, she asked, "So how did you and Hull meet?"

"Found him on the beach when he was a pup—a tiny, scrawny, shivery ball of mangy, matted fluff, near dead with exhaustion and hunger. Odds on he wasn't the only one in the litter dumped. Probably tied up in a sack full of rocks and thrown overboard. He's been crazy afraid of water ever since. Took him home, cleaned him up, fed him, and that was it."

"You saved his life and that doesn't make him your responsibility?"

"Never bought him, never sought him. Don't get me wrong, he's a great dog. And if he thinks you're a threat to me, he'd like nothing better than to tear you limb from limb."

"Me?" she said, flicking a quick glance at the now-snoring lump under the table. "A threat?"

Jonah shot her a flat look. She was the biggest threat he'd met in a long time.

By the rise and fall of her chest she got his meaning loud and clear.

Then, frowning, she slipped her fingers down the length of beads and stared at the little bits of pineapple bobbing on top of her drink. Most likely because of the elephant in the room. Or *not* in the room as he hadn't showed up.

Rubbing a hand up the back of his neck, Jonah wished he'd simply called Luke and asked where the hell he was. Or at the very least what his intentions towards her were, if any. Hell, he'd done such a fine job avoiding the woman, for all Jonah knew she and Luke could have been dating for days.

That thought clouded his vision something mad, but didn't put a dent in the attraction that rode over him like a rogue wave. The only right thing to do was leave. Walk away. Avoid more. At least until he knew where they all stood.

He quietly schooled his features, looked casually over the restaurant, towards the still-empty doorway. And set his feet to the floor as he made to leave her be.

When the waiter came shuffling up. "Oh, good, your company's finally arrived. Are you ready to order now?"

Jonah glanced back at Avery to find her blushing madly now, nose buried in the menu.

"Um…he's… I guess. Just… Can I have a second, please? Sorry!"

When she looked up at the waiter she shot him her sunshine smile, catching Jonah in its wake. The effect was like a smack to the back of the head, rattling his thoughts till he could no longer quite put them back in order.

"This is my first time here," she said. "What would you recommend?"

Jonah jabbed a finger at the rump steak. "Rare." Motioned to his friend under the table and said, "Two."

"Make it three," said Avery, picking out a pricey glass of red wine to go along with it.

When the waiter wandered off, she lowered the menu slowly, frowned at it a second, before taking a breath and looking up at him. Clearly bemused as to how they'd got there. Just the two of them. Having lunch.

He wished he knew himself.

Avery shuffled on her chair and said, "So, Jonah, did you always want to work with boats growing up?"

"Boats? We're really heading down that path?"

"Boats. The weather. You pick!" She threw her arms out in frustration. "Or you can just sit there all silent and broody for all I care. I was perfectly happy to have lunch on my own before you came along."

"Were you, now?"

She glared at him then, the truth hovering between them.

She grabbed her pink drink and slugged the thing down till it was empty. The fact that she thought she needed booze to get through lunch with him was actually kind of comforting. Then she licked her lips in search of stray pink drink. And Jonah had never felt less comfortable in his life.

He rubbed a hand over his jaw, hoping the prickle of stubble might wake him the hell up, but instead finding his cheeks covered in overly long scruff. The lack of a close shave was just about the only throwback to his old life. When the idea of lunch with a pretty girl was as normal to him as a day spent in the sea, not something fraught with malignant intentions and mortal peril.

He dropped his calloused fingers to his lap, so like his father's fingers.

She wanted to talk boats? What the hell. "My father worked on boats."

"Oh, a family tradition."

Jonah coughed out a laugh. His father wouldn't have thought so. As brutally proud as Jonah was of everything Charter North had become, he knew his father wouldn't have understood. The types of boats, or the number. Karl North had only ever owned the one boat, the *Mary-Jane*, named after Jonah's mother. And in the end she'd killed him.

"He was a lobster man," Jonah went on. "A diver. Over the reefs. Live collection, by hand." No big hauls, just long hours, negligible conversation, even less outward displays of affection, not much energy left for anything not on the boat.

Avery picked up on the *"Was?"*

"He died at sea when I was seventeen. He'd taught me a thing or two about boats before then, though. I could pull a boat engine apart and put it back together by the time I was fourteen."

"You think that's impressive? At fourteen I could speak French and create a five-course menu for twenty people."

"You cook?"

"I created the *menu*. Cook cooked it."

"Of course."

She grinned. *Sunshine.* And when she slid her fingers over the rope of beads, this time he felt the slide of those fingers somewhere quite else. "And your mother?"

"She left when I was eleven. I haven't seen her since. Hard being married to a man whose first love is big and blue. When the summer storms threaten to turn every boat inside out and upside down. When quotas laws changed, or the crops just weren't there. He went back out there the next day and tried again, because that's what men did."

And there you have it, folks, he thought, dragging in a breath. Most he'd said about his own folks…probably ever. Locals understood. Rach hadn't ever asked. While Avery dug it out of him with no more than a look.

Jonah shifted on his chair.

"My turn?" she said.

"Why the hell not?"

Grinning, this time less sunshine, more sass, she leaned down to wrap her lips around the edge of her glass, found it empty, left a perfect pink kiss in their place.

"My parents are both still around. Dad's an investment banker, busy man, Yankees fan—" A quick fist-pump. "Go Yanks! My mother earned her living the Park Avenue way—divorce—and is a fan of spending Dad's money. While I am the good daughter: cheerful, encouraging, conciliatory."

Jonah struggled to imagine this caustic creature being *conciliatory*. Until he remembered her snuggling up to Claude, bouncing on her heels as she waved to Luke. *Luke.* He frowned. Forgot what he was thinking about, or more likely shoved it way down deep inside.

"Even my apartment is equidistant from both of theirs," she went on.

"You're Switzerland?"

She laughed.

Chin resting on her upturned palm, she said, "Between you and me and this dog who's not yours, being Switzerland is exhausting. I didn't realise how much Switzerland needed a break till I came here. You know what my mother is doing right this second? Organising a *party* to celebrate the tenth anniversary of the divorce. Manhattan rooftop, over a hundred guests, yesterday she called to tell me about the comedian she's hired to roast my father, who won't even be there."

The waiter came back with her wine, which she wrapped her hands around as if it were a life ring. "Worst part? She actually thought I'd be dying to help. As if my relationship with my father—such as it is—means nothing."

Her eyes flickered, a pair of small lines creasing the skin above her nose. And when she shook her head, it was as if a flinty shell had crumbled to reveal a whole different Avery underneath. A woman trying to do the right thing in her small way against near impossible odds.

He got that.

With a shrug and an embarrassed twist of her sweet lips Avery gave him a look.

He opened his mouth to say…something, when Hull sat up with a muffled woof, saving him from saying anything at all. Seconds later the waiter arrived in a flurry. Hull's raw steak had been pounded into mush by the chef. Avery's and Jonah's sat in sweet and juicy seas of mushroom pepper sauce.

After the waiter left, Jonah said, "You know what Switzerland should do next?"

"What's that?" she asked, her hand flinching a little as she put her napkin on her lap.

"Eat," he said, shoving a chunk of steak in his mouth.

Her smile was new—soft, swift, and lovely. And Jonah breathed through the realisation that there couldn't *possibly* be any more last-minute saves.

The next time he nearly did something with this woman it would be all on him.

"So what's the plan for the afternoon?" Jonah asked later as they ambled onto the palm-tree-lined path that curled between the resorts and led back to the main street.

"Tropicana, I guess. Track down Claude. Sit on her so that we can get more than two minutes together in a row."

"How's she doing?" *Another scintillating question.* And yet he couldn't let her go. Not yet. The rubber-band feeling was back, tugging him away even as it pulled him right on back.

"Great. I think. Truth is, she's been so busy running the resort I've probably spent more time with you this holiday than her."

Her cheeks flushed as she realised what she'd said. And something swelled hot and sudden inside him. She'd spent more time with *him*. Not *Luke*. Meaning nothing had happened between them. Yet.

"Come on," he growled, pressing a hand to her back as he shielded her from a group of oblivious teenagers taking up the whole path as they headed towards the Punch Bowl.

Jonah kept his hand at her back as they continued along the now-secluded path. And she let him.

When they reached a fork in the path—one way headed straight to the beach, the other hooking back to the rear entrance to the Tropicana Nights—she turned towards him, and his hand slid naturally to her waist.

Wrong, he told himself, *on so many levels*. And yet it felt so right. His hand in the dip of her waist. Her scent curling beneath his nose. Her mismatched eyes picking up the earthy colours around her.

Her voice was breathless as she said, "Thanks for lunch. It was nice to have company."

Streaks of sunlight shot through the palm leaves above and shone in her pale hair and the pulse that beat in her throat. Through the thin dress he felt the give of her warm flesh beneath his rough palm. She leaned into his touch without even knowing it.

It finally drove him over the edge.

"Even if it wasn't the company you wanted?"

Her eyes flashed. Her cheeks flushed pink. Before she could move away, his second hand joined his first at her waist. And he pressed an inch closer. Two. Till their hips met. Her breath shot from her lungs in a whoosh and her top teeth came down over her bottom lip.

He lifted a hand to run his thumb over the spot, tugging the pink skin, leaving the pad of his thumb moist. "Luke is a fool," Jonah said, his voice so rough his throat hurt.

Her eyes widened, but she didn't deny it. Then they widened even more as she lifted her hands to press against his chest. "Is *that* why you had lunch with me? He couldn't come and sent you to soften the blow?"

"Hell, no," Jonah barked. "I'm nobody's flunky. And Luke's a stand-up guy. Doesn't mean that sometimes he doesn't know a good thing when it's right under his nose."

What the hell was he doing? Trying to talk her into the guy's arms? No. He was making sure she was sure. Because he was beyond sure that he wanted to kiss her. Taste her. Hell, he wanted to throw her over his shoulder and take her back to his cave and get it on till she cried out *his* name.

"He's your friend," she said, her fingers drifting to lie flat against his chest. Jonah's heart rocked against his ribs.

"Which gives me the right to call him out. And if the guy thought any place was better than being right here, right now, with a woman like you, who feels like you feel, and smells as good as you smell, and is into team sports as much as you—"

She laughed at that one, a dreamy gleam in her darkening eyes.

"He's worse than a fool," Jonah finished. "He's too late."

Avery's hands curled against his chest. He held his breath as he waited for her to take them away. Instead they gripped his polo shirt, her fingernails scraping cotton against skin, sending shards of heat straight to his groin. And he pressed back until she bumped against the white stuccoed wall beneath the palms.

Then, hauling Avery against him, with an expulsion of breath and self-control, Jonah laid his lips on hers.

He'd expected sweetness and experience—a woman couldn't be that gorgeous and not make the most of it.

What he didn't expect was the complete assault on his senses. Or the searing thread of need that wrapped tight about him, following the path of her hands as they slid up into his hair, deepening where her body arched against his, throbbing at every pulse point on his body.

Not a pause, or a breath, her lips simply melted under his, soft and delicious. And he drank her in as if it had been coming for days, eons, forever. He had no idea how long that kiss kept him in its thrall before he eased back, the cling of their lips parting on a sigh.

Slowly the rest of the world came back online until Jonah felt the warmth of the sunlight dappling through the trees, and the sound of the nearby waves lapping gently against the sand, and Avery, soft and trembling in his arms.

Then she looked up at him, shell-shocked. As if she'd never been kissed that way in her life. It was such an ego surge, it took everything in him not to wrap his arms around her, rest his forehead against hers, and just live in the moment. To forget about anything else. Anyone.

Hell, he thought, reality hitting like a Mack truck.

How readily he'd just caved. And kissed her. Avery Shaw. Claude's friend. Luke's…who the hell knew what? And until that point pain in his proverbial ass.

He dug deep to find whatever ruthlessness he'd once upon a time dredged up to take a dilapidated old lobster boat and turn it into an empire, and used it to put enough physical distance between himself and Avery that she wrapped her arms about her as if she was suddenly cold.

Her voice was soft as she said, "That was…unexpected."

Not to him. She'd been dragging him back to his old self—when he'd been wild, unfocused, all that mattered was following the sun—for days. Not that he was about to tell her so.

He looked at her sideways. "What was I supposed to do with you looking up at me like that?"

She blinked. "Like what?"

"Like Bambi when his mother died."

Her eyes opened as wide as they could go. "You kissed me to…*cheer me up*?"

"Did it work?"

Snapping back to factory settings, her hands jerked to her hips and her eyes narrowed to dark slits. "What do you think, smart guy? Do I *appear* cheerful?"

She *appeared* even more kissable now, her hair a little dishevelled, her lips swollen, and all those waves of emotion coursing his way. She also looked confused. And a little hurt.

Not so much it stopped him from saying, "I don't know you well enough to rightly say."

She reared back as if slapped. "Wow," she said. "I knew you were a stubborn son of a bitch, Jonah. But until right now I had no idea you were a coward."

And without once looking back she stormed away.

Rubbing a hand up the back of his head, he dragged his

eyes from her retreating back to find trusty Hull sitting at his feet, looking adoring as ever. No judgment there.

"She's partly right," he said. "I am a son of a bitch."

But he wasn't a coward. Not that he was about to chase her to point that out. In fact, considering that kiss, he considered himself pretty frickin' heroic for walking away. Until that point he'd been thinking all about him; why he should stay the hell away from her. Not once had it occurred to him she ought to stay away from him. Not until he'd felt her trembling in his arms.

While he'd made the decision to remain cemented in Crescent Cove for the rest of his natural life, emotionally he would always be a nomad. It was in his blood. Passed down from his flighty mother. His voyager father. To all intents and purposes he'd been on his own since before he was even a teen. Walked himself to school. Lived off what he could cook. Skating. Surfing. Nothing tying him to anything, or any place, except choice.

When Rach had sashayed into town he'd been twenty-three, living like a big kid in his father's house on the bluff, life insurance on the verge of gone. She'd been this sophisticated outsider, come from Sydney for a week, and he'd done everything in his power to win her over. The life might not have been enough for his mum, but if this woman could stay, to him it was incontrovertible proof that *his* was the best life on earth.

She'd moved in with him after three days, and stayed for near a year.

Inevitably, she'd grown bored.

And when she left he'd been left completely untethered. Banging about inside the old house like a bird with broken wings.

After his disastrous move to Sydney with its noise, and smog, and crush of people—he'd taken control of his life. Delivering on the promise of his father's hard work.

He might not have time to connect with the better parts of his old life—with the sun, and the sea, and the big blue—but he felt otherwise fulfilled. Better, he felt *redeemed*.

And he wasn't willing to risk that feeling for anything or anyone. No matter how kissable.

Avery was in such a red-hot haze she couldn't remember how she made it back to the resort. But soon the white steps were loud beneath her high heels as she made her way into the lobby.

Mere days before she'd been delighting in her ability to say *no* to the guy, as if it were some kind of sign that with a little R and R under her belt she might have the wherewithal to say the same to her folks one of these days. But *no*. One touch, one deep dark look, and she'd practically devoured him.

She lifted fingers to lips that felt bruised and tender, knowing that not being able to say no and wanting to say yes were two wholly different things, but it was hard to think straight while she could still *feel* those big strong arms wrap tight about her, his heart thundering beneath her chest, his mouth on hers.

Suddenly feeling a mite woozy, she slowed, found a column and banged her forehead against the cool faux marble. It felt so good she did it again.

"Avery."

Avery looked up, rubbing at the spot on her head as she turned to find Luke Hargreaves striding towards her in his lovely suit with his lovely face and that lovely way he had about him that didn't make her feel as if she were being whipped about inside a tornado.

Her invitation to lunch *had* been casual. An honest-to-goodness catch-up. Nothing more. As picture-perfect as he appeared she'd struggled to whip up the kind of enthusiasm required to campaign for more. Yet maybe this whole thing had been a sign. That she needed to up her game.

"Luke!" she said, leaning in for an air kiss.

"Don't you look a million bucks." He looked her up and down, making her feel…neat. If Jonah had done the same she'd have felt stripped bare. "Don't tell me today was meant to be our lunch date."

Yeah, buddy, it was. "Not to worry! I bumped into Jonah." *Argh!* "So he sat with me, and we ate. Steak." *Oh, just shut up now.*

"Was it any good?"

"I'm sorry?" she squeaked.

"The steak."

"Oh, the *steak* was excellent. Tender. Tasty." *Please shoot me now.* "If you get the chance to eat there, try it."

Nodding as if he just might, Luke ran a hand through his hair leaving tracks that settled in attractively dishevelled waves. Even that didn't have her hankering to run her fingers in their wake. Yet every time she saw a certain head full of tight dark curls it was a physical struggle not to reach out and touch.

"You know what? What are you doing right now?" he asked.

Trying not to make it obvious that my knees aren't yet fully functional after your friend kissed me senseless. You?

He glanced at his watch, frowned some more. "Miraculously I have nothing on my plate right this second, if you'd like to grab a coffee."

"No," she said, rather more sternly than she'd intended. But Avery was a Shaw. And Shaws didn't know the meaning of giving in. Look at her mother! She softened it with a smile. Then said, "Dinner. Tomorrow night. A proper catch-up." *A proper setting to see if something nice can be forged.*

"Perfect." He smiled. "Catch you then." It was a perfectly lovely smile. Her blood didn't come close to rushing; in fact it didn't give a flying hoot.

Avery made to give him a quick peck on the cheek, but instead found herself patting him chummily on the arm. Then he headed off, always with purpose in his stride that one. Unlike Jonah who, even as he got things done, had this air about him as if he had all the time in the world.

With a sigh Avery didn't much want to pick apart, she looked up and caught the eye of young Isis behind the reception desk. The girl waggled her eyebrows suggestively.

If only, Avery thought. Even Pollyanna gave a little yawn. By the time Avery slipped back to her room she collapsed on her bed and had the first nap she'd had since she was a kid. All it took to finally find the limit to her exhaustion was making a date with one man while the kiss of another still lingered on her lips.

CHAPTER SIX

JONAH SAT AT the small backstreet pub the tourists always seemed to miss—probably because it wasn't suffocated by a surfeit of palm trees and Beach Boys music. Self-flagellation being a skill he'd honed during the long months spent in Sydney, he'd invited Luke to join him.

"Thanks for filling in at lunch with Avery today, mate," Luke said.

And there went Jonah's hopes for a quiet beer.

Frosty bottle an inch from his mouth, Luke added, "I bumped into her in the lobby after I finally extricated myself from one of Claudia's presentations. All cardboard signs and permanent markers. She has a dislike for PowerPoint I'll never understand." His eyes shifted Jonah's way. "So how was lunch?"

"They do a good steak," Jonah rumbled, then chugged a third of his beer in one hit.

"So I heard."

He and Luke might only see one another once every couple of years these days, but they'd been mates long enough for Jonah to know he'd been made. *Dammit.*

He held his ground, counting the bottles of spirits lining the shelves behind the bar. Luke shifted on his chair to face Jonah. Until, thumb swishing over the face of his phone, Luke said, "In fact we have dinner plans for tomorrow night. Avery and I."

Jonah gripped his beer, even as he felt his cheek twitch in a masochistic grin. He tipped his beer in Luke's direction as he caught his old friend's gaze. "You're going, right?"

Luke pushed his phone aside, a huge smile creasing his face. "Any reason I shouldn't?"

"You stood her up once before."

Luke's smile fell. "Hardly. She'd told me she was having lunch at the Punch if I was around."

"Luke. Man. Come on. She thought it was a date."

"I don't think so, mate. You've got your wires crossed somewhere."

When had his old mate morphed from his wingman into this blinkered, workaholic monkey with a phone permanently attached to his palm? In fairness, it was probably about the time his ex-wife took his heart out with a fork.

Luke watched him a few long seconds before slowly leaning back in the leather chair. "Should be a fun night, though. Those legs. That smile. And that accent? It just kills me."

Jonah tried to sit still, remain calm, and yet he could *feel* the steam pouring from his ears. Luke clearly noticed, as suddenly he laughed as if he'd never seen anything so funny.

With a tip of his beer bottle towards Jonah, Luke said, "So, you and Miss Manhattan, eh?"

"There is no me and Miss Manhattan."

Luke grinned like a shark as he parroted back, "Jonah. Man. *Come on.*"

Jonah settled his hands around his beer and stared hard into the bubbles. "I'm right there with you on the legs. And the smile. And the accent." And the eyes. He'd had dreams about those eyes, locked onto his, turning dark with pleasure as she fell apart in his arms. "But she's my worst nightmare."

The raised eyebrow of his old friend told him he didn't believe it for a second. "From what Claude tells me, she's from money. So high maintenance, maybe."

"It's not that. She's…" Stunning, sexy, yet despite the big-city sophistication still somehow compellingly naive. She could swipe his legs out from under him if he wasn't careful. "A pain in the ass."

Luke thought on it a moment. "Then again, aren't they all?"

Jonah tapped the neck of Luke's beer bottle with his own.

"I've been around the block a few times now," Jonah went on. "I've made mistakes. I'd like to think I've learned when to trust my gut about such things."

"Since You Know Who?"

Jonah raised an eyebrow in assent. "And yet, I can't seem to…not."

"Then lucky for you the man she clearly wants is me."

At that, whatever morbid little tunnel Jonah had been staring down blinked out of existence. He leant back in his chair, and smiled at his friend. "Not as much as she thinks she does."

"Now what makes you think my charms aren't all-encompassing?"

"I have it on good knowledge that she's…in flux."

Luke's laughter rang through the bar. He sat forward. All ears. And, thankfully, not a lick of rivalry in his gaze. "I've been out of circulation too long. Since when does 'steak' stand for something else?"

"Calm down. Steak meant steak," Jonah rumbled.

"But *something* happened."

When Jonah didn't answer, Luke slammed the table so hard their beers bounced. "Jonah North, pillar of the Crescent Cove community, made out with *my* dinner date who is also apparently his worst nightmare. Was this before or after she asked me to dinner?"

Jonah's cheek twitched and his head suddenly hurt so much he couldn't see straight. "Hell."

Luke's laughter was so loud it echoed through the small bar till the walls shook. "Man, you have no idea how much I'm enjoying this. The number of times girls came up to me only to ask if the dude with the palm-tree surfboard was single… And then along comes a sophisticated out-of-towner, not instantly bowled over by your—to my mind— *deeply* hidden charms, and—"

Luke's words came to an abrupt halt as the parallel with the last great—not so great—relationship of Jonah's life came to light. Luke slapped Jonah hard on the back. "Walk away. Walk away now and do not look back."

"Sounds fine in theory."

"Yet far better in practice. Trust me," Luke said with the bitter edge of first-hand knowledge.

Jonah nodded. The *other* outsider had shaken up his whole life until it had never been remotely the same again.

But he'd been a different man back then. Barely a man at all. Alone for so long, with nothing tethering him to his life, that he'd mistaken lust for intimacy. Company for partnership. The presence of another body in his house for it finally feeling like a home again.

His foundations were stronger now. He was embedded in his life. There was no way he'd make the same mistake twice. If something happened between Avery and him, he'd be just fine. Which meant the decision was now up to her.

"You haven't heard a word I said, have you?" Luke grumbled.

"About what?"

"Battening down the hatches. And several other good boating analogies."

"What the hell do you know about boats? Or women, for that matter."

Luke stared into the middle distance a moment before grinding out an, "Amen."

Avery stood outside the elegant Botch-A-Me restaurant Luke had picked for their date, and took a moment to check her reflection in the window. Her hair was twisted into a sleek sophisticated up-do. Her platinum-toned bustier was elegant and sexy, her wide-legged black pants floaty and sensual. Her favourite teardrop diamond earrings glinted in the light of the tiki torches lighting the restaurant with a warm golden glow.

The man didn't stand a chance.

Pity then that as her focus shifted as she looked through the window, she imagined for a second she'd seen a head of darkly curled hair.

Seriously? After the way Jonah had acted as if that kiss was some kind of *consolation* prize. Forget *him*. It was why she was here tonight after all. Only her damn heart wouldn't give up on him. Pathetic little thing couldn't think past the kiss at all.

Suddenly the dark curls moved and Luke's face came into view, and Avery's stomach sank. She wasn't imagining things. Jonah was there. With Luke. And they were clearly a couple of drinks down. Avery's stomach trembled even as it fell to her knees.

"Hey, kiddo! Sorry I'm late."

Avery turned to find Claudia beside her, peering through the window, her wispy blonde hair caught back in a pretty silver clip, and—for once out of uniform—looking effortlessly lovely in an aqua maxi-dress that made her blue eyes pop.

"Late for what?"

"Ah, dinner? I begged Luke to use the Grand Cayman

back at the Tropicana—the new chef I just hired is fantasmagorical. But *he* insisted *we* need to check out the competition. Everything okay? You look a little unwell."

"No. Everything's fine," Avery said, while the truth was she now shared Claude's urge to slap Luke across the back of the head. As for Jonah? Knees and soft body parts came to mind. All four of them at the same table was going to be a disaster.

Her usual MO would be to bounce about, create some cheery diversion to keep every faction distracted before it escalated into something she couldn't control. It was what she'd do back home.

Or she could face the music.

Taking a deep breath, Avery slipped a hand into the crook of Claudia's elbow and dragged her inside. Avery motioned to the host so that she could see her dining party and made a beeline for the table near the edge of the room, her heart beating so hard she could hear the swoosh of it behind her ears.

Luke saw her coming first, and gave her an honest-to-goodness smile that started in his mouth before landing in his lovely brown eyes. She might have forgiven him if not for the fact that she knew the moment his companion noticed it too. Jonah's buff brown forearm with white shirt-sleeves rolled to his elbows moved to slide across the back of his chair, as his head turned and his eyes found hers.

Nothing like a polite smile there. In fact, Jonah was scowling at her as if the fact that he'd trapped her into a kiss gave him some kind of right to be upset with her for making a date with another man.

Gripping her sparkly purse so he couldn't see her trembling, Avery dragged her eyes from his and found Luke standing. Such a gentleman, unlike certain others who were giving her a once-over that made her feel as if her sophistication had been peeled all the way back to skin.

"Lovely to see you, *Luke*," she said.

"Evening, Avery. Don't you look stunning?"

"Thank you. As do you."

Jonah coughed beside her.

With a smile she leant into Luke for a kiss. With a light hand on her hip, he pressed his lips to her cheek. *Nice lips*, she thought. *Firm*. The hand on her hip brief but sure. And he smelled great. When he pulled away she waited for that lovely feeling of bereftness that came when a lover was no longer close enough to touch.

And realised with a sense of impending doom she'd be waiting forever.

"Good evening, Avery," said a deep voice to her left.

Avery looked into the deep grey eyes of Jonah North. He'd stood. *Belatedly.* And yet she had to knock her knees together to hold back the tide of heat that swept over her at the mere sight of him.

"Jonah," she managed.

All she got for her effort was a flicker of an eyebrow, and a slow smile. She leant in for a perfunctory kiss, trying not to remember with quite so much clarity the other kiss. Failing spectacularly as his hand landed on her hip like a brand. The touch of his stubble against her cheek was a delicious rasp that she felt at the backs of her knees. And when he pulled away she felt not so much bereft as bulldozed.

She blinked. And when a smile finally reached his eyes, making them crinkle, making them gleam, she realised that she probably looked exactly like she felt.

"Claude," said Luke, "looking just as lovely."

Claudia stood behind her chair at that, her lips tightening as if she was waiting for the "but." But when it didn't come she gave Luke a quick nod. His eyes darkened, before, with a tilt of his lips, he returned the nod.

Then, Mr Oblivious proceeded to help *Claudia* into her

chair. Meaning Avery had to put up with Jonah doing the same for her, leaving her feeling every inch of exposed skin in her shimmery strapless top.

Then Luke sat on one side of Avery looking intently at the menu, Jonah sat on the other staring her down, while Claudia's eyes smiled in relief over the top of a cocktail she must have ordered before she'd ever arrived.

Oh, well. She'd admit romantic defeat where it came to the estimable Luke Hargreaves, but that didn't mean she couldn't have a very nice catch-up with the boy she'd once known.

And if that pissed off the man on the other side of the table, well, he could lump it.

An hour later, Avery was so exhausted from being charming she could barely sit up straight. Taking a breather, she let the fifties torch song in the background and the chatter of the three friends float over her.

"You okay, Ave?" Claudia asked, the second Avery closed her eyes.

"Shh," she said, opening one eye, "I love this song."

Claudia listened. Then hummed in agreement. "Don't make 'em like they used to."

When the men had nothing to say to that, Claude jabbed them both in the arm. "Talk about not making 'em like they used to… Come on. One of you please ask the poor woman to dance."

"Claude—" Avery blushed. And blushed some more when Luke pushed his chair back and held out a hand. With a cock of his head towards the dance floor he invited her to join him.

She felt Jonah's eyes on hers, but stopped herself from looking his way. With a smile she put her hand in Luke's and lifted to her feet before following him to the dance floor to find they were the only ones there.

Without preamble he swung her out to the end of one arm before hauling her back. She grabbed him tight, breathless with laughter, her fingers gripping his upper arms. And then with a grace she couldn't have hoped for he calmed them into a perfect sway.

She glanced over his shoulder to find Jonah watching her, his white shirt doing its best to cage all that well-earned muscle, the collar slightly askew as if he'd torn the top button open in a hurry, his eyes dark and shadowed in the low lighting. Her stomach sparked, her skin tightening. When he lifted his drink in salute, she knew she'd been staring.

Luke felt…nice, safe. He smelled…clean. He danced… really well. The tiki torches about the edges of her vision wavered and gleamed, catching on jewellery, on sparkles in women's clothes. It would have been such a nice story to one day tell their grandchildren…if only she didn't find it easier to wax lyrical about her surroundings than the man in her arms.

Luke started, and turned them both to find Jonah behind him, a finger raised to tap Luke's shoulder. Yet the interloper's deep grey eyes were only on Avery's as he said, "May I cut in?"

Eyebrows raised, a not-so-surprised smile on his face, Luke turned back to Avery for an answer. "What do you think?" he asked. "Should I release you into the clutches of this ragamuffin?"

Should he? Avery felt as if her world were tipping on its axis. But when her eyes slid back to Jonah's and she felt her entire body fill to the brim with sparks, she knew with a finality that tightened her stomach into a fist that nice and safe weren't in her near future.

She must have nodded, or maybe she simply drifted into Jonah's arms. Either way, she didn't even feel Luke slip away, just that Jonah was there. She had one hand in his, his other hand burning a palm-print into her lower back—her whole body melted.

On the edge of her consciousness, the song came to an end. But they didn't stop swaying. Her eyes didn't leave Jonah's. And his didn't leave hers.

He pulled her closer still, till—without either of them breaking any indecency laws—every bit of her that could touch every bit of him did. When he lowered his hand so that his little finger dipped below the waistline of her pants, her breath hitched in her throat.

"Avery," he said, his voice rough and low.

"I know," she said, and as his arms folded around her she leant her head on his chest, the deep thundering of his heart more than a match for hers.

Whether it was the cocktails Claude was knocking back or Avery's sudden rose-tinted view of the world, she couldn't say—but the rest of the night Luke and Claude seemed to get along without sniping at one another. Which was *nice*. Or it would have been if Jonah hadn't kept finding ways to touch Avery. The slide of his foot against hers, resting his hand on her knee, drifting a finger over her shoulder. At that point *nice* was no longer in her vocabulary.

When the last dessert plate was cleared, and the bill had been paid, Claude sat back with a hand over her stomach. "Who's going to roll me back to my big beautiful home that I adore so very much?" She glanced at Avery before her gaze slid to Jonah. "Forget that. I'll be just fine on my own."

With a sigh, Luke pushed back his chair before collecting Claude with a hand under her elbow. She whipped her elbow away as if burned. But Luke took her hand and threaded it through his elbow and locked it there tight. "Come on, sunshine. Let's get back to our crumbling white elephant before it falls into the sea."

"She's not crumbling. She has…elegant patina."

Luke shot Avery a smile, Jonah a told-you-so look, then, with Claude babbling about fresh paint and passion, they disappeared through the door.

Jonah stood and held out a hand. This time there was no hesitation as Avery put her hand in his.

Outside the air was still and sweet, the road back from the beach devoid of crowds, the moon raining its brilliant light over the world. And as soon as Avery's eyes met Jonah's they were in one another's arms.

The moment their lips met, she felt parts of herself implode on impact. Heat sluiced through the gaps, her nerves went into total meltdown until she was a trembling mass of need, and want, and unhinged desire.

The sweet clinging kiss of the day before was a mere memory as Jonah plundered her senses with his touch, with the insistent seduction of his lips, the intimate rhapsody of his tongue.

Desperation riding them both, Avery's back slammed against a wall, the rough brick catching on her top, her hair, her skin. But she didn't care. She merely tilted and shifted until the kiss was as deep as it could be.

It wasn't deep enough.

All those clothes in the way. She tugged his shirt from his jeans and tore the thing open, her eyes drinking in the sight of him as her hand slid up his torso, through the tight whorls of hair, palming the scorching-hot skin, loving the harsh suck of his breath and the way the hard ridges of muscle jumped under her touch.

With a growl he lifted her bodily, till she wrapped her legs around him, her head rolling back as his mouth went to her neck, to her shoulder, the sweet spot behind her ear.

When he tugged her top down an inch, his nails scraping her soft skin, his tongue finding the edge of her nipple, she froze, the tiniest thread of sense coming back to her from somewhere deep down inside. It might be near midnight, but they were in a public place, her legs around his waist, one arm cradling his head, the other beneath his shirt and riding the length of his back.

"Jonah," she said, her voice a whisper on the still night air.

She felt him tense, then relax, just a fraction, but enough that he lifted his head to rest it against her collarbone, his deep breaths warming her bone deep.

Avery opened her eyes to the sky.

When Jonah had asked her to dance Luke hadn't been surprised. He'd been waiting for it. Which meant it hadn't been spur of the moment. Hadn't been some kind of He-Has-Girl-So-I-Want-Girl reaction.

This big, beautiful, difficult, taciturn, hard-to-crack man had staked his claim.

And scary as the feelings tumbling about inside of her at that knowledge were, the brilliance of them won out.

"Take me home, Jonah."

He held his breath, his chest pressing hard into hers so that she could feel the steady thump of his big strong heart.

"You sure?"

She slid a hand into the back of his hair, the tight curls ensnaring her fingers.

He growled, and she trapped the sound with her kiss as she strove to make the best mistake of her life.

CHAPTER SEVEN

AVERY'S FIRST GLIMPSE inside Jonah's place—a shack tucked away in the hills behind the cove—held no surprises; the place was a total man cave.

Surfboards and a kayak lined up on hooks in the entrance hall. Battered running shoes lay discarded on a small pile of sand under a top-of-the-range road bike. A slew of mismatched barstools shoved under an island bench in the utilitarian kitchen the only dining option, and along with a big dark sprawling lounge were a recycled timber coffee table covered in boating magazines and mug rings and a projector screen taller than she was.

Avery glanced back towards the front door; but as the last time she'd checked there was still no sign yet of the man himself.

Right in the middle of a pretty full-on make-out session on his porch, Hull had let out a gut-curdling yowl before taking off into the forest. And if Avery's heart hadn't already been racing like the Kentucky Derby from that kiss, the sight of big brawny Jonah staring in distress after his dog—sorry, not *his* dog—had made her heart flip twice and go splat.

She'd given him a shove. "Go."

After a brief thank-you kiss he'd gone, leaping off the porch, grabbing a man-sized torch from his big black muscle car, and run off into the forest like some kind of superhero.

No telling how long he'll be, she thought as she distracted her nerves by scoping out the rest of his home. Down the solitary hall was one seriously cool bathroom with a fantastic sunburst mosaic covering an entire wall and an old brass tub—the kind you sat in with your knees up to your chin. Leaning against the doorjamb of his small office, with its big wooden desk, a wall of shelves filled with books and knick-knacks, another covered in old maps, star charts, pictures of boats, she admitted that, while the house might be a total bachelor pad, with not a feminine touch in sight, it was seriously appealing. Simple and raw, woodsy and warm. Lived in.

It was Jonah.

Pushing herself away from the wall, she walked unthinkingly through the last door to find herself standing in a bedroom.

Jonah's bedroom.

Her next breath in was choppy, her palms growing uncommonly warm as her eyes skittered over the chair in the corner covered in man clothes. The bedside table—singular—had at one time been a beer barrel, and now boasted a lamp with a naked bulb, a book—pages curled, face down—and a handful of loose change. No curtains shielded the windows, which were recycled portholes looking out over what would no doubt be a spectacular Pacific view.

Her heart beat wildly as her eyes finally settled on the biggest thing in the room: Jonah's bed. It was big. *Huge*. And unmade, the white sheets a shambles. It wasn't hard to imagine his long brown limbs twisted up in the bedding.

Never in her wildest dreams would she have imagined that she'd be in such a position with a man like Jonah North. A man who made her twitch. And scramble. And think twice. And want. The *want* she felt around him was crazy, wild, and *corrupting*.

A man who couldn't even commit to a dog…

Insides twisting, Avery knew the smart thing to do would be to walk away, before the want became something else, something more. She could already feel it happening, encroaching. Heartbreak loomed with this one. Way better to find herself that cabana boy and piña colada and spend the rest of the summer in blissed-out inactivity.

Too late, she thought as warmth skittered over her skin. Jonah was back.

She turned to find him standing in the bedroom doorway, his broad shoulders blocking out the light from the hall. He'd ditched his shoes, and his shirt, and his eyes were as dark as coals.

Any doubts she might have harboured about what she was doing there went up in a puff of smoke. "Everything okay?" she asked, her voice so husky it was barely intelligible.

"All sorted."

"No baby birds to check on? Stray cats to nurture? Just saying I could go watch a DVD or something till you're… ready."

Jonah's smile was swift. Sexy as hell. And predatory.

And Avery was done thinking. The sound of a zipper rent the air; and when Avery's bustier sank forward into her arms she let it dangle from two fingers before dropping it to the floor.

Jonah's smile disappeared. And Avery's stomach quivered as his dark gaze raked her from head to toe.

When her hand went to the side zip of her floaty pants, Jonah shook his head. Just once, but it was enough for her fingers to fall away.

All man, this one. Never asked permission—not to rescue her, not to kiss her. The only time he'd asked was when he'd wanted to dance. As if he'd known that her acceptance was as significant as kicking down a brick wall.

When Jonah took a step her way, her breath caught in her throat, and in the low light his mouth hitched into a grin. She scowled back, which only made him laugh; that deep masculine *huh-huh-huh* that near took her knees out from under her. Lucky for her, suddenly he was there, an arm at her back, his nose rubbing gently against hers.

Then with a nudge he tilted her chin and captured her mouth with all the ease and honeyed smoothness of a man who'd done so a million times before.

Sparks flittered prettily at the edges of her vision before morphing into a deep delicious warmth that curled down her back and into her limbs. And without another thought Avery's hungry hands roved over all that smooth bare skin. The man was beyond beautiful. He was pure, raw, masculine heat, as if he'd trapped thirty years' worth of sun beneath his skin, till the heat of it pulsed inside him.

She moved, just a fraction, sliding her belly against the erection burning between them, breathless with expectation that she'd be thrown back onto the bed and ravished senseless. Then whimpered when Jonah pulled back. Not entirely, just enough to add air between them, allow breath to escape. Till she was left hyper-aware of the smallest touch, every erratic change to the beat of her pulse.

Then his lips were on her neck, and gone.

On her collarbone, then gone.

On the edge of her mouth, coaxing, teasing, then *gone*.

All the while his hands didn't stop touching, sliding over her back, his rough, calloused thumbs riding the curve of her waist, slipping under the edge of her bra, heading south...

Just when she thought she might melt into a puddle of tormented lust, Jonah took advantage. Completely. His tongue dipping into her sighing mouth to slide along hers, one warm hand cupping her backside pitching her closer, the other delving deep into her hair, capturing her until she was in his complete thrall.

Then his thumbs dipped into the waistband of her pants, finding a heretofore unknown sweet spot at the edge of her hipbones until she curled away from him, gasping. Leaving him all the room he needed to lick his way down her neck, her collarbone, his teeth grabbing the edge of her bra and tearing it away so that he could take her breast in his mouth.

She slipped a bare foot around his calf, keeping him hooked; she dug her hands into his hair, keeping him there, keeping him from ever leaving—ever—as his tongue and teeth and hot breath drove her wild. Until he pulled the other half of her bra away with his fingers, his rough, warm, sure fingers, and, caressing her as if she were something precious, sent the most intense pleasure looping inside her belly it near lifted her off her feet.

When his mouth once more found hers, he kissed her till she felt on the verge of drowning. And her knees finally gave way from under her and she landed on his bed with a thud and a bounce. She flung an arm over her closed eyes in an effort to find her balance.

When she opened them it was to find Jonah standing at the end of the bed, half-cocked grin on his gorgeous face. All golden-brown rippling abs. And dark whorling chest hair. Ropey muscle across his shoulders, veins slicing down his smooth brown arms. A deep tan line from his diving watch wrapping about his wrist.

"You are something else, Jonah North," she said, shaking her head back and forth.

The grin deepened, and his eyes roved over every inch of her. "When you find a name for it, let me know. As I'm totally in the dark about you, Avery Shaw."

And crazy as it sounded, that felt perfectly all right with her.

She hauled herself up, curled her fingers into his open fly to drag him closer only to discover the tan line at his wrist was matched by another. This one was a perfect horizon that split the dark trail of hair leading into his pants.

She kissed the demarcation, relishing his sharp intake of breath. She kissed a little lower to find his skin there scorching hot. She pulled back and licked her lips as if burnt to find they tasted like sun and salt and sharp sea air. Like him. When she went in for another lick he slid his finger to her chin, lifted it so she'd look him in his smoking-hot eyes, then bent towards her.

It seemed forever before his lips found hers. Enough time for all her compressed want to collide with what felt like years and years of unmet need and rustle up a very real shot of fear. Fear that this was about to be so good she might never recover.

Then he unhooked her bra with a practised flick, and the fear was smothered to death.

"Done that before have we, champ?"

Her hands sank into his springy curls as he smiled against her ear before taking her lobe between his teeth for a nip. "One of my many skills."

"Many?"

He lifted his head, moonlight through the porthole window slanting shadows across his crooked nose, his hooded eyes, his beautiful mouth. "You asking me to list them?"

"You seem more like a doer than a talker to me."

She got a grin, a slash of white teeth in his swarthy face, before he lifted an eyebrow in mercurial promise and set to it.

Avery wrapped herself about him as he kissed his way down her belly, his chest hair skimming her bare breasts, then he rid her of her pants and G-string in one smooth yank, and his mouth was on her inner thigh, his teeth grazing her hip, his tongue dipping into her navel.

"Lie still, woman," he demanded, his deep grey, eloquent eyes boring into hers.

She bit her lip and tried, really she tried. But the deep scraping pleasure was nearly too much to bear. And then she completely lost control—her control anyway; she was clearly helpless under his—as his rough hands skimmed over her sensitised breasts, caressed her flinching waist, dug into that sweet spot at her hips, then easy as you please pressed her thighs as far apart as they would go.

As soon as he broke eye contact her eyes slammed shut, red and black swirls of light and dark beating the backs of her eyelids as his breath fanned over her a split second before his tongue dipped deep inside.

That was where thought was lost to her as her world distorted into beats of purest pleasure. Of breath, touch, taste. The near painful rasp of his stubble on her most sensitive skin, the gentle wash of his warm breath, the glorious graze of his tongue, and her own heat, collapsing in on itself until all sensation balanced on the head of a pin before exploding into shards of light to every corner of her universe.

He gave her a scant few seconds to just enjoy it, to bask in the wonderment of such a bone-melting orgasm; enough time to get naked and sheath himself in protection before he kissed and nipped his way up her belly, her overwhelmed nerves crying out, her tenderised muscles jumping at every touch.

When he positioned himself over her, she had the ambitious thought to flip him over and give him the ride of his life, but he'd rendered her so completely limp all she could do was slink her body against his, to rain a series of soft kisses along the spiky underside of his jaw, and run her hands down his back till she found two handfuls of glorious male backside.

Then, wrapping her legs about him, she nudged her sensitised centre against his remarkable erection, and kissed him long and hard and wet and deep while she took him deep inside.

Her gasp was lost as he kissed her back, taking more, taking everything as he deepened the connection. Deeper, deeper, filling her with sensation so intense, she was absorbed. Lost in him.

When her eyes caught on his, she felt herself swirling, tumbling, drowning. She held him tighter, drew him deeper, his intense gaze her only anchor. As they—

"Oh, God!" she cried as she split apart before she even felt it coming.

When Jonah pushed himself to the hilt, and again, and again, finding sweet spots the likes of which Avery had never known, every ounce of pleasure was wrung from her. Too vast, too much… She found yet another peak as Jonah's muscles hardened beneath her touch, heat reaching a fever pitch as he came with a roar that shook the walls.

"Hell, Avery," he said an eon later, his voice muffled in the mess of sheets at her back.

"You're telling me."

He laughed, the sound still muffled. While she ran a quick finger under one eye before smoothing a hand down his back, biting her lip to stop any more tears from falling. Pure emotion, exhaustion, the last threads of tension that had built over the past few weeks back home finally finding a way out.

With a manly groan, Jonah rolled away, one arm flung above his head, the other lying between them. After a long moment he moved his arm closer, close enough his pinky finger spun sweet lazy circles at her hip.

Breathing deep, Avery took his hand, lifted it, and

kissed the palm till the heat of him sank into her like a brand. And then empty, like a vase just waiting to be filled, and wrapped up in layers of delicious afterglow, she fell deeply asleep.

Jonah woke slowly, dragging himself out of a deep sleep with the feeling that he'd been in the middle of a really good dream. When he shifted to find the sheets at his hips rather resembled a teepee, he knew; whatever he'd dreamt it would have been nothing on the very real delights of one Avery Shaw.

With a groan that told of muscles well used he rolled over, only to find the other side of his bed wasn't only empty, it was cold. Meaning she'd been up for a while.

Jonah yawned, scratched his belly, then lifted onto his elbow and listened for sounds of her. Felt with his sub-consciousness for a sense of her. That particular snapping heat that sizzled about her like an electric current. But there was nothing.

"Avery!" he called, his voice husky, his legs not quite ready for dry land. "Come back to bed, woman!"

When his voice echoed off the walls and he got no response, the warmth in his limbs started to dissipate.

"Avery?"

In the distance he heard a scratching. Hull at the front door. He'd locked the dog inside the night before, after the odd run for the hills that had worried Jonah something fierce. But that scratching was coming from *outside*.

Avery. She'd let him out. When she'd left.

Jonah lowered himself back to the bed, laid a forearm over his eyes, slid another to the aching bulge between his legs and swore.

Of course she was gone. What had he expected—to be woken with coffee and bagels? That all it would take was one night to render his flinty little American all sweetness and light?

No. He hadn't. But he also hadn't expected her to run for the hills.

The myriad reasons why he'd managed to keep his hands off her till now had meant that instead of going at it like rabbits, they'd got to know one another in the past couple of weeks. While he wouldn't say they were *friends*—the word was a little too beige for the kinds of feelings the woman engendered—they knew enough about one another he'd have expected a little respect.

Jonah opened his eyes and stared at the first tinges of gold shifting across the ceiling. It had taken him months to realise Rach hadn't respected him. That while he'd been imagining a future, she'd seen him as free board and great lay. A man suitable for a season, not forever.

One night together and Avery had skulked out at God knew what time without having the grace to say *Thank you and good night*.

"Dammit," he swore, hauling himself upright to run two hands through his hair. And despite himself he couldn't help going to that place inside himself he'd worked his ass off to leave behind. The part of him that would always be small town, a lobsterman's son. That knew no matter how many boats he owned, how many homes, how many helicopters or tourism awards or dollars in the bank, to a city girl like Avery Shaw he'd never be enough.

Rachel. A girl like *Rachel*. He'd lived with *her* for a year. He'd slept with Avery once. There was no comparison. None at all.

Punching out enough oaths to make a boxer blush, Jonah hit the floor, tore the sheets off the bed, threw them down the hall to be washed. He didn't want to hit his bed that night and catch her scent, even if it was all he deserved for letting her in. To his head and his home. Thankfully his heart was tough as an old boot.

Still didn't mean it wasn't a smart idea to scrub her scent from his skin, her image from his head, and her presence from his heretofore perfectly fine life. If he saw Avery Shaw again in the weeks she spent in town it would be too soon.

When the cab dropped Avery at the Tropicana, the sun was barely threatening to spread its first golden streaks across the dawn sky.

She slid her room card into the slot at the front of the resort, opened the door and padded across Reception, which, due to the hour, was even more quiet than usual.

Except that Claudia was behind the reception desk.

Before Avery could think up an alternative escape route, Claudia looked up with a start; slamming shut her laptop, and looking as guilty as Avery felt.

"Hi!" said Claude.

"Morning!" chirped Avery. "What are you doing down here so early?"

"Oh, nothing. Just…bookings. *So-o-o* many bookings."

Claude's hair was a little askew, her eyes a little pink. She had gone hard at the cocktails the night before and yet here she was pre-sunrise, hours before check in, and all decked out in her polyester Tropicana Nights finest.

More importantly, though, she seemed distracted enough not to notice Avery's walk of shame.

"Okay, well, I'll catch you later then—"

"Wait."

Dammit. Avery turned to find Claudia looking anything but distracted, her eyes roving over Avery's shimmery top, her swishy black dress pants, the ankle breakers dangling from her fingers.

"Yo ho ho! Avery Shaw, you hot dog. You got yourself some Jonah!"

"Shh."

"Who's going to hear? The pot plants? Come," said Claude, scooting from behind the desk to drag Avery over to a sumptuous leather couch where sunlight was starting to hit patches of once-plush rug. "So what happened? Why the pre-dawn crawl home? After all that sexy touching and tractor-beams eyes you two had going on last night I'd have thought you'd have set the bed ablaze. Was it terrible? All smoke no fire?"

Avery sniffed out a laugh. Then laughed some more. Then laughed so hard she got a stitch. Clutching at her side, she bent from the waist and let her head fall between her knees. Nose an inch from an old wad of gum stuck on the underside of the couch, she sighed. "It was…spectacular. Claude, I can't even begin to describe the things that man did to me. On a cellular level."

"Ha!" Claude clapped her hands so loud it echoed through the gargantuan space. "Awesome. But if it was so spectacular why aren't you at Jonah's shack doing the wild thing with that man right now?"

Because it was only ever going to be a one-night thing? Because her itch for him had finally been scratched? Because she knew Jonah well enough to know he'd give his right pinky not to have to go through a talky-talky morning after?

Avery heaved herself to sitting and stared into nothingness. "Because I am a common-or-garden-variety coward."

Claudia took Avery's hand between hers, and waited till Avery's eyes were on hers. "You, my friend, are generous and kind. To a *fault*. But even the best of us trip over ourselves once in a while. Find your feet again, and you'll be fine."

Avery plucked a mint leaf—left over from some cocktail or other from the night before—from Claude's hair. She just had to figure out which direction her feet ought to be going.

She wondered if he was awake yet. If he knew she was gone. If the decision as to what her summer entailed was already out of her hands.

"So it's all over for you and Luke," Claude said, "one would think."

Avery laughed, then cringed. "Do you think he had any idea that I had…intentions?" Vague, and reactionary, as they'd been.

Claude's mouth twisted in an effort not to smile. "If it makes you feel any better I had a huge case of the hero-worships for the guy when I was a kid."

"Re-e-eally?"

Claudia slapped her on the arm at her saucy tone. "That was, of course, until I realised he was a robot. Thank goodness for Jonah or you might yet have married Luke and moved to wet old London and made robot babies."

Claudia shivered—but whether it was the thought of London weather or making babies with Luke, Avery couldn't be sure.

"What about you? Seeing anyone? Since Raoul?"

"Too busy," Claude said with a wistful sigh. "No time. No energy. Especially for the likes of Raoul."

"Stuff Raoul. Stuff Luke. You should have a fling with some hot blond surfie type, who has big brown muscles and never wears shoes and says dude a lot."

"Not leaving much room for movement there."

"It's a beach. In Australia. Walk outside right now and you'll trip over half a dozen of them."

Claudia checked her phone as if checking the time to see if she could squeeze in a quick fling, then saw she'd missed a message. And her whole demeanour changed:

back stiffening, her eyebrows flying high. "It's Luke," she said. "He's gone."

"What? Where?"

"London."

"When?"

"Some time between when he dropped me back at the resort last night and now. *Dammit*. We had the best conversation we've had all summer last night. About the old days, the mischief we used to get up to behind the scenes in this place, and the crazy plans we made for when we got to take over the resort, and how we used to watch *The Love Boat*.... And *then* he ditches me...*us* faster than a speeding bullet?" Frowning, Claudia pressed a thumb to her temple. "Jerk."

"Why?"

"Why is he a jerk? Let me count the ways—"

"No, why did he leave?"

Claudia waved her phone at Avery, too fast for her to catch a word. "'Important Work.' More important than here? His birthright? This place is the entire reason he's as successful as he is!" Claudia nibbled at a fingernail, her right knee shaking so hard it creaked, and stared over at the desk. "I'd better get back."

Avery's eyes glanced off her friend's less than perfect chignon, the dark smudges under her sunny blue eyes. The curve of her shoulders since Luke's message. It was obvious things weren't as peachy as Claude was making out; even Avery could see the resort wasn't as busy as it ought to have been at the height of summer. But she knew her stubborn little friend well enough to know that Claude would come to her in her own time.

Till then, Avery worked her magic the way she best knew how. She took Claude's stressed little face in her hands, removed a bobby pin, smoothed the errant hair into place, and slid the pin back in. "There, there. All better. Now, my clever, inventive, wonderful friend, go get 'em."

Claude sighed out a smile, and then tottered off, her hips swinging in her shiny navy capris, the yellow and blue Hawaiian-print shirt somehow working for her.

Good deed for the day done, Avery lay back on the couch. Unfortunately the second she closed her eyes the night she'd been holding at bay came swarming back to her.

Jonah's mouth on hers, tasting her as if she were precious, delicious, a delicacy he couldn't get enough of. His calloused touch making paths all over her body.

She snapped her eyes open, early morning light reflecting off the white columns and walls.

At least Luke had had the good grace to let Claudia know when he'd done a runner. Avery had dressed in the dark, called a cab and split. Even if none of her expensive schools had given classes on Mornings After, she was well aware that it was just bad form.

She pulled herself up and padded back to her room. She needed a shower. She needed a coffee. Then, as usual, it was up to her to put the world back to rights.

CHAPTER EIGHT

AVERY REALLY GOT the hang of the right-hand drive in Claudia's car—a bright yellow hatchback named Mabel with Tropicana Nights's logo emblazoned over every possible surface—about the time she hit Port Douglas.

The GPS on her phone led her to Charter North's operations, down a long straight road past a bright green golf course, million-dollar homes, and ten-million-dollar views.

She eased through the high gate and pulled to a halt by a security guard in a booth.

To her left was a car park big enough to fit fifty-odd cars, with a dozen gleaming sky-blue Charter North charter buses lined up beside a neat glass and brick building. Oceanside was a perfect row of crisp white sheds, as big as light airplane hangars, the Charter North logo on each catching glints of sunshine.

She knew the guy owned a few boats. And a helicopter. And a shack. Now nautical empire didn't seem such a stretch.

"Ma'am?" the security guard said, bringing her back to earth.

"Sorry. Ah, Avery Shaw to see Jonah North."

He took down her licence plate and let her through with a smile. She pulled into a car park in time for a super-friendly man in chinos and a navy polo shirt—who introduced himself as Tim the office manager—to point the way to a big white building hovering over the water. To Jonah. She would have known anyway, as right in a patch of sun outside lay Hull.

The sun beat down on her flowy shirt, and her bare legs beneath her short shorts. Her silver sandals slapped against the wood of the jetty and Hull lifted his speckled head at her approach.

"Hey, Hull," she whispered. His tail gave three solid thumps—meaning he at least wasn't about to eat her alive for dissing his master—then he went back to guarding the door. Her heart took up the rhythm; whumping so loud she feared it might echo.

The door was open a crack so she snuck inside—and understood instantly why Hull was stationed outside. Jonah had said the dog hated water, and inside huge jetties criss-crossed the floor and a ways below the ocean bobbed and swished against the pylons holding the building suspended above the waves.

A few boats were hooked to the walls by high-tech electrical arms, one in the process of being fixed. Yet another was getting a wash, and spray flew over the top and onto the jetty.

Not seeing any other movement, Avery eased that way, taking care where she stepped as the wood beneath her feet grew wet.

Until against one wall she saw a familiar surfboard. Silvery-grey, like its owner's eyes, with the shadow of a great palm tree right down the middle, and her heart beat so hard it filled her throat.

Because she knew why she'd fled in the middle of the night. Somehow in the odd sequence of meetings that had led her to Jonah's bed, she'd got to know the guy. And despite his ornery moods she even *liked* him.

She'd woken up terrified that those feelings would unleash her Pollyanna side upon him—*Like me! Love me!*—

like some rabid pixie hell-bent on smothering the world with fairy dust. Not quite so terrified, though, as what it might mean if Pollyanna still didn't show up at all.

Her feet felt numb as she came upon a curled-up hose, water trickling from its mouth. Then around the bow of the boat she found suds. And at the end of a great big sponge was Jonah. Feet bare, sopping wet jean shorts clinging to his strong thighs, T-shirt clinging wet to the dips and planes of his gorgeous chest.

As Avery's gaze swept over him, over his roguish dark hair, over the curve of his backside, his athletic legs, she didn't realise how dry her mouth had become until she opened it to talk. "You could hire people to do that, you know."

Jonah stilled. Then his deep grey eyes lifted and caught on her. She felt the look like a hook through the belly—yet he gave nothing away.

A moment later, he turned off the hose, threw the sponge into a bucket at his feet, wiped his forearm across his forehead, and slowly headed her way.

And when he spoke his deep Australian drawl twisted the hook so deep inside she was sure it would leave a scar. "I have hired people to do this." A beat, then, "But today I find being around water a damn fine release of tension."

Avery considered picking up the sponge herself. "Well, that's why I'm here, actually."

"To wash my boat?" His voice skittered down her arms like his touch—coarse and gentle all at once. How did the guy make even *that* sound sexy?

"To apologise."

"For?"

He was going to make her say it, wasn't he? *Not nice.* Not nasty either, though. Just…plain-spoken. Direct. True.

"For leaving. This morning. After—" She waved a hand to cover the rest.

"After you fell asleep in my bed, exhausted from all the hot lovin'."

"Jonah North," she muttered, throwing her hands in the air in despair, "last of the great romantics."

"It was sex, Avery," he said, walking towards her again. "Good sex. Nothing to apologise for."

He didn't stop till he was close enough she could feel his warmth infusing the air around her. Could see his eye-lashes all spiked together with water, as they had been that first day. And that his face was a picture of frayed patience, also as it had been that first day.

But the difference between that day and now was vast.

"It was more than good," she said, her voice as jerky as a rusty chainsaw.

One eyebrow lifted along with the corner of his mouth.

"It was freakin' stupendous."

His mouth tilted fully into a smile so sexy it made her vision blur. Then he ran a hand up the back of his hair and said, "Yeah. I'll give you that."

Then he moved nearer, near enough to touch. But instead of touching her, he reached out for a towel draped over a mossy post near her feet. She closed her eyes and prayed for mercy, lest she drool and lose the high ground completely.

Jonah wiped the towel over his face, and down his arms, smearing the sweat and suds.

"Why, then, did you run?"

"I didn't run. I caught a cab."

By the way his brow collapsed over his eyes, she was pretty sure that being flip wasn't going to cut it. But there was no way on God's green earth she was about to tell him she ran because of *how* much she wanted to stay. She'd been very careful till now not to let anyone have that much sway over her desires. Keeping things light, happy, above the surface. The flipside was unthinkable.

"Just hit me with it, Avery," he said, throwing the towel over the back of his neck and holding onto the ends, his biceps bulging without any effort at all. "It's about Luke."

"What? No! Luke was…a brief flirtation with finding a way to distract myself from the goings-on back home by dipping my toes back into the past. But from pretty much the moment you hauled me out of the ocean and manhandled me back to shore and glared down at me with your steamy eyes…" Okay, heading off track now. She breathed deep, her cheeks beginning to heat with a slow burn that showed no signs of stopping, and said, "I want you."

Jonah didn't so much as twitch. He let her sway in the wind. Getting his money's worth. Till finally he said, "Okay, then."

"Okay, then?" That was it? That was all she got? For basically telling the guy he turned her to putty?

He took a step her way but Avery planted her feet into the floor so as not to sway back. "Was there something else?"

"Yeah. You're an ass, Jonah North. A gorgeous ass, one I can't seem to get out of my head no matter how much I try, but still an ass. I'll see you 'round."

She turned and walked away, waving a hand over her shoulder that might have had a certain finger raised. But she'd given her apology and *that* was all that was important. She had the high road. He only had her pride.

Then suddenly he was walking beside her.

"So," he said, "I was just about to head up to the Cape to check on a tour-boat operation I'm thinking of buying."

"How nice for you."

"Avery," he said, his voice a growl as he slid a hand into her elbow, forcing her to stop and look at him. She crossed her arms and glared, as if facing all that sun-soaked skin, and those deep grey eyes, and that pure masculine beauty were some kind of chore.

He tipped his face to the ceiling and muttered, "God, I'm going to regret this. Would you care to join me?"

Pollyanna showed up long enough to flip over and waggle her happy feet in the air. But Avery's dark side, her careful side, pulled Pollyanna's plaits and told her to shut the hell up for a second.

This wasn't as simple as being forgiven. *This* was the tipping point. Her chance to hole up with her heart and spend her summer reading, and swimming, and refilling her emotional well; or to dive into uncharted waters with no clue as to the dangers that lay beneath.

"Are you asking me on a date, Jonah North?"

He watched her for a few seconds, his eyes sliding to settle on her mouth, then with a hard heavy breath he said, "I'll let you decide when we get there."

Because there was no choice really. She *was* going with him. He knew it, and she knew it too.

Avery leant against the battered Jeep that had brought them to the edge of the crumbling jetty on the side of the marshy river, watching Jonah grumble his way through a business call.

He shot her the occasional apologetic glance, but honestly she could have stayed there all day, watching him pace, listening to that voice; it was nearly enough for her to forgive him the hat—a tatty Red Sox cap that he'd foraged from who knew where, as if the fates one day knew she'd be owed some payback.

Avery turned when she heard a boat. It appeared through the tall reeds; not as fast and streamlined as the boat to Green Island, or sleek and sexy as the one Jonah had been washing down back at Charter North HQ. This was squat, low riding, desperately in need of a paint job.

And had Cape Croc Tours written on the side.

While Jonah chatted with the tour operator, Hull—

who'd been pacing back and forth by the Jeep, one eye on the water the other on the man-who-was-not-his-master—huffed at her with a definite air of *You asked for it*.

Jonah rang off, slid the phone into the back pocket of his shorts, and came to her, long strides eating up the dusty ground. While she subjugated her panic beneath a smile.

"You okay?" he asked, and she dialled the smile back a notch.

"Fine! What girl doesn't dream about the day a guy offers to take her on a croc tour? Okay? No. I'm not okay. Are you freakin' kidding me?"

A grin curved across his mouth. Then he reached into the cabin of the Jeep and pulled out an old felt hat and slapped it on her head. Not the most glamorous thing she'd ever worn.

"Can they climb in the boat?"

"The crocs? No."

Hull huffed as if to say Jonah was pulling her leg. Avery glanced back to find him lying in a patch of shade by the Jeep, his head lying disconsolately on his front paws. In fact, maybe she ought to keep him company—

"Ready?" Jonah asked.

"As I'll ever be."

Avery took Jonah's hand as she stepped into the boat, gripping harder as the boat swayed under her feet. Jonah didn't let go till he sat her on a vinyl padded bench at the rear of the vessel.

Feeling a little less terrified, she caught his eye and smiled. "I like your shirt, by the way."

He glanced down at the faded American flag with the eagle emblazoned across it, pulling it away from his chest for a better look and giving her an eyeful of his gorgeous brown stomach.

"Were you thinking of me when you picked it out this morning?"

His deep eyes slunk back to hers, then in a voice deeper than the water below he said, "Believe it or not, princess, I go entire minutes without thinking of you."

Her smile turned into a grin. "Good for you."

He flipped some keys into the air, and caught them, then moved to sit on what looked like a modified barstool up near the helm.

"You're driving?" she called.

"Yep."

"Shouldn't we have a chaperone?" She earned a lift of two dark eyebrows for her efforts. "I mean because the boat's not yours."

Jonah glanced back at the dock. "If we go down he can have the Jeep. And the dog."

"The dog that's not your dog."

His eyes slid back to hers with a sexy smile.

"Fine. Whatever," she said, tipping her hat lower on her head and squinting against the sun. Just the two of them, heading off into the wilderness, where crocs were near guaranteed. She *really* hoped he'd forgiven her for sneaking out on him.

The engine turned over and the boat shifted in the water, giving her a fair spray of river water in the face. Gripping the bench, she looked back over her shoulder and saw how low the boat actually was. The edges of the thing looked real easy to scale. With an agility she wasn't aware she had she scuttled up to take the stool next to Jonah's.

"Happier there?"

"Better view." Her disobedient gaze landed on his muscular arms as he put the boat in gear, eased it into the middle of the thin river, and took the thing along at a goodly pace. *Yep, much better.*

"So, feel like a date yet?" he asked, and her insides gave a hearty little wobble.

"This is textbook. In New York a date isn't really a date if there aren't wild animals involved."

And just like that she and Jonah North were officially on a date. And she was okay. Not deeper than her limits. Just…about…right. Feeling unusually content about her world and everything in it, Avery propped her feet on the dash; the wind whipping at her hair, the sun beating down on her nose, the deep rumble of the engine lulling her into a most relaxed state. Till the hum, and the heat, and *eau de Jonah* had her deep in memories of the night before.

"I hate to think what you're conjuring up over there, Ms Shaw."

She nearly leapt out of her skin. "Nothing. Just soaking it all in. Thinking."

"Dare I ask what about?"

To say it out loud would be pornographic. "I really liked your shack."

A surprised smile kicked up the corner of his mouth. "It's hardly the Waldorf."

"Why would you want it to be? It's unique. And cool. It suits you."

After a few beats, Jonah added, "It was my father's house."

"Were you brought up there?"

He nodded. "Never lived anywhere else." He frowned. "Not true. I spent three months in Sydney a few years back."

"You? In Sydney?" She was already laughing at the idea by the time she noticed the twitch in his jaw and the sense that the air temperature had slipped several degrees towards arctic. *Okay…* "Was it for work? Play? Sea change…in reverse?"

"My ex-fiancée lived there."

Well, she'd had to go and ask!

A deep swirly discomfort filled her up and she struggled

to decipher if her reaction was shock at the fact a woman had managed to put up with him for any length of time, or that she'd been wrong about his lone-wolfdom. There was a woman out there that this man had at one time been prepared to *marry*. A fiancée. *Ex*-fiancée, her subconscious shot quickly back.

"I'm assuming things didn't turn out so well," she said, her daze evident in her hoarse whisper.

But he was clearly caught up in thoughts of his own. She jumped a little when after some time he answered.

"She came here on holidays and stayed. Then she left. I followed. Got a position with a shipping company to manage their freight in and out of the harbour. Told myself water was water."

Clearly it hadn't been, as here he was. Mr Not Quite So Thoroughly Unattainable After All.

On a date.

With her.

"Wow," she croaked, "Sydney." Yep, she was focusing on the easier of the two shocks. "Try as I might I can't picture you living in the big smoke."

Storm clouds gathered in his eyes, his jaw so tight he looked liable to crack a tooth.

"Jonah—"

"Don't sweat it, Avery. You're not the first woman to think me provincial."

And *that* came from so far out of left-field Avery flinched. "Hold on there, partner, that's not what I meant at all. I'm sure you made a huge splash in Sydney."

"I didn't, in fact." He took the boat down a gear so that the change in engine swept his words clean away.

"Rubbish," she scoffed, imagining the looks on her friends' faces if she'd ever turned up with this guy on her arm. Those Manhattan blue bloods would take one look at those delicious eye crinkles, those big shoulders, and drop their jaws like a row of cartoon characters. And it wasn't just the way the guy looked—it was in his bearing, how obviously he lived his life to as high a standard as any man ever had. "I don't believe that for a second."

Jonah glanced up, the storm clouds parting just enough for a spark to gleam from within. A spark that met its twin in her belly.

"What I *meant*," she said, *now* choosing her words with care, "about me not being able to imagine you in *Sydney*, is that you seem like you were made for this place—the scorching sun, the squalling sea, the immense sky. Sydney would be a big grey blur in comparison. Which sounds ridiculous now I've put it into words—"

"No," Jonah said, frowning and smiling at the same time. "No."

"Okay." Avery hugged her arms around her belly to contain the tumbly feelings as they softened down to a constant hum. "So what happened with you and—"

"Rach? Real life."

"It has a way of getting in the way of things."

"You ever come close?" Jonah asked. "Marriage. Kids. The whole calamity."

"Me? No. Not unless you include Luke, of course, and he wasn't even aware of our impending plans."

Jonah laughed. An honest laugh. Confident, this man. Why wouldn't he be, though? Look at him. One hand resting casually on the wheel, a shoe nudged against the foot of the helm, eyes crinkling in the sunshine as he eased the boat around the reeded bends of the river.

This was a man who knew where he belonged.

The boat hit a wider stretch and Jonah slowed the engine to a throaty hum.

Maybe she still had to figure out where she really belonged. Not here. A ride on a dilapidated old boat at the top of Australia was probably a bit of a stretch considering where she'd come from. But here, so far away, made her realise how much of her life she spent trying to sort out her parents' lives. And the seed was now sown; to find her place. It would be hard. It would mean unravelling a decade's worth of ties before weaving them into something new. Something better.

Later, she thought as her throat began to constrict with the thought of it. Right now, the summer was hers. All hers. Nobody else's. And she no longer had any doubts about how she wanted to spend the time she had left.

Avery slipped off her stool and slipped under Jonah's arm, finding a perfect spot for herself between his knees. She rested a hand on his chest; the other took the cap from his head. His slow intake of breath and the darkening of his eyes created pools of heat low in her belly.

"So, Jonah North, what do you say we put all that behind us and just have some damn fun? No promises. No regrets. Do you want to be the man who makes my summer holiday one to remember?"

A muscle ticced in his jaw a moment before he grabbed her by the waist and drew her into him, covering her mouth with his. No finesse this time, no interminable teasing, just pure unleashed desire.

Lust rushed through her, unfettered, thick and fast, and she kissed him back, the heat of his mouth, the slide of his tongue driving every thought from her head but *more, now, yes*!

She threw his hat away—the man was hot but kissing a Sox fan would be sacrilege—and tucked her hands under his T-shirt, revelling in the warm skin, the rasp of hair, the sheer size of him. He was so big and hot and so much man he made her feel so light, like a breath of fresh air. As if nothing else mattered but here, now, this.

He tugged her closer, the ridge of his desire pressed

against her belly, and her head fell back as anticipation shivered through her with the surety of what was to come.

"What time do you have to have the boat back?"

Holding her close with one hand, Jonah grabbed his phone with the other, punched in a message, waited a long minute for a response, then with a wolfish grin said, "Never. The boat's mine."

Avery's knees near gave out. In her life she'd been wooed with bling, with tables at impossible-to-get-into restaurants, *never* had she had a man want her so much he'd bought the real estate under his feet in order to have her.

In one swift move he lifted her floaty top over her head, taking the hat with it. "Hell," he said, spying her bikini top which was made of mostly string a shade or two paler than her skin.

"You like? I found it in this wicked boutique in the Village—*oh*..."

Jonah proceeded to show her just how much he liked it by yanking it down to take her breast in his mouth. When she thought herself filled with more pleasure than she could possibly bear, his mouth slowly softened, placing gentle kisses over the moist tip.

And the thumb at her hip dipped below the beltline of her shorts. He found her button, snapped it open; the slide of her zip rent the quiet river air like a promise.

His hand slid an inch within. Her breath hitched, then he lifted his hand to run the backs of his knuckles over her stomach and her breath trembled out of her.

When his hand sank into the back of her shorts, the calloused pads of his palm cradling her backside with such gentleness, such reverence, she bit her lip to stop from crying out.

Using his teeth, he pulled the other half of her bikini top free, and took her nipple in his mouth, his tongue circling the tip but not quite touching. Right as his hand dived into her shorts and a finger swiped over her, once, then twice, then found her centre with the most perfect precision.

She gave in then, crying out. The crocodiles, wherever they might be, would just have to deal.

The gentle moans that followed sounded as if they were coming from a mile away but they were all her. Coming as they did with every slide of his finger, every lathe of his tongue.

Warmth spread through her, building to a searing heat where he touched, where he caressed, where he coaxed her higher, higher, till she reached a peak of insane pleasure. And there she stayed hovering, aching, for eons. And as she felt herself tip, as she began to spill over the other side he took her mouth, his tongue and touch guiding her all the way until she was left shaking in the strongest arms.

He held her there long after while she found herself gripped by mighty aftershocks. He pulled back only when she had stilled. Lifted her face with a finger to her chin, and kissed her. Eyes open. Such deep, absorbing eyes.

She reached between them, caressed the impressive length of him, wondering how on earth she'd coped with all that the night before. Her pulse quickened with anticipation at doing so again.

Grunting, he pulled his wallet from his back pocket, produced a small foil packet, which she snapped out of his grip. And with as much reverence as he'd shown her, she peeled away his pants and sheathed him, stopping every now and then for a sweet kiss, a swipe of her cheek, a lick.

With a growl he pulled her back upright, turned and backed her up against the dash. His eyes were like mercury, all slippery silver as he rid her of her bikini top and her shorts, leaving her naked.

The sun beat down on her shoulders, the dials dug into her back, and there was the occasional splash, the occasional bump of the hull, a possible deadly beast coming to say hello—but she didn't care.

All that mattered was Jonah, eyes roving over her as if he couldn't quite believe it. His hands followed, running over her so gently, tenderly, as if he was memorising her shape.

With a hand to his shoulder, she pulled him close, lifted a leg to hook around his hip, and then with a bone-deep sigh he was inside. Filling her slowly, achingly slowly, a sweet scrape that built till she couldn't stand it. He pulsed inside her, deeper, deeper, deeper than she'd ever been touched.

He came with a ferocity that made her head spin, and half a second later she followed right behind. Sensation imploding until all she could feel was the pulse between her legs. In her belly. In her heart. And Jonah's heart, thundering beneath her ear as she rested her head on his chest.

As they both struggled to drag in breaths, Jonah laughed, and Avery joined him. She lifted her head to find something fleeting and warming lighting his eyes.

Before she could pin it down he shook his head, hitched his shorts into place, then slumped back on the floor of the boat and lifted his face to the sun. "You're not the only one having a summer to remember, Miss Shaw."

Avery kneeled down to kiss him, then stood and spun about the boat butt naked. While Jonah lifted onto one elbow to watch, appreciation and wonder playing about his face.

And Avery wondered where she'd been her whole life.

Jonah took his time heading back.

One hand on the wheel, the other resting on Avery's lower back as she leant over the dash in her wild bikini top and short shorts. Sunlight flickering over her through the trees lining the marshy bank; her eyes otherwise cloaked in shadows from the brim of his ancient Akubra, her lush mouth tilted up at the corners.

It was so quiet out on the river, the scenery so rugged and raw they could have been the last two people on earth.

Then a telltale splash tugged at his instincts, and he squinted against the sun beating off the water. "Look," he said, his voice rough from under-use.

Avery blinked, followed the line of his arm, and saw. A croc. Its long brown body floating below the water snout, beady eyes, and a few bumpy scales cutting through the surface.

She stood taller, her fingers gripping the console till her nail beds turned bright pink. "It's huge."

"Twelve feet. Fourteen maybe."

She tipped back her hat—which had left a red mark slicing across her forehead. "It's looking right at me. No doubt thinking 'there's lunch.'"

"Don't blame him."

She flicked Jonah a glance, then licked her lips to cover a grin that made itself felt right in the groin. Then she turned, leant her backside against the dash, her long legs crossed at the ankles. "If, heaven forbid, I fell in right now you'd save me, right?"

"From a croc? Not on your life, princess. If he took you under that'd be it. They don't call it a death roll for nothing."

Her laughter was shocked, but the gleam in her eye was not. "How do the ladies resist you, Jonah North?"

"Resist me? Why do you think I let Hull skulk at my heels? Without him I'd be beating them away with a stick."

Her eyes narrowed a fraction, as if the idea of hordes of women coming after him was not one of her happier thoughts. "Ye-ea-a-ah," she said. "I actually half believe you. It's counterproductive, though, you know. Only adds to the tragic Heathcliffian mien you have going on."

"The what?"

"Nothing," she deadpanned.

Laughing under his breath, he ran a thumb along the red line on her forehead left by the hat. When her eyes flared at the touch, her breath hitching, her cheeks filling with blood, he tucked his hand back around the wheel.

His parents hadn't been demonstrative. Till then he'd figured he'd inherited the same. But the urge to touch Avery was strong. Too strong. So he did something he understood, reaching and slipping a hand around her waist, pulling her into the cradle between his legs.

His voice was rough as he said, "I notice Hull didn't scare you away."

"I notice you didn't beat me away with a stick."

The noticing beat between them like a pulse, until he pulled her in for a kiss. Her hand dived into the back of his hair, tugging till his skin thrummed with the sweet pleasure of her touch.

It took him longer than was smart to remember he was navigating croc-infested waters. He pulled away, thoughts all crooked. The intimacy part of this thing with Avery was so fresh, after keeping off every touch like an electric shock.

And yet he already found himself thinking towards the day her summer ended, while his simply kept on keeping on. Which was all he'd ever wanted. To belong here. In this paradise on earth. Where too much of a good thing was daily life.

The boat finally bumped against the riverbank back where they'd started, and Avery stretched away from him, yawning, leaving him to tie off. And get some space. Not that it seemed to help any. Her imprint lingered. Would do so for some time.

"Well, that was way more fun than I'd expected."

"Can I quote you for the website?"

The yawn turned into a grin. "Your slogan can be Satisfaction Guaranteed."

The tour operator called out a cheery welcome back, which stopped Jonah from giving her any kind of comeback. Leaving him to watch her head to the back of the boat to collect her stuff, her short shorts giving him a view of a hell of a length of leg.

She might have felt satisfied, but he felt as if his balls were in a vice.

The taste of her, the scent of her, the feel of her stamped on his senses like a brand. So much so he couldn't remember what any other woman of his experience felt like. Eyes on Avery, it was as if the rest had never existed.

But they did exist. And had taught him valuable life lessons. That things like this always ended. That advance bruise he felt behind his ribs was a good thing. Because this time he knew what was coming. This time it was in his control.

"Hull?" Avery said.

Yanked from his trance by the hitch in Avery's voice, Jonah looked past her to find Hull, not at the Jeep, but at the edge of the river, pacing back and forth so close to the edge his paws kept slipping into the water.

"Hey, boy," he called out. "No panic. We're back safe and sound." But Hull's whimpers only increased.

Jonah leapt off the boat the second he had it tied off. But instead of coming to sniff his hand Hull bolted to the Jeep, big paws clawing at the doors.

Flummoxed, Jonah looked to Avery, who hopped off the boat behind him and shrugged. He didn't know anything about dogs. He'd never had one as a kid—his father had never been home enough for it to be possible.

Jonah eased up to the dog, asked him to sit, which he did, which crazily made his heart squeeze. Then he ran gentle hands down Hull's legs, over his flanks, under his belly, checking to see if he might be hurt. Red-bellied black snakes liked water. Hull was tough. He'd survived being dumped. Survived where his brothers and sisters hadn't. He'd be fine.

"He doesn't look hurt to me," said Avery behind him. "He looks like he's pining."

"What?"

Avery's mouth twisted, then her eyes brightened. "Do you think he's found a lady friend?"

Jonah spun on his haunches, ready to shoot her theory down in flames. "He's three. A little over."

"That's twenty-one in dog years."

Jonah thought of himself at twenty-one and rocked back on his heels. "Aww hell."

"Unless of course he's neutered."

Jonah winced. "Hell, no!"

"Well, then, if your dog has knocked up some poor poodle, it's as much your responsibility as it is theirs."

"He's *not my dog*." But even as he said it he remembered the way he'd run after Hull into the forest the night before, panic like a fox trap around his chest. Thoughts catching on the burr of how blank his life would be without Hull in it. "You really think that's all it is?"

Avery snorted. "When the impulse can no longer be denied…"

Jonah's eyes swung back to the woman behind him. Her eyes liquid from the bright sun. Her clothes askew. Her skin pink from his stubble rash. Living proof of impulse no longer denied.

He looked back to his furry friend. "Hull." The dog looked up as he heard his name; all gentle eyes, wolfish profile, wildly speckled fur. "You missing your girl? Is that the problem?"

Hull licked his lips, panted, and Jonah swore beneath his breath. "What am I going to do with you, mate?"

Avery made snipping sounds that had Jonah clenching his man bits for all his might.

He whipped open the car door, and with a growl said, "Get in."

Hull leapt first, Avery followed.

Jonah took the keys back to the operator waiting in the hut, gave him Tim's card, and explained his man would get the lawyers together, then jogged back to the Jeep where a hot blonde and a hot-to-trot canine awaited him.

And he wondered at what point his well-managed life had gone to the dogs.

CHAPTER NINE

HALFWAY THROUGH AN early morning run up the beach path, Hull at his ankles, Jonah pulled up to jog on the spot. In the far distance he spied the ice-cream van that lived permanently on blocks in front of one of the dilapidated old beachfront homes that housed a half a dozen happy surfers.

Not that he felt like a half-melted ice cream. It was the blonde leaning into the thing that pulled him up short. Long lean legs, one bent so that her backside kicked out behind her, fair skin that had taken on the palest golden glow, long beach-waved hair trailing down her back.

Gone were the huge hat and fancy shoes that had been Avery's hallmark when she'd first arrived. In their place she wore the odd little fisherman's hat she'd picked up on Green Island and rubber thongs the local chemist sold for two bucks a pair. But the wild swimwear was all her—this one was strapless, the top a marvel of modern engineering, the bottom barely anything but a saucy frill that bounced as she lifted onto her toes to talk to the ice-cream guy who was now leaning out of the window, grinning through his dreadlocks.

And there but for the grace of God went he. Once upon a time *he'd* been one of those surfers who sat on that same porch, doing not much at all. It sounded nice in theory. Truth was it had been nice, and for a good while. Until it hadn't been enough.

Now he tried to carve an hour out of his work day every few weeks for a paddle, the way this kid no doubt carved an hour out of his surf time to put in an appearance at the dole office. The same kid who had all the time in the world to chat to a pretty tourist. And for the first time in years Jonah wondered who really had the better life.

Avery's laughter tinkled down the beach, and adrenalin poured through Jonah as he took off at a run.

She'd been in his bed near every day for the past week. Staying over more nights than not. And even while it was just a fling, Dreadlocks over there needed to know he wasn't in with a hope in hell. It was only neighbourly.

In fact *"just a fling"* had become somewhat of a mantra around his place, during those moments he found himself wondering when next he'd find her sitting at his kitchen table, draped in one of his shirts, one foot hooked up on a chair, hair a mussed mess as she smiled serenely out of the window at the forest-impeded ocean views beyond.

Unlike Rach, who'd set her treadmill up in his office, a small TV hooked to the front of it so she could watch the Kardashians, Avery soaked *every* moment in. Whether it was sitting on the jetty at Charter North watching him tinker with a dicky engine or on a bed of sketchy beach grass on Crescent Cove beach throwing a stick to Hull. She'd immersed herself in Crescent Cove.

Watching the cove through her eyes reminded him why he'd worked so hard to work himself back into the fabric of the place. And how little time he spent savouring it. What was the point of living in the most beautiful place on earth if you never even noticed?

Avery turned as he neared, hands wrapped around a cone. At the sight of her tongue curling about the melting ice cream, he missed a step and near ended up ass up. She looked up as he righted himself, grinned, and lifted her melting ice cream in a wave.

Hull peeled away to say hello and she crouched down to give the dog a cuddle about the ears. Even offered him a lick of the ice cream from her wrist and laughed when he took it.

When she stood Hull bounded back to join Jonah but from that point Avery's eyes were all on him as he jogged on the spot. He knew her odd eyes were dilated, even from the other side of the street. Knew they coursed over him, paused on the parts of him she liked best.

The urge to go to her, to kiss her, to throw her over his shoulder, and lock her up in his shack on the cliff was so thick, so all-encompassing, so *disquieting* he gave her a quick wave then kept running, just to prove he could.

"You!" said a woman who appeared as if from nowhere—her face red as a tomato.

Jonah only pulled up when he realised she wasn't talking to him, she was talking to Hull. "Ma'am, can I help you?"

"Don't you *Ma'am* me, sonny! Is this your dog?"

Jonah's cheek twitched with the urge to say no, but when Hull started whimpering in a way that made Jonah's insides go all squidgy, he heard himself say, "I'm his…main person."

"What the hell does that mean?"

It's all I've got for you, lady.

"Whatever you are, your…mongrel has been sniffing around my Petunia and you need to make him stop."

"Your—"

At that moment Avery appeared at his side. He caught her scent, her warmth, the zing of her travelling down his left arm before she even said a word.

"Hey, little thing. Petunia, is it?" she cooed, leaning towards the crazy woman's handbag where Jonah only just noticed a bald-headed little thing so overbred it could barely be labelled canine. Avery reached out to pat the thing's head, but it grew fangs and went in for a nip. She pulled back and sank down an arm around Hull's head, muttering loud enough for all to hear, "Really, Hull. Her?"

Jonah barely had a moment to note how much calmer Hull was with Avery all snuggled up to him before the woman stuck herself back into his line of sight. "Petunia is in heat."

Jonah snapped back to the present. "Do not tell me she's knocked up."

"No, she's not *carrying*! Thank goodness. And the last thing she needs is for your mutt to ruin her chances of producing champion offspring."

"My dog's not a mutt. While yours is—"

"Cute as a button," said Avery, standing at his side. "And champion, hey? Wowee. If she was my dog I'd take extra special care to keep her away from lusty male suitors. They can be temptation incarnate when they're all big and hairy like this guy."

Her voice was so kind, consoling, with that sophisticated New York measure, that the woman's face twitched as though she had a glitch in her regular programming. Then her eyes slid away from Avery and back to Jonah. And she looked at him as if she hadn't really seen him before. More precisely, looked hard at his big and hairy chest.

Jonah took a step back and the woman shook her head as if coming out of a trance. "Just keep your mutt on a leash. Or I'll sue. Or I'll have him put down."

At that Jonah regained his lost step and more, leaning in and forcing the woman to look up and up and up. "Hang on a second, lady. If you kept your Pansy—"

"Petunia," Avery muttered.

"Petunia—*whatever*—at home while she's in heat rather than schlepping her out in your bloody handbag, then my dog wouldn't have looked twice at her. And I'll have you know he's not a mutt. He's a superb dog. A smart dog. A loving, loyal, kind dog. You and your little rat would be lucky to have him in your life!"

The other woman stormed off with her shivering critter in tow.

"Wow," Jonah said, running a hand over his sweat-dampened hair, knowing not all the sweat had been from the running. He glared down at Hull, who looked up at him with a kind of despair as the object of his affection was whisked away.

"Your dog."

Jonah glanced at Avery to find her back to licking her ice cream, a rogue smile gleaming deep within her mismatched eyes.

"I'm sorry?"

"You said Hull was *your* dog. There's no going back from that."

She tipped up onto her toes, placed a cool hand on his bare chest, and kissed him, a seriously hot lip lock that tasted like summer and ice cream and everything sweet and wholesome. Everything about the cove that made it feel like home. Then her hand trailed down his chest, her nails catching in his chest hair in a way that was the opposite of wholesome.

She walked backwards, back towards the resort, the frill of her bikini bottom bouncing up and down as if it were beckoning him to follow. Then said, "Your dog's a big softie, Jonah North. Just like his owner."

"Didn't I just hear you tell that woman I was temptation incarnate?"

She didn't even pretend she was talking about Hull. "I'm in PR. Which more often than not means taking not naturally pleasant products and talking them up till they smell like roses. Now you know I'm good at it."

Hips swinging, hair swaying, cheap thongs slapping on the hot concrete, she left him feeling anything but soft.

With a growl he turned and ran. And ran. And ran.

* * *

Avery headed into the Tropicana Nights, all aglow after her little run-in with Jonah.

Intending to take a long cool shower to wash off the sunscreen and ice cream and smirk before checking in with her mother, she took a short cut past the pool. Middle of the day and there was nobody there. So she gave her sticky hands a quick wash in the crystal-clear pool, then nearly fell in when she saw she wasn't alone—Claudia was all curled up on a white sun lounge.

"Hey, stranger!" Avery called out as she neared.

Claudia came to as if from far away. "Hey, kiddo! What's the haps?"

Avery parked her backside in the lounge next to Claudia's and filled her in on the unlikely Petunia.

"So you and Jonah are getting along quite well, then," Claude asked.

"We are," said Avery, and even she heard the sigh in her voice. So she qualified, "I mean, if you could create the perfect man for a summer fling, he'd be it, right?"

Claudia nodded wistfully. "Can't fault your logic there."

Avery nudged Claude's chair with her foot. "Which is why it kind of shocks me that he was *engaged* once upon a time."

"That he was," Claude said, the nods slowing. "Are you digging?"

"Frantically," Avery admitted.

"Her name was Rachel."

"Got that."

"She lived here, with him, for several months."

Months? Several?

"She was gorgeous, too. Uber-tanned, luscious dark hair, legs that went on forever. Amazonian, really. Like a half-foot taller than you. Fitness freak too, a body that would make you weep. And charismatic! Reserves of energy like nobody I've ever met—"

"Right, okay," Avery said, leaning over and slamming a hand over Claude's now-laughing mouth. "I get it. She was perfect."

Claude ducked away, grin intact. "She was a cool chick. But she was totally wrong for Jonah."

"How?" she asked, wondering how much it had to do with her being a city girl, him being a beach boy. Wishing she didn't care about the answer so very much.

"Turned out she was only waiting out her time here till her boss back in Sydney offered up a big enough package to lure her back."

"But weren't they engaged?"

"I think she'd have happily taken him back to Sydney and kept him there if he didn't do that big, strong, tree man thing better than any man I've ever known. She never saw beyond the hotness and the stubbornness to his big heart." Claude's eyes narrowed a fraction, then she said, "You see it, though, don't you?"

"What?" Well, sure she did, but that was beside the point. "No. Don't you go getting ideas now."

"I had to try."

"Wouldn't be you if you didn't."

Claudia took Avery's hands and squeezed, as if making sure Avery was paying attention before she said, "You need to know, though, that I've never seen him smile as much as when he's with you. While you…" Claude's eyes roved over Avery's face. "You, my friend, are glowing."

Avery flapped a "shut up" hand at Claude, and lay back in her sun lounge. Staring up at the cloudless blue sky, more questions came to her only when she looked over at Claude it was to find tears streaming down her face. She leapt to Claude's sun lounge, wrapping an arm about her shoulder. "Claude! Are they happy tears? Tell me they're happy tears!"

Claudia perked up, swiped under her eyes, and smiled. It was a pathetic effort. At least now her friend might be ready to tell her what the hell was really going on.

"That's it," Avery said, "enough of this stoic crap. Tell me. Are your parents okay?"

Claude shook her head so hard her wispy ponytail slapped her in the cheeks. "No, nothing like that. It's just while you're having the best summer of your life I can safely say this has been my worst. The resort... You must have noticed how quiet we are."

Avery looked across the vast pool that curled beneath the balconies of dozens of empty rooms. "When I said I was coming you said something about renovating, so I just thought—"

Claudia laughed, and sniffed. "We can't renovate. We have no money. The resort's bust, or near enough. I've been scraping by since I took over, but so much needs fixing and there's nothing left to fix it."

"Why didn't you tell me all this before?"

"Because I wanted you to have a good time. And I'm pissed off at my parents for not being here to give me any advice. And now I just don't know what else I can do."

Avery's stomach turned at the fear in Claudia's big blue eyes. "Luke's the advertising guru, right? What plans has he put in place?"

"Robot just sent me an email," Claude said, flashing her phone at Avery before curling it back into a tight grip. "He's given me an ultimatum. Get the resort in the black or he's taking over."

"What?"

"He wants to turn it into some flashy Contiki-style re-sort with a swim-up bar, and toga parties catering to hordes of drunken twenty-somethings."

"He does not!"

"He has figures, graphs, a business plan."

"But that's not what the Tropicana Nights is about. It's kitsch. Family fun. Like a cruise ship without the sea-sickness."

"Yes! You get it and you've only been here twice. He grew up here and still—" She couldn't get the words out.

"What an ass," Avery said.

And Claude coughed out a laugh. Her laughter turned to more tears, but it was better that than staring into space as she had been the past minute. "Wasn't this the same man you were set to ride off into the sunset with not that long ago?"

"I saw the error of my ways just in time."

"Thank goodness for Jonah."

Yeah, thank goodness for Jonah. But she didn't have time for that now. In fact she'd been a horrible friend all summer, letting Claude get this far without bringing her into the loop.

Avery took Claude by the arms and gave her a shake. "What do you need me to do?"

"You can't do anything."

"I can do quite a lot, as it turns out. I didn't get a first-class education for nothing."

"There's no time."

"Not for a complete turnaround, sure. But what if we could stall Luke? To convince him to give you a stay of execution?"

A flicker of hope came to life in Claude's eyes. "But you're busy."

"Doing what?"

"Jonah."

"Funny girl."

Claude gave a watery smile.

"Claude, I'm not about to walk away from you for some

hot summer loving. You're family." *And family comes first.* How many times had her mother said that, using it as a hook to drag Avery back into the fold any time she looked ready to stray? This time it was true.

Claude's mouth flashed into its first full smile. "Is it as hot as I imagine?"

"Hotter. And yet, here I am. What do you need?"

Sighing long and hard as her glassy gaze wafted over the huge, near-empty resort surrounding them all sides, Claude admitted, "A miracle."

"A party," Jonah repeated as Avery used his warm bare chest as a pillow. Together they lay on a massive hammock strung between two leaning palm trees down on his secluded private beach at the base of his cliff while the tide lapped a lullaby against the big black rocks cradling the small patch of sand.

"Not just a party," Avery said on a blissful sigh. "*The* party. I'm a New Yorker, Mr North. One who has spent nearly every August of my life in the Hamptons. My mother is on so many charity boards it would make you wince. And I am quite the PR savant. So I, Mr North, *know* how to throw a party."

Ironic, considering a party was why she'd fled her home country in the first place. Another reason why the party to relaunch the Tropicana Nights Resort was going to be the most upbeat party ever thrown.

"And it's you, young Jonah, who gave me the idea."

"I seriously doubt that," he murmured, his deep voice reverberating through her chest.

"Way back when, you told me the cove was more than a tourist town—it's a real community. I figured, why not let that community rally around the idea of an 'under new management' icon? So we've invited everyone who has any influence on where people stay in this town. And, using one of the great secrets of the human condition, we'll make them desperate to come by charging an absolute packet for tickets, thus giving Claude's coffers an immediate boost! We are going to put the Tropicana Nights Resort back on the map."

He lifted his head and cupped her chin so he could look her in the eye, clearly less excited than Claude had been. "So what you're really telling me is that you'll be busy the next couple of weeks."

Oh, that's why. "Some."

"Hmm," he growled, lowering himself back down. And wrapping her up tighter. She was near sure of it.

And even while every inch of her craved nothing more than to spend every second of her summer she had left in the arms of this man—converting him to her beloved Yankees—Go Yanks!—watching him let himself love Hull, and just swimming deep in the tumble of feelings she'd never come close to feeling before, Claude was her oldest friend.

And thus, miles from home, she'd once again found herself caught in the perennial tug of war between responsibility and aspiration.

In the past responsibility won, every time. It wasn't even a question. She'd lost count of the dates she'd broken because her mother had called her on her way to a nervous breakdown. But far from the epicentre of that life, she could see that she'd been perfectly happy to indulge in her mother's emotional blackmail. The ready excuse had been a *relief.* Beneath the Pollyanna effervescence, she'd been paralysed by fear of getting hurt.

But here, now, for the first time in memory she felt as if the choice was totally up to her. And while helping Claude in her time of greatest need was a no-brainer, she was all in with Jonah for as long as she had him.

"I'll be busy," she said, shuffling till she fell deeper into his grooves. "But not all the time."

Getting her meaning loud and clear, Jonah ran a lazy finger up and down her bare back, making her spine curl.

"In fact, I foresee many more days like this before my time here is at an end."

His hand stopped its delicious exploration as she felt him harden beneath her, and not in a good way. She shifted to look at his face to find the muscles in his jaw working overtime and his eyes glinting with silver streaks.

She took a careful breath, and had even more careful thoughts. They didn't ever talk about her leaving, but only because they hadn't needed to. It was simply there, a big beautiful prophylactic against the times she found her softer self wondering if being "all in" was less about time and more about the connection between them. Those moments when she caught him looking at her in a way that made her feel something sweet and painful, when it bloomed so sudden and bright within her it took her breath away.

Needing to change the subject, Avery said, "Speaking of hammocks."

"Were we?"

"Yes," she said, waiting for him to agree to pretend they hadn't both been thinking about The End.

With a short expulsion of breath he nodded. "Hammocks."

"Can we borrow yours?"

"For what?

"The party! Have you not been listening to a word I've said?"

"Hard when you keep wriggling against me like that."

This they could do, Avery thought, curving her spine to meet his hand, breathing out long and hard when it went back to its lazy trawls up and down her back. The sexy stuff left little room for thinking, much less over-thinking.

"That's not the only way you're going to help, either," she said, running a hand over his pecs, his beautiful brown skin rippling under her palm.

"Who said I was going to help at all?"

"I did. You are buying tickets for the entire Charter North office. And I've already messaged Tim a list of the boating decor you'll be loaning us for the evening."

The sexy touching stopped as he moved to glare into her eyes. She wondered how she'd ever found that look infuriating. It was seriously hot. "You sidestepped me to go through Tim?"

"He's nicer than you are. He doesn't argue. He compliments me on my shoes. I think he likes me more than you do too."

"Not possible," he said without thinking, and the bittersweet bloom of feelings inside her ratcheted up to cyclonic levels. "He's gay, you know. Tim. Has a boyfriend. Going on three years now."

"Fabulous. Buy the boyfriend a ticket too."

At that Jonah laughed—finally!—the glare easing to a gleam. Then, by way of an answer, he kissed the corner of her mouth, then the other one, with a gentleness that the gleam in his eyes concealed. Grouchy Jonah was hot, but gentle Jonah, the one who snuck up on her at the least expected moments, was the one who could tear her apart.

She'd miss him when she left—more than it bore thinking about—but she'd never regret leaping into the wild wonderful world of Jonah North. And *that*, she decided in a brilliant epiphany, was the key. It wasn't the looming sense of loss that would define life after this summer, but how she dealt with it. She would not feel sorry for herself. She would not harp on it. And life would go on.

She pulled back to trace the bump on his nose, the ridge

of his cheekbone, the crinkles at the edge of an eye. His skin was so hot, so real.

Jonah's eyebrow raised in question.

Since she knew the surest way to have him leaping from the hammock and running for his life was to give him any indication what was going through her head, she scored her hands through his hair, his glorious dark curls, and drew his mouth back to hers. And with the ocean clawing its way onto the beach below, the sun baking the earth around them, she kissed him till she felt nothing but him. But this. All this.

For now...

Later that evening, curled up in a big round cane chair on Jonah's back porch, Avery found herself thinking more and more about home. Wondering if the best thing to do would be to book her flight back so that it was done.

Instead—as if *that* were the lesser of two evils—she Skyped her mother. She'd been avoiding it all week. Ever since she and Claude had started organising the party, in fact. Because it would come up. And then so would the *other* party. And distraction and avoidance had worked brilliantly so far, so why mess with it?

By the time her mother answered—her neat ash-blonde bob and perfectly made-up face flitting onto the screen—Avery's throat was so tight she wondered if she'd get a word out at all.

Lucky her mother was on song. "Who are you and what have you done with my daughter?"

Avery glanced at the small version of herself in the bottom of the screen, and realised for the first time since she'd arrived it hadn't occurred to her to dress up for the call. She had shaggy beach hair, freckles on her nose, wore a bikini and nothing else.

But that wasn't why she couldn't drag her eyes away

from her own image. Her mouth was soft. Her shoulders relaxed. Her eyes content. Somehow in the past few weeks she'd shed her air of quiet desperation and she looked... happy.

The tapping away of a computer keyboard in the office behind the open window farther down the porch brought her back to the present.

Blinking, she dragged her gaze back to the main screen. "You hate the tan, right?"

Caroline Shaw—she'd kept her ex-husband's name—rolled her eyes, careful not to wrinkle. "So long as you're using sunscreen. And moisturiser. And toner. And—"

"I'm having a fabulous time, thanks for asking."

When her mother smiled at the hit, Avery went on to fill her in on the happenings around the cove—about Claude, and Isis and Cyrus, and Hull and his lady friend. Not about the party, though. Or the man taking up most of her time.

"What about that man?" her mother asked, glancing away to grab a china cup hopefully filled with tea as Avery jumped.

It took everything in her power now to glance towards the glow of Jonah's window as she asked, "What man?"

"The hotelier. We came to know his parents all those years ago."

"The... *Luke*?"

"Mmm. I Googled him when you brought him up at one time. Handsome fellow. Eminently eligible. Divorced," she said with the usual hiss that implied, "but redeemable, one might hope. You haven't mentioned him in a while so I wondered, if perhaps..."

Avery had forgotten that her mother was like a human tuning fork, trembling in aggravation any time she thought her only daughter might be cast aside by some evil man as she herself had once been.

It would have been easy to pretend, just as it had been

easier to walk away from every romantic relationship than to think about why that was. But, for the first time in re-callable history, she said to her mother: "No. I'm actually seeing someone else."

Her mother paused with the teacup halfway to her mouth. "And who is this lucky young man?"

Avery's heart beat hard as she watched her mother's every facial movement for signs of a meltdown. "His name is Jonah. He's a local. We met in the ocean. Hull—the dog with the lady-friend—is his."

Good grief. Could she have offered a less interesting version of the man? But this was a watershed moment and she was doing her best.

"As handsome as the other one?" her mother asked gently as if she knew that Avery was struggling not to gush.

"More."

Her mother smiled softly, sadly, and Avery suddenly wished she hadn't said anything at all. Dealing with her mother as she raged at the world was one thing, seeing her wistful was like a knife to the heart.

Avery heard the shower start up, meaning Jonah was done with whatever he'd been working on in his office and was getting ready for bed. This *handsome* man she was seeing. Hearing it inside her head she saw how vanilla that sounded, how weak a description for what had happened to her this summer.

And she felt with a sharp keening deep inside her how little of that summer was left.

She feigned a yawn.

Her mother attempted to raise an eyebrow, which, considering the years of Botox, was a near impossibility. "Sleepy, darling? You'd be heading out now if you were back here."

The idea of heading out paled into insignificance compared with what was awaiting her by staying in. "Life's different here. It's slower. Gentler. It revolves around the sun. It's…" This time she couldn't stop herself glancing towards the window down the way, the light spilling out onto the rough wood and mixing with the unimpeded moonlight. "It's curative."

When Avery looked back at her mother's image on the screen, it was to find her mouth open, her forehead pinched, as if she was about say something; something Avery wouldn't like. Avery's stomach clenched. *Please*, she begged silently, not sure what she was pleading for. Time? Understanding? Amnesty? Release…?

Then her mother said, "Love you, baby girl. Take care. Come home soon." And signed off.

Avery breathed out hard.

She put Jonah's tablet on the kitchen bench inside and padded into his bedroom to find his en-suite shower—hot the way he liked it, filling both rooms with steam. And the man himself stripping bare.

Her eyes trailed his beautiful form, the movement of muscles across his back, the perfect pale backside between the deep golden-brown of his back and his thighs, like a hint of sweetness amidst all that raw testosterone.

She went to him and ran a hand over each cheek, kissing her way across his shoulder blades, grinning against him as his muscles clenched deliciously at her touch.

"You all done out there?" he asked, turning, his scrunched up T-shirt warm and soft between them.

"Mmm-hmm," she said, trailing fingers over the bumps of his biceps.

"All good?" he asked, his voice tight.

She glanced up to find his eyes were dark. His energy reined in. She couldn't wait for the moment it wasn't.

"As good as can be expected. My mother did wonder one thing…"

"What's that?"

"She wondered why I wasn't planning on going out."

"What did you tell her?"

"We're close, but we're not that close." With that she lifted onto her toes, sank her hands into his hair, and kissed him, melting from the outside in when he dropped the T-shirt and held her, his naked heat against her bikini-clad skin.

Lifting her lanky self into his arms as if she weighed nothing at all, he walked her into the bathroom, and dumped her in the shower, her head right under the hot spray. Laughing, she pushed her hair out of her eyes and grinned up at him. The grin fading to a sigh, when she caught the heat in his eyes.

Curative, she thought as he enfolded her in his strong arms, and kissed her till she saw stars. Making her wonder just what Jonah North might be curing her of.

CHAPTER TEN

AVERY NEVER DID get the chance to book that plane ticket home as the next week and a half of her life was consumed by the organising of The Party.

Claude had picked the theme—*Beyond the Sea*. Leaving room for exactly the kind of kitsch fun of the Tropicana Nights she had in mind along with a hefty dose of glamour, elegance, and old-world nostalgia, Avery Shaw style.

Dean Martin crooned smoothly beneath the sounds of laughter and chatter of the guests. Champagne, locally brewed beer, and pineapple punch flowed, served by a cute-as-a-button mermaid and a total hottie merman. Frangipani flowers and silver tea lights floated in the pool and above it all hung a web of lobster nets from which glinted strings of pure white fairy lights.

Jonah—by way of Tim the office manager—had donated the nets, life-preservers for the wait staff, and life rings for decorations, and the dozen vintage rum barrels currently serving as occasional tables. But the yacht? That was pure Jonah. A gorgeous black and silver thing reposing with lazy elegance on stumps in one corner of the pool deck, it had arrived at the resort the day before, complete with a crane to put it into place. There'd been no word as to where it had come from, just a note: "Raffle it. Knock 'em dead, kiddo." From the raffle tickets alone Claude had already made enough money to keep the resort afloat for a month.

Claudia leaned her head on Avery's shoulder as they took a rare breather from hostess duties. "I couldn't afford to throw a beach ball much less a party, but look at this."

Avery lifted her beer bottle in salute. "And this is only the beginning. Once the travel bloggers start trickling in for their free stays word will really get out that you offer something really special here, Claude. And people will come."

"I don't know how I can do all that without you, Avery."

Avery held her hand. Hard.

She'd always thought her attraction to PR was a natural extension of all those years playing Pollyanna with her mom and dad. But standing there with her best friend in the whole world, seeing their efforts about to come to fruition, felt pretty different from… What had she said to Jonah? *Taking not naturally pleasant products and talking them up till they smelled like roses.*

Avery drew Claude's arm close. "Go mingle. Thank. Drum up clients. A hotelier's work is never done."

Claudia pulled herself up straight, and went to do just that.

Which was when Avery felt a hand land on her lower back. She knew instantly it didn't belong to Jonah—no spark, no warmth, no drizzle of sensation that hit the backs of her knees and stayed even after his touch was gone.

She spun to find Luke—clean-shaven, neat as a pin, resplendent in his slick suit.

"Luke!" She leaned in and kissed his cheek. "Wow. No tie. It must be a party. Does Claude know you're here? She'll be thrilled you made it back in time to see her glory unfold."

"Sure about that?"

"Absolutely. And this is only a taste of the kinds of ideas

she has going forward. So you need to cut our girl some slack or you'll have me to deal with. Don't even think I'm kidding. I'm a New Yorker, remember. I know people."

Luke tapped the side of his nose. "I'll take it into consideration. Where is she?"

"She was heading to… Oh."

Avery caught sight of Claudia's wispy blonde ponytail. She was dancing with a dark-haired, dark-eyed, snake-hipped man who held her very, very close. It could only be Raoul.

Avery turned to Luke to point her out. By the look in Luke's eyes she didn't need to.

Tunnel vision down to an art form, Luke said, "Nice to see you, Avery," then made a beeline for his business partner.

Avery made to follow, to play intermediary, till she felt a pair of hands encircle her waist from behind, and this time there was no doubting who they belonged to. She leant into Jonah's warmth, sighing all over as she sank into his touch.

"How's Luke?" he asked in that deep, sexy, *sexy* voice of his.

"Had you worried there, did I?"

"Not for a New York second."

"A New York second, eh? You do know that's like a tenth the length of a Crescent Cove second."

"You're really going there?" His tone was joking, but the dark thread wavering beneath it curled itself around Avery's heart and pulled tight. But the thing was, the time was coming when she *would* be going there. They couldn't avoid it forever.

Beer, adrenalin, and the fact that she wasn't looking into his eyes gave her the guts to say, "Afraid you'll miss me so desperately when I go?"

He sank a kiss into her hair, his lips staying put. "No point. Without me around the moment you get home you'll fall down a sewer hole and never be seen again. And then I'll have to console Claudia. She'll insist we build a memorial. And I'm a busy man, don't you know?"

She knew. And she also knew how much time he'd carved out for her these past few weeks. The late starts, the early afternoons, the long delicious nights. Avery's stomach clenched so hard she put a hand on her belly. Jonah's hand landed quietly over the top. And there they stayed a few minutes, simply soaking in one another's warmth.

Then Jonah's chin landed on her shoulder, his breath brushing her ear. "Ms Shaw, are you actually drinking a beer?"

Avery lifted the bottle to her mouth and took a swig. Jonah growled in appreciation.

"I'd have thought you'd like women with a bit of tomboy in them. Women who can hoist a rigging. And swing an anchor. And lift a… No. I'm done."

There was a beat, like a moment lost in time, before he murmured, "I like you."

And while Avery's heart near imploded, she somehow managed to say, "Took your sweet time."

He laughed, the *huh-huh-huh* tripping gorgeously down her arms, before casual as you please he unwound his arms and ambled away.

Avery's breath shuddered through her chest as she stared after him. Watching him ease through the multitude, stopping to chat whenever anyone called his name. Such a man. A *good* man, she thought, her gaze glancing off all the extras he'd donated without having been asked. The yacht he'd given simply because he could. No fanfare. No drama. Just honest, down-to-earth decency.

And this man *liked* her.

She liked him too. She felt full around him—light and safe and important. She felt desired. She felt raw. In fact she liked the Avery she was around him. The one who didn't have to try so hard all the time.

The sexy, pulsing thrum of The Flamingos' "I Only Have Eyes For You" hummed from the speaker near Avery's feet. A burst of laughter split the night from somewhere to her right. A drip of condensation slid from the cold beer bottle clasped gently in her grip to land on her foot.

As just like that, between breaths, between beats, between one second and the next, Avery Shaw fell in love for the first time in her life.

Jonah watched Avery laughing it up with Tim and his boyfriend, Roger. Playing referee between Luke and Claude. Mesmerising the ice-cream-van guy and the rest of the Dreadlock Army who'd managed to wangle tickets from who knew where—though by the number of nubile young female tourists fluttering around them it had probably been a smart move to bus them in.

Not that he did any more than notice the others. Not with the way Avery seemed to fill his vision. Her dress a shimmery cream concoction of ruffles that made her skin gleam. Her hair a shining waterfall down her back. String of tiny silver beads sparkled on her wrist throwing off light every time she moved.

And it took every bit of self-restraint he had not to drag her away and find somewhere quiet, somewhere private, even if just to mess her up some.

Instead he downed a goodly dose of beer.

For these feelings were not fun. They were bloody terrifying. For this Avery wasn't the one he knew. In her place was some kind of professional miracle worker. What she'd done in whipping the slow-moving folk of the cove into a near frenzy to throw the bash of the century in such a short space of time was nothing short of miraculous.

She was something else—not that *his Avery* hadn't tried to tell him as much on many an occasion: competitive swimmer, life spent travelling the world, PR whiz in what was no doubt the toughest market in the world, with a life bigger, brighter, snazzier than he could possibly know.

Like knocking on a brick wall with a feather, it had been. Because he hadn't wanted to see it. Preferring to focus on her futile resistance to his charms. How readily she'd made room for him in her life. The ease with which she'd fitted into his. And how, for the first time in a half-dozen years, he'd found a reason big enough to carve time away from his business.

But tonight there was no hiding from the stark reality before him.

The Avery who'd snuck under his skin, made herself right at home, who looked as if she were born in a bikini, was at her heart a social butterfly, a Park Avenue Princess. She *glowed* out there, under the bright lights and attention.

While at his very essence he was a beach bum who'd had no plans beyond living off his father's meagre life insurance until a kick in the pants had brought his life to the very crux of survival.

Like a hard tug on the cord of an abandoned outboard motor, that resting survival instinct coughed and spluttered back to life, and Jonah took a step back, near tripping over a vintage rum barrel. One of his. Collector's items; he'd seen them, wanted them, and just had to have. So he'd made them his.

An offshoot of thriving so stridently. He'd become cocky. Proven by the fact that he'd seen Avery, wanted her, and hadn't let anything stand in the way of having her. Not the fact that she was a tourist. Not the fact that she drove him around the bend. Not even when her ridiculous notion of Luke had given him the best possible out.

All signs he'd ignored; when Avery and her kisses and

sweet skin and nothing to do but him were gateway drugs back to the old days. When he'd taken pleasure for pleasure's sake. When he'd had no responsibilities. When he'd had nobody left in his life to set him any boundaries. When things had felt simple, and easy, and free.

As if she'd sensed him watching, whatever she'd been saying came to a halt. Her cheeks pinked as her eyes lit on his and sparkled. She lifted the beer in salute. And by the time someone stepped in between them, blocking her from view, Jonah's lungs felt as if they were filling with water.

Avoiding the rum barrel, Jonah turned and walked away. Stopping only when he found a place he could think straight. He found it amongst the girls from the Tea Tree Resort of Green Island. They clearly didn't care that he didn't join in their conversation, which was something about men in boots.

Charming girls, he thought, their familiar accents earthing him. Charming like the cove. But the cove was too far away from the rest of the world to hold any but the most determined, the most dug in, forever. Avery would go back where *she* belonged and he'd be left rattling around in his big house. His big life. His full life.

A life that had felt like more than enough.

Until he'd gone looking for something he felt was missing that fateful morning, and found Avery.

His survival instincts were roaring now, propelling him fast and hard in the right direction. The other stuff, the stuff he didn't want to think about any more, he shut down piece by piece.

It was a trick he'd learnt after his mother had left. A trick he'd utilised, every night after, waiting past dark for his father to come home, never entirely sure that he would. Until the night he'd not come home at all.

In that state of numbed relief he'd remain. At least until the day Avery Shaw finally flew out of his life. And then, as before, he'd claw his way back out, using the restorative air of his home to bring him back to life again.

It was near three in the morning when Avery made it back to the Tiki Suite and floated inside, the gratification of success, a couple of late cocktails with an ebullient Claudia, and the wild blow of feelings for Jonah giving her wings.

She wished he were there to help her work off her adrenalin, but he'd disappeared at some point around midnight. Once the girls from Green Island had imbibed enough cocktails to start following him around and calling him Captain Jack, she'd known he'd only last so long.

Instead she decided to call her mother. It would be the afternoon before the other party. The flipside. Evil to Avery's Good. Even as it made her tummy flutter, it would be heartless not to let her mother know she was thinking about her, hoping it went…not disastrously. So why not do so while she was full of beer and joy?

Lying on her bed, moonlight pouring through the window, she pressed the phone to her ear.

"Hey," Avery said when her mother answered, her voice croaky from all the *talking, talking, talking*.

"Darling," her mother said, her voice so weary Avery quickly checked her phone to make sure she hadn't got the time wrong. "What time is it there?"

"Middle of the night. But that's okay. I'm just home from a party Claude and I threw. A Tropicana reboot. And it was fabulous."

"I have no doubt."

Avery swallowed. "Are you all ready for yours?"

"Hmm?"

"Your party?"

"Oh. Didn't I mention…? I cancelled it."

Didn't she…? *What?* Wow! And no. But good, right? Maybe even a breakthrough! The very idea of which swam through Avery like a wave of hope, of possibility that maybe things were changing on both sides of the world—

"Are you sitting down?" her mother asked, breaking into her reverie.

"Um, sure," Avery lied, lifting up onto her elbow at least.

"I have some news I was hoping to save until your return, but I don't want you to hear it on the grapevine, so... Darling, your father's getting remarried."

Avery's elbow shot out from under her.

"Darling?"

"I heard." Avery dragged herself to sitting, leaning forward over her crossed legs, the back of a hand on her suddenly spiking-hot forehead. Her father...getting remarried? "Oh, Mom."

"You seemed so happy when we Skyped last week, so content, I couldn't... But you had to know some time, so there it is. Phillip's getting *married*," her mother said again, and this time Avery heard more than just the words. She heard the deep quiet, the gentle sorrow, the *fresh* heartbreak. *Oh, Mom.* "Are *you* okay?"

"I'll be fine. Aren't I always?"

Avery could have begged to differ, but she let that one lie. Saying no to her mother was a lesson she had to learn, but that was not the time.

"Maybe this is a good thing..." Avery offered up, feeling sixteen all over again as she squeezed her eyes shut tight. "Maybe now you can move on."

"Sweet girl," said Caroline, making no promises.

And for the first time since their family fell apart, Avery kind of understood. There was a fine line between love and...not *hate* so much as exasperation. Avery knew how that felt. Jonah had taken her there these past weeks, right to the tipping point and back again, with his stubbornness, self-assuredness, neutrality. How long it had taken for him to even admit he *liked* her?

It was a scary thing, the tipping. But the reward so was worth it. Every time she saw in his eyes and felt in his touch that what was happening between them was so much bigger than *"like."*

Maybe that was why her mother had hung on as long as she could. Not out of some kind of predisposition to hysteria, but because when it had been good it had been beyond compare.

Avery bit her lip to stop the emotion welling up inside her.

"Darling," said her mother, into the silence, "just this one last thing. Something to tuck away for one day. When you find the one it's not all hearts and flowers—it's two separate people trying to fit into one another's lives. Which can feel nearly impossible at times. But no matter how hard it might be to live with them, it's far harder to live without them."

One day? Avery thought. Wondering if across the miles her mother had a single clue that her *one day* was *this day*. So much philosophy from her mother to take in at three in the morning, Avery pressed her fingers to her eyes.

"Now, just forget about it. Go back to enjoying your holiday. Is it sunny there?"

Avery looked at the moonlight shaving swathes into the darkness. "Sunny like no place on earth."

"Cover up. Hats and sunscreen. Don't ruin that gorgeous skin of yours. You're only young once. Blink and it's gone."

That was when the tears came. Big fat ones that left a big wet patch on her party dress.

"Love you, Mom."

"Love you too, baby girl."

Avery hung up her phone and held it in her lap. Shoulders hunched, she looked out at the moonlit sky. The same moon that would rise over New York the next night.

She imagined herself standing outside JFK airport, icy wind slapping her coat against her legs, the sharp scent of the island making her nostrils flare, the sound of a million cabs fighting for space.

Shaking her head she replaced the view with the angel in Central Park, with the stairs of the New York Public Library, with her favourite discount shoe shop deep in the canyons of the financial district. The colour of Broadway. Her favourite cocktail bar in the Flatiron. Laughing with her friends, sharing stories about people they all knew, had known all their lives.

She blinked and suddenly saw Jonah's face, his eyes crinkling, white teeth flashing in his brown face, his dark curls glistening with ocean water, sun pouring over his skin. She closed her eyes on a ragged sigh and felt his hand on her waist, sliding over her ribs, scraping the edge of her breast. She opened her mouth to his taste. His heat. His desire.

And his difference. Everyone took Avery at face value. Happy go lucky. Always with the smiling. With Jonah she'd never been anything but herself. Good, bad. Delighted, irate. Whatever that was at any given moment.

And her heart clenched with such a beat of loneliness, a foreshadowing of what she'd be—who she'd be—without him in her life.

Because she'd soon find out.

Her mother might be putting on a brave face, but, for all the drama of the past decade, this would be the hardest thing she'd gone through. And Avery had to be there. Not to do cartwheels and tell her everything was going to be okay. But to give her mother a hug. And let her know *she* was loved. Just the way *she* was.

Not because it would keep the peace, but because it felt like the right thing to do.

She opened her eyes, and lay slowly back on her bed, wrapping her arms about her stomach.

It was time for Avery to go home.

Late the next morning, Avery hung up from her dad.

He'd sounded...if not *over the moon* about his upcoming nuptials, about as close to as Phillip Maxwell Shaw ever got when not talking about the Dow Jones or the Yankees batting line-up.

She'd also discovered that he *knew*. He knew her mother still pined for him, had known for the past ten years that her feelings hadn't flagged, which was probably why he hadn't put out a cease and desist order the times she'd gone past the edge of reason.

Avery sank her face into her hands, letting the darkness behind her eyelids cool her thoughts.

Maybe the life lesson she'd been meant to learn from them *wasn't* that love was a perfect storm of emotional vertigo teetering on the precipice of destruction. Maybe it was just to be *honest* about it. Because if her mother and father had just had a candid conversation in the past ten years they could have saved themselves a hell of a lot of trouble. And *her*.

Her phone beeped. She breathed in a lungful of air, eyes refocusing.

You up for a swim? I can practically guarantee your survival.
Jonah.

Seeing his name was like an electric shock, shooting her from nonplussed to high alert. She'd wondered if the barrage of news, and the bright light of day, might dim her feelings. But if anything they'd taken on a new sharpness. A new veracity.

And the thought of going home, of saying goodbye, of never seeing him again, made her hurt. But she was going home. It was what happened after that that remained a big gloomy blur.

Her palms felt slick as she answered.

Meet you on the beach in ten.

She couldn't feel her feet as she made her way through the halls, through Reception, and outside.

She found Jonah leaning against his sleek black car, his naked torso gleaming in the shadows, his surfboard leaning beside him, Hull making circles in the grass beneath a palm tree before he sat with a *hurumph*.

Jonah looked up, took in her short white shorts, slinky black wraparound top, her strappy sandals. Her lack of a towel.

He pushed away from the car, his mouth kicking into a half-smile even as his eyes remained strangely flat. "I get that you're a city girl, but earrings?"

He looked so gorgeous. Her heart slammed against her ribs and she perched on his bumper to catch her breath.

Jonah joined her. Close enough to catch his scent, his warmth, far enough not to touch. As if he knew she was leaving. And how much she didn't want to.

She turned to find him looking back towards the Tropicana. "Jonah, I've booked my flight home."

Air filled his chest, his nostrils flaring, a frown darting across his brow before he looked down at his bare toes. Then finally, finally he looked her way, his grey eyes unreadable. His mouth so grim she could have been mistaken for thinking it had never learned to smile at all. "When?"

"Early this morning."

"No, when do you leave?"

"Oh." Her cheeks pinked. She felt so raw, so terrified by his reaction or lack thereof.

"Three days."

He breathed out. Nodded once. As if it was no surprise. And yet a world-weariness settled over him, adding a grey tinge to the golden halo that made him always seem more than a mere mortal. She could only hope that it was because he felt some fraction of what she felt for him. One way or the other, she'd soon find out.

"I'd like to come back. Soon." Deep breath. *Be honest.* "I'd like to come back to see you."

He didn't comment. Didn't even blink. A muscle ticcing once in his jaw as he looked across the road.

"Or maybe you'd like to come visit me."

She shrugged, as if it didn't matter either way. When really her heart was now desperately trying to take its leave of the space behind her ribs and jump into his hands and say, *Do with me as you please, because I'm all yours!*

"I can show you around Manhattan. I think you'd love the park. And Liberty Island is a pretty special place. I promise not to drag you around Saks.'

As the words spilled out of her mouth she even began to see how it might work. How a long-distance relationship was actually…not impossible. They both had the means.

They both just had to want it enough.

Her want was palpable, running about inside her with such speed she had to hug herself so it didn't escape. All that aching hope was what finally woke Pollyanna. She gave a yawning stretch, stood to attention, brushed the dust from her hands, about to say, *Right, let's get this thing done*! But before she could open her mouth, Jonah came to.

"Avery," he said, his voice ocean-deep. "This has been fun. But we both knew it was only going to last until it was time for you to go."

Avery uncurled her spine and sat up straight, all the better to breathe. "That was the plan, sure. But plans can change. I'm saying…I'd like the plan to change."

There, Avery thought, breathing out hard.

Jonah shot her a glance, so fleeting it brushed past her eyes and away, but long enough she caught the heat, the ache, the want. Then said, "Not going to happen."

"Why?"

"Because I have a job here, Avery. One that's been getting short shrift of late. I have ties here. Because I have responsibilities I'm not about to turn my back on. Because *this* is where I want to be."

Avery flinched as his voice rose. "I know that. I'm not asking you to *move*. Or give up anything. Or change who you are. Just to spend some time. With me."

The look he shot her told her he didn't believe her for a second. Been there, done that, lived to regret every second.

"Jonah—"

"Avery. Just stop," he said, exasperation ravaging the edges of his voice.

She shifted on the bumper bar till her knees bumped his, the scoot of heat nothing in the quagmire of frustration and fear riding her roughshod. "This," she said, "from the man who came over huffy when he thought I had intimated he might be parochial! The cove is wonderful. I give it that. But I've travelled. I've seen a hundred places equally gorgeous. So why are you *really* hiding out at the end of the earth?"

His expression was cool, his voice cooler, as he said, "I'm not hiding, Avery. I'm home."

She snorted. Real ladylike.

But at least it seemed to snap him from his shell. "I've tried it out there, Avery. It's not for me."

The urge to scoff again was gone before it ever took

hold once she realised—by *out there* he didn't mean Sydney. He meant *love*.

He'd put his heart *out there*, and had it sent spinning right on back. She wanted to tell him she wouldn't do that. Wouldn't leave him like his mother. Wouldn't pretend to feel something as his ex had. Wouldn't let him flounder while she got on with her life like his dad had done.

But by the stern set of his jaw she realised he wouldn't believe her.

No snorting then. Just a sudden constriction in her chest as she saw the raw honesty in Jonah's clear grey eyes. The determination. The conviction that this was no different. She was no different.

God, how she wanted to hit him! To thump his big chest till he got it. That for them summer could go on forever. They…both…just…had…to…want…it.

And then it hit her, like a smack to the back of the head. She might want it enough for the both of them. But—as proven by events on the other side of the planet—it would never be enough.

"This can't be it," she said, the words tearing from her throat.

"Honey," he said, and this time it felt so much like a real endearment she opened her eyes wider to halt the tears. He saw. Right through her, as always. But instead of doing what the twitch in his jaw told her he wanted to do—to run his thumb underneath her eye, to slide his big hand over her shoulder, to haul her in tight—he sniffed out a breath of frustration and ran two hands down his face. And said, "This summer has been a blast. But like every summer before it has to end. It's time for you to go home. And soon you'll look back and thank your lucky stars you did."

Avery shook her head, her fingers biting into the hot metal at her backside.

Not having Jonah in her life would *not* be better than having him in it. She hadn't needed to hear her mother say it to know *that* for sure. But he looked at her with such clarity, such resolution.

"How can you just switch off like that? Tell me. Because I really want to know how to make this feeling—" She slammed a closed fist against her ribs, the surface hurt nothing on the tight ball of pain inside. "How can you make it just go away?"

"Avery—"

"I'm serious. *Can* you turn it off? Just like that? Honestly?"

He looked at her. Right into her eyes. As tears of frustration finally spilled down her cheeks. He looked right into her eyes, not even a flicker of reaction to her pain. And he said, "I can."

Then he leaned over, wrapped an arm about her shoulders, kissed her on top of her head, lifted himself from the back of his car, grabbed his surfboard, and took off for the water at a jog.

CHAPTER ELEVEN

HE COULDN'T.

The night of the party Jonah had convinced himself that the only way not to feel like crap at being left was by doing the leaving himself. As if *that* was the common denominator of the shittiest times of his life; the fact that they had been out of his control.

Turned out it didn't matter a lick. Two days on, walking away from Avery still bit. Like a shark bite, a great chunk of him missing, the wound exposed to the salty air.

"Storm's a coming."

"What?"

Tim backed up to the office door, two hands raised in surrender. "Nora said you were in a snit. I said, 'More than usual?' She said, 'Go poke the bear and you'll find out.'"

Jonah pinned his second in charge with a flat stare. "Consider me poked."

Tim lolloped into the office and sat. "Want to talk about it?"

"I'll give you one guess."

"Avery," Tim said, nodding sadly.

Right guess, wrong answer. Knowing Tim well enough to know the only way out of this was through, Jonah ran two hands over his face and turned his chair to look out over the water. The sun glinted so fiercely through a mass of gathering grey clouds he had to squint.

"She's really leaving, huh?" Tim asked.

A muscle twitched in Jonah's cheek. "You'll find that's what holidaymakers do. Keeps the tourist dollars spinning. Pays your wage and mine."

A pause from Tim. Then, "She's been doing the rounds of the entire town. Saying goodbye. And leaving little gifts." Tim held up his hand, a plaited friendship bracelet circling his arm. "It matches Roger's."

"Lucky Roger."

"What did she leave you?"

The knowledge that he'd been knocked around more times than he could count in his thirty-odd years on earth and hadn't learned a damn thing.

Jonah pushed himself to standing and grabbed his keys from the fish hook by the door. "I have to go. Appointment. Tell Nora to transfer calls to my mobile."

Tim saluted. "Aye-aye, Cap'n."

Jonah jogged through the offices. His staff were smart enough to leave him be.

Truth was he did have an appointment; one he'd made a week before. Once outside and at the Monaro, as he pressed the remote lock Hull apparated from nowhere to appear at his heels, his liquid eyes quietly sad, as if he knew what he was in for.

When the sorry truth was he was probably pining for Avery. Whole damn east coast was apparently pining for Avery.

Jonah clicked his fingers and Hull jumped in the back of the car. Jonah gunned the engine, the wild rumble of the muscle car matching his mood to perfection. He wound down the windows, thumbed the buttons till he found a song on the radio that had a hope in hell of numbing his mind. Then he set off for the vet.

For big Hull was getting the snip.

He'd be better off castrated. For one thing he could go

through life never again noticing the Petunias of the world. No more urges that were as helpful as a hole in the head.

For half a second Jonah was envious. An operation might be pushing it, but he'd take a pill if it meant ridding himself of the ache behind his ribs that refused to let up.

With a rumble of gears, he hit the freeway leading down the coast towards the cove.

Towards Avery. Yeah, she was still out there somewhere— lazing on the beach, drinking those coconutty things she couldn't get enough of, wearing some delectable excuse for swimwear, laughing in that loose sexy way of hers—

She hadn't been laughing, or smiling, when he'd last seen her. He'd been harsh. He'd had to. Even as she'd floated the idea to keep it going, he'd felt the same pull so strongly it had threatened to take him under. Because what he'd had with her was better than anything he'd ever had with another human being in the entire history of his life on earth.

But he'd had to make a clean break.

He lifted a hand to shield his face from the burning sun shining through the driver's side window, and pulled into the fast lane to overtake a semi-trailer. The road shook beneath him, rattling his teeth.

After his mother left, his childhood had been waylaid by waiting for the other shoe to drop. By the expectation that more bad things were to come. And they had, when his father had died. He'd realised too late that waiting for it to happen hadn't made it any easier. So with Rach, instead of waiting he'd leapt in, held on tighter. Not because *her* leaving had been that much of a shock—but because he was looking for a connection, *any* connection, something to prove he was more than a dandelion seed caught on the wind.

Half an hour later he pulled up at the shack. Jogging up the steps, he went inside to grab Hull's new lead, copies of the paperwork he'd recently filled out to register Hull with the local council as his dog, and Hull's favourite chew toy.

And there, right in the middle of his sun-drenched entryway, he stopped dead. Looked around. And felt Avery everywhere. He felt her in the tilt of his kitchen chair, better angled to the sun. Felt her in the throw rug draped over his couch, the one she wrapped about her feet that always got cold at night.

He stared at Hull's chew toy in his hand; Avery had ordered it online—a rubber hot dog in Yankees colours.

Poor Hull who was about to get the snip. Who'd never again have the chance to find himself a girl. The *right* girl.

Jonah was running back to the car when the first raindrops hit.

Only to find Hull was gone.

"Jonah! Excellent. You staying?" Claudia asked as she saw Jonah taking the front steps of the Tropicana two at a time.

"Where?"

"Here! Storm's a coming, my friend. A big one!" Claude poked her hand outside, captured a few stray raindrops in her palm. "Can't hate a storm when it brings a town's worth of guests through my front door to use my cellar as a safe area! Would it be poor form to hand out brochures with the water?"

He shook his head. "Claude, I'm looking for Hull."

"Not here. Why?"

"Doesn't matter." Jonah rocked on his feet; half of him keen to look for Hull, the other half somewhat stuck. "Everyone's down in the cellar?"

"Everyone who's anyone. I'm thinking it's the perfect chance to show off what the Tropicana Nights is all about."

"Natural disaster management?"

"Fun," she glowered. "Submarine theme, perhaps.

Caveman, maybe. Mum and Dad had an awesome collection of faux animal skins back in the day."

A themed bunker, Jonah thought. *Heaven help them all.* And then his thoughts shifted back to where they'd been moments before. Where they constantly strayed.

He couldn't ask—he didn't have the right after what he'd done—but it came out anyway. "Avery there already?"

Claude shot him a flat stare. "She's gone, Jonah. No thanks to you."

"Gone where?"

"*Gone* gone. Back to the U. S. of A. To the bright lights and freezing winters and her suffocating mother and neglectful father. I thought we had her this time. That our beautiful butterfly had finally realised she had wings. But no. Flight to JFK leaves in…fifteen minutes. Or left fifteen minutes ago. Not sure which."

Time slowed, then came to a screeching halt. Avery was gone. Out of his life for good. As the full realisation of all that meant wrapped about him like a dark wet cloak, Jonah was amazed he could find his voice at all. "But she wasn't due to leave for a couple of days."

"Time to get back to *real life*," Claudia said, taking a moment to glare at him between happily ticking off the list on her clipboard. "I tried to make her stay despite it, but I wasn't the one who could."

"Meaning?"

"There's a *storm* a coming. I don't have time for all this. Use that brain in that pretty little head of yours and think!"

Think he did. So hard he near burst a blood vessel.

Why? Why was he making himself feel like crap when he didn't need to? Fear she'd some day make him feel like crap and he wanted to get there first? Life had taught him some hard lessons. Some at a pretty early age. And there was no certainty there wouldn't be more hard lessons to come.

Didn't mean he couldn't buck the system. He'd done it

before, in dragging himself up by his bootstraps. He could do it again. Damn well *should* do it again, if that was what it took to have the life he wanted. To be happy.

"Don't worry about Hull," Claudia said, drawing him out of the throbbing quagmire inside his head. "He'll have found a safe haven somewhere hiding out from the storm. Dogs are smart."

"What storm?"

"Storm!" she said, taking him by the cheeks and turning his face to look through the huge front doors across the street and over the water where grey clouds swarmed like an invasion from the skies.

Where the hell had that come from? How had he not known? He owned a fleet of boats, for heaven's sake. Phone already at his ear, he called Charter North. "Nora. Get Tim to—"

Jonah listened with half an ear as he pounded down the front stairs, his eyes on the menacing clouds overhead. Turned out Tim had somehow known he might not be quite on his game and had done all that had to be done. Good man. The second he next saw him the guy was getting a promotion.

Jonah hung up and looked to the skies. And his heart imploded on the spot.

Avery was flying into that?

"If you see Hull," he called out, his voice sounding as if it were coming from the bottom of a well, "get him under cover. Don't dress him up in any way, shape or form."

"Count on it!" Claudia called back. "Where are you going?"

"To bring our girl home."

"'Atta boy!" she said, then shut the front door.

Hull was strong. Hull was smart. He'd be somewhere dry, waiting out the wet. Just as Jonah had planned to wait out the heartache of letting Avery go.

Only the storm in his head, in his heart, was of his own making. And as he set off to rescue his girl, he did so with a slice of fear cutting through him the likes of which he'd never felt. And hope.

He reached his car right as raindrops hit the road with fat slaps, and when the skies opened and dumped their contents on the cove he was already headed to the airport.

Avery sat in the cab, which had been stuck in the same spot for over an hour, the rain outside lashing the windows.

"Car accident," the cabbie said.

"Mmm?"

"Radio's saying car accident. Hasn't rained here for weeks. Oil on the road gets slick. Accidents happen." He leant forward to peer through the rain-hammered window and up into the grey skies. "Any luck your flight's been cancelled."

When he realised Avery wasn't in a chatty mood, he shrugged and went back to his phone.

She didn't mind. The shushing of the rain was a background of white noise against her disorderly thoughts.

She'd been thinking about moving, actually. Farther down the island. It would be healthy to keep some of the distance the trip had given her from her family.

Her apartment was a sublet, after all. Her job freelance too, despite numerous headhunters desperate to secure her. Even her house plants were fake. Heck, she'd only bought a one-way ticket on her holiday, ambivalence stopping her from even committing to when she might return.

She'd felt holier than thou that Jonah couldn't commit to a dog? She'd never even committed to her life.

Why not some real distance? she thought, shifting her thoughts. In San Diego the weather was spectacular. And she did have a huge bikini collection she'd hate to see go to waste.

No. Not San Diego. Too much blue sky, too much sea air, too many reminders of here.

Head thunking against the head rest, Avery thought back to that afternoon in the hammock, blithely admitting to herself that she'd sure miss Jonah when she left. As if admitting she cared meant it was somehow in her control. But it never had been. From the moment he'd yanked her out of the ocean, he was doomed to invade her heart. And now that he'd retreated, her poor abandoned heart hurt like a thousand paper cuts.

What she wouldn't do to have her hands around his neck right about then. Squeezing hard. Then softening, sliding over his throat, the rasp of his stubble against her soft palms…

She sat up straight and shook her head.

A fresh start was what she needed. A clear head with which to start her own life, one not all tied up in her mother's troubles, her father's impending nuptials, or her own heartache.

She ran both hands over her eyes that felt gritty with lack of sleep.

Yep. When she got home changes would be made. She'd soak in the moments as they happened. Do work that truly satisfied. Give her mother a daughter's love, and hold the rest of herself back so that there was something left over. Enough that she could offer it to somebody else. Somebody she loved who loved her back.

Because she'd learned all too well these past weeks that home wasn't where you laid your hat; it was whose hat lay next to yours. Those mornings waking up in Jonah's bed—to find him breathing softly, his deep grey eyes drinking her in as if she was the most beautiful thing he'd ever seen—were the most real, alive moments of her life.

A half life wasn't enough for her any more. She had to be thankful for that.

A crack of thunder split the air, rocking the cab with it. "Whoa," said the cabbie with nervous laughter.

But Avery's mind was elsewhere. Flittering through the past few weeks, to the tentative way she and Jonah had begun, circling one another like dogs who'd been kicked in the teeth by love their whole lives. How they'd come together with such flash and fire, only to blithely pretend that it was everyday. That it was normal. That they could go about their daily lives afterwards.

She couldn't. Being with Jonah had pried her open, forced her to reach deep inside and grab for what she wanted. Made her feel deeply, broadly, inside outside upside down and so thoroughly there was no going back. Not even if she wanted to.

And she didn't.

She didn't want to go back at all.

She wanted Jonah. And Hull. And the cove. She wanted that life. And the Tropicana Nights. And to help Claude. And heat and sunshine. And storms that looked as if they could rip trees from the ground. She wanted passion and light and life. Even if it was dangerous. Even if it was hard.

It was her best life. Her best moments. Her happiest self. But none of that existed without him. Which was where she came full circle yet again.

Not that she'd out and out *told* him that she loved him. She'd hinted. She'd hoped he might notice and make the first move into forever.

Jonah whose mother had left him behind. Jonah whose father had never had time for him.

"Here we go," the taxi driver said, warming up the engine once more.

When they started towards the airport, Avery looked back in panic. "Wait."

"Wait what?"

"Can we please turn around?"

"Not go to the airport?"

She shook her head. "Crescent Cove," she shouted over the sound of the rain now pelting against the car from all angles. "Whatever your fare ends up being, I'll double it."

She felt the car accelerate beneath her backside, and her heart rate rose to match.

Her parents had never been fully honest with one another, which had led to ten years of suffering. No matter what else she got wrong in her life, she'd not make *that* mistake.

She was going to find Jonah, and this time she was going to tell him how she felt.

And if Jonah was so sure he didn't feel the same way he'd just have to tell her he didn't love her back. Right to her face.

"I have to call Jonah," Avery said, panting as she trudged inside the Tropicana Nights with her sopping-wet luggage in tow. She peeled a few random leaves from her skin, and wiped away as much sand as she could.

The weather was wild out there. So much so she knew the only reason the driver had been stupid enough to keep going was the double fare she'd promised at the end of it.

Claude—wearing a moth-eaten ancient faux bearskin over her head and holding what looked mighty like a cavegirl club—quickly shut the door behind them. "He went looking for you."

Avery stopped wringing water from her hair and looked at Claude, who was by then trying to drag her into the resort. "For me? Why?"

Claude looked at her as if she were nuts. Then when Avery continued to be daft said, "Because the woman he loves was about to fly away and out of his life? The man might be stubborn as an ass, but he's not stupid."

"He told you he *loved* me?"

Avery took a step back towards the door before Claude took her by the upper arms and looked her dead in the eye. "Storm, Avery. Everything else can wait."

She looked over Claude's shoulder to the empty foyer beyond. The lights were low, the place dark as the sun was completely blocked out by the storm. "Will you be okay?"

"We'll be fine. She's a tough old place. Strong. We're a safety point," Claude said. "Wine cellar, foods storage bunkers. Enough room to fit a hundred-odd people underground."

Avery gave her a hug and without further ado walked out into the storm.

Her clothes slapped against her limbs and the sand in the swirling winds bit at her skin. The double row of palm trees lining the beach path were swaying back and forth with such ferocity it was amazing they weren't uprooted.

She was halfway down the stairs before she realised the cab had gone.

Dammit.

Dragging her slippery hair out of her face, she took two more steps down to the path, looked up the deserted beach and down, before making to turn around, go inside. To dry out her phone. To call—

Which was when she saw a figure huddled under a tree in the front yard of a cottage overlooking the beach. A wet, bedraggled, speckled four-legged figure.

"Hull?" she called. The dog glanced up then sank deeper against the tree. She called louder this time. "Hull! Come on, boy. Come inside!"

But Hull just sat there, in the squall. This dog who *hated* water. What was he doing out in this craziness?

Lifting the back of her shirt over her head, she jogged down the steps, down the footpath, and into the front yard, slowing in case Hull was hurt. In case the hurt made him lash out instead of accepting comfort. She knew his owner, after all.

"Come on, boy," she said, sliding her arm around his wet neck. He whimpered up at her, his tail giving a double beat against the sodden ground. But he dug his heels in and bayed up at the window of the house whose yard he was camped in where the curtains flickered ominously.

When she realised he had no intention of moving, Avery sat down next to him, the shade of the tree giving them no respite at all from the onslaught. Soon she was soaked through to the skin. A little later she began to shiver.

"What are we doing here, Hull?" she asked, when the rain got so hard she could no longer see the beach at all.

He whimpered and turned to look forlornly up at the house outside which they'd camped. A small, white, flat-fronted brick cabin, with a picture of a familiar dog in an oval frame on the front door.

"No, Hull. Seriously?"

A storm was raging about them, and here Hull sat, crooning outside Petunia's house, pining for his love.

"Where did you come from, kid?" she asked, hugging him tighter. "I can't even get your owner to admit he cares for me at all."

Hull gave Avery's hand a single lick. She ran her fingers down his wet snout. And there they sat, getting drenched, ducking out of the way of the occasional falling branch, watching in bemused silence as lawn furniture went tumbling down the street. Till Avery began to fear for more than her poor heart.

Yet it all faded away when she heard the throaty growl of Jonah's car before she saw it come around the bend. She waved, and the car pulled to a halt in the middle of the street, the wheels spinning as he ground to a sudden sodden halt. It screeched into Reverse, backed up, then mounted the kerb as it pulled up across the driveway.

As Jonah leapt from the car Avery pulled herself to standing, her legs frozen solid. She tripped as she tried to walk, her legs cramped into a bend.

Jonah was there to catch her.

"Jonah," she said, wanting to tell him, to ask him, to show him…

But then she was in his arms and he was kissing her and bliss sank through her limbs. He kissed her as if his life depended upon it. As if she were his breath, his blood, his everything.

When he pulled back, he drew her into his chest and rested his chin atop her head. They both breathed heavily, rain thundering down upon them, but the sound of his heart was the only thing she heard.

When she looked up, he held her face between his hands. Emotion stormed across her eyes, too deep, too violent to catch.

"I found your dog."

"I see that," he said and his eyes smiled as they roved over her face, raking in every inch as if making sure she was really real.

"I rescued him, in fact."

"You rescued him? From a little rain?"

She slapped his chest, her hand bouncing off the hard planes before settling there, her nails scraping his wet T-shirt, her heart kicking against her ribs. "From being sued by a crazy woman."

Jonah's brow furrowed. Avery tilted her head towards the cottage. "Hull's girl lives here."

Jonah's eyes finally left hers to take in the front door with its picture of a tiny, near bald, shivering scrap of flesh that was barely rat, much less a dog. Jonah's eyes swung back to her, and he used both hands, both big, warm, rough hands, to gently peel the lank hair from her cheeks.

When Avery began to shiver harder it had nothing to

do with being thoroughly drenched. And as his hands
roved down her arms, and up again, she was heading very
quickly from lusciously warm to scorching hot.

But knowing he'd need encouragement, a place to feel
safe to tell her what she needed to hear, Avery nudged.
"Is that why you were driving around? You were worried
about Hull in the rain and all?"

Jonah breathed deep through his nose, his clear grey
eyes glinting. "I trusted he'd take care of himself. You, on
the other hand—"

"What about me?" she said, rearing back. Not far,
though. Enough to show her chagrin while still being plastered well and truly against him. "I'm perfectly capable of
taking care of myself."

"I know. You're plenty tough, Avery Shaw. And yet I
can't seem to fight the urge to look after you. In fact, I'm
done. Done fighting it. Done fighting how I feel about
you."

Avery swallowed hard while her belly flipped and
started singing the Hallelujah chorus.

"Avery, I barely got halfway to the airport when I heard
there was an accident. The thought that it might have been
you, that you might be hurt—there are no words to explain
how that felt. I called Claude. And she said you were here.
And I can't possibly explain the relief."

Try, she thought. "Why were you going to the airport?"

"To *find* you, woman. To haul you back here. Or, hell,
to go with you, or ask if you'd care to try living trans-
continentally, if that's what you wanted. So long as you
were where you belong. With me."

"You'd leave the cove? For me?"

"Not for you, Miss Shaw. With you… If it meant being
able to do this—" he kissed the corner of her mouth
"—and this—" he kissed the other corner "—and also
this—" he placed his mouth over hers with infinite gentle-

ness, infinite subtlety, until Avery felt as if the only thing holding her cells together were his touch.

When she shivered so hard her teeth rattled, Jonah scooped her up and deposited her in the back seat of his car. He joined her there. The curtains in the cottage continued to flicker, yet Hull kept up his vigil beneath the tree.

In the dry hollow of the car, Avery turned to face Jonah. Water glistened in his gorgeous curls, turned his lashes into dark spiky clumps, and gave his lips a seductive sheen that made her clench in deep-down places.

Raindrops still sluiced down her nose, running in rivulets beneath her now-muddy clothes. She was bedraggled. And yet he didn't seem to mind. In fact he was looking at her as if she were his moon and stars.

And then he had to go and completely tear her apart by saying, "I'm in love with you, Avery Shaw. And even if you live on the other side of the world, I'm going to keep on loving you. And if you think that's something you can live with, then we have some figuring out to do."

Could she live with it? With being loved by this man? This man who made her feel so much she couldn't contain it?

She threw herself at him so thoroughly she banged her knee, rocking the car. But pain was way in the background beneath the million other far more wonderful sensations pelting her all over as she kissed the man she loved for all that she was worth.

"I'm assuming this means you're all in favour?" he asked, when he came up for air.

"I love you. I love you, I love you, I love you!" she said. Laughing, shouting, fogging up the windows with all that beautiful, *beautiful* kissing.

The storm disappeared as quickly as it had come.

When Avery and Jonah left the cocoon of the car—

having broken several public indecency laws—they managed to encourage poor Hull away, and the three of them made their way over to the beach to check out the damage only to find the cove looking as if nothing had happened at all.

But everything had happened.

Jonah took Avery's hand and pulled her down onto a patch of sand in the shade of the palms. Her cheeks hurt from smiling and with a sigh she looked out over the waves of the Pacific. It was a completely different ocean from the one back home, and yet it didn't feel so far from everything at all. Because everything she wanted more than anything else was right here.

EPILOGUE

AVERY STOOD OUTSIDE the Tropicana Nights, eyes closed, arms outstretched, soaking up the blissful warmth that made this part of the world so famous.

Jonah grunted behind her as he dragged her bags out of the car. She had more luggage this time; she was staying longer, after all. Forever, in fact.

"Avery!" Claude said, running down the stairs, her Tropicana Nights uniform shirt brighter than the sun, her clipboard flapping at her side, Hull at her ankles.

"God, am I glad to have you back! This dog of yours pined the entire month you were gone."

Hull came bounding up, spry as a puppy, with a big new collar around his neck. Avery checked the label—a doggy bone with his name engraved into the front. On the back, *Property of Jonah North*.

"Want one?" Claude said low enough for only her to hear with a grin when Avery motioned to the tag. "How was your holiday?" she added, this time for all to hear. "Did I say how glad I am you're back? Did Jonah grumble the whole time?"

Yeah, Jonah had grumbled, Avery thought, turning to watch him crouch to take his dog—*their* dog—in a huge cuddle. Hull's tongue lolled out of his mouth as Jonah boxed him about the ears, and when Jonah laughed the dog wagged his tail so hard he near dented the car.

New York was so grey, Jonah had noted, and too cold, too many people, air so thick you could choke on it, the Hudson a poor substitute for the Pacific Ocean. But then again she found his particular brand of manly grumpiness kind of hot, so she was all good.

Also, he'd completely charmed her mother, who seemed to have come blinking into the light now that her father had truly moved on. Jonah had kept toe to toe with her dad, talking baseball stats as if he were born to it. As for her father's new fiancée, she'd turned out to be pretty nice. It had been no shock when half her friends fell in lust with Jonah on the spot, and he'd let her take him to shows, and to all the tourist traps, and when they'd stayed at the top of the Empire State Building for hours it had been his idea.

Then the Yankees won their first three exhibition games three out of three, which pretty much trumped the rest.

"The place is looking great, Claude."

"Isn't it?" She looked up at the freshly whitewashed façade, gleaming in the sunlight.

"We heard there were more storms while we were away."

"Mere rain. Though it gave me the chance to do a vampire theme party in the bunker. I sent Luke the link to the blog post with all the photos. I've yet to hear back."

"So the stay of execution is still in play?"

"He's given me a year. So the work's only just begun!"

"I love work. Bring on the work." Knowing how close Claude had come to losing her business, her home, she'd forced Claude to hire her without pay—she had a trust fund after all, and no longer any compunction about using it. Not for such a good cause.

"The press we had after the party was unbelievable, and the website guy you set me up with is awesome, and we have bookings flying in. This place is going to be as amazing as it was in its heyday."

"More amazing! Is Luke back to help?"

Claudia frowned so hard her cheeks pinked up in an instant. "Forget about Luke. All we have to concern ourselves with is making this resort the premier family destination in Far North Queensland."

"That's the spirit."

"Now, I've ordered a whole bunch of uniforms in your size—"

"Oh, not necessary, really. I've brought so many great clothes—"

"Nonsense. You are one of the team now. Uniform's a must. All about the brand."

Avery grimaced at Jonah, who grinned back, and even the thought of spending her working hours in Hawaiian print shirts and polyester capris couldn't dampen her spirits. Because, oh, she loved that smile. And the man behind it. The way those deep grey eyes of his saw through her, right to the most vulnerable heart of her, and loved her in a way she'd never dared hope she could be.

"Claude," Jonah called, his voice deep with warning.

Claudia looked over Avery's shoulder at him. "Hmm?"

"Leave the woman alone. The last time she tried to do anything strenuous while dopey with jet lag she nearly drowned."

"I did no such thing," Avery started. "I'm—"

"An excellent swimmer," Jonah joined in. "Yeah, I know."

"Fine, yes, of course!" Claudia said, backing up. She clicked her fingers at Cyrus.

The lanky kid grabbed a trolley and ambled over to Jonah's car, heaving the bags into place. Cheek twitching, Jonah dragged them all off again and set about doing it right.

"Are you sure you're right to stay here?" Claudia asked as both women watched Jonah at work, arm muscles bunching, teeth gritting, the hem of his T-shirt lifting to showcase the most stunning set of abs ever created.

"Of course!" Avery said nice and loud. "Wasn't it you who said we have a lot of work to do?"

"Yeah, right," Claude muttered. "I give it a week before you're living at his place with that huge dog of his sleeping on your feet."

"Yeah," Avery said with a grin. Mention in passing the spotting of a man-eating spider in her room perhaps, and he'd turn up and throw her over his shoulder and whisk her away to his castle in the forest like her own personal knight. "I can't wait."

Claude scrunched up her nose. "Each to their own."

Claude grabbed one arm of the trolley and dragged it and Cyrus along the path around the side of the resort to settle Avery back home.

Home.

Sea air tickled Avery's nose, heat poured and prickled all over her skin. She watched Jonah lift his face to the sky, the Queensland sun glowing against his golden-brown skin, infusing him with life.

Yeah, her guy might have wowed 'em in New York City, but he wasn't built for city living. He was built for this place. This raw, majestic, lovely, warm place. Lucky for them she could handle living in paradise.

Lucky for Avery, Jonah was also built for loving her.

Sensing he was being watched, he tipped his head to look at her. All dark curls and strong jaw, might and muscle and heat and hotness. And hers.

Feeling like she was sixteen all over again, full of hope and love and zeal, Avery ran and jumped into his arms. He caught her, swung her around, and held her tight as his lips met hers in a kiss that sank through her like melted butter.

"I love you, Jonah North, and don't you ever forget it."

"Yeah," he said, his arms wrapped about her tugging

her tighter still. "Couldn't if I tried. Now, come on, princess, time to get you to bed."

"Feisty."

"Insurance. I was serious about you getting some sleep after last time. I wouldn't put it past you to get it in your head to try parasailing for the first time. Hell, I might even strap you into bed so you don't do yourself damage."

"Extra spicy feisty." The effect of her sass was dampened when the last word was swallowed by a massive yawn.

As they walked through Reception Avery noticed at the edge of her mind that the place was busier than the last time she was there. Not bustling, but better.

Isis gave her a cheery wave. She waved back before her mind focused in on more important things, like the fact that Jonah's hand had moved down her waist until his fingers were at her hip.

Cyrus was leaving the Tiki Suite as they arrived. Yawning again, she fished through her wallet for a tip, came up with a twenty and tucked it into Cyrus's pocket, then trudged to the centre of the room and fell back on the bed with a thud.

Through the slits of her eyes she saw Jonah glare at Cyrus to make him leave. Which he did. Jonah locked the door behind him.

"That kid has a thing for you," Jonah said, thumb jerking at the door.

"I know. It's sweet."

Jonah turned slowly to stare at her, his eyes flat. "Honestly, how did you survive twenty-six years on that island without getting nabbed?"

"Street smarts. And the deep-down knowledge that I'd only ever get nabbed if the right man did the nabbing."

"Oh, yeah?" Jonah said, sliding his hands into his pockets even as he edged her way.

She lifted her weary self up onto her elbows as she was suddenly not so weary after all. "A handsome man, he'd be. A little full of himself, but understandably so." Her eyes roved down his torso, his long, strong legs to his feet, which were nudging off his shoes. "A successful man too. Helicopter an absolute must. As is…" her wandering gaze landed on the impressive bulge in his jeans "…heft."

"Heft?" he coughed out, laughing in that deep, delicious *huh-huh-huh* way that made her spine tingle and then some.

"Cerebral heft. Emotional heft. General…heft."

Jonah and his heft left a mighty dent in the mattress as he lowered himself over her, a halo of sunlight around his gorgeous curls. His dark eyes on her mouth. His knee sliding between hers and up, and up.

"Whoever this perfect man is, he can shove off, because he's too damn late. From the moment I pulled you out of the water, I owned you, Avery Shaw. You're mine—" he punctuated that one with a kiss, a long, slow, hot, bone-melting kiss "—all mine."

"Okay!" she said, sliding her arms around his neck to pull him down for more.

Jet lag be damned. The only drowning she planned to do that day and every day forth was in bliss. Pure, unadulterated bliss. Starting right now.

Because saying Yes—capital *Y* intended—had never felt more right.

* * * * *

THE HEAT OF
THE NIGHT

AMY ANDREWS

*To Ally Blake for her indefatigable
enthusiasm and getting this duet off to
an incredible start with two wonderful
characters in Jonah and Avery.*

And for getting me hooked on Pinterest.

Amy Andrews has always loved writing, and still can't quite believe that she gets to do it for a living. Creating wonderful heroines and gorgeous heroes and telling their stories is an amazing way to pass the day. Sometimes they don't always act as she'd like them to – but then neither do her kids, so she's kind of used to it. Amy lives in the very beautiful Samford Valley, with her husband and aforementioned children, along with six brown chooks and two black dogs.

She loves to hear from her readers. Drop her a line at www.amyandrews.com.au.

CHAPTER ONE

Luke Hargreaves had never seen such an unholy mess in all his life. Uprooted trees competed for space amidst the smashed and splintered building debris. Dangerous electrical and glass hazards lay strewn everywhere. Only one out of the dozen buildings that made up the five-acre property where the Tropicana Nights had sprawled for forty years had survived intact.

Holy crap. The resort was never going to recover from this.

It was hard to believe standing underneath the perfect untainted blue of a tropical north Queensland sky, listening to the gentle kiss of waves as they lapped at the crescent beach fringing this idyllic tourist spot, that weather could be responsible for such violence.

That the light breeze could build to cyclonic, that the cloudless sky could blacken with ominous intent and the calm ocean could rage and pound.

Sure, cyclones were one of the hazards of living on the northern Australian coastline and the resort had sustained damage in the past from such events that regularly stalked the coast from November to March.

But never like this.

This one had been a monster and Crescent Cove's number had been up.

A decade in the UK had anaesthetised him to the dangers of tropical storms, but, looking at the destruction now, it was a miracle no one had been killed.

All thanks to Claudia.

Luke's gaze trekked from the devastated resort to the devastated figure standing on the beach, her back to the ocean as she surveyed the damage. Avery had told him Claudia was taking it all in her stride. But he knew Claudia Davis well. Too well. And her look of hopeless despair was evident even from this distance.

Somehow inside his head, despite the march of time, she'd always been a skinny six-year-old with blonde pigtails and skinned knees. And there was something just as gut-wrenchingly innocent about her today. Her ponytail fluttering in the gentle breeze, her petite frame encased in the God-awful polyester Tropicana uniform that hadn't changed since the seventies, that damn stupid clipboard she always carried around clutched to her chest.

The intense little wrinkle of her brow as if she was trying to wish it all better from the power of her mind alone.

He sighed. He was *not* looking forward to this.

He shucked off his shoes and stripped off his socks leaving them at the row of lopsided palm trees that formed a natural demarcation between beach and land. Or what was left of them anyway.

Crescent Cove's beloved palm-tree avenue, which hugged the long curve of beach, was looking equally devastated. Whole trees had been ripped out by the roots, plucked clean from the ground and thrown around as if they'd been mere matchsticks, some still lying on the path or beach wherever they'd been hurled.

It would take a lot of years to build it back to its former glory.

The hot sun beat down on Luke's neck, a far cry from chilly London, and he shrugged out of his jacket too. He undid his cuffs and rolled up his sleeves on his business shirt. He turned his phone to silent and slipped it in his back pocket. He didn't want to be disturbed when he spoke to her and he'd already had three urgent texts from the office. Taking a deep, fortifying breath, he stepped onto the beach and headed towards the woman he'd known nearly all his life, his footsteps squeaking in the powdery sand.

Claudia stared at the wreck before her, a sense of helplessness and despair overwhelming her. She should have known that only a cyclone named Luke could cause this much damage.

She refused to give into the harsh burn of tears scalding her eye sockets.

She would not cry.

Crying was for wimps and she was *not* a wimp. She'd spent a year of her life renovating her beloved family resort and just because it lay in a shambled ruin in front of her didn't mean it was time to give into a fit of girly histrionics.

She held tight to the comfort of her clipboard. They *would* recover from this. They *had* to.

But how? a little voice asked somewhere in the back of her brain, bleating away in time to the distant drone of generators that had filled the air for days now. The same voice she'd been hearing every time she stood on the beach and was confronted by the true horror of the destruction of the only home she'd ever known.

Well, there was the main resort building—the original structure—for a start. Even now its white stucco façade gleamed beneath the full morning sun like a beacon amidst the rubble, its sturdy stone construction having somehow miraculously survived Mother Nature's fury with only minimal damage.

How, Claudia had no idea.

How had the dinosaur—or White Elephant as Luke had coined it—managed to survive when the newer edition bungalows, made to the highest ever cyclone specifications, had perished?

It didn't make any sense. It had been four days since Cyclone Luke, a huge category-five juggernaut, had crossed the coast right on top of them, and it still didn't make any sense.

None of it did.

Tears threatened again and Claudia blinked them back. She refused to cry as Avery had done. Tears wouldn't get the Tropicana back on its feet and Claudia was determined to hold it all together if it killed her. She'd been doing that since Luke had deserted her to run the place by herself, since their respective parents had handed the keys over to them and entrusted twenty years of their life's work to their children.

She would not be cowed by the mammoth task ahead of her just as she'd refused to be cowed by Luke's ultimatum this time last year to have the resort turned around in twelve months—or else!

She hadn't needed him to elaborate on his threat—and it really hadn't been an issue because she *had* turned it around. They'd had a bumper summer, there was money in the bank and they'd been poised to welcome their best ever winter season in over a decade.

And then along came Cyclone Luke. As determined as the other Luke in her life to take away everything she'd ever known and loved.

'Bloody hell, Claude. You're never going to recover from this.'

Claudia blinked as the eerily familiar voice behind her caused everything inside her—her heartbeat, her breath, the metabolism in her cells—to come to a standstill.

Luke?

She turned and there he was. Standing right there. Every tall, lean, clean-shaven inch of him. Close enough to touch. Close enough to feel a very familiar pull down deep and low.

Luke.

The boy she'd hero-worshipped, the teenager she'd crushed on, the man who'd disappointed her more than she'd ever thought possible when he'd turned his back on their legacy.

You're never going to recover from this?

His words were like a jolt to the chest from a defibrillator and then everything surged back to life. Her lungs dragged in a swift harsh breath, her heart kicked her in the ribcage with all the power of a mule, her cells started metabolising again at warp speed.

You're never going to recover from this?

Oh, no! He had to be kidding. This *had* to be a monumental joke. *A very bad one.*

But no, here he was, in a freaking business shirt and trousers. *On the beach.* Gloating. A tsunami of emotion Claudia had been stuffing down for four days—hell, for the last year—rose in her chest and demanded to be expressed.

'What the hell are you doing here?'

Luke's eyes widened at the distinct lack of welcome turning her normally chirpy voice deeper. Darker. He shrugged. 'I saw it on the tele…I just…came.'

And he had. As much as he'd resented the weird pull this place still had over him, he couldn't *not* put in an appearance. Escaping to the other side of the world a decade ago, immersing himself in a completely different life had dulled the pull, but one look at the devastation and it had roared back to life.

Claudia blinked at his explanation, then let loose a laugh that bordered on hysteria. But if she didn't laugh she was going to cry. And it wasn't going to be dainty little London tears he was no doubt used to from his bevy of gorgeous sophisticated Brits, it was going to be a cyclonic, north Queensland snot fest.

And she'd be damned if she'd break down in front of *Luke*.

'How'd you even get here?' she demanded. 'The road is still cut in both directions.'

'Jonah picked me up in his chopper from Cairns airport.'

Claudia vaguely remembered hearing the chopper a little while ago and she silently cursed Jonah for being so damned handy. She made a mental note to tell Avery to withhold sex from him as his punishment for fraternising with the enemy.

Because as far as she was concerned, Luke Hargreaves was public enemy number one.

Not that Avery would—those two were still so loved up it was sickening.

'Well, you came, you saw,' she snapped. 'Now you can leave. Everything's fine and dandy here.'

Fine and dandy? Luke looked at the unholy wreck in front of him. It was the complete antithesis of fine and dandy. He shoved his hands in his pockets. 'I'm not going to do that, Claude.'

Claudia gave an inelegant snort. 'Why not? Isn't that what you do? Leave?'

'I thought I could…' Luke flicked his gaze to the flattened resort '…help.'

'Help?' Her voice sounded high even to her own ears. '*Now* you want to help?'

'Claude…' Luke sighed, unsurprised she was still carrying a grudge that he hadn't wanted anything to do with their parents' giant folly when they'd decided to retire and pass on the management to their children last year. 'I can help with the clean-up. And there will be partnership decisions that need to be made.'

A sudden surge of anger burned white-hot in Claudia's chest. *Partnership decisions?* What the hell? Did he think she'd be too distraught to not understand the true meaning behind such a casual announcement?

She drew herself up to her full five feet one inch, and jammed a hand on her hip. 'You think you have *the right* to waltz in here—'

Claudia broke off as a pressure—rage and something more primitive—built in her sinuses and behind her eyes. It threatened to explode and robbed her momentarily of the ability to form a coherent sentence.

'To just…*sweep* in when everything is such a bloody mess…and think you have a *right* to any decisions? You forfeited any rights when you walked away from the Tropicana last year.'

Luke tried to stay calm in the face of her anger. But Claudia always had driven him more nuts than any woman in the history of the world. She'd always been a firecracker where the resort was concerned, her petite, perennially cheerful disposition slipping quickly to growly Mummy bear when her precious Tropicana was threatened.

He kept his hands firmly buried in his pockets lest he succumb to the urge to shake her. Part of the reason she was in this mess was because she'd refused to listen to reason. If they'd gone the way he'd wanted to go with the resort they'd have been making money hand over fist as part of a bigger chain and therefore sheltered financially from such a monumental disaster.

But no. Claudia had wanted to keep the resort completely independent. Run it the way their parents had in some grand vision of yesteryear.

And he'd been too busy dealing with the disarray left by his ex, both personally and career-wise, to really care. But this mess was going to require some big decisions.

'Well, actually, that's not entirely true, is it?'

Claudia knew exactly what he was alluding to and hated that he was right. *Hated it.* But his name was still on the partnership agreement their parents had made them sign and he did have equal say—he just hadn't been interested in claiming it before today.

Claudia sighed, feeling utterly defeated all of a sudden. 'Look, I get it, you're here out of some misguided sense of responsibility. But you really don't need to worry. Everything's fine and dandy. Just go back to London. I can only deal with one Luke at a time.'

Luke was torn between picking her up and dumping her in the ocean and pulling her into his arms. 'I'm staying. I have a week off. I can help with the clean-up.'

This time Claudia's laugh did not *border* on anything—it had lapsed into full-blown hysteria.

'A week?' she demanded, her voice high and shaky. 'Well, gee, Luke, thank you for sparing *seven lousy days* out of your busy and important life to help out poor old Claude.'

She shook her head in disgust at him, the urge to slam the clipboard down on his head riding her as hard as the threatening tears. She *would not* cry!

'Take a look at this place,' she demanded, flinging her arms wide to distract from the crack in her voice. 'Do you think this is going to be cleaned up in a week?'

Luke looked. He doubted it would be cleaned up in a month. But he had a major account on the hook, one that would erase for ever the big one he'd lost because he'd foolishly trusted the woman he'd loved. He couldn't afford to spend a lot of time away. Hell, he couldn't even afford *seven lousy days*.

But he was here, wasn't he?

'Let's just take it one day at a time,' he suggested, holding onto his temper.

Claudia glared at him. 'Don't patronise me. I have an entire army of people ready, willing and able to help me clean up when we get the all-clear. We don't need someone whose heart isn't in it and who doesn't give a damn about the Tropicana.'

Luke clenched his fists in his pockets. Just because he hadn't chosen to slavishly devote himself to a forty-year-old white elephant, didn't mean he didn't care. He glared at her. 'And I suppose walking around with that damn clipboard and wearing that God-awful Hawaiian shirt and those polyester capris proves your level of give a damn?'

Claudia gasped at his insult. The uniform had been around since the beginning—it was *iconic*, damn it! But it gave her something else to focus on other than the prickle inside her nose caused by building emotion. 'I'm on duty,' she snapped.

It was Luke's turn to snort. 'For what? There's nobody here, Claude.'

Claudia held herself erect. 'I'm never off duty.'

And that, as far as Luke was concerned, was one of her problems. She was twenty-seven years old and, apart from her brief sojourns overseas with Avery every couple of years, the resort had been her entire focus.

'You really need a life,' he muttered, still smarting from her stinging judgment of him.

'*I* need a life?' She laughed again, all high and shaky. 'This from a man who wears a freaking suit to the beach.'

'I got the first flight I could,' he said. 'I went straight from work to Heathrow. I know it's hard for you to believe but there are other people in this world just as dedicated to their jobs as you are to yours. Although I think manic obsession probably fits better in your case.'

'The Tropicana isn't a *job*. It's our legacy,' Claudia snapped.

Luke shook his head as a storm of frustration and disbelief raged in his gut. God, her doggedness was infuriating.

'It's not *our legacy*. It's just an old-fashioned relic from a different time and *everybody*'s moved on but you. You're not in *Dirty Dancing*, Claude, and this—' he threw his arms wide at the destruction before him '—isn't freaking Kellerman's. Johnny Castle isn't going to drop by and demand that nobody puts you in a corner.'

Claude blinked. A pain flared in the vicinity of her heart as he took everything she believed in and crushed it into the hot, white sand. Yes, she was sentimental and a romantic and she not only believed *but had proved* that there was a market for the style of resort he was so disparaging of. She just hadn't realised he'd thought so little of the things that were important to her.

It made her feel small. Insignificant. Unvalued.

And so very sad. For her and for him. His divorce sure had made him cynical.

And it was her undoing. Her vision blurred, the emotion she'd been holding back for days coming now whether she liked it or not. A solitary tear spilled down her cheek.

Luke saw the tear threaten, then fall and wished he could cut his tongue out. He'd been angry and frustrated and his words had been harsh and ill considered. Strands of her blonde hair had loosened and blew across her face, sticking to the wet tear track and her mouth.

'Claudia.' He took a step towards her.

Claudia shook her head and held up a hand to ward him off, swiping at the tear with the other, angry that he was a witness to it, that she was being weak and *sentimental* in front of him. 'Just go back to London, Luke.' She turned away, marching off, needing to get away from his toxic disregard as more tears ran down her face.

Luke watched as she turned away, marching back up the beach, her spine straight, her ponytail barely bouncing as she held her head high. He cursed his insensitivity.

That went well. *Not.*

CHAPTER TWO

AVERY, JONAH, ISIS and Cyrus looked up from the reception desk that had been turned into a mini war room as the glass entrance door was yanked open and a red-eyed, tear-streaked Claudia stalked inside the cavernous lobby. Jonah looked at Avery with a question in his eyes as Claudia steamed straight past them.

'Claude?' Avery called after her, her American accent echoing around the large, deserted foyer. Claudia didn't stop or reply.

'Claudia.'

This time Claudia hesitated slightly before throwing an, 'I'm fine,' over her shoulder and, 'I just need some time alone,' before hitting the wide elegant staircase that would have been perfectly at home in some maharajah's palace.

There was a worried silence as four sets of eyes watched her beat her hasty retreat to her first-floor suite.

'What was that about?' asked Cyrus, a young local guy employed at the Tropicana as a bellhop.

'I don't know,' said Isis, his sister, who usually worked Reception.

The siblings, products of hippy parents, were uncannily similar with their striking red hair and freckles.

'I think I do,' Avery said, her eyes narrowing as Luke strode up the wide front steps.

Luke, his shoes and jacket in hand, glanced at the reception desk as he entered the lobby. None of the people behind it looked very receptive.

He made his way across the expanse of mosaic tiles swirling together to form a tapestry of rich sandy tones. He diverted around colossal rugs, cushy lounge chairs and potted palms. Huge beige columns rose to the two-storey ceiling and bordered the domed mural on high. It showcased a midnight sky twinkling with stars, the edges decorated with palm leaves.

As a kid it had fascinated him endlessly; now it seemed just another relic of yesteryear.

'Luke Hargreaves,' Avery said, her voice full of accusation as he approached the desk. 'Did you make Claude cry?'

Luke glanced at Jonah, standing behind Avery, who was sending him *run away now* signals with his eyes. Jonah knew as well as Luke that Avery was Claudia's fiercest champion.

'I'm rather afraid I did.' He grimaced as he approached the desk.

Much to Luke's surprise Avery's shoulder's sagged and she said, 'Oh, thank God for that. She needed a damned good cry.'

The group all nodded in agreement, even Jonah. 'Oh, yes,' Isis agreed. 'She's been saying she's *fine and dandy* for days now.'

'Fine and dandy,' Cyrus repeated. 'Like a cracked record.'

'Well…' Luke shrugged '…mission accomplished.'

Luke was glad that little group were more relaxed and looking less like they wanted to hang, draw and quarter him. Apparently an upset Claudia was a good thing. But it didn't help his guilt…the things he'd said had been fairly unforgivable.

He felt about as low as a man could feel.

He remembered all too well how it'd felt to be idolised by her and he much preferred that feeling. Although he'd certainly developed feet of clay as far as she was concerned since declining the opportunity to give up his entire life in the UK—no matter how shambolic—and manage the resort with her.

He glanced up the stairs behind him, then back to the group. He had to go and apologise. 'Think I'll go and see how she is. Say sorry.'

Avery shook her head. 'No. That would be bad.'

Jonah agreed. 'You should give her some time to cool off, man.'

Cool off? As if anyone could cool off in this God-awful heat without the electricity that usually cooled the vast lobby into a blissful paradise. The frustration that had ridden him down at the beach returned for a second spin and a sudden rush of bone-wearying tiredness joined the mix.

He was jet-lagged to hell and sweating like a pig in his inappropriate clothes, but he had to *fix* this.

'Why didn't you tell me on the chopper ride she was this fragile?' Luke demanded of Jonah.

'She's not fragile,' Avery said, rising quickly to Claudia's defence.

'You could have fooled me,' he snorted.

'She's been working day and night organising everything like a Trojan, getting things into place so when the official all-clear comes tomorrow we can start the clean-up, not to mention having to deal with the two hundred guests we were expecting over the next few weeks.' Avery glared at him. '*And* she's been helping out in the town and at the other resorts. She's been strong, she's been a leader. She is *not* fragile.'

'Then why is she bursting into tears?'

Avery shook her head at him and Luke felt lower still.

'Because she's exhausted. Because she's stressed and worried. She's barely slept a wink in five days. Because her entire life just got blown all to hell and maybe, just maybe, she'd thought you might be the one man who really understood her devastation. None of us here can truly understand how this disaster in this place she loves so much has wounded her. Except you. Is that what you did, Luke? Did you go down to the beach and tell her you understood?'

Luke avoided the doubt and reprimand in Avery's gaze as guilt rode him again. 'I asked you how she was doing,' he said, turning to Jonah. 'You said she was fine.'

Jonah nodded. 'She is fine. *And dandy.* Considering everything she's worked for this last year has been flattened to a pulp. She's been keeping busy and putting up a good front for us all. But you're *family*, man. Your opinion has always mattered more than anyone else's.'

Luke scowled, hating that Jonah was right. He had lashed out and hurt her. 'Right,' he said after a moment. 'So I'd better go and fix it, then.'

Avery made a tutting sound and it was Luke's turn to glare. 'What?'

'I know you're a man and all and it's in your DNA to *fix* stuff but she doesn't need that. She told us she needed some time alone and a smart man would just let her do it. And probably after that she needs you to shut your mouth and just hug her.'

Jonah nodded. 'Give her some space, man. I wouldn't add insult to injury if I were you.'

Luke knew it was good advice. But he couldn't bear the fact that she was upstairs all alone crying because of the things *he'd* said. Claudia wasn't a crier—never had been. She was bouncy and cheery and peppy.

She was a ray of freaking sunshine.

And he'd made her cry. *He* was responsible for her tears.

Luke shook his head. 'Nope, sorry, can't.'

And then he was gone and four sets of eyes watched him bound up the stairs following in Claudia's footsteps.

Avery sighed. 'And I thought he was smart.'

Jonah slid a hand onto Avery's shoulder and squeezed as he pulled her gently back against his chest. 'Even smart men can be stupid where women are concerned.'

She smiled and slid her hand over the top of his. 'That's true. You were pretty dumb.'

Jonah chuckled and dropped a kiss on her temple.

'That's not going to end well, is it?' Cyrus asked his sister, agog that *anyone* would go against Claudia's express wishes.

Isis shook her head. 'His funeral.'

Luke's feet took him without conscious thought to the door of the Copacabana Suite, the room where Claudia had lived with her parents since she was six years old. He and his parents had lived next door in the Mai Tai Suite. He hesitated before he knocked—maybe she didn't reside here any more? Maybe she'd downgraded now her parents had moved on? It wasn't as if a single woman needed a massive two-bedroom suite.

But the thought was only fleeting. Claudia Davis was as sentimental as they came. No way would she have passed up the nostalgia of her childhood home. Or the view from the balcony.

He knocked. No answer.

He knocked again. Louder. Still no answer.

'Claude, I know you're in there. Open up.'

No answer.

'I can stand out here all day and knock,' he warned, even if the thought made him weary to his bones. 'Hell, I can just sit down here and wait for you to come out. You're going to have to eventually. But I'm not going back to England. I'm not going anywhere for a week so you might as well get used to it.'

Still no answer. The door remained stubbornly closed. Luke sighed and slid down the door, propping his back against the dark grain wood. He was too bloody tired to stand upright. Despite the luxury of business class he hadn't slept much on the plane—worry about the resort, *about Claudia* had unfortunately kept sleep at bay.

Luke rubbed his eyes and scrubbed at his face with his hands. He could hear the faint rasp of stubble already fighting back against the quick shave he'd managed in the restroom aboard the plane. He was used to keeping it ruthlessly smooth, and it bothered him—he really should do something about that.

After a shower. And a sleep.

In fact his whole appearance bothered him. His sleeves were rolled up haphazardly, his top three buttons were undone, his expensive business shirt felt sticky against his sweaty chest and his bare feet were still coated with traces of sand.

Luke prided himself on his appearance. He believed it had a lot to do with his success. If you looked professional clients were more likely to part with their money.

He rapped again on the door, his knuckles connecting with the wood just above his shoulder. 'Claude.'

Still no answer.

Luke looked back at his feet and rubbed his toes together to displace the sand. A fine sprinkling of gritty powder dusted the thinning, aged carpet with its palm-tree print that had graced this hallway for as long as he could remember.

As a kid roaming around the resort he'd never been without sand between his toes. He'd rarely even noticed it, for ever being chided by his mother for tracking it into the suite. He'd loved it back then.

But like everything else today, it bugged him and he leaned down with his fingers to brush it all off. His phone buzzed in his pocket and he rubbed his hands together to remove the last trace of sand before quickly answering the text.

A pair of work boots filled his vision as he hit send and he glanced up to find Jonah looking down at him dangling a key—yes, they still had real bona fide keys at the Tropicana, *of course*—from his fingers.

'This might help,' Jonah said. 'And if you tell Avery I gave it to you I will deny everything.'

Luke put the phone away and took Jonah's offering. It was the keys to the Mai Tai. He smiled. 'Thank you.'

Jonah and Luke had been friends a long time so when he reached out a hand Luke grabbed hold gratefully and let

Jonah haul him to his feet. 'Don't screw it up,' Jonah warned before retreating.

Luke made his way next door and slid the key into the lock. For twenty years the Davis family and the Hargreaves family had not only run the resort but lived right next door to each other. Somehow, *miraculously,* they'd made it through twenty years in business together and still come out as friends. Even choosing to take their trip of a lifetime together.

Luke stepped inside the suite, which looked more worn and shabby around the edges than ever. A familiar smell of old carpet, starched linen and the hibiscus air freshener that was synonymous with his childhood embraced him. He'd grown to hate that smell as his desperation to see the big wide world had grown more intense, but today it was soothing to ragged nerve endings.

He *must* be tired.

He glanced at the big king-sized bed covered in its colourful Hawaiian-style bedspread and was surprised by the overwhelming desire to leave Claudia alone as she'd requested and get some much-needed sleep. Tackle her when he could count on more than two functioning brain cells. But that solitary tear played in slow motion through his head and he placed temptation firmly behind him as he stalked to the connecting door.

A long-forgotten memory made Luke hesitate before sliding the key into the lock. When their parents had run the resort, the door was never locked. In fact it was usually left chocked open. On a hunch, he just reached for the handle.

The knob turned and the door opened.

And there, dead ahead, on a matching king-sized bed, lay Claudia, all curled up and very definitely bawling her eyes out. She was crying so hard and so loud, he didn't think she'd even heard the door swing open.

Hell, it sounded as if she were crying for Australia and going for gold.

Another spike of guilt drove a stake right between his eyes. *Crap.* He hesitated before he crossed the threshold into her room but *what the hell*? He'd come this far.

The curtains that matched the bedspread were pulled back and the balcony doors were thrown wide, admitting the magnificent tropical view. A cool ocean breeze tickled at the open neck of his shirt as he tentatively edged inside, and felt heavenly against his sweaty skin.

'Claude?'

Claudia almost leapt out of her skin as Luke's deep, rich voice reached straight into the middle of her misery and yanked her out by the roots of her hair. She sat abruptly, her tears temporarily forgotten.

'Jeez,' she said, her hand clutched to her rocketing heart, 'are you trying to scare me half to death?'

Luke stalled where he was, holding up his hands at the frightening sight of a puffy-eyed, wild-looking Claudia. Her hair was half in, half out of her ponytail, the loose bits clumped together into some kind of bird-nest-like creation, her nose and cheeks were red and she was surrounded by piles of well-used tissues.

'Sorry…I didn't mean to startle you.'

'Who gave you a damn key?' Claudia demanded, ignoring his apology. 'No, don't worry, it was Jonah, wasn't it? Bloody traitor.'

Luke took a tentative step closer. 'I just wanted to see if you were okay,' he said, avoiding selling out Jonah.

'Do I look okay?' she snapped.

Luke shook his head. She looked as if she'd been dragged through a hedge backwards. She looked angry and sad and tired.

She looked defeated.

And that probably kicked him the hardest. Claudia was a glass-half-full kind of girl.

'Oh, just go away,' Claudia groaned as the fright wore off and the surge of adrenaline mixed with her already precarious emotional state to make her feel even more edgy and vulnerable. Emotion clogged her throat and the hot scald of tears pricked at her eyes again.

She fell back against the mattress, resuming her former foetal-ball position. 'Just let me cry in peace,' she said, dragging another tissue out of the box.

Luke was torn between leaving and not having to listen to her cry and staying put, being some kind of emotional support for Claudia. Or *trying* at least.

Neither prospect thrilled him.

But the part of him that had run barefoot through the resort with her and swum with her in the ocean just across the pathway and played hide-and-seek with her amidst the resort gardens won out.

He shut his eyes, sending up a brief plea to the universe that she wouldn't jab him in the ribs or knee him somewhere a little lower as he moved around the other side of the enormous bed and climbed on.

Claudia frowned as she felt the bed give behind her. She looked over her shoulder as Luke approached on his hands and knees. 'What are you doing?' she demanded.

'I'm doing what I should, according to Avery, have done down on the beach. I'm going to hug you.'

Claudia blinked and swallowed against another threatening tide of tears. She gave an inelegant sniffle. 'If you hug me I'm just going to cry harder.'

Luke chuckled at her husky threat as he settled in behind her, slipping his arm around her waist. 'I guess that's probably kind of the point.'

Claudia's breath caught at the light tease in his voice and she looked away from him, turned to face the doorway over the other side of the room. Her back was all smooshed against his front—his big, broad, hard front—his breath was a warm caress at her neck, the slight scrape of stubble skating delicious shivers to dangerous places.

She shut her eyes, her heart racing now for an entirely

different reason. How many hot, fevered dreams had she had as a teenager about exactly this? Lying with him like this?

Minus their clothes, and her inhibitions?

Luke shut his eyes as his exhausted body revelled in being horizontal. Claudia felt stiff as a board but it was bliss to lie down and he could already feel the tug of sleep pulling at the hazy hold he had on consciousness.

How many times had they lain in her parents' bed as kids, watching reruns of Claudia's favourite television show, *The Love Boat,* while their parents finished up for the night? She'd always offered to let him watch something he wanted to but he hadn't minded—as long as whatever they were watching had ads, he was happy.

How many times had Tony, the head chef, who had been at the Tropicana for all its forty years, personally brought them up his speciality Hawaiian pizza? And how many times had he woken to his dad picking him up and carrying him to his bed next door?

But so much had happened in the intervening years to put distance between them. He'd gone away—far away. He'd rarely been back as he'd fought to establish himself in a dog-eat-dog industry. He'd got married. *And divorced.* He'd refused to come back and play when the resort was handed to him. He'd disagreed with her vision.

In short, he'd changed.

But Claudia? Claudia was still the same girl she'd always been. He'd thought less of her for that this last decade but, lying here with her now, he was immensely pleased that she was still the same old Claude.

Except she was so quiet and rigid. Taut as a bow. He wished he knew the right words to comfort her. The time when they'd been close and their conversations had been easy seemed a million years ago now.

He'd spent a decade in the cut-throat advertising game where men and women alike fought tooth and nail for an account. There wasn't a lot of softness, of emotion, in the advertising business. Nobody comforted you when you lost an account—if anything there was a certain degree of triumph at someone else's misfortune, the scent of an opportunity in the offing.

God knew he'd witnessed the pointy end of it three years ago after being the golden-haired boy for so long.

None of that helped him with right here, right now. None of that equipped him to deal with a grieving Claudia.

'Was it awful?' he whispered.

Claudia tensed as the whisper seemed to punctuate the silence like a blaring trumpet. She'd been trying not to think about that night. Trying to keep busy and organise. Trying to look ahead, not back. Not think about the howling wind and the sounds of destruction that not even a large underground cellar had insulated them from.

Her face scrunched up in a most unpleasant fashion as the fear rolled over her again and she was pleased he was behind her. A tear rolled down her cheek as she relaxed back into him.

'I was so scared,' she said, choking on a lump high and hard in her throat, trying to hold it all back but failing because Luke was here. 'I knew we were all safe down in the cellar but…it was so loud. And it destroyed everything.'

Claudia paused as the next thought formed. It was too awful to speak aloud. 'What if I can't do it?' she whispered. 'What if I fail? What if I let everybody down?'

She started to cry again and Luke finally understood the true root of her anxiety. Claudia had spent her whole life keeping everyone happy—their parents, the locals who relied on the resorts for their economy, the tourist industry. She'd spent her entire adult working life at the resort juggling all these responsibilities.

And, if she wasn't careful, she was going to crack up under the pressure.

'Shh,' Luke said, his arm tightening around her waist as he absently kissed her neck. 'Shh.'

Claudia cried harder then. It felt so good to have him here. To lean against him for a while. To feel his lips brushing against her neck as he assured her over and over he was here. *Right here.* She felt as if she'd been juggling so many things alone for so long, trying to make the place a viable concern. Trying to be true to their parents' vision and prove to him it could be done.

And it was nice that he didn't say anything else, didn't try and fix things so she'd stop crying. Throw out some trite words about her being strong and how *she could do it.* Because deep down she knew she was strong; she knew she could do it. She was just having an extraordinarily weak moment, and his being here, putting his arms around her and letting her cry was exactly what she needed.

So she cried. She cried until there were no more tears left and she drifted off to sleep.

CHAPTER THREE

LUKE SLEPT TOO. Unfortunately not the deep, dreamless sleep of the severely jet-lagged. The sleep his body was craving. Whether that was the total chaos his diurnal rhythms had been thrown into or the fact that he was draped around warm, soft woman he wasn't sure. But his sleep was disturbed with fevered images cavorting through his head.

Difficult to understand, impossible to hold onto.

They slipped elusively through his fingers like strands of the silky blonde hair fluttering in and out of his reach.

There was a woman in a long, sheer gown. He was chasing her but she was always too far away to catch, to really see her. She was laughing, the tinkly sound echoing through his dream in time with his heartbeat. Every time he got close to her she'd disappear like mist only to reappear again in the distance.

She was naked under the gown, glimpses of her buttocks, the bare arch of her back and the side swell of her breasts taunting him. He was conscious of his arousal as he gave chase, as his legs pumped towards her, the desire to hold her, to kiss her, drumming through his veins.

His body ached with anticipation, his head spun with desire, his breath rasped and not just from the demands of the chase. She laughed again and he ran faster.

Claudia woke to a whirl of sensation spiralling deep and low inside her and sinking lower still, tingling between her legs and dragging heavy fingers down the backs of her thighs. Her eyelids fluttered open and she blinked, trying to orientate herself through eyes that were gritty, the skin around them simultaneously tight and puffy.

Something weighed heavy across her hip and thighs. And her breast. She was aware of heat at her back and hardness nestled between the cheeks of her bottom as she looked down at the hand no longer at her waist but cupping her breast instead. She froze.

Luke.

His hand moved in a circular motion then, gentle and firm all at once, and her nipple responded with blatant enthusiasm, scrunching tight.

Luke groping her.

Claudia's heart thundered behind her ribcage and echoed like gunshots through her ears. She was surprised he couldn't feel it considering how closely acquainted he was becoming with that area of her body.

How long had it been there?

Long enough to have her belly twisted into knots!

She raised her head and looked over her shoulder. He was sound asleep, his leg thrown carelessly over her hip, his thigh trapping hers, weighing her down. His mouth was still at her neck where she remembered it, his hips well and truly aligned with hers and about as close as was humanly possible with clothes on.

She watched as a frown flitted across his forehead, then stared at the stubble covering his jaw, a little darker now. It was surprisingly sexy and Claudia took a slow steady breath to expel any thoughts of sexy from her brain.

She was worried if she moved a hair, a single muscle, if she breathed too deep she would wake him and he'd find himself in this compromising position and then where would that leave them? Their relationship had become fraught enough this past year.

But she needn't have worried. He didn't budge, his body remaining heavy against hers in slumber, effectively trapping her slighter frame.

He wasn't waking and she wasn't going anywhere.

She turned away from him then, slowly placing her head back on her pillow and shutting her eyes. Willing herself not to think about the press of him along the length of her. About the wild tango her hormones were performing. About the persistent tug down low morphing into something else. Something more.

She just revelled for a moment. *This* was how it would feel to be with Luke. To be cherished by him. Comforted. Protected. *Loved.*

This was what she'd fantasised about during all her teen years. Hoping he'd see her as more than the little sister he never had. Hoping he'd kiss her, look at her as if she was a woman rather than a child, take her to his bed.

Hoping he'd stay.

He shifted against her slightly and Claudia held her breath. She expelled it on a quiet whimper as the delicious friction between their bodies ramped up another notch. The roughness of his barely there stubble scraped at the sensitive patch of skin where shoulder met nape and sensation prickled from the point of contact right down to her nipples, tightening them.

His hand squeezed in some kind of subconscious response because he was definitely still heavily asleep. Claudia's eyes practically rolled back in her head as her nipple blazed with hot, fiery need. She pushed back slightly, trying to ease the ache between her legs.

Oh, God. She swallowed. She should move—now! She should get the hell away. She *should not* be using his unsuspecting body as some kind of scratching pole!

Her resort had been declared a disaster zone and Luke was only here for a week.

But neither of those things seemed to matter right now.

She just wanted to push back a little more. Maybe rub herself against him a little. Arch her back, slide her arm up around his neck, pull his mouth down on hers.

Or maybe she could just roll over and press her mouth to his. Beg him for just one time in his arms.

Once was all she needed.

And then her mobile rang.

Luke could hear the chiming of a bell and the woman from his dream faded from sight altogether as his subconscious pulled him back through the layers of sleep.

He came out slowly, groggily, completely disorientated, his brain cells still heavily mired in fatigue. The sunny room wasn't remotely familiar, the ocean sounds weren't familiar, the smell of salt and apple blossom weren't familiar.

He shifted slightly, struggling out from the steely tendrils of his dream. Where were the heavy blackout curtains, the traffic noise, the smell of percolating coffee?

None of it was familiar.

The weight of something warm and distinctly female filled his hand and he squeezed tentatively.

The breast was *definitely* not familiar. The last time he'd woken to a woman in his bed it had been his wife and she washed her hair with expensive shampoo that smelled like designer perfume, not sweet and fresh like apples.

He pulled away, his hand releasing the breast, his leg sliding off the woman's thighs as it all came rushing back.

'Claude?'

Claudia lay frozen for a few seconds; her phone blaring out 'Summer Nights' from *Grease* alerted her to the fact it was Avery calling. Her friend was probably wondering where the hell she'd got to.

Just lying on my bed letting Luke grope me in his sleep. Sheesh!

Claudia didn't answer him or even look back as she snatched up the phone and scrambled off the bed, keeping her back firmly turned on Luke.

'Hi, Avery,' she said chirpily as she picked up the call.

Luke half sat in the bed, his eyes on her back as the memory of Claudia's—*Claude's!*—breast, her very erect nipple, burnt a hole in his palm. He might have been only semi-awake but he'd been fully aware of its arousal, and that was going to be impossible to forget. Especially with his hard-on pressing insistently against the zipper of his trousers. He wanted desperately to adjust it but there was no way he was touching himself with her right there—back turned or not.

He slid off the bed on the opposite side, not really paying any attention to what Avery and Claude were talking about. He needed some space. Some distance.

For adjusting.

For thinking.

For mental flagellation.

Luke stalked to the open balcony door and stepped grate-fully through the curtains and out into the sunshine, easing things inside his underwear as best he could. The harsh sun-light blinded him a little and he squinted against it, raising his arm to block it out.

The ocean was still flat and listless, swishing quietly against the sand, and he took several deep breaths of salty air, filling his lungs with sand and ocean, cleansing it of London smog, wishing it were as easy to cleanse his brain. Erase the mem-ory of Claudia all warm and soft, her nipple stiff and ready.

He turned his back to the vista, the brightness too much for his tired eyes. He shut them but then the edges of his dream fluttered seductively in the periphery of his mind and his eyes snapped open as his erection surged again.

Crap.

What had he done?

He shook his head. No. He'd been having a normal male physiological response to an erotic dream and Claudia just happened to be in the wrong place at the wrong time.

Nothing more, nothing less.

For God's sake, they'd grown up practically siblings.

She was like the kid sister he'd never had. Following him around. Getting into all kinds of mischief and strife with him. Sometimes bratty, always devoted. There'd never been *anything* between them.

He'd *never* felt *anything* other than brotherly towards her.

Except the heat in his palm didn't feel very brotherly. The memory of her softness, *of her hardness*, felt pretty damn carnal.

Which begged the question—why *hadn't* they ever got together? Never had a fling? Never even shared a quick teenage pash? It made sense with their proximity. Of course, she'd been sixteen and he'd been twenty-one when he'd left over eleven years ago but there'd been plenty of times since.

Hell, the only time they'd kissed that didn't revolve around a hello/goodbye was on New Year's Eve—and that had never been anything other than a quick chaste peck on the cheek.

'I have to go,' Claudia said, stepping briskly out on the balcony in a very businesslike manner, tucking her shirt into her awful polyester capris. But Luke wasn't fooled. She forgot he knew her better than anyone and she was as flummoxed as he was about the whole *groping* situation.

'I'm sorry…about before,' he said. Luke knew there was only one way to really deal with what had occurred on her bed.

The same way he dealt with everything.

Head-on.

'Oh…don't worry about it,' Claudia dismissed, looking at the balcony tiles and nervously pulling at the wisps of her hair at the nape of her neck. 'It was nothing.'

'It was not nothing, Claude. It was not my intention to… molest you in my sleep when I crashed in the bed with you. I don't think I can be held entirely accountable for my actions given that I wasn't aware of what I was doing, but I believe in taking responsibility so…I apologise.'

Claudia peeked up at him through her fringe and gave him a vigorous nod. 'Right…yes…good,' she said. 'Now do you think we could never speak of it again?'

Luke laughed then. He'd forgotten how endearingly funny Claudia could be. 'Deal,' he said and stuck out his hand.

She shot him a nervous-looking smile but returned the nice firm grip and he lingered for a moment longer than he would normally have. 'Why didn't we ever…?'

Claudia frowned. 'What?'

'Why didn't we ever…get it on?'

Claudia pulled her hand from his at the unexpected question. He was so sophisticated now. So different from the boy she'd known. Even the way he spoke had changed. Gone were the broad, flat Aussie vowels. He sounded more cultured now, more anglicised. His voice had taken on a smooth richness that poured over her like thick double cream.

Why hadn't they ever got together? Was he insane?

Because you were never interested, idiot.

But even as she thought it Claudia knew it wasn't that simple. There was more to it than that. Much more. Stuff that had never been spoken but somehow she'd known intuitively.

'Too…complicated.' She shrugged. 'We couldn't have just had a fling where we spent some time together and then went our own separate ways because it wouldn't just be us getting together, would it? It'd be our parents too. And if something happened…'

Luke nodded as she trailed off. 'They'd have to take sides. It could ruin a friendship that's somehow survived twenty years of being in business together.'

And if Luke knew one thing it was how easily work relationships turned to dust, and the long-reaching consequences that could have. He was still paying for the faith he'd put into his.

And he'd vowed to never stick his head in the mouth of that lion ever again.

Claudia shrugged. 'We couldn't do that to them. It wouldn't be fair.'

Luke nodded. She was right. Their parents' friendship was a very good reason why he needed to forget how it felt to have Claudia smooshed up against him. To have touched her breast. Felt it respond. He shut his eyes to block the mental image even as his palm tingled. He turned around, grabbing the railing hard as he stared out over acres of calm ocean.

Hell. He *must* be jet-lagged.

Get a grip, man.

Claudia let her gaze wander over the contours of his back. She supposed he didn't have a tan any more. He used to. Surfing every day with Jonah, he used to go a dark nut-brown. His hair used to be long and shaggy.

And then he'd left.

Claudia dragged her mind back to the present. 'I have to go,' she said. 'Avery needs me. Jonah can take you back to Cairns later if you like. I believe there's an afternoon Qantas flight to Heathrow.'

Luke's shoulders tensed and he counted to ten before he turned back to face her. 'I'm not going anywhere for a week,' he said. 'I'll help with the clean-up as much as I can. You might as well just go on and get used to it.'

Claudia regarded him for a moment. His jaw was rigid and his mouth was set in that obstinate line she remembered so well. She'd forgotten how stubborn he could be. And the reality was, she could ill afford to knock back help.

'Fine,' she said. 'Stay. See if I care. I need every bit of muscle I can get my hands on anyway. But we're doing this my way—do you understand? I,' she said, pointing to herself, 'am the boss. You—' she pointed at him '—are the muscle. Got it?'

Luke suppressed the twitch of his lips at Claudia's Little Miss Bossy Britches act. He nodded without saying a word. He'd never been known as *the muscle* before but it brought a whole new connotation to her dominatrix spiel. She narrowed her eyes suspiciously at his easy capitulation but said nothing before turning on her heel and leaving.

His gaze was drawn to the swagger of her butt in those terrible capris.

Who knew polyester could suddenly seem so enticing?

CHAPTER FOUR

THE NEXT DAY they got the all-clear to start the clean-up and for five long days Claudia and the whole crew worked like Trojans to clear the mountains of debris whirled up, ripped to shreds and dumped back down again by the cyclone.

Five long days from sun up to sun down—picking up, chopping up, loading, dumping and starting all over again. Crashing exhausted into bed each night with aches and pains and blisters galore. Waking early to do all again the next day.

Too busy to do any of the leisure things that could usually be indulged in at a beach resort. Too busy to relax on the beach or go surfing after shift end. Too busy for long, boozy chats late into the night. Too busy to take a day off and go out fishing in one of Jonah's charter boats.

Too damn busy for sure to psychoanalyse a very weird moment that should never have happened. Too busy to question it. Too busy to barely say a dozen words to each other.

But when she shut her eyes, all bets were off and Claudia spent a lot of time fantasising about just where that moment could have gone. If she *had* shifted against him, slid her arm around his neck. If he had kissed her, if he'd pushed his hand under her shirt.

This was what happened when there were unfulfilled sexual fantasies. They just grew and grew in the deep, dark recesses of the imagination until a person could barely sleep from the wondering.

Maybe they should have *got it on* as he'd put it. Done it early, rid it from their systems. Hell, their parents would never have even known if they'd had some wild pash one night down on the beach.

It probably would have been one of those awful, soggy, teeth-clashing kisses. *Probably.* And that would have been that.

Because she sure as hell was spending a lot of her supposed sleep time wondering about a wild pash with Luke now.

Too much bloody time.

On the sixth day Claudia was busy inside, ostensibly going over the strategic plan, plotting their progress, seeing what else had to be done/arranged and making some phone calls to local suppliers.

And it really had started out that way.

But from the reception desk she had a bird's eye view of the pool. The pool that Luke had decided was on his to-do list today. She'd actually put it on Cyrus's list but clearly they'd swapped. So there he was in a pair of boardies. And nothing else.

He didn't have that deep nutty tan any more. Although, he had toasted to a light delicious golden colour even in the short time he'd spent back under the north Queensland sun. His chest was as hairless as she remembered, just a sprinkling around his nipples and a fine trail that arrowed down from his belly button.

All the way down.

Her work largely forgotten, Claudia, her handy clipboard clutched to her chest, watched Luke clear all the large debris that had been dumped in the previously sparkling water of the large resort pool that meandered its way all around the outside of the main building. He stood on the edge and pulled it all out with a large net. From leaf matter to building wreckage to about a zillion dead insects.

There was no sign of the mobile phone he had practically glued to his hip the entire week. Taking phone calls from

London at all hours of the day and night, downing tools while he dealt with whatever matter was deemed urgent enough by the person at the other end to interrupt his week off, then picking up again and getting on with it.

Nope, as he waded into the pool with the hand-held industrial vacuum cleaner the phone was nowhere to be seen. Just Luke and his boardies and a pair of reef shoes to protect him from any glass hazards that could still be lying on the bottom of the pool, hidden by the slightly murky water.

With her occupational health and safety hat on, Claudia was pleased to see Luke being cautious. But that wasn't what was causing her to openly ogle him.

No.

That would be the way water droplets clung to his arms and chest, glistening distractedly. The midday sun shone down on him, sparkling in the droplets, and he was literally dazzling to her eyes.

Claudia swallowed as she watched his broad shoulders and powerful quads get to work, sweeping at the layer of silt and sand on the bottom of the pool.

'Hey.'

Claudia almost jumped out of her skin as Avery's voice sounded right near her ear. 'Do you have to creep around like that?' she protested, pressing her hand to her pounding heart.

Avery frowned. 'What's wrong?'

'Nothing,' Claudia muttered, quickly turning back to the desk.

But it was too late. Avery turned to see what had been holding Claudia's attention. And found it.

Or him, as the case may be.

She grinned. 'Well, well, well,' she teased. 'Were you perving on that gorgeous hunk of man flesh, Miss Claude?'

Claudia refused to look up and give anything away. 'Just checking he was wearing the appropriate shoes. That's an accident waiting to happen,' she fobbed.

Avery grinned again. 'Uh-huh.'

Claudia glanced at her friend sharply. 'I was.'

'Uh-huh.'

Claudia shoved her hand on her hip. 'What the hell is that supposed to mean?' she demanded.

Avery shrugged in that gorgeous retro Hollywood movie star way of hers. 'Nothing. I think it's great that you can't take your eyes off Captain Sexypants.'

Claudia blinked. Only Avery would come up with such a fanciful nickname. 'Captain *Sexypants*?' Of all the… 'Just because you are all loved up, Avery Shaw, does not mean the rest of the world is similarly interested.'

'Uh-huh.'

Avery got that dreamy look in her eyes again—the one that had been an almost permanent fixture on her face since she and Jonah had become an item—and Claudia rolled her eyes, returning her attention to the paperwork in front of her.

'You can tell me, you know, Claude. We've been friends a long time—you know you can talk to me.'

Claudia glanced up as Avery turned serious, her American accent more pronounced when edged with worry. The thing was she knew she could. Or she used to be able to anyway. But then the resort got dumped on her as a sole responsibility and, even though Avery had been there by her side throughout it all, the onus still fell directly on Claudia's shoulders. Trying to keep it altogether, make it all work, had forced Claudia into an almost permanent state of seriousness, with no time for frivolous girly chatter.

And then Avery had hooked up with Jonah and how could Claudia possibly dump her problems on her friend's shoulders? Avery was happy—she didn't want to bother her with trivial stuff.

The days of their girlhood confidences had been well and truly squashed by her very adult responsibilities.

So now she wasn't sure how she could say, well, actually, Avery, Luke sleep-groped me a few days back and I'm so sexually frustrated I think I might die from it or at the very least jump the next guy who walks through the door.

How could she even voice that, think of her own petty desires, when the world around her had gone to hell and there were so much more important things to deal with?

And it was just as well she didn't as Jonah chose that moment to walk through the door and Avery's face lit up as if he were dipped in chocolate and rolled in sugar.

'I know, Avery,' Claudia said, and smiled at her best friend in the whole world. 'I know. I just have a lot on my plate.'

Avery gave her shoulder a squeeze. 'You need a break.'

Claudia nodded. 'Later.' She tapped a pen against the resort plans in front of her. 'After.'

But then Jonah's, 'Where are those refreshments, woman?' boomed across the foyer and Avery said, 'I'm just going to organise some drinks for the workers.'

Claudia nodded absently. ''Kay. See you later.'

Claudia watched as Avery took off in Jonah's direction and smiled as Jonah swept her up and pressed a very indecent kiss on Avery's mouth. She looked away.

Outside. To the pool.

Luke was boosting himself up on the side, his back to her. Water sluiced off his hair and down over his shoulders and the perfectly delineated muscles of his back. For a man who had an office job, he was in excellent shape. In one smooth movement he'd twisted and sat on the coping of the pool. The broad expanse of his chest was exposed to her view now and Claudia drank it in. Firm pecs, flat abs and that distinct trail of hair that arrowed from his belly button down...

Before she could follow it all the way to its destination, Luke turned again and pushed up through powerful quads into a standing position.

Her gaze was drawn to those legs. Lightly haired, his calves firm without being bulky. And then there were his boardies. His *very wet boardies* that clung in all the wrong places, outlining the hardness of quads beneath but also the part of his anatomy she'd felt up close and personal only days before.

Claudia's mouth suddenly felt as dry as day-old toast.

He chose that moment to look up and suddenly she was looking straight into his eyes. Eyes that, despite distance and the barrier of glass, seemed to pierce right to her centre. Their gazes locked and held and Claudia's heart banged around in her chest. Her breath hitched. Her mouth went from dry to arid.

There was a frankness to his gaze and in that instant she knew, *she just knew*, he'd been aware of her interest all along. A part of her wanted to hide behind the desk, hide from the directness in his gaze, but he chose that moment to sweep a flat palm up his belly to his chest and her eyes helplessly followed.

She couldn't look away.

He motioned to her then, inviting her to join him and, God help her, she wanted to. *Really freaking bad.*

But the phone rang, dragging her back from the edge, and she leapt on it as if it were the last life buoy left on a sinking ship, picking it up and brandishing it at him, barely stopping herself from kissing it.

He looked at her long and hard for a moment before shrugging and nodding and she turned away gratefully, catching her breath as she greeted the caller, her usual chipper phone manner lost in the mental images of a half-naked Luke.

Captain Sexypants indeed.

Later that evening, with the bulk of the clean-up finally completed, Claudia threw an impromptu luau down on the beach for all the volunteers. Back before the resort was blown to hell, every Saturday night was luau night. It was one of their most popular themed events amongst their largely family clientele as well as Crescent Cove locals.

This wasn't going to be anywhere near as fancy as that.

There wouldn't be drums and ukuleles to hula to and there wouldn't be the usual feast but then, there wouldn't be two hundred people either. There was only a dozen to cater for and, given that there was enough raw material to make a bonfire big enough to be seen from space, all they really needed was some fresh seafood and some cold drinks.

Jonah had been tasked with taking one of his boats out and catching some fish, which he'd done most admirably. Tony, their chef, who was still with them after all these years, had cooked the fish along with an amazing rice-in-coconut-milk concoction and piping-hot fresh bread. Avery had dug out the leis and a CD of Hawaiian music.

And even if partying was the last thing Claudia and her aching body felt like, she put on her uniform, plastered a smile on her face and was the chipper Claude that everyone knew and loved because these people had helped out and worked like dogs, out of the goodness of their hearts, and she owed them.

But it felt good to sit down on one of the logs that ringed the fire and just listen to the chatter and the swish of the ocean. To not do anything. It felt like the first time she'd sat and done nothing for over a week.

She buried her toes in the cool sand and let the bliss take over. Hull, Jonah's hulking great hound, had collapsed on the sand beside her.

She tipped her head from side to side to stretch out aching neck muscles. She rubbed at the left side with her hand and winced as her index finger twinged. She looked down at her hands. They were in bad shape from a week of hard labour—some old blisters on her palms in various stages of healing, her fingers rough and dry from pulling out a zillion splinters.

She'd kill for a day at one of those fancy spas.

Iron out the kinks with a massage. Get a pedicure. Sit in a sauna and soak half the day. Maybe one of those full-body scrubs.

Nearby laughter pulled her out of her fantasy and Claudia smiled as she watched Cyrus and Isis perform a rather good hula. Jonah in his boardies and Avery in a tangerine bikini with a matching sarong low on her hips danced a much closer, sexier number in the shadows further away, lost in each other.

A pang of jealousy bit Claudia hard in the chest.

'They look good together.'

Claudia looked up, all the way up, to find Luke looking down at her. He was in boardies as well—dry this time, *thank goodness*—and his chest was covered with a form-fitting T-shirt. She resolutely ignored the wetter, less dressed image of him that floated in her mind's eye but his eyebrow kicked up and he looked at her as if he knew exactly what she was thinking.

'Yes, they do,' she said and hoped like hell the words didn't sound as squeaky as they'd felt leaving her throat.

She was relieved when he broke eye contact, handing her a frosty bottle of beer. She took it gratefully as he stepped over the log and lowered his butt, plonking down beside her.

Claudia shifted to make some room for him.

Or put some space between them, anyway.

She looked back at the fire, which had settled from a blazing inferno to a dull roar, as they both took some swallows of their beers, neither saying anything for a few moments. Until Luke mentioned the elephant sitting next to them at the fire.

'I was hoping you'd join me in the pool today. Just like old times.' Luke had been acutely aware of her eyes on him today and his blood had flowed thick and sludgy through his veins as her gaze had continued to linger.

Claudia kept her eyes firmly fixed on the flames that danced before her. Why had he hoped that? Surely after a sleepy grope he knew they'd progressed far beyond the innocent pool games they'd played as kids? Even through the glass of the window she'd felt the pull of him, had been aware of him like no other man.

'I don't do much swimming these days,' she dismissed.

'What, not even in that magnificent ocean right on your doorstep?'

She shook her head. 'Too busy.'

Luke took a swig of his beer 'That's a shame...I seem to remember you looked good in a bikini.'

Claudia faltered, her pulse flickering madly in time with the flame as she glanced at him. What was she supposed to say to that? Since when did you pay any attention to how I looked in a bikini? Or, not as good as you do in wet clingy boardies?

Or maybe, more aptly, *don't flirt with me*?

'I leave the bikinis to Avery,' she said, dropping her gaze to the fire again. 'There's too much to do at the moment to bunk off for a cool dip.'

Luke tutted at her dismissal. 'The clean-up's essentially done,' Luke said. 'I'm sure you could have squeezed in a quick, dirty swim.'

Claudia, who almost choked on her beer, was shocked into looking at him again. He laughed at her scandalised look, then winked. 'I was referring to the state of the water.'

She narrowed her eyes at him, wondering how many beers he'd consumed. Maybe the jet lag was hitting him in one large wallop and taking over his mouth.

Either way, she chose to ignore his comment and the direction he seemed to want to steer the conversation. 'The outside is largely complete but there's still a long way to go,' she said. 'We have to keep moving forward.'

Luke sighed at her determination to stay serious. He'd hoped as he'd sat beside her that she'd loosen up a little—relax as everyone else was doing.

But no. The uniform should have been a clue.

'So what's next?' he asked as he reached down and absently petted a mellow Hull.

Claudia took a mouthful of her beer before she answered.

'Back to the drawing board. Starting again. Working out how much I can do with the insurance money.'

'It's not going to cover it all?'

Claudia shook her head. 'It may have been enough twenty years ago, not today. Hell, it'd probably have been enough for just a normal cyclone but…'

Luke took a swig of his drink and watched Claudia's toes, painted a cute shade of pink, wiggle in the sand.

'So you want to talk about where we go from here?'

He felt her tense beside him and her toes stopped their wriggling. 'I'm not selling to some consortium, some…giant hotel chain, Luke.' She glared at him and Luke couldn't decide if the flare in her eyes came from her sudden well of pissed off, or the fire.

'If you've stopped by to butter me up about that you might as well keep on going.'

Luke knew it was important to stay calm and frankly he was too wrecked from a week of hard yakka to get into an argument. 'Okay, so what *are* we going to do?'

'The Tropicana has been here for forty years. *Our parents* ran it together for twenty of those years. And it will be again.'

'Complete with Tiki Suites, salsa nights and lei stringing?'

Luke felt her hostile glance shoot bullets of disapproval straight into his chest.

'Yes. What's wrong with those things?' she demanded. 'I know they probably don't seem very sophisticated to Mr Hotshot Ad Exec, but the Tropicana has always been a family resort—that's the way our parents wanted it. And that's the way it's going to stay.'

'And what about *you*, Claude? What do *you* want?'

Claudia frowned. Where was the man who had teased her about a bikini before? He was looking at her as he had by the pool earlier, as if he was trying to see all the way to the inside. And now, as then, it discomforted her.

'What do you mean?'

'I mean if you were given a bottomless bucket of money and told you could build whatever you wanted—*anything*—what would you build? Not what our parents wanted, not what the town wants, not what's always been. What Claudia Davis wants.'

Luke watched her intently as she opened her mouth to say something and then shut it again. Conflict crinkled her brow. Wisps of blonde hair had loosened from her ponytail and the ocean breeze blew them gently across her face. The firelight played across her features complementing their fineness but it also illuminated her internal struggle, backlit her doubt.

She chewed on her bottom lip, contemplating the question as if he'd just asked her to tell him the meaning of life in ten words or less. The firelight glowed in the moisture she was creating and his gaze dropped to her mouth briefly before returning to the fire, tuning into the background noises of surf, laughter and hula music.

He drank his beer and waited quietly for her to figure it out. Was the question really that difficult?

Claudia contemplated the rim of her beer bottle, conscious of the time ticking away. She didn't know. She'd been so caught up in her parents' vision it had become her own. And she loved the kitschy, retro feel they'd created. But *was* it what she wanted?

What *did* she want?

She rubbed absently at her neck again and the muscles protested. 'A day spa,' she said on a whim. 'A place for people to be pampered.'

Luke blinked, both surprised and excited by her answer. 'Yeah?'

For a brief moment their eyes met and the spark in his caused a flutter of possibility inside Claudia's chest. But reality intruded and snuffed it out. She shook her head. 'The people we attract here can't afford that kind of decadence, Luke. We're the affordable alternative.'

'Can't we be both?'

Claudia frowned. 'Being good at one thing is better than being half-arsed at two.'

'So then let's not be half-arsed. Let's be some kind of hybrid resort where we cater to both ends of the market.'

'I think that'll be really confusing to the market, don't you? High-ticket clients aren't going to want to be bothered by a bunch of screaming kids and salsa lessons on the beach.'

Luke shrugged. 'So we keep them separate—we have enough land. Why shut ourselves off to another, potentially very lucrative, source of income?'

Claudia could feel that flutter again and her pulse picked up slightly as her imagination started to run a little wild. Avery would be great at managing and running a spa business. Temptation shimmied possibilities in front of her—typical that Luke would be an integral part of that, enticing her with firelight and his strange but lovely accent like a big, fat, juicy apple.

She dragged her gaze off him and looked into the fire. Bad enough that he'd reminded her of how she'd perved on him in the pool today, but now he was waving a shiny new future in front of her.

Get behind me, Satan.

Luke was encouraged by Claudia's contemplation, the little flare of interest he'd seen in her gaze. He nudged his thigh against hers and a quiver of something hot and sinful spread all the way up to his groin. 'Just think about it, Claude. You don't have to rush into anything.'

Claudia looked down at his thigh, all warm and muscled in the firelight. And tempting. Oh, so tempting. It was hot against hers and she didn't think it had anything to do with the fire. Did he feel it too or was it just her? She wondered what he'd do if she slid her hand onto it. If she slowly moved it upwards.

Right. To. The. Top.

She blinked as the image formed in real time in her head

and stood abruptly, shocked by the ferocity of the urge to follow through. 'I'll think about it,' she said, looking straight ahead. Not down at him. And his eyes. And his smile.

And his outrageously sexy accent.

Luke smiled at the stiffness of her stance. 'Good,' he murmured.

Claudia nodded. 'Right, well…I think I might turn in,' she said, still not looking at him.

Luke chuckled. 'Sweet dreams.'

Claudia swallowed as she thought about the dreams she'd been having this last week.

Not one of them sweet.

'See you in the morning,' she said with as much nonchalance as she could muster before she fled the beach for the safety of the Copacabana Suite, far away from men with sexy accents and delectable thighs.

CHAPTER FIVE

CLAUDIA BARELY SLEPT a wink. It was as if Luke had tripped some switch in her brain and a hundred different possibilities for what the Tropicana *could* be had bombarded her. And frankly it was a relief to think about something other than the way Luke's hand had felt on her breast. The way his boardies had clung to him in the pool.

The way his thigh had sizzled against hers.

By the time morning rocked around, her head was buzzing. And she needed to share! Avery and Jonah weren't on her radar—she'd walked in on them too many times to know that spontaneous bursts of shared creativity were off the table.

But the one man who had inspired them was just through a connecting door and he was in there alone.

She rose at six, climbed into her uniform—the skirt for a change—and made copious notes. When she was all spent she took to the floor, pacing it until the clock ticked over to seven—a perfectly reasonable hour. After that, all propriety was off. She rapped once on the door before pushing it open, knowing in her gut that Luke wouldn't have locked it.

The room was like a black hole when she pressed inside but that didn't deter her. It was only eight in the evening in the UK—still a perfectly decent hour. She marched over to the curtains from familiarity alone and yanked them back with a harsh squeal along the railing. Another impossibly sunny day greeted her and was surprisingly buoying.

Luke's eyes scrunched up as he stirred. He rolled on his side and prised open an eyelid to check the time on the clock beside his bed. 'What the hell?' he groaned, rolling on his back, knowing it was Claudia in his room without having to sight her. 'There better be another cyclone on the horizon,' he griped, 'because I thought this was our day of rest.'

'Sorry,' Claudia chirped although she didn't sound very sorry at all.

'Shut the curtain,' Luke said. 'Nowhere has the right to be this bright so early.'

'You're such a city boy now,' she scoffed as she acquiesced and closed half the curtain.

'I'm still on London time,' he protested.

'Whatever, city boy,' Claudia dismissed. 'Wake up. I've been up all night and it's all your fault.'

At another time, when he wasn't exhausted from hard physical labour and the remnants of jet lag, Luke might have taken that as a compliment. Might have raised his eyebrow and shot her a little *oh, really* look. But he was having trouble prising his eyes open.

And this was Claude. He didn't think about Claude in that context. *Or he never used to anyway...* Thinking about keeping her up at night was just plain wrong.

'Come back in an hour and tell me then,' he muttered, rolling on his side and plonking a pillow over his head.

Claudia glared at his covered head. 'Hey,' she protested, marching to his side and whisking the offending pillow away, tossing it on the ground. 'I know you're flying back to London tomorrow but I have ideas. Lots of ideas.'

Luke groaned. So did he. None of them sane. All of them X-rated. But she looked very awake. Very no-nonsense. Very determined. He sighed, resigning himself to his fate, pushing himself up into a semi-upright position against the head of the bed, his hands rubbing at his eyes.

'Okay, fine,' he said when he could just make her out through bleary eyes tortured by the kind of sunlight he'd never been privy to in his ten plus years in London. How quickly eyeballs forgot!

Then of course they were subjected to further torture by Claudia standing at the end of his bed in that horrendous uniform that somehow seemed to get sexier the more he saw her in it.

'What have you got?' he demanded with a gruffness that he was fairly sure had some kind of sexual genesis.

Claudia narrowed her eyes. He didn't look very awake. 'Do you need coffee?' she demanded.

Luke snorted. There were about a hundred things he needed, including dragging her into bed and stripping her out of her awful clothes, pulling out that damn ponytail and kissing her till she stopped growling and started purring.

Coffee didn't even rate.

Clearly his sanity was of much greater concern.

'Just speak,' he griped. '*You* woke me. And now I'm vertical and reasonably awake. So speak.'

Claudia tsked. 'I remember a time when you would have been up and on your surfboard catching a wave somewhere by now.'

'Claude.'

The warning in his voice told Claudia she'd stretched his patience long enough and she opened her mouth, prepared to get down to business, to launch into her spiel, and then his state of dress registered. Or, undress, to be exact. He was sitting up looking all big and broad with a very naked chest leading to a very naked abdomen and that very, very nice happy trail meandering downwards to what she began to suspect might be a very naked everything else.

'Are you…wearing *any* clothes?'

Luke looked at her for long moments and didn't answer and Claudia wished she could bite her tongue off. She hadn't meant to voice her concerns but she was so used to speaking her mind around him she'd forgotten that they were all grown up now. That some things just weren't said.

'No. I always sleep naked. Why? Don't you?'

Claudia snorted. 'No.'

'What, not even after sex?'

Heat rose in Claudia's cheeks. She really didn't want to discuss her sexual habits with Luke. 'That's none of your damn business.'

Luke couldn't agree more. Thinking about sex and Claudia in the buff were not places he wanted his mind to wander.

Clearly he needed more asleep

'You're right,' he sighed. 'I apologise. Now can we please just get this over with?'

Claudia folded her arms across her chest as she stared at his. 'I'd really prefer you to not be naked when I'm talking to you.'

And he'd prefer her to be a lot more naked than she was. Irritation needled him. 'Well, we don't always get what we want.'

Claudia dragged her gaze up. Fine. Tiredness was making him belligerent. She'd show him she could be cool about talking to a naked man. Who was in bed. With bed hair. And a shadowy hint of stubble along his jawline.

She wasn't some middle-aged prude. She was perfectly fine with nudity.

And bed hair. And stubble.

Luke rubbed his hand over his jaw, the rasp loud in the silence. He needed a shave. After some more sleep. 'Claude, I swear if you don't say something I'm just going to go to sleep sitting up.'

Claudia nodded. Speaking. She could do that. She cleared her throat. 'I was thinking about...' His bare chest was distracting in her peripheral vision. 'The whole spa idea. About...' He rubbed at his jaw again and the rasp went straight to her nipples. They tightened in blatant response, almost as if he'd scraped his chin over the sensitive tips, and she was thankful for the palm-tree pattern disguising their reaction.

Dear Lord, where was she? She cleared her throat again. 'Catering to that end of the market.'

'Yes?'

His slight accent dragged sticky fingers across her belly and she absently placed her hand on her midriff, pressing slightly to relieve the tingle. 'I was thinking about how we could offer the spa customers a fuller service, including exclusive accommodation. Have you seen those deluxe tents with four-poster beds that sit on raised wooden floorboards and are draped in the most luxurious georgette screening? They open to the ocean and look like something out of *Arabian Nights*?'

Luke knew the type Claudia was talking about—one of his clients dealt exclusively in that style of accommodation— but her hand resting where it was had become very distracting. Her fingers drummed against her belly as she spoke and he was beginning to have very bad thoughts indeed.

Which was not conducive to his nakedness.

Also, *this was Claudia!*

He pulled his legs up, tenting the sheet. 'I think it sounds perfect for the Tropicana—we have enough land to make it a really exclusive set-up.'

Claudia nodded, temporarily forgetting in her enthusiasm Luke was wearing nothing but a sheet. She even took a step towards his bed and propped her knee on the end of the mattress. 'If we set it up right the two parts of the resort could be kept separate but co-exist quite happily.'

Luke chuckled as Claudia's blue eyes shone like polished topaz. 'You look exactly like you used to on Christmas Eve,' he teased.

Claudia smiled back. 'I can't remember being this excited about anything since that Christmas I got that amazing bike from Santa but I was more interested in the clipboard your parents gave me. Do you remember? I think I was ten.'

His smile broadened into a grin at the memory. It must have cost his parents next to nothing but she'd loved that damn thing. 'And you walked around pretending you were Julie from *The Love Boat*.' He laughed.

'And hardly ever rode the bike,' Claudia said, laughing too.

They laughed together for a while until it petered out and the intimacy of the situation invaded again. They were alone in Luke's room and one of them was naked.

Claudia withdrew her knee from the bed. 'Anyway… sorry for waking you, I just…'

Luke waved her apology away with his hand. 'You're forgiven. Just make sure you bring coffee next time.'

'What makes you think there'll be a next time?'

'You mean you're *not* going to make a habit of barging into my room at ungodly hours?'

Claudia rolled her eyes. 'It's seven. And you're leaving tomorrow, remember?'

'I'm still on holiday today.'

'Some holiday,' she snorted. And then they were grinning at each other again.

'Get out of here,' Luke said as their grins faded.

Claudia crossed her arms again. 'You're not going back to sleep, are you?'

'Nope. I'm getting out of bed and hitting the shower. I just figured you wouldn't want to be here when I peeled this sheet back.'

Claudia couldn't help herself—her gaze dropped to the sheet covering his tented knees. Suddenly the familiar easiness between them evaporated and a more loaded atmosphere took over.

'Right. No,' she said, willing her legs to move, but somehow remained rooted to the spot. 'That would be…too much information.'

Luke chuckled at her understatement. 'Amongst other things.' He waited for her to move and chuckled again when she remained stationary. 'Claude?'

Claudia sprang into action this time, embarrassed by her inertia. 'Right. Yes,' she said, pulling down the hem of her skirt a little and brushing imaginary lint from her sleeves. 'I'll just…I'll catch you…later.'

She didn't wait for his reply and two seconds later Luke was practically staring at her dust. He fell sideways onto the mattress with a groan.

He didn't like this...*vibe*...between them now. He and Claude just didn't do vibes.

It would be good to go home tomorrow. Put some distance between them and get back to his job, to a career that was finally on the up again. Especially now Claudia and he were on the same page for the direction of the resort.

An image of Claudia's fingers drumming against her belly slid into his mind.

He reached for a pillow and pulled it over his head. Tomorrow couldn't come soon enough.

'Surprise!' Avery said as Claudia entered the large bright dining room populated with potted palms and an underwater-world mural taking up one entire wall. She couldn't get used to seeing it so empty, bereft of the usual bustling morning breakfast crowd.

Both her and Luke's parents grinned at her from a nearby table.

Claudia almost dropped her clipboard at the sight. She'd told them not to dare cut their big adventure short, that there was nothing they could do here anyway. When the cyclone had been building and finally hit, the intrepid adventurers had been out of reach on safari somewhere in the Great Sandy Desert and hadn't even been aware. But as soon as they'd returned to civilisation and seen the news they'd been on to Claudia.

They'd insisted on coming home but Claudia had begged them not to. She didn't need to worry about four grey nomads driving a massive RV at breakneck speed, especially when they were over five thousand kilometres away and the roads were still a treacherous mess.

But damn...it was good to see them.

An immediate lump lodged in her throat and she forced it

down—she'd done her crying. No more tears. 'Mum? Dad? When did the road open?'

'This morning.' Lena, her mother, smiled.

'You didn't have to come,' she said. 'We're managing.'

'We know. But we couldn't not.'

And then she was swept into their arms and there were hugs all round and everyone talking at once. The whole disaster and clean-up was retold as Tony served breakfast then sat at the table and ate with them, adding his own embellishments about the worst storm he'd seen in all his forty years.

'Where's Luke?' Gloria, his mother, asked. 'He's not still asleep, is he? It's not like him to lie in.'

'I think the jet lag's really knocking him around,' Avery said.

'We've been working him pretty hard. Getting those soft office hands all dirty.' Jonah grinned.

Cyrus, Tony and Brian, Luke's father, laughed. 'He should be down soon,' Claudia interrupted. 'He was getting up to have a shower when I left him.'

The table fell instantly silent and every set of eyes swivelled to her. It took a moment for Claudia to figure out why until she glanced at Avery's huge goggle eyes.

'Oh…not like that,' she said hurriedly. 'I was just telling him about my ideas for the resort. I thought he was an early riser too. I didn't think he'd be asleep when I went through the connecting door.'

More silence. 'He was asleep?' Gloria finally asked.

'Like a log,' Claudia confirmed.

Luke's parents looked at each other and Claudia was struck as per usual by how Luke was a perfect combination of both of them. His father's build, his mother's brown eyes and gorgeous complexion. 'Does he still sleep in the buff?' Brian asked.

Claudia averted her gaze as a tide of heat rose to her cheeks, missing the wink Brian shot Jonah. 'Apparently,' she said, forcing her voice to sound normal and not crack as she thought about those abs.

That happy trail.

She glanced at Avery, preferring not to be looking at Brian as she thought about his almost naked son. Brian who was very much the blueprint for Luke. Avery was sharing a loaded look with Gloria.

'He's leaving on the evening plane tomorrow,' she blurted out. Claudia wasn't exactly sure why she'd said it but it seemed important for them all to know that Luke wasn't part of the Tropicana equation.

Wasn't part of *her* equation.

'Well, that's a shame,' Gloria said.

Claudia couldn't agree more but for some strange reason she felt compelled to defend him. 'His career is important to him.'

Gloria patted Claudia's hand. 'Yes, dear, we know. Now…' she picked up her cup of tea '…tell us about these plans you were discussing with Luke.'

Pleased for the change in subject, Claudia launched into her spiel with enthusiasm. There was so much she didn't know yet, so much she still had to figure out, but she couldn't deny the excitement that fizzed through her veins.

The last year or so she'd felt as if she'd been going through the motions. Sure, she loved the Tropicana *unconditionally*, had never thought to change a single thing, but now change had been forced upon her whether she liked it or not.

It had been a revelation realising that she'd never been particularly challenged here—she could do what she did in her sleep with her clipboard tied behind her back.

It had been a revelation realising that she *wanted* change.

Still, she was nervous. Ownership of the resort wasn't hers—their parents had just handed over management rights. She had to convince them. Get them on board.

Their enthusiastic nodding helped put her mind at ease. Avery was over-the-moon excited.

'And Luke supports this too?' Gloria asked.

'He sure does,' came a voice from behind them.

Claudia watched as first his parents then her parents embraced Luke. It was heartening to see how close he was with her family too. He was wearing another pair of boardies and a T-shirt and the hem lifted a little to reveal a peek of those smooth abs she'd seen in full Technicolor not that long ago. She dragged her gaze away.

When the greetings were finally done he pulled up the chair beside her and gave her a smile. 'It's like a family reunion,' he said.

Claudia smiled back, forgetting the abs for a moment. It had been a long time since they'd all sat down to a meal together and she felt strangely nostalgic.

'So you're leaving tomorrow?' Lena, Claudia's mum, asked. She was petite and blonde like her daughter and always cut straight to the chase.

Luke nodded. 'No need for me to stick around. The cleanup is largely done and Claude and I are both on the same page with the direction of the resort. I can leave it in her very capable hands and we can communicate via email.'

Luke didn't notice the look his mother and Claudia's mother shared with Avery. He was tucking into the bacon that Tony was renowned for. Claudia didn't either. She was trying to not think about eating bacon off Luke's abs.

CHAPTER SIX

BY THE END of the day Claudia had almost burned through their entire download quota as she madly surfed the net for any information on spas and the kind of exclusive accommodation and experience she had in mind for the new and improved Tropicana. Thank goodness the web was up and running after a week without.

She and Luke talked extensively, working together in the brief time they had left to throw ideas around, and she made copious notes. She refused to dwell on the fact that he'd be gone tomorrow, that the resort still meant so little to him that he could just walk away, especially after it had been so devastated. If anything the disaster that had befallen the Tropicana had only brought her closer to the grand old dame.

This was where she belonged. Right here.

Walking away just wasn't an option.

Occasionally Claudia glanced up to find her and Luke's mothers in a huddle with their fathers or with Avery or with Avery and Jonah. Sometimes with Isis and Cyrus involved. Even Tony had come out of the kitchen at one point. But she figured they had a lot of catching up to do and everyone was still going about their assigned chores so who was she to complain?

It wasn't until they were sitting around eating their evening meal that night that she began to suspect there was more at play.

'You two were very busy today,' her mother murmured, flicking her glance over them both.

'Lots to plan.' Claudia shrugged.

'How soon do you think you can get started?' her father asked.

'Not sure, Harry,' Luke said. 'Nothing can really be accomplished until the insurance money comes through. The government and the insurance companies have promised the industry that claims will be processed speedily but...' he shrugged '...that doesn't mean it'll actually happen.'

Her father nodded. 'So it could be quite some months before we're back on the road again.'

Claudia looked up, alarmed. 'No...Mum, Dad.' She reached over and squeezed her mother's hand. 'Brian and Gloria,' she said, looking at them both individually. 'Go back to your trip. You guys slogged your guts out here for twenty years and this is supposed to be your retirement. Your dream trip. We'll be just fine without you, won't we, Avery?'

'Hmm,' Avery said noncommittally, avoiding Claudia's gaze. 'I suppose...'

Claudia frowned at her friend, who'd been wildly enthusiastic this morning, before turning back to face the parents. 'We'll be fine,' she assured.

'Of course you will be, darling,' her mother said, squeezing her hand back. 'But...we can't just leave you to do it on your own. Not with your management partner heading back to London. That wouldn't be fair.'

Claudia glanced at Luke. She wished he weren't leaving but the truth was she'd managed without him for over a year and she wasn't going to pressure him into staying.

'I'm not on my own. I have Avery.' Claudia glanced at her friend, who wasn't looking so confident all of a sudden. Maybe she was thinking how much time it was going to take away from her relationship with Jonah?

'We turned the resort around last year,' she said. 'We can rebuild it.'

'No.' Her mother shook her head. 'We'll have to stay. We can't just abandon you. Rebuilding is different from refurbishing—it's a much bigger undertaking. No,' she declared again with a determined shake of her head. 'With Luke gone we'll stay as long as it takes to get the resort on its feet again.'

Luke's mother nodded wildly in agreement. 'Of course, we really don't know anything about the kind of high-end stuff you're talking about doing so we may have to…modify some of the things you were talking about. I mean, the Tropicana clientele really don't expect to be pampered like that when they're here with their kiddies. I'm not sure we should be so…exclusive. We don't want to put anyone off.'

Claudia could feel it all unravelling as Gloria and her mother nodded in unison. She glanced at Luke to find the same kind of alarm written all over his face.

'We're hoping to attract a different clientele,' Luke said through a forced smile.

'Well, of course, darling,' Gloria said. 'But it's not really the spirit of the Tropicana, is it?'

'I agree,' Harry said. 'One of the resort's charms is that it's not pretentious.'

'And surely the objective is to get the place up and running as soon as possible?' Gloria added. 'We can do that blindfolded if we keep it the way it was. Creating this whole new…concept will add a lot of burden to the process.'

'I think your mother's right,' Brian said, sliding his hand on top of Gloria's. 'I think the resort is a little too old to be changing its spots now. It's increasingly difficult to attract the tourist dollar. I surely don't need to tell an ad man that, do I, son? I think if we stay we're better off sticking with the devil we know.'

'I guess we could turn one of the rooms into a massage parlour,' Lena added. 'We could employ some of those lovely commune people down at the markets who offer fifteen-minute neck and shoulder massages. You know how we feel about local employment.'

Claudia watched as her shiny new dreams disappeared slowly into the ether; her shoulders sagged a little. 'Well, of course…it's still your place,' she said carefully. 'We can't do any of it without your support. If you'd prefer we keep it as is…then, of course, that's what we'll do.'

It had been a long shot anyway. Pie-in-the-sky stuff. And their parents were right—why mess with a winning formula?

Luke could feel Claudia's dismay without even having to look at her; it rolled towards him on a heavy cloud of doom. She'd started the day, her eyes sparking with possibility and now she was practically hunched over her untouched meal.

He looked at his parents, then at hers.

They had to go.

In one brief conversation they'd sucked all her joy away.

'Or you could place some faith in us and let us do our thing. Go back to your holiday and trust us,' he said.

'But it won't be *your* thing, will it?' Lena said. The rebuke was gentle but Luke heard it nonetheless. 'You'll be in London and it'll just be poor Claude left to cope and carry all the responsibility. No.' Lena shook her head. 'She's twenty-seven years old—she's too young for that kind of pressure. We're not going to let Claude start from scratch all on her own, not with such a big venture.'

It was on the tip of Luke's tongue to remind them they'd already left her all on her own. But of course they hadn't, had they?

He had.

'Mum, I'm fine,' Claudia dismissed.

Lena smiled at her daughter. 'Of course you are, darling. And you will continue to be so because we're going to be here every step of the way.'

Claudia smiled at her mother wishing she didn't feel suddenly trapped and smothered by their love and thoughtfulness. She'd never felt it before, but then she hadn't had this much freedom before. She'd been running things solo since their parents had taken off and that had been really freeing.

She wasn't sure she wanted to go back.

Claudia's head throbbed at the thought. 'Actually, if no

one minds, I think I'm going to turn in. I've got a bit of a headache.'

'Of course not, darling,' her mother said as Claudia stood. 'Have you got some tablets you can take?'

Claudia nodded. 'Yes…thanks.' She smiled at the group sitting around the table, deliberately avoiding Luke's gaze. 'I'll see you in the morning,' she said.

Luke glared at them all as they watched her go. 'I hope you're all happy now,' he said.

'What on earth do you mean, Luke?' his mother asked.

Luke stood. 'Forget it,' he said, throwing his napkin on the table, and took off after Claudia.

The table waited until Luke had left the dining room before they grinned at each other and Avery leaned across the table and high-fived Gloria.

Luke caught up with Claudia on the stairs. 'Claude, wait,' he said, taking them two at a time. She kept going. 'Claudia,' he called again and she stopped as he caught up with her.

'I'm fine, Luke,' she said wearily. 'Just tired.'

'Fine and dandy, huh?' he mocked.

Claudia didn't deign to answer. She turned away from him and continued up the stairs.

'You should fight for what you want,' he said as he followed a step behind her.

Claudia concentrated on her feet. 'It's their place, Luke.'

'Is that what it is?' he demanded. 'Or are you just too chicken? You've had an original idea that just might turn this giant white elephant of theirs around but you don't have the guts to go for it. You're running scared.'

Claudia stopped as a well of anger rolled through her. She turned abruptly, narrowly avoiding a collision with Luke. Even with him on the lower step he was still taller than her. She clenched her fists to stop herself from placing them on his chest and pushing him down the stairs.

Or possibly tearing his shirt off.

This close she could see every fleck that made up the brown of his eyes, every single eyelash, every individual whisker valiantly trying to push through the skin to freedom before he once again ruthlessly mowed them down.

He couldn't taunt her in that hybrid accent of his—not about this. 'I think you're the only one running around here, Luke.'

And then she turned again and ran up the remaining stairs, putting as much distance between them as possible.

When she got to her room she thanked her lucky stars her parents had decided to take a different room rather than reclaim this one. She didn't fancy sharing with them again—not tonight anyway. And God knew, there were plenty of suites to choose from at the moment!

She didn't turn the light on. She didn't have a shower, she didn't brush her teeth, she didn't even put on her pyjamas. For the first time in her life, Claudia stripped straight out of her clothes and left them discarded on the floor where she stood before walking to the bed, yanking back the sheets and crawling between them.

She sighed as the thick, crisp sheets folded her in cool starched bliss. It felt heavenly even though she knew in this sticky tropical weather she was bound to wake up in a few hours with body parts sticking together. But right now she was just too damn exhausted—physically and mentally—to care.

And hey, if it was good enough for Captain Sexypants…

His outrageous accusation on the stairs came back to her and Claudia shut her eyes to ward it off. She took five deep breaths, tuning in to the gentle swish of the ocean floating to her on a breeze that rustled the balcony curtains. She would not let Luke under her skin. He was leaving tomorrow and things here would return to business as usual.

She shifted around in the king-sized bed trying to get comfortable, not sure this whole naked thing was conducive to sleep.

Sex, maybe, but not sleep.

Hot, sweaty, dirty sex.

She shut her eyes, trying not to think about anything hot, sweaty or dirty or how long it had been since she'd had any.

Not with Captain Sexypants right next door.

It was Luke's turn to stay awake all night staring at the ceiling, turning the dinner conversation over and over in his head. Claudia's disappointed face burned into his retinas. Her accusation taunted him on automatic replay.

I think you're the only one running around here.

He couldn't stay, for crying out loud. His career was at a crossroads. He was back to the point he had been a few years ago before his *wife* had screwed him over. He just needed to lure this one big client, to bring their multimillion-dollar account to the firm, then he'd be back on top again.

He was almost there.

People depended on him at work—both his clients and his team. He couldn't abandon them.

But could he really abandon Claudia now?

Again?

Sure, she had a team too, a very devoted team, but he couldn't bear the thought of her stuck in the resort-that-time-forgot where it was Groundhog Day twenty-four-seven. Not after the excitement—the anticipation—he'd witnessed today.

It was as if he'd taken her to the gates of paradise and opened them a crack so she could see inside…and then clanged them shut in her face.

Claudia would let their parents have their way. After all, she'd always loved the place just the way it was.

And she was a pleaser.

But would she still have that verve and bounce she was renowned for as each year went by and the if-onlys set in? If-onlys could cripple a person—he knew that better than most. If only he hadn't been so trusting of Philippa. If only he'd been paying more attention to the signs. If only he'd followed his own advice about the stupidity of office relationships.

If only he hadn't been such a fool…

If-onlys could eat you up inside. They could make you bitter; they could make you hard; they could wear you down.

He hated even the thought of that picture—Claudia with all the fizz and bubble gone. No more bounce. Lines around her eyes. A strained smile.

Hanging onto that damn clipboard of hers for dear life because if she didn't she might just smash it over the nearest hapless tourist's head.

He wouldn't wish if-onlys on his worst enemy.

Goddamn it.

He rolled over and punched his pillow hard. He was responsible for building up Claudia's expectations. He couldn't walk away from it now.

He was going to *have* to stay.

CHAPTER SEVEN

AFTER A NIGHT of tossing and turning and with his decision made, it was Luke's turn to barge in on Claudia. He'd heard the pipes in her shower going earlier so he knew she was up and about.

He knocked briefly on the interconnecting door then entered the room.

Except, she wasn't up and about.

The room was lit only by a slice of sunlight peeking through curtains ruffled by a stiff ocean breeze, but it was enough to see she was very much in bed. Very much asleep. And, he froze on the spot…

Very, very much naked.

For long moments he didn't know what to do—too shocked for any rationality as his brain tried to compute what he was seeing and his body waged a war with his conscience.

What are you doing, jerk? Get the hell out of here.

But…

She'll kill you if she wakes up and finds you staring at her like you've never seen a naked woman before.

But…

You are acting like a dirty perv. Stop it now!

And Luke knew it was true but he just didn't seem to be able to drag his eyes off Claudia's nakedness. He'd spent twenty-plus years of his life not thinking about her *like that* at all and within the space of a week he'd subjected her to a sleepy grope, was having erotic dreams about her and now he was perving at her in the buff.

He really needed to get the hell out.

But he couldn't move. Her breasts drew his gaze like

some horny fifteen-year-old boy at a peep show. She had both arms up over her head, one resting across her face, which drew her breasts up very nicely indeed. And there they sat, small, yes, but pleasingly pert with that enticing side-swell he'd felt in his hand a few days ago.

His palm tingled again in Pavlovian response.

Caramel-coloured areolas and nipples crowned the tips majestically and he swallowed as his blood sugar plummeted suddenly, his body craving a sugar hit.

A caramel hit.

Frightened by the urge to indulge, he fisted his palms as he dragged his gaze down. Her bare skin was pale and he absently wondered how she'd accomplished *that* living on top of a beach from the age of six. She'd told him she didn't have time for swimming but he hadn't thought she was serious.

Her waist was slender, boasting an equally petite belly button that sat out like a little pearl, just begging to be licked. Sucked.

He swallowed again.

Her hips flared into a gentle curve before the sheet hid the really interesting parts from his view. Although one leg was hidden in a tangle of fabric it managed to drag on the sheet enough to expose most of the other leg. His gaze wandered over her pink toenails, her delicate calf and one well-defined knee then all the way up to where the sheet stopped just shy of her groin.

He expelled a shaky breath. Claudia Davis was one sexy little package.

How the hell had he missed that?

A gust of wind blew the curtain, billowing it out, and the door creaked loudly behind him, dragging him out of his inertia.

Leave, leave now!

He turned to go. But another strong gust snatched the handle away just as he reached for it and the door slammed. Loud enough to wake the dead.

Sure as hell loud enough to wake the naked woman he'd been ogling.

He glanced over his shoulder as she sat bolt upright in bed and Luke's heart slammed as well. Louder than the door. Louder than the clanging chimes of doom that were ringing madly in his head.

Claudia woke with a start, her heart thundering in her chest, her startled gaze flying to the windows, momentarily confused. Was it another cyclone or was she still caught in the nightmare from the last one? The noise didn't come again and her pulse settled, her wild, dilated eyes constricting down to a more useful size. She looked around, her vision clearing to reveal a Luke of a different variety in her room.

He was standing still with his back to the bed. She frowned. 'Luke?'

He held his arms up as if in surrender but didn't turn around. 'I'm sorry,' he said. 'I thought you were awake. I didn't realise you were…'

Claudia frowned again. 'Asleep?' she clarified when it didn't appear as if he was going to finish his sentence.

He seemed to hesitate before saying, 'Er…yes…'

Claudia shrugged. 'Well, I'm awake now…kind of.'

Luke doubted it. He'd know the second she woke up fully.

Claudia yawned as she ran a hand through her hair. 'You might as well stay and talk to—'

Luke didn't have to wait much longer. The muscles in his shoulders tensed.

'Oh…my…*God*!'

Yep. *Now, she was awake.*

Claudia looked down at herself in horror. She was *naked*? She covered her breasts with an arm as she made a wild grab for the sheet, the quick impulsive tumble into bed the night before coming back in all its stupid glory.

She glared at Luke's back, the full implications sinking in pretty damn quick as she dragged the sheet right up to her chin and scuttled back until she was sitting ramrod straight against the bed head.

He'd seen her like this.

'How much did you see?' she demanded.

Luke, relieved to hear the rustle of the sheets, dropped his hands. 'I...' He was caught between lying to make her feel better and blurting out the truth.

Too bloody much.

He was never going to see her as that skinny six-year-old any more.

'Oh, God,' Claudia wailed, his silence more damning than any words. 'Please tell me I had the sheet on.'

'You did.'

He turned to assure her he hadn't seen *everything* but her frantic, 'Don't you dare turn around,' had him swivelling back to face the connecting door again.

Claudia clutched the sheets harder. 'What did you see?'

'Claude...'

Claudia wasn't in any mood to be placated. 'What. Did. You. See?'

'Just a...little bit of your...upper...part.' Luke waited for the lightning bolt to strike him dead.

Claudia shut her eyes. *Oh, dear God.* He'd seen her breasts. Within a handful of days he'd not only touched them but he'd seen them as well.

Damn, damn, damn.

'I'm really sorry...' Luke continued. 'I thought you were up...I thought I heard your shower pipes. I *did* knock.'

'How long were you standing there for?' she demanded.

Again Luke wasn't sure what the right answer was—the truth sure as hell wasn't pretty. 'Not...long...'

His hesitancy did not fill Claudia with confidence. 'Oh, God...you were, weren't you? Just standing there staring at me—*naked*—while I was asleep.'

'I...' He went to turn again.

Claudia pulled the sheet closer. 'Stop right there!'

Luke stopped mid-turn. 'This is ridiculous, Claude.'

Why was he facing the door when she'd obviously covered herself? He wanted to be able to plead his case and he needed to look at her for that. He needed her to know that he hadn't snuck into her room purely to perve on her.

Even if he had, in reality, not been able to tear his eyes off her.

But it hadn't been premeditated.

'I'm turning around,' he announced.

'No, you're not,' Claudia squeaked.

'Yes,' he said grimly. 'I am.' And did just that.

'Luke!' she gasped, outraged.

'Oh, relax,' he chided. Claudia had the sheet hiked up to her chin. 'You're more dressed than you were five minutes ago.'

Claudia blinked. 'Oh, nice, real nice, Luke,' she said scathingly.

Luke took a deep breath. 'I'm sorry,' he muttered, holding up his hands in a sign of contrition. 'But you're perfectly decent and I promise I'm not going to leap across the space between us and rip the sheet away so just ease up on it a little or the bloody thing will tear in two and then we'll be back at square one.'

'Yes.' Claudia nodded vigorously. 'With you gawking at me,' she said caustically, but she eased off, lowering the sheet to just below her chin.

Luke glared at her. 'I didn't…I wasn't…' He stopped because he *did* and he *was*. But it wasn't how she made it sound. Her eyebrow kicked up at his hesitancy and he shoved a hand through his hair in frustration.

Like with the grope incident, he was once again on the back foot. And like with the grope incident the best way to settle things was head-on.

'I came in to talk to you. I thought you were up and about. When I realised you were asleep, realised you were…naked I was *temporarily* rendered incapable of movement. I was… surprised.'

In shock was probably a better word. She'd told him just the other day when she'd been so scandalised by his own nudity, that she didn't sleep in the buff. It was a safe bet to assume that even if he had caught her in bed, that she'd at least be fully clothed and not *completely starkers*.

'I may have…probably…looked longer than I should have…' *Way longer.* 'I apologise. It wasn't my intention to…'

'Gawk? Perve? Ogle?'

Luke nodded. 'Yes. To all three.'

Claudia had to admit it was a fairly comprehensive apology but she wasn't sure she was ever going to be able to look at him again and not be aware of the fact that he'd seen her naked. She almost wanted to demand that he strip just so she could even the score.

More heat crept into her face at the thought—*how would that solve anything?* Didn't that make her just as pervy?

And what about those moments after she'd woken the other day to his hand on her breast and his erection snuggled against her? Hadn't she pushed back a little? Hadn't she stayed where she was instead of moving away? Hadn't she lain there wondering how good it might be if he slipped his hand under her shirt?

Could she claim to be so innocent where a sleeping Luke had been concerned?

The situation was too much and Claudia rested her forehead on her knees, feeling decidedly conflicted. How had they found themselves here?

'I really am sorry, Claude. What if I promise to permanently delete what I saw here today from my memory cells?'

Claudia blinked at the ludicrous offer—as if that were going to be possible. And then suddenly disbelief turned to affront. Wait. *Was that possible? Could he do it?* Did her assets leave that little an impression? She knew they were small but they were quite perky even if she did say so herself *and* in a push-up bra they looked even better.

Despite her embarrassment she felt more than a little miffed.

'Just like that?' she asked waspishly. 'My breasts are really that forgettable?' It was completely irrational to feel as if her femininity had been insulted.

She was supposed to still be mortified!

Luke frowned, trying to keep up with the sudden about-face. *What the—?* She was pissed at him now because he was offering to do the gentlemanly thing? Or was it just some trick question? Did she want him to remember it? Because frankly he didn't think there was enough will in the world to erase the memory of those delectable caramel nipples.

He was pretty sure they were going to feature in many future fantasy scenarios.

'No.' He shook his head 'God, no. Absolutely not.'

'Damn straight,' she muttered.

Luke frowned again. 'So...you don't want me to forget them?'

Claudia glared at him for rationalising something that had no rational basis. 'Yes, I do. Just maybe don't look as if it's so damn easy,' she grouched.

Luke knew this could be funny if it weren't so confusing. How could she sit there with the sheet pulled up to her neck like some Victorian virgin and look cranky and embarrassed and accusing all at once? As if her being naked were his fault?

He didn't think any man with a recent dose of jet lag should have to figure out the workings of the female brain.

'Oh, God,' he begged, rubbing his temples. 'I'm too tired and suspect I may have a Y chromosome too many for this conversation. Can we please just start again?'

Claudia noticed the cornered-male look on Luke's face and the absurdity of the situation hit her. If she weren't buck naked under the sheet, she might even have laughed. She felt the tension ease from her shoulders even if the heat in her cheeks didn't.

'Fine,' she huffed as her shoulders sagged and her lungs deflated. 'I'm sorry...I'm just...this isn't really in my playbook, you know?'

Hell, yeh, he knew. Walking in on a naked woman he could handle. Walking in on a naked Claudia—not so much. 'Well, if it's any consolation, it's not in mine either.'

Claudia smiled despite herself. 'Maybe this could be another of those things that we never speak of again?' she suggested.

Luke nodded vigorously. 'I think that's a very good idea.'

'Also, how about we both agree to knock and *wait* for an answer in future?'

'Deal.' Normally he would have held out his hand for a shake but he doubted she'd remove her grip from the sheets for anything. 'So I'm just going to go and pretend like this never happened.'

Claudia gave him a rueful smile. 'Sounds like a plan.'

It wasn't until he was halfway through the door that Claudia realised she still didn't know why he'd come to her room in the first place. 'Wait. What did you want to talk to me about?'

Luke turned at the unexpected question. With everything that had happened, he'd forgotten all about why he'd come to see Claudia in the first place. 'I'm going to stay. Help you manage the resort. At least until the spa is up and running anyway.'

Claudia stared at him for a moment, her heart beating almost as hard as it had when the door had slammed and scared the bejesus out of her. 'Really?'

Luke grinned. 'Really. Get dressed. I'll meet you downstairs. There are things to plan.'

Claudia didn't know what to say. Or do. If she hadn't been naked and just made a complete idiot of herself she'd have leapt out of bed and hugged him. As she'd hugged him hundreds of times in the past.

Instead she said and did nothing, just watched him disappear and the door shut after him.

Then she sank down onto her back and, grinning like a loon, pulled the sheet over her head and threw herself into a full naked body shimmy, squiggling her shoulders, arching her back off the bed and drumming her heels on the mattress.

She was getting her spa!

CHAPTER EIGHT

CLAUDIA'S HEAD WAS buzzing by the time she'd had a quick shower, thrown on her uniform and hightailed it downstairs. Not even the embarrassing thought of what had transpired in her room was enough to stop her from seeking Luke out. She found him breakfasting with everyone else.

'There you are, darling,' her mother said. 'Luke's just been telling us what you two have been up to.'

Claudia paused mid-sit, startled at the announcement as everyone beamed at her. Luke, sitting in the seat beside hers, gave her a wink.

'Has he now?' she murmured.

She knew he wouldn't have said anything about the…incident, but her mind couldn't help but go there. Especially as Luke was clearly amused at her mother's choice of words. His warm brown gaze was level with her breasts and she sat quickly to quell the memory as her nipples firmed against the fabric of her bra.

'It's wonderful,' Avery agreed, the excitement in her voice sharpening her accent.

'Yes,' his mother agreed. 'You are sure your firm will understand, though?' Gloria pressed.

Luke gave a short nod because he knew his decision to work remotely would not be popular with the partners. Major adjustments would have to be made to accommodate it. Not to mention he'd be working two demanding jobs. Long days at the resort would be backed up by long hours into the night when clients were awake on the other side of the world.

He couldn't see himself getting much sleep.

But these were extenuating circumstances and at least these days they had the technology to run with something like this so, why not? The Internet made distance a non-sense—email, iClouds, Skype, teleconferencing—anything was possible.

'It'll take some setting up,' he dismissed, 'but it shouldn't be a problem.'

'There now,' Avery said to two sets of parents. 'You can get back to your holiday.'

Claudia wanted to kiss her. 'That's right,' she agreed quickly. 'You guys retired so other people could wait on you for a change. You really don't have to worry about the Tropicana.'

Her mother beamed. 'Excellent. I feel so much better knowing the two of you will be doing this together.'

There was general conversation over breakfast about the new addition but Claudia felt inadequately prepared to answer a lot of the questions raised. 'To be honest,' she admitted, 'I've never been to a spa and I think I've only ever had one massage in my entire life.' She looked at Avery, who was more accustomed to the day-spa life. 'That time in Bali… on the beach…do you remember?'

'Oh, yes.' Avery smiled. 'Your masseuse was an ancient woman with hardly any teeth.'

Claudia nodded. 'And yours was that buff young guy wearing a shirt that showed off every perfect muscle in his abs.'

Avery's smile turned dreamy. 'Oh, yes,' she sighed. '*Incredible* fingers too.'

Jonah looked unimpressed. 'I hate him already,' he murmured, gliding a possessive hand onto Avery's shoulder, and Claudia felt a pang hit her square in the chest at Jonah's caveman display. She glanced quickly at Luke, then glanced away again.

Avery smiled at Jonah and the look they shared took the pang into chest-pain territory. 'We'll have to do some tours,'

Avery said enthusiastically as she dragged her gaze away from Jonah. 'See what's out there. See what's new and innovative and popular.'

'That will be impossible for a while,' Claudia dismissed. 'We have one hundred rooms upstairs that all need to be assessed one by one and given a good clean so we can at least offer them to the public and have some income again.'

All their efforts last week had been concentrated on the outside clean-up. Apart from a cursory examination of the rooms that had been thankfully largely untouched, they hadn't worried about them at all. But they were going to need to be electrically checked at the very least.

'We'll have to discount them,' Luke said. 'This place isn't exactly paradise any more.'

Claudia nodded automatically at Luke's shrewd business assessment, ignoring her emotional response to his words. If she thought too hard about their paradise lost it would break her heart, and they needed to be practical.

'And before anyone comes we'll have to put in all new landscaping,' she said. 'The resort may be a long way off its established old self but I'd like to make a good impression when we welcome back our first guests.'

'We can pitch in and help you with that stuff,' Lena said.

'Harry and I can help with the landscaping,' Brian said.

'And your mother and I can contact all cancelled and future guests and see who might still be interested in a basic cheapy holiday,' Gloria confirmed.

Lena nodded. 'We're here, we might as well put ourselves to good use, if you'll have us. And then when the guests start to arrive we can push off again and let you kids get on with it.'

'Of course we'll have you,' Claudia said reassuringly. 'This is your place—you don't need to ask permission to stay. There will always be rooms here for you.'

'Good to know,' Brian said gruffly. 'But we've got at least a year left on our trip so don't keep them blocked for us.'

'You'll come back for the opening of the spa, though?' Claudia insisted.

Brian patted her hand. 'Try keeping us away, love.'

Claudia smiled at Luke's father—she'd always had a soft spot for him. 'Thank you.'

'So it could be a while before we get to check out spas,' Avery said wistfully.

'Not necessarily,' Jonah said. 'The best time to go will be before the paying customers come back. You and Claude might be able to squeeze something in.'

'Cairns is the best place,' Isis added.

Claudia doubted they'd have time to scratch but she nodded anyway. 'We'll see how we're tracking.'

An hour later Luke had made a list of things he was going to need to set up a makeshift office in the Mai Tai. Jonah was taking the chopper into Cairns for business and had offered him a ride. He was coming down the stairs as Claudia was heading up, her clipboard clutched to her chest.

They slowed as they neared, her on the step below him. 'I'm off to Cairns with Jonah for a quick trip. Anything you need?' he asked, waving his list in front of her.

Claudia shook her head as she looked up at him. *Way* up. 'Thanks. I've given him a list already.'

Luke nodded. 'You off to assess the rooms?' he asked

'Yes. I'm tackling the suites. Isis is doing the first floor. Avery the second.'

'And the ground-floor rooms?'

'I'll do them after I've done the suites.'

Claudia shifted her feet nervously. Her gaze was level with his chest, the T-shirt he was wearing gracing its lean musculature like a velvet glove. She remembered how hard that chest had felt behind her the other day. Then she remembered what had happened *today*.

It was hard to believe on this grand staircase in this voluminous foyer that she could suddenly feel claustrophobic.

She looked down at her clipboard, confused by the skip in her pulse. She dropped it slightly away from her body, relieved to have something else to look at even if it was just pages and pages of pristine maintenance reports awaiting her neat handwriting.

'We're just taking notes today,' she said for something to say in case his head was where her head was at. 'Don, he's a local electrician, is coming in two days for the electrical checks. He's crazy busy but we did him a good deal on his daughter's wedding here a few years back so he's squeezing us in.'

'Yay for Don.' Luke smiled. The clipboard movement had pulled down her blouse slightly revealing her usually well-covered décolletage. From his vantage point he could see some swell rising out of a soft-looking emerald-green fabric edged with black ribbon.

Was that satin?

It *looked* like satin, soft and shiny.

And then he was thinking about her breasts again. When, true to his word, he *had* been trying hard not to.

Crap.

Who knew Claudia favoured sexy lingerie beneath her awful uniform? He'd never look at her polyester blouse the same again.

Claudia took a step to the side so she could walk around him, then hesitated for a moment. Her eyes glued to the clipboard, she murmured, 'I haven't really said thank you.'

Luke shrugged. 'It's okay. I owe you for being such a stubborn bastard last year. I should have done what I'm doing now back then. It's just that things at work were…'

Luke didn't really want to get into it but he'd still been under the gun from losing the account his wife—*ex-wife*—had stolen from him. It was the main reason he'd wanted the resort handed over to a big chain—his career was in crisis and the resort had been an unwanted distraction.

'Were?' she prompted softly.

Luke grimaced at the familiar bitter taste the memory left in his mouth. A flash of black ribbon caught his eye again and yanked him out of the past. 'It doesn't matter. The point is I'm here now and I'm in.'

'And I'm very, very thankful.' Claudia smiled. 'We'll have to remember this day and celebrate it next year as the day we really put our mark on the Tropicana.'

Luke smiled back before the full import of her words sank in. His smile slowly faded. 'You do know this is only temporary, Claude? I did say just until the spa was up and running. I'm not staying for good. I'll be heading back to the UK as soon as things are settled here. You're more than capable of managing the place solo.'

Solo. Claudia swallowed. Why did that word sound so bloody lonely?

'Yes…of course,' she said with a dismissive shake of her head. 'Of course.'

Even though she felt like a complete idiot. He'd said this morning it was just until the spa was open but she'd been off building castles in the sky. Spinning fantasies of them running the resort together for the next twenty years as their parents had done.

Luke wasn't sure about the overly bright light in her eyes. The last thing he wanted to do was to get her hopes up. 'My life is there, Claude,' he murmured.

Claudia forced a smile onto her face, determined not to show him how much those five words hurt, no matter how gently he'd said them.

My life is there, Claude.

His life was there. Hers was here. She'd do well to re-member that over the coming months.

'Of course,' she assured him, her voice more definitive this time. 'I know. And you're right, I'm perfectly capable of managing the Tropicana.'

Luke nodded, satisfied. 'No one better.' He grinned as soft green satin taunted his peripheral vision.

Claudia grinned back even though it felt as if it had been slashed into her face with a carving knife. 'Well,' she said as she put her foot on the next step, pulling the clipboard back to her chest. 'Guess I'd better get on. I'll see you when you get back from Cairns.'

Luke nodded, disgusted in his disappointment that the cleavage show was over. 'Yep. Should be back in a couple of hours.'

'Okay,' she said.

Visions of green satin, black ribbon and caramel nipples taunted him as he continued down the stairs.

CHAPTER NINE

TWO WEEKS FLEW by. Two weeks of getting rooms and grounds ready to open again. All the rooms had escaped major damage. Some power points had blown and three rooms had sustained some minor water damage to the carpet when their windows, despite the cyclone taping, had cracked under the force of the wind and allowed water to trickle in.

But three out of one hundred was good going, considering the other accommodation blocks on the property had been completely smashed.

The landscaping was a big job hampered by transport difficulties due to the state of the roads. The extensive Tropicana gardens that had taken forty years to establish and made guests feel as if they were living in a tropical paradise had been about fifty per cent destroyed in a matter of a few hours.

They would take many years to get back to the way they were but thankfully some of the older trees and vegetation had been left intact so they didn't have to start from scratch.

The problem was supply of raw material. Mature plants and trees and things like mulch were in high demand postcyclone and difficult to source, which meant the landscaping would be an ongoing job. But they managed with what they could get, transforming the grounds from decimated to rejuvenated in an amazingly short time.

Gloria and Lena worked the phones like the true veteran hotel professionals they were. Claudia was thankful that they'd stayed on to lend a hand, knowing the process would have been much longer without them and it also freed her up to help Isis and Avery get everything shipshape on the inside.

Next week they were welcoming their first trickle of guests—fifteen rooms booked. And the week after that they had a further twenty. Claudia had set a target of fifty per cent occupancy by the time the spa opened a few months down the track and hoped to be back at full occupancy for the summer season at the end of the year.

It was March—it was doable.

They were never going to have the numbers they had before simply because the accommodation units that had been scattered throughout the property had been flattened and were not going to be replaced.

The hope was that the higher-end customers would make up the shortfall.

Claudia and Luke set a couple of hours aside each afternoon to work on plans for the spa. They'd contacted a local builder who Claudia trusted to do the job and consulted a local architect. They just needed to get plans drawn up and then council approvals and other such legalities under way.

They kept things businesslike between them, barely talking outside what was needed for the Tropicana and rarely seeing each other outside anything to do with the plans. Unlike their childhood, the interconnecting door was *not* chocked open and they *never* entered each other's rooms without knocking and receiving clear direction to do so!

It was a grope-free, nudity-free zone.

And things could have been awkward between them had they not been so busy. But everyone was busy, everyone had their heads down, so it was easy for them to just follow suit and pretend there wasn't time for chit-chat.

Luke was probably busiest of all working two jobs. After a back-breaking day out landscaping, he was up late into the night working on UK time in the world of advertising. He rarely got into bed before two a.m. And if he was tired, well, he knew there was a queue he could join. Everyone was working hard. Everyone was tired.

On Friday morning at breakfast, Avery slipped a sheaf of papers across the table to Claudia. 'I spent a few hours on the net last night and I think we should check out these three day-spas in Cairns.' She looked at Luke. 'You too. Seeing them firsthand is much better than getting second-hand descriptions.'

'Yep. Count me in,' he said.

Claudia flicked through the printed pages. 'These look good.' She handed them to Luke.

'I can make a booking for us to have something different at each one for tomorrow?' Avery said.

'Tomorrow?' Claudia worried her bottom lip. 'Do you think we should be tripping off for mani-pedis with the first guests arriving on Monday?'

'It's the perfect time,' Gloria encouraged. 'There's nothing much to do between now and then and you won't get a chance after Monday.'

Claudia nodded. 'I suppose.'

'Jonah can take us all in the chopper, make a bit of a day of it,' Avery suggested.

'You kids have worked really hard,' Brian said. 'Why don't you make a night of it? Get away from here for twenty-four hours and relax? Stay in a swanky hotel, be waited on. You're going to be the ones doing all the waiting soon.'

'Oh, yes,' Avery said, clearly warming to the subject. 'We could go dancing,' she said, turning to Jonah, gliding her hand onto his forearm. 'It's been ages since we danced.'

Jonah smiled and kissed the tip of Avery's nose. 'Yes, it has.'

Avery squeezed his arm. 'Claude, what's the name of the hotel where Raoul hangs out? That has that Latin dancing on Saturday night?'

Luke frowned. Raoul? Why was that name familiar?

'The Quay,' Claudia said, wondering how a trip to a day spa had suddenly become twenty-four hours of debauchery complete with Latin dancing.

'Yes, that's it,' Avery exclaimed. 'Oh, let's do that,' she enthused, looking first at Claudia and then at Jonah.

Luke looked at Claudia. He didn't want to dance with her. Getting that close after what had transpired between them didn't seem like such a good idea. He turned to Jonah. 'No,' he said to his friend. 'I have to work tomorrow night.'

'It's Saturday.'

'My job's twenty-four-seven.'

'Good thing you're so attached to your phone, then,' Jonah said mildly.

Luke shot his friend a measured stare. 'I don't dance.'

Jonah grinned at Luke. 'So don't.' Then he smiled down at Avery. 'Your wish is my command,' he said.

'Oh, I'm not sure—' Claudia started.

'Oh, go on, darling,' her mother quickly interrupted. 'It's a brilliant idea. You guys have been working yourselves into the ground. Go and let your hair down for a night.'

'Right, that's settled, then,' Avery announced as she scraped her chair back and stood. 'I'm going to go book us in at the spas and then the hotel.'

She looked directly at Claudia and Luke, who were sitting next to each other in the seats that had somehow, by silent majority, been relegated to them. 'Do you guys want separate rooms or are you okay with twin share?' she asked.

'Separate,' they both said in unison.

Avery shot them a mischievous grin before she practically skipped out of the room, and Claudia narrowed her eyes.

'Guess we're going dancing.' Jonah grinned as he watched Avery go.

A flash of green satin trimmed with black ribbon floated through Luke's mind. There was no way he was getting on that dance floor.

* * *

'So what are you wearing out dancing?' Avery asked Claudia later that evening as she sat on Claudia's bed almost at the bottom of her second glass of wine and watching a movie on cable TV. It had become a regular thing for them ever since Avery had come to work at the Tropicana over a year ago—Friday night was girlfriend night.

It was something that Claudia always looked forward to and appreciated that Avery still tore herself away from the lovely Jonah to spend some quality time with her bestie. But tonight, Claudia wished Avery had let Jonah talk her into staying home.

'Hadn't thought about it,' Claudia dismissed, hoping her voice sounded light and disinterested and didn't betray the mass of nerves screwing her stomach into a tight ball.

Avery frowned at her. 'What? I don't believe it. You love to dance.'

Sure, she loved to dance. That was how she'd got involved with Raoul. Raoul ran the dance lessons at the Tropicana and had been her occasional lover for the last five years. But she didn't want to sit all night and watch Luke dance with other women either. 'Guess I'm just not in the mood,' she said.

'Oh, come on,' Avery teased. 'Raoul could be there. How long has it been since you guys hooked up?'

Claudia didn't have to think about it—she knew exactly. 'Since just before the resort got handed to me.'

Avery sat up, nearly spilling some of her wine. 'That was nearly eighteen months ago.' She sounded horrified.

'So?'

Avery gaped at her nonchalant reply. 'That's an awful long time to go without some lovin', Claude.'

Claudia gave an exasperated sigh. 'I know you're all loved up,' she said, her tone as dry as powdery sand under a hot midday sun, 'but, trust me, you don't die from lack of sex, Avery.'

'Yeah, but...what's the point of living?'

Claudia laughed then, she couldn't help herself. Avery's expression was priceless. 'I've been a little busy,' she finally said.

Avery waggled her finger in front of her friend's face. 'All work and no play makes Claude a dull girl.' She placed her wine glass down on the bedside table and slipped off the bed. 'Let's see what's in your cupboard that might get Raoul's pulse racing.'

Claudia watched her go, her enthusiasm for that idea utterly underwhelming. 'I'm not going to *hook up* with Raoul in front of Luke,' she grouched as Avery pulled open the cupboard doors.

Avery turned, a frown marring her forehead. 'Why not?'

Claudia squirmed a little. The reason sounded stupid in her head—she could only imagine how dumb it was going to sound out loud.

'Claude?' Avery prompted.

Claudia knew that tone in her friend's voice all too well. 'It'll be too...weird with Raoul...in front of Luke.'

Avery blinked. 'Why?'

Claudia shook her head—she wished she knew. 'I don't know. It just would be.'

A sudden speculative spark flared to life in Avery's shrewd eyes and she forgot the wardrobe as she returned to the bed and sat on the edge with one leg tucked up under her, the other firmly on the ground.

'Is there something going on with you and Captain Sexypants?' she asked.

Claudia almost laughed out loud, both at the nickname that seemed to have stuck and the preposterous suggestion. Something going on with her and Luke?

Impossible.

Even if he did know what she looked like naked *and* what her breast felt like. 'No,' she said.

Avery dropped her head slightly to the side as if she was trying to see deep into Claudia's heart. 'I think there's stuff you're not telling me, Ms Claude.' She folded her arms. 'Spill.'

Claudia thought long and hard about keeping what had gone on between her and Luke to herself, but a part of her wanted to get it off her chest so badly, to analyse it to death in that secret girly-gossip way she used to enjoy with Avery, she could hardly bear it any more.

So she spilled. About the grope incident. About her walking in on him naked. About him walking in on her naked. And it felt so damn good to unburden it. It felt just like it used to do when they'd been teenagers, sharing all their angsty, hormone-ridden secrets.

'So you *do* have a thing for Captain Sexypants?' Avery, who had been remarkably quiet throughout, said.

'No,' Claudia denied, and when Avery gave her that *watch it, Pinocchio* look she just said, 'I can't. He's *Luke*. He's a friend I've known for ever. Our parents are *best friends*. He's divorced and bitter on love. *And* he lives on the opposite side of the world.'

Claudia shook her head at Avery's *what-else-have you-got?* eyebrow-raise. 'He's *leaving,* Avery.'

Avery reached out and grabbed her friend's hand. 'So was I,' she said. 'But I didn't.' Then she sprang off the bed. 'It ain't over till the fat lady sings,' she said, sounding more American than ever. 'And besides, I don't think there's any harm in letting Captain Sexypants know *exactly* what it is he's leaving behind.'

Claudia watched her friend return to the wardrobe, pulling out dresses, wishing she had just an inch of Avery's confidence. 'I know just the one,' she said.

Resigned to her fate, Claudia watched. 'There's that royal blue one I wear to our voodoo nights,' she said.

'Oh, no, no, no,' Avery said, throwing dresses on the ground now. 'I know exactly the one. The red velvety one. It flutters around your ankles, fits you like a glove, has that halter neck and huge side split.'

Claudia blanched at the suggestion. 'I think that's a bit OTT, don't you?'

Avery's voice was muffled as she disappeared into the cupboard a little more but Claudia could still make out her friend's denial. 'Nope. Raoul goes a little crazy every time you wear that dress and that's exactly the effect you're after.' And then a few seconds later, she heard the proclamation, 'Aha!'

Avery walked out of the cupboard brandishing the dress in question. 'This one.'

Claudia shook her head. 'No.'

Avery ignored her. 'We're going dancing. *This* is your dancing dress.'

'It is?'

'It is now.' Avery grinned at her. 'Try it on.'

'Avery…' Claudia glared at her best friend. 'No.'

'You know I'm just going to harp on about it all night until you do, so you might as well get it over with now.'

Claudia sighed at the truth of it. Avery could be very persistent, particularly after two glasses of wine. 'Fine,' she huffed, climbing off the bed. 'Give it to me.'

Claudia took the dress from Avery and marched into the bathroom, quickly stripping off her uniform and throwing the dress over her head before marching back out again.

Avery beamed at her as she appeared. Then she reached over and pulled Claudia's hair out of her ponytail, fluffing it up a little.

She grinned. 'Well, hello, Kryptonite.'

CHAPTER TEN

THEY WERE AT the first day-spa venue at nine o'clock the following morning. Jonah had left them to spend the morning checking up on Charter North, his exceedingly successful charter business, which he'd been neglecting to help the Tropicana back on its feet. He had a good second in command so he wasn't worried, but he felt as if he should at least look in and check on progress. He was to join them again for lunch.

The first two spas were attached to hotels and the managers were happy to show them around. Avery and Claudia had a manicure and a pedicure at the first one while Luke sat at a table with his phone and his laptop. The second one they both indulged in facials and again Luke had the phone glued to his ear.

They caught up with Jonah at the marina for lunch. It was more of a business lunch with lots of constructive conversation about the pros and cons of what they'd seen so far and they were only interrupted once by Luke's phone.

'It'll be interesting to see what the next place is like by comparison,' Avery said as she sipped at an icy cold mineral water. 'It's a stand-alone and is *very* exclusive.'

'More the kind of thing we'll be doing,' Luke said.

'Yep.' Avery nodded. 'I've booked us all in for massages.'

Luke frowned. 'What? I don't want a massage.'

Claudia thought if anyone could do with a massage right now it was Luke. He'd been working all morning at his computer on some crisis or other that had cropped up overnight in London.

Avery shot him an exasperated look. '*You* need a massage more than all of us combined,' she said and Claudia hid a smile behind her napkin at Avery in bossy mode. 'You've been saving the world all morning on your damn phone, not to mention both you and Jonah have been doing some pretty hard physical labour these last couple of weeks. I'm sure there are some kinks that could do with some ironing out and I've booked it for you and you *will* have it and what's more you better bloody enjoy it.'

Luke glanced at Jonah, who also seemed to be having trouble keeping a smile off his face. He held up his hands in surrender. 'It's a massage, man. There are worse ways to spend an hour.'

Luke shook his head in disgust. 'You are so whipped.'

Jonah grinned back at him. 'That I am.'

Luke rolled his eyes. 'I guess I do have some kinks.'

Claudia almost spat her orange juice all over the table. Yeah, like groping and perving on sleeping women.

Avery beamed. 'Atta boy,' she said, reaching over and patting his arm. She flicked a quick glance at Claudia. 'Just think, you'll be all loose and limber for when you spin Claude around the dance floor tonight. Win-win.'

Luke sensed Claudia tense beside him. An echoing tension crept into his shoulders.

Looked like they both needed that massage.

When they arrived at the spa they checked in and were all given a tour of the facility. Then they were ushered into separate change rooms to undress and get into the robes provided in preparation for their massages. Jonah and Luke were shown the male change rooms. Luke's phone rang the second his shirt was off.

'You miss your massage and Avery is going to be very displeased,' Jonah said as Luke reached for it.

Luke looked at the London number on his screen. 'This won't take long,' he said. 'Go on without me.'

Jonah clapped Luke on the shoulder. 'You know she'll come in and get you if you take too long.'

'Two minutes,' Luke said as he pushed the answer button.

Ten minutes later, Luke stepped out of the change room, swathed in soft white towelling. Despite his earlier protest he was actually looking forward to it. He was hyper-aware of the tension in his neck that had cranked up during the phone call and his muscles *did* ache from all the physical activity he'd been doing.

He'd become unaccustomed to that kind of heavy labour. Sure, he worked out at the gym regularly and jogged along London streets in the early morning most days—he loved the pavements that ran alongside the Thames, even in winter—but he hadn't been this physically challenged in a long time.

An attractive brunette met him. 'Hi, I'm Sherry,' she said. 'I'll be doing your massage today.'

Luke nodded. 'Nice to meet you.'

She smiled at him and Luke got the impression she wasn't going to find his massage a chore in any way, shape or form. He smiled back. Jonah was right. There were worse ways to spend an hour.

'This way,' she said and gestured for him to follow her.

Sherry walked down a carpeted hallway with subdued lighting and opened a door to the right at the end of the corridor. She smiled at him again as she indicated he should precede her. A light floral aroma greeted him before he even entered and Luke noted the subdued lighting extended into the interior of the room as he put his foot over the threshold.

Then several things registered all at once. The presence of two tables, one empty, the other with a person—a female person. She was lying on her belly with nothing but a towel covering her butt and acres of bare, glistening skin exposed to his gaze. Candlelight glowed in the oil covering her body and a man worked said oil into the backs of her legs.

Claudia?

And then while his brain desperately tried to compute the

images in those first few surprising seconds he heard, 'Oh, dear Lord in heaven, that's *soooo goooood*.'

Actually it was more a groan. She'd definitely groaned it. *Claudia* had groaned it.

He watched the male masseur's hands slide all the way up from the back of Claudia's knee to the top of her thigh—a little too close to where it joined her butt for Luke's liking.

'What the hell?'

Even in Droolsville, the low growl yanked Claudia out of her bliss. She gasped as she half raised her chest off the table and then remembered she was wearing only a towel that wasn't currently covering much of her at all.

Caught in flagrante again!

She lowered herself, looking over her shoulder at Luke looking better than any man had a right to in a white fluffy gown.

'What are you doing in here?' she snapped, heat in her cheeks—was she destined to suffer from a terminal lack of clothing around him?

'What am *I* doing in here? This is where I was brought. What are *you* doing in here?'

'Oh, I'm sorry,' Sherry said, looking as confused as the rest of them. 'I think there's been a terrible mistake. I thought this was a couple's massage? Like the other two? I thought the other woman said…I thought you were…together.'

Luke glared at the guy whose hands had stilled on the back of Claudia's thigh. The masseur removed them, eyeing Luke warily. 'No,' Luke said tersely. 'We're not.'

'Oh, dear, I'm terribly, terribly sorry,' Sherry apologised, wringing her hands, looking more mortified than Luke had ever seen another living person. 'No worries,' she said, 'I can rebook you. It'll need to be tomorrow—we're fully booked today.'

'I won't be here tomorrow.'

'Perhaps another day,' Sherry the mortified asked.

Luke's jaw clenched. 'I don't need a massage,' he said and turned to go.

Claudia frowned as a wave of crankiness accompanied Luke's dismissive statement. Oh, no. Avery was right—he *did* need a massage. Now more than ever—*clearly*! And she'd be damned if she was going to be the one to stand in the way of it.

'Wait,' she said as he neared the door. 'You stay and I'll go. You're working two jobs and long hours. You need the massage more than I do.'

Luke stopped and turned to face her. 'I'm fine, Claude.'

'No,' she said. 'I insist.' She craned her neck around further until she could see the man whose fingers had been working magic until this rather abrupt interruption.

'Can you cover me please, Marco?'

Marco went to shift the towel from Claudia's derrière and Luke stepped forward on an alarmed, 'No.' Marco stopped and shot Luke a puzzled look. Claudia was looking at him as if he'd lost his mind as well. But he'd seen more than enough of her skin for one day.

In the few weeks he'd been home he'd seen more than enough of Claudia to last him a lifetime.

'You've had more stress than all of us combined,' he said. 'And besides…' Luke glanced at Marco. 'You *sounded* like you were enjoying it. Very much.'

Claudia couldn't deny how much she'd been enjoying it. How much she'd been looking forward to a massage ever since Avery had mentioned the spa idea yesterday. And to deny herself Marco's fingers would be a particularly heinous form of torture.

'Oh, for God's sake,' she said, suddenly annoyed at him and herself for acting as if they were in some Victorian melodrama. It wasn't as if they hadn't already seen each other in next to nothing. 'The table's here, Sherry is here…we shared a bed for years. Just lie down already.'

Luke was aware of the two masseurs exchanging looks.

'We were kids,' he clarified to Sherry. And then flicked his gaze back to Claudia. 'I'm fine.'

Claudia glared at him. 'And dandy?' And then when he didn't look as if he was going to give in she said, 'You're making me tense just looking at you.'

Which really wasn't a lie. The thought of what he had on under that robe was making her really freaking tense. They'd asked her to strip everything off so she assumed he had too...

Luke held Claudia's gaze for long seconds. 'Fine,' he muttered again. He turned to Sherry. 'Where do you want me?'

Claudia wasn't sure if he was being deliberately provocative but she gritted her teeth as she placed her face back in the hole on the massage table and prepared to go back to her happy place.

Not easy to do with six feet four inches of pissed-off man right beside her.

Naked pissed-off man.

Luke found it difficult to relax even under Sherry's expert hands. Everything in the environment around him was conducive to a state of relaxation—the low lighting, the essential oils, the rainforest music—he just couldn't find it. All he could see behind his shut lids was big male hands on the backs of Claudia's legs, slippery and kneading.

And they *weren't* Marco's.

Luke tensed even more as the deep melodic timbre of Marco's voice reached him. 'I'll lift the towel if you want to turn over to your front.' Claudia's table creaked slightly and he swallowed as he tried not to think about her turning over.

Do not think about Claudia naked and jiggling.

'You're very tense,' Sherry murmured somewhere near his ear in the same melodic timbre that blended with the music and ambience.

He was pretty sure he heard Claudia snort. 'My boss has had me working like a lackey these last two weeks,' he murmured.

Another snort from Claudia's direction.

Luke smiled to himself as silence descended upon the room again. He wondered what the hell Sherry and Marco thought of *this* particular couple's massage. He could just picture them raising their eyebrows at each other and shrugging their shoulders. They were undoubtedly more used to couples holding hands and bringing their own CDs of Gregorian chants than a couple who could barely say a civil word to each other.

Claudia was grateful for the warm cloth that Marco placed over her eyes. She'd copped an eyeful of Luke's broad smooth back as she'd turned. Sherry's hands glided all over the expanse of him, and she was alternately turned on and jealous.

She could massage the hell out of that back. She'd been told she gave a mean back rub and Luke's muscles looked as if they were made to be kneaded.

Her heart crashed around in her chest as unhelpful images sprang to mind. No matter how hard she tried to let the drugging massage take her away, to concentrate on the long smooth strokes from expert hands, the image of *her* hands on Luke's back—and his legs, and his chest—kept her well and truly anchored to the room.

To the man lying less than two metres away.

'I'll hold the towel so you can flip over.'

Claudia tensed and held her breath as Sherry's command to Luke seemed loud in the room. What would he see when he turned over? Another man's hands massaging oil into her legs? Her bare shoulders and chest? The towel clinging precariously to nipples and just skimming her upper thighs? Her exposed legs?

A lot of skin. Oily and slippery as his had looked, the flicker of flame casting a warm glow over it, bathing it in golden light.

Would it remind him of *that* morning?

Would he even look?

'Just the back's fine,' Luke said.

Luke took a deep steady breath. The last thing he needed was to turn over. He'd spent twenty minutes trying not to think about the fact that a naked woman was having her body oiled and kneaded right beside him.

And not just *any* woman.

Claudia.

He'd tried really hard not to think about them being alone at the end of this, all slippery and oily and essentially naked. He closed his mind off to wondering how much weight one of these tables could bear. And he'd definitely not let himself go down the mental path of I-wonder-if-these-doors-have-locks.

He'd got this far without an erection but he knew he had a precarious control on his libido and he didn't trust himself to turn over and not glance Claudia's way one more time.

His libido didn't need that kind of trouble.

'Are you sure?' Sherry asked.

He'd never been surer of anything in his life. 'Positive.'

'Well, let me work a bit more on your neck,' she offered. 'I'm surprised it hasn't snapped right off your shoulders it's so taut.'

'Thank you,' he murmured.

Because his head *was* about ready to snap right off. And he was damned if he was going to leave this room before Claudia did. He was keeping his head down and his face firmly jammed in the cut-out until Claudia and her robe had departed.

CHAPTER ELEVEN

'AVERY SHAW, YOU switched the dresses.'

'Ah…yes. I can explain that.'

Claudia gripped the phone. 'Oh, really? How?'

'I had a hunch you'd chicken out on the red dress so I performed a little…switcheroo this morning.'

'You did what?' Claudia blustered into the mouthpiece. 'When?'

'Well, I enlisted—'

'Jonah,' Claudia said in disgust, the incident that had momentarily puzzled her this morning now making sense. She should have gone with her instincts when Jonah required her assistance to choose which font they were going to use on the new garden signs.

As if he gave a rat's arse about fonts.

'Don't blame him,' Avery pleaded down the line, jumping to Jonah's defence—as if the brawny, muscle-bound, lovesick fool needed it.

As if he gave a rat's arse about Claudia's displeasure. He was clearly too busy thinking about *his own* pleasure.

'I cajoled him into it,' Avery continued.

Claudia snorted. 'I bet it didn't take much.'

'He told me he didn't think I should interfere.'

Claudia wasn't swayed by Avery's standing-by-her-man act—even if it was the sweetest thing. 'He's a clever guy,' Claudia said dryly.

'I'm not interfering, Claude…not really…'

Claudia touched the crushed-velvet fabric laid out on her

hotel room bedspread and tried not to be seduced by its glamour. 'You booked us into a couple's massage!'

'I *did not* book you in as a couple,' Avery protested for the umpteenth time. 'I can't help it if Sherry got the impression you two were…together.'

'And then,' Claudia said, ignoring Avery's arguments because they both knew damn well who had planted those impressions in Sherry's head, 'you sabotage my wardrobe.'

'We're going dancing—you need your dancing dress.'

Claudia glanced at the dress again, then firmly turned her back on it. 'The blue one is fine.'

'Of course it's fine. But the red one…' Claudia heard Avery sigh loud and clear across the connection and rolled her eyes. 'The red one is *ooh-la-la*. Every man's head is going to turn when you walk into the room in that thing. Every man is going to want to dance with you. Your dance card will be full.'

'I don't want every man's head turning,' Claudia said waspishly. 'I don't want to dance with every man in the room.'

There was a pause for a moment before Avery's voice said softly in her ear, 'Just the one?'

'Avery,' she warned. 'Forget about Luke and I.'

There was another silence during which Claudia could almost hear the thoughts whizzing around in her friend's head.

'We can never have that kind of relationship, Avery,' Claudia said, gentler his time. 'We've known each other too long. Too well. And he's too cynical about love.'

It helped to say the words out loud, and not just for Avery's sake. 'It's never going to happen.'

A brief pause followed this time but Avery was never one to be kept down. 'So that's even more reason to go out and let your hair down,' she enthused. 'You deserve a night on the town. So go knock 'em all dead in that dress.'

Claudia turned back to face the dress. 'I don't know, Avery…I'm kind of tired.'

It was a lie, of course; the massage had rejuvenated her from the inside out and it had been such a long time since she'd danced...and if Luke wasn't going to be there she'd definitely be up for a party.

She stroked a finger down the deep V of the halter neck.

'Oh, come on, you know you'll have fun once you get into it.'

'I suppose...'

Avery tutted in her ear. 'Suppose? Phfft! You know you'll love it. Now, say it out loud. I, Claudia Davis, will put on my red dress and shake my booty all night and I *will* enjoy it.'

'Avery.'

'Say it!'

Claudia sighed and repeated the requested phrase. 'Louder,' Avery said. 'Say it with feeling.' Claudia said it louder. And with feeling.

'There, now, doesn't that feel better?' she asked.

Claudia smiled. 'Yeah, it does.'

'Good,' Avery chirped and the triumph in her voice was infectious. 'Now, what have you learned from this incident?' she asked, then gleefully supplied the answer to the rhetorical question. 'That Avery's always right.'

Claudia laughed. 'No. Try never trust someone who has access to your door key.'

Luke almost had a heart attack when he called on Claudia to pick her up right on the dot of seven as they'd prearranged. She was swathed head to ankle in slinky dark red velvet. Like crushed raspberries.

And he was starving.

Her hair was in some kind of messy up-do that trailed blonde wisps down her nape, her shoulders were bare, her *cleavage* was bare—*do not think about her breasts*—and she had on some strappy shoes with ten crimson toenails flashing at him in all their sinful glory.

She looked as if she'd been shrink-wrapped from chest

to hips into the dress before it flowed around her thighs and calves.

'You're wearing *that*?'

Claudia supposed she could have taken offence at his rather rude greeting, but she wasn't stupid and she didn't believe in acting obtuse around men. It was clear she'd stunned him and her feminine ego swelled dramatically.

'And good evening to you too,' she murmured, pulling her door closed.

Luke ignored the gentle reprimand. He looked into the depths of her cleavage. 'Don't you have some kind of...' he waved his hands in the general direction of her shoulders and cleavage '...wrap?'

Claudia's chin rose. 'No.'

'Don't you think you should?'

Claudia smiled and shook her head. 'You do know I'm not six years old any more, right?'

Luke blinked as she swept past him and headed for the lift, the dress clinging to every microscopic movement of her body. The palm that had held the softness of her breast tingled.

'I'm hardly likely to forget in that outfit,' he called after her.

Luke's breath hitched as Claudia looked over her shoulder at him and gave him a wink.

They ate a sumptuous meal in the aptly named Rumba Room and Claudia was pleased that Avery had thought to book one of the tables that ringed the large dance floor. The entertainment here was always spectacular and being this close they wouldn't miss any of the acts.

The restaurant was crowded and the food was delicious. Avery and Jonah were happy to lead the conversation and Claudia let them go. She spoke where required, as did Luke, but neither of them were very engaged. Claudia was too aware of the strange vibe between her and Luke. He brooded away in her peripheral vision, also responding perfunctorily to verbal cues in between glaring at any man who dared look at her.

It was off-putting to start with but after a couple of glasses of wine Claudia actually started to enjoy it. It was a fairly pointless exercise but knowing that he found her attractive after years of secretly drooling over him was something of a head swell.

And he was looking particularly dashing tonight. He'd teamed a pair of dark trousers with a retro button-up shirt in a paisley print of dark greens, purples and greys. It was open at the neck and the sleeves were rolled up to his elbows and it had been left hanging out.

It was very funky. *Very London.*

His whiskers had been shaved to within an inch of their lives and while she wished he'd just let them grow, become the shaggy and scruffy stubble of her fantasies, a part of her was just as attracted to the whole *London suit* thing he had going on.

She wanted to reach out and feel for herself that a man's face *could* be that deliciously smooth. Trail her finger along his chin. Push her nose into the underside, where neck met jaw, and rub her lips against all the satiny smoothness she knew she'd find there.

And then maybe she could get a better whiff of his sweet but spicy aroma. She'd been trying to place it all night. Not that she was a connoisseur of men's aftershave but she did appreciate a man who smelled good.

'I thought your ambition was to have your own agency by now, Luke?'

Claudia sensed Luke tensing beside her and tuned back into the conversation. What was Avery saying?

'So it was,' Luke said, his lips tight. 'And if it hadn't been for Philippa screwing me over, I would have.'

It was Claudia's turn to tense at the mention of Luke's ex-wife. She held her breath and waited for him to elaborate, to talk more about what must have been a fairly low point in his life. To tell them something about his ex-wife. The mysterious Philippa.

She'd never once had a conversation with him about the woman who had, according to Gloria, broken her son's heart and almost destroyed his professional reputation. One minute he'd been married at a London register office without bothering to even tell his mother and the next it was all over.

Two years was all it had lasted. He'd been going to bring Philippa out to meet them all but they were always too busy and it had never eventuated. And then it had all fallen spectacularly apart.

'Oh, I'm sorry, Luke,' Avery said as Jonah frowned and almost imperceptibly shook his head at Avery. She reached out to touch his hand. 'That was insensitive of me.'

'It's fine,' Luke dismissed. 'I'll get there again. I plan to be out on my own—*completely on my own this time*—in two years.'

Jonah nodded at his friend. 'Well, you can have my account,' he said. 'I haven't been happy with my advertising mob for a while now.'

Luke chuckled, his taut muscles relaxing. 'Well, I'm flattered but you can't just hand over a huge account like that,' he said. 'What if you don't like what I can do?'

'Can't be worse than I have now. I've been a little distracted lately,' he murmured, trailing his finger up Avery's arm, 'to care. I've really let the ball drop in that department. Besides, you forget, I know what you can do with that awful plastic-cheese crap. If you can sell that you can sell anything.'

The whole table laughed this time and Luke joined in. He'd won a national jingle competition when he'd been eleven years old, not long after his parents had partnered with Claudia's to run the Tropicana. It had been to sell pre-wrapped cheese slices and he'd been hooked on advertising ever since.

Luke shrugged. 'I can have a look if you like.'

Jonah nodded. 'That would be good.'

The long, low sultry note of a saxophone oozed out then, interrupting their conversation, and a murmur ran around the room. Claudia felt her heart flutter a little.

Bring on the dancing.

Spotlights from up above flicked on, one at a time, illuminating circles on the dance floor; other instruments joined the saxophone until a raunchy tune was playing.

'The samba,' Claudia announced to no one in particular.

And then a half-dozen couples twirled onto the floor from the wings. The women were dressed in tight, sequined dresses with huge slits that fitted like a second skin and the men were dressed in skinny trousers that fitted across narrow hips, formed a sash across flat abs and flared slightly at the hem. Their white silky shirts bloused and flapped, a little like pirates', the buttons mostly undone.

They found their positions and, as one, they all commenced dancing.

Really dirty dancing.

Bumping and grinding. Big male hands all over petite, scantily clad, female bodies. Spanning waists, gliding down legs, skimming breasts.

They twirled and turned and practically floated across the dance floor, light as feathers. When the music ended, the male dancers dipped their partners with dramatic flair, the spotlights cutting out, and the room burst into applause.

'There's Raoul,' Avery called across the table, raising her voice to be heard over the clapping.

Claudia nodded. She'd noticed. And he'd noticed her too, giving her a quick wink as he'd sambaed past earlier. He'd be over when he finished his set.

Luke frowned. *Raoul.* His eyes searched the dance floor for the man that Avery and Claudia were talking about as the lights came back on again and the dancers started up a tango. He spent the next fifteen minutes checking out each of the incredibly talented dancers wondering who the mysterious Raoul was. And what his relationship to Claudia might be.

He didn't have long to wait.

As the performers finished their last dance they all split up and headed for the tables, cajoling people to dance with them. A tall, dark-haired man with very white teeth, a perfect tan and designer three-day growth made a direct beeline for Claudia.

Raoul, he presumed.

CHAPTER TWELVE

CLAUDIA STOOD AS Raoul approached. It had been such a long time and she'd missed watching him dance. He had the swagger that all good-looking men possessed and combined it with that loose-hipped sway of a dancer. And it would have been quite something had Claudia not known that Raoul was aware of every single pair of female eyes following him across the floor.

He was beautiful and he knew it.

Sure, Raoul was great to dance with and a fun occasional lover but Claudia had never entertained anything serious with him. When—if—the big L happened *she* wanted to be the centre of that man's world. She needed a man who loved her more than he loved himself.

She *deserved* that, damn it.

Claudia was hyperaware of Luke's gaze on her as Raoul closed the distance between them and swept her into his arms.

'Raoul,' Claudia exclaimed. 'It's so good to see you again.'

Raoul slid a hand onto her waist as he kissed both of her cheeks. '*Mi querida*. You look *magnifica*,' he said, then stood back slightly to admire her dress.

Claudia knew that Raoul's Spanish accent could be used like a lethal weapon on unsuspecting women but she also knew it came and went with remarkable ease. But she didn't care—not tonight.

Luke clearly did though. She could feel the disapproval radiating off him in waves and she felt just a little triumphant.

'You like?' she asked, performing a sexy pivot from side to side for full effect, flirting just a touch.

'You make all the men go a little crazy here tonight, I think.' He grinned. 'What you say, Miss Avery?' he asked.

'Definitely.' Avery smiled as she greeted Raoul. He held out his hand and she placed hers inside, grinning when he kissed it.

'Raoul,' Jonah said, half standing as Raoul's attention shifted and the two men shook hands.

'And who do we have here?' Raoul asked as his gaze came to rest on Luke.

'This is Luke,' Claudia said, jumping in before Luke, who didn't look inclined to chit-chat, could say anything abrupt. 'Raoul's company runs our Latin dance classes and Latin nights at the Tropicana,' she said.

She thought it was best not to introduce Raoul as her lover, no matter how much she wanted to make Luke squirm. Truth was it had been too long to claim him as that any more.

'Ah,' Raoul said. 'This is the famous Luke.' He held out his hand. 'Nice to finally meet you. I have heard much about you.'

Luke vaguely remembered now seeing Raoul at a function when he'd come back last year to work out what they were going to do about being handed the management of the resort. He shook the other man's hand when what he really wanted to do was to demand that *Raoul* remove his other hand from Claudia's waist.

There was no way that hand said anything other than *mine*.

'Darling,' Raoul said as he dropped Luke's hand and returned his attention to Claudia. 'They're playing a cha-cha. Your favourite.'

Claudia didn't need to be asked twice. Luke might disapprove but she'd been dying to dance the second she'd slipped the gorgeous red dress over her head. And she was going out there to shake her booty with the best dancer in the room.

'Lead the way,' she said, ignoring Luke's glowering, and allowed herself to be swept onto the dance floor.

Luke stood there stewing, watching as the other man walked off with Claudia.

His Claudia.

And he did not like what he saw as the dancing began. The dance floor had cleared a little around Claudia and Raoul as people stopped dancing to watch—consequently he could see every move they made. Thankfully the cha-cha didn't appear to be a dance where the couples got too close and Mr Glitterpants seemed to be all about the rules of posture and body space and maintained his ruthlessly— Luke had seen enough clips from *Strictly Come Dancing* to know that.

But hell, if he had Claudia that close in that dress, the rules be damned.

He shook his head of the useless thought.

'She's good, isn't she?' Avery enthused from across the table.

Luke, who was about ready to gouge his own eyes out, was grateful for the interruption. He turned back around to face Avery. 'Yes, she is. Where'd she learn to dance like that?'

'Raoul taught her.' Avery gave him a wink. 'Private lessons, I think.'

Luke bet he had. His lips tightened. He did not want to think about Raoul and Claudia having private lessons.

'We're going to dance,' Avery said, standing up, Jonah taking her hand and following suit. 'You should ask Claudia to dance.'

Luke shook his head. 'I don't dance.' Not like that anyway.

'Sure you do,' Avery teased. 'All you have to do is hang on tight and shuffle your feet. That's what Jonah'll be doing.'

'You got that right.' Jonah grinned.

The cha-cha music came to an end and another tune

started up. 'Oh, I love this one!' Avery exclaimed and dragged Jonah onto the dance floor leaving Luke to his indecision.

Luke wasn't entirely sure what *this one* was but as Raoul's swivel hips got a bit too near Claudia's it was evidently going to be a lot more up close and personal than the cha-cha.

A little *too* up close and personal for his liking.

Before he knew it he was on his feet and storming onto the dance floor.

Claudia shut her eyes, pleased to be losing herself in the music and the syncopation of the dance. Raoul had taught her all she knew and was an excellent dance partner. Luckily on the dance floor he let all his ego and pretentions drop and just became one with the rhythm. Dancing with him was like dancing with the notes as they floated in the air.

And then Luke came along and ruined it. She heard a firm, 'May I cut in,' and opened her eyes to find Luke tapping Raoul *very* firmly on the shoulder while staring at her.

Raoul, who'd also been lost in the dance, looked momentarily puzzled, but he was much too indoctrinated with the code of the dance floor to deny Luke his request. There was an insane moment when she wanted to cling to Raoul's shoulders and beg him not to leave her.

Luke didn't really want to dance. He just didn't want her to dance with Raoul. In her dress. *With no wrap.*

And there was also something slightly wild about Luke tonight. He didn't look in the mood for anything light-hearted.

But then Raoul was bowing slightly and saying, 'Of course,' and moving away and Claudia was left facing Luke on a crowded dance floor. One hand had slid onto her hip and she couldn't decide if the skin beneath burned or tingled.

'I didn't think you could dance,' she said waspishly.

Luke nodded. 'I can't dance like that,' he said. Raoul was

all about keeping the frame and executing the moves perfectly. He was a dancer.

Luke wasn't.

'But I can dance like this,' he said and yanked her body hard against him.

Claudia gasped at the sudden intimate contact. It was completely out of left-field and she hadn't had time to prepare for the impact. And then he started to move and things rubbed and there was friction and it felt so good—better than any expert dance move Raoul could pull—and she knew he felt it too as his hand tightened on her hip.

She wasn't sure she could do this with Luke. This was twenty years of friendship on the line.

'This isn't dancing,' she murmured, the husky note in her voice cutting straight through the music.

'No. But it's real. It's not some fake display for Raoul to advertise his business.'

Claudia looked up into his face. Way up. She'd forgotten how tall he was. Or at least how much taller he was compared to her. Raoul, for all his Spanish good looks, didn't quite make six foot and she had to readjust her centre.

His smooth jaw was just there and she could smell his spicy-sweet aftershave and if they'd been lovers, God help her, she would have stood on tiptoe and licked from the hollow of his throat all the way to his chin.

But they weren't.

'Why does me dancing with Raoul bother you so much?'

Luke, who had been trying desperately to look anywhere else but Claudia, found himself looking down at her.

A mistake.

Two ripe swells of cleavage greeted him, pushed up and out of the V of her halter dress from the way he was holding her all smooshed up against him.

He wished he knew the answer to her question but all he had were bone-headed Neanderthal reactions. Gut reactions.

Because I can't stand the thought of him looking at your

breasts. Any man here looking at them. I can't stand knowing that he's touched them.

Not when I haven't. Not thoroughly anyway.

Yup. So not going to say that.

He dragged his gaze up to her face, her blue eyes glittering like polished turquoise in the spotlights. 'I don't know why it bothers me,' he said. 'It just does.'

Claudia would have been knocked on her butt had she been sitting near a chair. She hadn't expected such raw honesty from him and she didn't know how she felt. Part of her wanted to run and hide. The other part *really* wanted to lick his neck.

So she did the mature thing: she unlocked her gaze from his, dropping it to the patch of shirt that was right in front of her, and decided to change the subject. She cast around for something that would completely lampoon the warm buzz she could feel gathering down low as the delicious friction between them ramped up.

'Why don't you ever talk about Philippa?'

Luke stumbled slightly at the unexpected question. Bloody hell. She sure knew how to kill the buzz. 'There's nothing to say,' he said tersely, keeping his gaze trained on a spot over her shoulder.

Claudia refrained from rolling her eyes. That statement in itself was a big blaring warning signal to his mental health. 'What happened with you two?'

Luke's jaw. 'I don't really think it's any of your business,' he said.

Thinking about Philippa's betrayal, her infidelity, always left Luke feeling a little emasculated and he didn't need that while dancing with a beautiful woman.

Even if it was Claudia. Who he shouldn't be thinking about in relation to his masculinity.

Claudia fell silent for a few moments and just swayed to the music, but that was worse. Because that left her thinking and her thoughts were far from pure.

Far from sensible.

All she could think about was how her breasts rubbed against his chest, how hard and meaty his shoulder felt in her palm and the crazy thump in her groin as their bottom halves rubbed together and things got a little heated down there.

'You broke your mother's heart, you know?' she said.

Again, another comment out of the blue but it was something she'd always wanted to say to him. Marrying Philippa and not inviting his parents had really hurt Gloria. She'd made a big deal out of being understanding but Claudia had been just outside the door when Gloria had broken down on her mother's shoulder and it had been heart-wrenching to hear.

Maybe it wasn't a fair thing to say but Luke had lived a fairly selfish life for a decade, far away from how many of his decisions had affected them all. Moving to the UK the first chance he got, getting married, not wanting anything to do with the resort.

It was his life and these were his decisions to make but they still had an emotional ripple effect.

Luke kept his eyes firmly fixed over her shoulder. 'When I moved to London? I know.'

Claudia shook her head. 'No. When you married Philippa and didn't invite her to the wedding.'

'What?' Luke forgot about not looking at her as he searched Claudia's face, forgot about dancing. 'We didn't invite *anyone* to the wedding. It wasn't a...*wedding*...' he spluttered, 'with the dress and the cake and the...other stuff. It was a quick trip to the register office in our lunch break then back to work. We didn't even go on a honeymoon for three months.'

Claudia blinked at him and barely managed to suppress a shudder. It sounded horrible. No wonder Philippa had left him. She'd known exactly the kind of wedding she wanted from the age of six. A full-on romantic affair on the beach just outside their doorstep and a huge reception at the Tropicana.

'You know your parents would have travelled halfway round the world to be there with you when you got married regardless of how you chose to go about it.'

A spike of guilt lanced Luke as the truth in Claudia's words found their mark and slashed hard. 'We didn't invite anyone,' he reiterated. 'Not even Philippa's parents.'

Claudia shrugged. 'Okay.'

'Mum seemed okay with it when I spoke to her.'

It had never been his intention to hurt his mother and if he'd had any inkling that would be the outcome he would have paid for them both to fly over.

Claudia rolled her eyes. 'Of course she did, you idiot. You were blissfully happy and she didn't want to burst your bubble or burden you with her disappointment. She's your mother—she was never going to put a guilt trip on you.'

'But I suppose you have no compunction?'

'Strangely enough, tonight I don't, no.'

Luke glared down at her. He knew exactly how she felt. 'It's a strange old night,' he said.

A trill undulated in her belly at the intensity in his gaze. 'Amen,' she muttered.

Their eyes locked momentarily before they glanced away from each other. Luke resumed dancing and Claudia followed suit. He *had* been happy, he remembered. *Blissfully happy*. It seemed like a long time ago now and time had mired it in such bitter memories, but he'd really thought Philippa was the one.

'Maybe that's why it failed...your marriage.'

Luke faltered again slightly but kept going. Dancing with Claudia like this was the sweetest torture. All soft and warm against him despite her sharp tongue and prickles.

'Oh, this ought to be good,' he said derisively. 'Please *do* share why you think my marriage failed.'

Claudia shrugged. 'All women want the fairy tale, Luke.

The dress, the cake, the bridesmaids. Where's the romance in a register office?'

Luke snorted. Not Philippa. Her lack of interest in a big event had puzzled him at the time—most women he knew wanted the fancy party, the whole shebang. But not Philippa. Of course, it had become evident only two years later why she hadn't been bothered.

The bitter memories rose to the surface again and twisted a knife in his gut. 'Dear little Claude,' he said, 'still on board the *Love Boat,* I see.'

Claudia froze as his patronising words slid down her back like cold slime. She'd thought he'd finally seen her as a woman tonight—not some adoring little lapdog that followed him around and hero-worshipped him. Not some silly romantic girl with her head in the clouds.

She stepped out of his arms and glared at him. 'I think I'm done with dancing.'

Luke glared back. 'Me too.'

CHAPTER THIRTEEN

AN HOUR LATER Claudia was still royally pissed off.

Lying on her bed in the dark, her red velvet dress twisted around her, she stewed away like some sappy freaking Cinderella who hadn't got the prince after the clock had struck twelve.

Occasional flashes of lightning from the storm brewing outside slanted into the room in strobe-like bursts, illuminating her misery.

God, maybe she was as pathetic as Luke's words had suggested.

Why weren't life *and love* as simple as *The Love Boat*?

Why, more importantly, hadn't she just kept her big mouth shut? Yes, she'd spoken some home truths, things he'd needed to hear, but who'd died and left her in charge of things Luke should know?

And what on earth had possessed her to spout on about where his marriage had gone wrong when she knew hardly anything about it? In fact, until tonight, all she'd known was the name of his ex and that they'd worked together at the same firm.

She'd seen a photo, of course—a tall, gorgeous, curvy brunette. Worldly and sophisticated. The *exact* opposite of her.

But that was it.

And she'd told Luke it was because their wedding hadn't been romantic enough. She, who had been married exactly zero times, was dishing out marital advice!

Argh!

But, man, he'd been especially...infuriating/sexy/irritating tonight. Coming over all *do you think you should be wearing that?* and treating her as if she were some recalcitrant teenager who needed her virtue protected.

She laughed suddenly at the absurdity of it. Her virtue had been lost some time ago. Ironically on a cruise she and Avery had taken together when they'd been nineteen.

She knew he liked her in the dress. His eyes had practically bugged out of his head, for crying out loud. She knew he'd been aware of the delicious friction between them as they'd danced. So why didn't the jackass just accept it for what it was and let it go?

Smile, dance, flirt a little.

Just because there was an attraction there didn't mean it had to be acted on. They were both adults, for crying out loud—not some hormone-riddled teenagers. Surely they could merely enjoy the buzz?

The fact they were both aware of it, the fact that it was taboo, ramped up the buzz even further. It felt like some delicious, unspoken secret between them. Made it sexier, somehow. Made her insides quiver and her outsides hyperaware of the way velvet felt against her skin—soft but abrasive at the same time. How it rubbed at her nipples, tickled her belly, smoothed over her hips.

Things shifted inside her and Claudia squeezed her thighs together to suppress the sudden tingle that had started between her legs. She squirmed against the bed to relieve it.

It didn't help.

If anything it reminded her how damn long it had been since anyone had been between her legs and she wished she were someone who could just go out and find anyone to scratch an itch. If she were, she'd march down to that ballroom right now and drag Raoul back to her room.

And he'd come willingly.

But she couldn't lie down with Raoul while Luke was on

her mind. It wouldn't be right. And probably not very conducive to a satisfying sexual experience.

But, God help her, if she didn't have a satisfying sexual
experience soon she was going to have to invest some serious cash in a latex boyfriend—the best one on the market.

The phone rang and she groped for it in the semi-dark,
snatching it up, pleased to be relieved from having to think
about the depressing state of her sex life.

Her *non-existent* sex life.

'Avery, if this is you I hope Jonah is there to protect you
because I swear to God I'm going to throttle you. The red
dress? Bad idea.'

'It's not Avery.'

Claudia shut her eyes as the deep tones, made even sexier
by the touch of English class, undulated directly into her ear.
Damn.

'The red dress wasn't a bad idea.'

She opened her eyes. 'Luke…don't…'

'You looked hot in the red dress.'

Claudia's belly flopped over inside her. 'Luke.'

There was silence for a few moments. 'I'm sorry I was
a giant arse,' he said.

'No,' Claudia sighed. 'I'm sorry. I shouldn't have gone
on about stuff that was none of my business.'

More silence until Claudia began to wonder if he hadn't
hung up or nodded off.

'There's a *Love Boat* marathon on cable.'

Claudia rolled her eyes. 'You're just screwing with me
now, right?'

He chuckled and goose bumps marched down the side of
her neck and the length of her arm. 'Hand on heart, pinky
swear, I'm not. Turn on your TV.'

Claudia reached for the remote, which sat beside the
phone. 'Which channel?' she asked as she pushed the power
button.

'Two six three.'

Claudia scrolled through until she found the channel and there, before her eyes, was Julie with her clipboard. The electronic guide told her they were running back-to-back episodes until six in the morning.

'I think I've died and gone to heaven,' she murmured.

Luke laughed. 'Tell you what, I have a bottle of wine. How about I come to yours and we watch it together?'

'You hate *The Love Boat*.'

'Consider it my penance.'

'Lying on a pillow-top mattress in a five-star hotel, drinking wine and watching television is penance?'

'I know, right?' he said and Claudia could hear the laughter in his voice. 'I don't know how I'll bear it.'

Lost in the sheer sexiness of his voice all low and smiley in her ear, Claudia didn't say anything for a few moments.

'Oh, come on,' he cajoled. 'For old times' sake?'

Claudia knew that could be dangerous. Wine and nostalgia. *Not a good mix.* But if he was willing to try and put the strange dance-floor incident behind them and get back to where they had been—lifelong friends—then she could at least meet him halfway.

'Okay, a couple of episodes but I'm coming to yours.' At least that way she was in control of the situation. She said how long she stayed and what time she left. And she could leave if things got weird again.

Or if her libido demanded she throw caution to the wind and jump Luke's bones.

'You had to wear the dress?' Luke said as he opened the door to her five minutes later. *Was she trying to kill him?*

'You're still in your clothes,' she pointed out.

'Yes.' But he didn't look like *that* in his clothes. 'I thought you'd be more...casual.'

She shrugged. 'I let out my hair. What did *you* do?'

'I...shaved,' he said.

Claudia snorted. *Of course he had.* God forbid his whiskers should ever poke through his skin. 'Well, it was the dress or my pyjamas.'

Luke stepped aside so she could enter. 'Pyjamas would have been fine,' he said as he watched her velvet-swathed derrière sway enticingly back and forth.

'The dress covers more,' she said.

Luke's eyes stayed glued to her shrink-wrapped butt— technically the dress might have covered more. It did, after all, fall to her ankles, but it left *nothing* to the imagination.

Dear God, in the name of all that is holy, let her be wearing underwear.

'Pull up some mattress,' he said. 'They've just started a new episode. It's one of the Christmas ones. I'll pour you some wine.'

Claudia should have hesitated about lying on his bed, especially with what had happened earlier but, as he said, it was just like old times. Him, her, some ham and pineapple pizza and *The Love Boat*.

'Is there a Hawaiian pizza on the room-service menu?' she asked as she kicked off her shoes and took the unrumpled side of the bed.

Luke laughed. 'Nope. Already looked.'

'It's okay,' she said, her eyes drawn to the flickering television screen, which had been muted. 'I'm too full anyway.'

Luke approached with the glasses of wine. 'Cheers,' he said as he handed one over and they clinked them together.

'Are we supposed to be lip-reading?' Claudia asked as Luke pushed the remote and TV guide aside and got comfortable on his side of the bed.

'I thought we could do that thing you see on comedy shows sometimes, where we make up the dialogue as it goes along.'

'Ha. Funny guy,' she said, reaching for the remote that was stranded in what she supposed was the no-go zone between them and unmuted it.

He chuckled as the volume returned. 'You've seen these episodes enough to know them word for word, surely?'

'Shh,' Claudia said, ignoring his quip. 'I'm trying to listen.'

And after that they didn't really speak much. They passed the odd comment about how dated it seemed and about some of the more lurid seventies and eighties fashion.

Claudia yawned as the credits rolled on the second episode. She'd snuggled down amongst the pillows more and was lying on her side, her head propped on her open palm, her elbow bent. 'I should go,' she murmured.

She was feeling kind of mellow though after two glasses of wine. The lightning had ceded to rain and it beat steadily against the windows lending a cosiness to Luke's easy companionship. It was nice and familiar and Claudia was beginning to think she'd imagined the tension earlier.

This was how she remembered her relationship with Luke—nice and easy. Uncomplicated. Maybe this was all they had? All they were destined to have?

Maybe they were at their best when they were stuck in this *Love Boat* time warp?

'I really should go,' she said again.

But then the opening song finished again and the scene opened with Julie and Gopher chatting. 'Oh, I always wanted them to get together.' She sighed. 'Do you remember?'

'Yeah, I remember,' he said.

'They took their time about it,' she muttered, her gaze firmly fixed on the television.

Luke chuckled and she dragged her eyes off the screen. 'What?' she asked.

'Nothing.'

Claudia shot him a wry smile. 'You hate it, don't you?'

Luke shook his head, his gaze roaming her face. 'I love watching you watch it.'

The comment should have been sweet. Uncomplicated.

But his gaze brushed her mouth and suddenly the nice and easy evaporated.

Maybe this wasn't all they were destined to have...

'Pleased I amuse you,' she said, deciding to just ignore him. She laid her head on the pillow and snuggled in letting *The Love Boat* take her away to a far less complicated world.

Where a woman with a clipboard *could* get her man.

When she woke several hours later the room was darker, quieter. No television to spread a flickering light or fill the room with noise. Only the digital clock numbers cast a pall on the situation.

And the situation was not good. She'd fallen asleep. So had he.

They *really* needed to stop doing this.

She was still on her side but had wriggled right down and her dress had ridden up a little and tangled around her knees. One hand was tucked under her cheek, the other hand was lying palm down on Luke's chest.

He had also shuffled down, lying supine with his head rolled in her direction, both his hands lying loosely beside him. His hair was too short to be rumpled but that wasn't where she was focused. The red glow from the clock drew her attention to his mouth. It illuminated his lips, slack in slumber, and showcased them for what they were—nicely full, perfectly delineated.

Just like the warm muscles she could feel beneath her hand.

Her fingers itched to touch his ruthlessly smooth face. To move along his jaw as if she were reading braille, carefully seeking out any patch that he might have missed with his razor. Even if it was just a single solitary scrape against the pads of her fingers.

His chest rose and fell evenly beneath her palm and she could feel the thud of his heart—sure and regular. The same could not be said for her own. Her pulse tripped madly,

knowing this…voyeurism was wrong. Knowing even thinking about touching him was wrong.

Her breath turned ragged at the mere thought of crossing that line. But…

He'd done it to her, hadn't he? Watched her while she'd
slept?

Watched. An angel had suddenly appeared on her shoulder. *He didn't touch.*

But you were naked. A devil sat on her other shoulder
whispering tempting truths.

And it was true. At least Luke was fully clothed.

That doesn't make it okay, the angel insisted.

Go ahead, it's fine, the devil urged.

Claudia had never been more tempted in her life. It was
just a tiny touch to his face, after all. Light as a feather. He
was sound asleep. He probably wouldn't even feel it.

And then with no conscious control, her hand was moving
anyway. Slowly, tentatively, as if he might wake any second.
Her fingers made landfall at hard jaw, the pads practically
sliding down the slope of his throat his face was that smooth.

She paused, tensed, waited. Held her breath.

Her heart thundered.

Nothing happened. He didn't move. He didn't shift in his
sleep. He didn't wake and demand to know what the hell
she was doing.

Claudia eked out a ragged breath that sounded freaking
cyclonic in the heavy silence of the room. Then, when she
was sure he was staying asleep she trailed her finger from
the angle of his jaw to his chin. It was less than a touch, more
like a butterfly whisper across his skin, a flutter.

And not a single patch of rough whisker to be found.
He was baby smooth, talcum soft. Like his lips. Her gaze
zeroed in on the two perfect pillows, illuminated to perfection by the red digital glow.

How many times had she fantasised about kissing that
mouth? Too many to count.

And there it was, right in front of her.

Her pulse kicked up another notch as the devil whispered, *Kiss him,* and she contemplated doing just that.

That would *definitely* wake him up.

But what if he rejected her advances? It would be embarrassing and awkward. For a *very* long time. It would probably even kill her. She'd probably die of mortification on the spot.

It would certainly be hard to come back from.

Another sinful whisper. *But what if he doesn't?*

Her finger inched towards his mouth, the very tip lightly touching the bow of his top lip. He shook his head slightly as if a mozzie had buzzed him and Claudia froze. His tongue darted out and swiped along where she had touched. But he settled back to sleep again quickly.

Her heart was beating so loudly now she was surprised it alone hadn't woken him up. Hell, she was surprised it hadn't triggered a tsunami.

The possibilities of what could happen here scared the living daylights out of her—the number of ways he could reject her and crush her spirit made her cringe. But she realised something else as she waited like a scared rabbit in the shadows for her heart rate to settle. In a few short months Luke would be heading back to London, and the thought that she might never get another opportunity to show him how she felt suddenly scared her a hell of a lot more.

Screw it.

And the devil smiled.

CHAPTER FOURTEEN

LUKE DRIFTED UP out of the many layers of sleep to a pair of lips brushing along his. Light and gentle but definitely a mouth. Definitely a kiss. His lips responded on autopilot to the pressure before his brain could compute the facts.

He opened his eyes. Claudia?

'Claude?' he murmured, her lips so close they brushed against each other again.

Claudia pulled back abruptly, clearly startled. 'Oh, God,' she whispered. 'I'm sorry…I just…I…'

Every cell in Luke's body stood to attention. Claudia was kissing him? 'You just decided to…kiss me?' he clarified.

Claudia shuffled away a bit, put some distance between them as she rolled back onto her elbow, propping her head up with her hand. She could feel the heat in her face and was grateful it was too dark to see the resulting pink in her cheeks.

'I'm…I don't know what happened. I was just…no.' She shook her head. 'There are no excuses for it.'

Luke was fully awake now. Claudia had kissed him. A delicious buzz took up residence in his lips as the tension from the dance floor revisited. He rolled up onto his elbow too, facing her, his gaze drifting to her breasts where a decent amount of soft swell made the cleavage interesting.

His breath hitched a little.

His pulse spiked a lot.

'Oh, I don't know,' he said. 'I think I'd like to hear them.'

Claudia swallowed as her nipples hardened beneath his blatant gaze and part of her just wanted to grab his hand and bring it to one of them, feel him squeeze it again as he did that night all those weeks ago now.

But she was in more than enough trouble.

'You're always so…clean shaven…so smooth…I was trying to find out if you'd missed a patch…or something.'

'So, you were checking my *lips* for stubble as well? With…your mouth?'

Claudia cringed at how bad it sounded. She'd known this was going to be humiliating but had that stopped her? No.

Stupid devil.

Stupid. Stupid. Stupid.

'No.' She shook her head. 'Your mouth…God…your mouth…' Claudia shut her eyes. How could she explain this?

Tell him you lost your mind temporarily and apologise, the angel demanded.

Screw that, the devil butted in. *Tell him it looked so goddamn pretty and kissable in the glowing red light.*

Claudia groaned, wishing they'd both shut the hell up.

Luke felt a leap in his belly as the tortured little moan escaped her mouth. Every one of her words had gone straight to his groin and stroked. He wanted to kiss her very badly, to put her out of her misery, but the moment was too drenched in seething sexuality to let her off that easily.

He wanted to hear what she had to say about his mouth. And then he was going to put it on her cleavage and suck her nipples deep inside it.

'My mouth?'

Claudia's eyes snapped open at the prompt that sounded more growl than request. He was really going to make her say it.

'I was…curious, all right? I've thought about it…about kissing it…for ages. And suddenly…there's this devil on my shoulder and it was saying how pretty your mouth looked in the light from the clock and it did…it really did. And then I was…'

Luke chuckled. He was sure she wasn't the first person

to use the-devil-made-me-do-it defence but she sounded so damned confounded by it, he couldn't help but be amused.

And flattered. He was flattered all the way to hell and back.

Yeah…he knew a little about that devil.

Luke reached out, bridging the short distance between them, sliding his hand onto her nape, drifting his thumb up and down. It came into contact with the knot at her neck where the halter straps of her dress tied and it took all his willpower not to undo it.

'How long?' he asked, his gaze dropping briefly to her mouth. 'How long have you wanted to kiss me?'

Claudia knew this was the perfect opportunity to lie. He couldn't see inside her head. He didn't know the truth. She could just say ever since that day you groped me. Or since last week. Or something flip. But his gaze was heavy and it seemed to bore straight to the root of her honesty.

And besides, this seemed a moment for honesty. No matter how much it might come back to bite her in the butt.

She swallowed, her throat suddenly tinder dry. His thumb at her nape was seductive and she fought against the downward flutter of her eyelids.

'Most of my life,' she admitted. It sounded so…desperate said out loud and Claudia wished she could snatch the words straight back. 'Kinda pathetic, huh?'

'No,' Luke whispered. 'Sweet.'

Claudia gave a half snort, half groan. He couldn't have chosen worse words if he'd tried.

Luke felt the sudden tension in her neck. 'What?' he asked.

Her eyes opened fully. 'I'm so sick of being sweet old Claude.'

Luke nodded slowly. 'Okay. So what *do* you want?'

Claudia glared at him. What the hell did he think she wanted? 'I want you to shut up and kiss me,' she said not quite managing to keep her exasperation to herself. 'What do *you* want?'

Luke shook his head. 'Oh, you don't want to know what I want.'

Claudia bristled further. 'I'm not a kid, Luke,' she said, staring at him with as much pissed off in her eyes as she could muster. 'I can handle *whatever* it is you want.'

Luke had had a semi hard-on since waking to Claudia's kiss but now it flowered to its maximum potential at her definitive assertion. He held her blazing gaze for a moment before dropping his to her mouth, her breasts, her belly.

'I want to rip this damn dress off you and feast on your breasts while I bury myself inside you. I want to make you come loud enough for Jonah and Avery to hear four floors away. And when I've done that I want to do it all again. I want to do it with you. All. Night. Long.'

Claudia wouldn't have thought it possible for her throat to get any drier—she was wrong. Every cell in her body practically went into a dehydrated torpor at his frank gaze and his even more frank admission.

'Well,' she said, licking her lips as she finally found her voice. 'How about we start with mine and graduate to yours?'

Luke smiled at her then and she smiled back. 'Good answer,' he muttered before closing the distance between them and claiming her mouth.

And claim it he did. Deep and hard, no finesse, no gentle initiation, it was full-on from the second their lips touched. Masterful and demanding, explosive and searing, sucking away her breath and her very ability to reason. It spoke of lust and longing and desires too long denied. It commanded capitulation and she submitted eagerly.

'God,' he groaned against her mouth. 'I want you.'

And before she even had a chance to answer he rolled her onto her back and then he was over her and then on her and he was kissing her again. Deep, wet, open-mouthed kissing, pushing her into the mattress with every thrust of his tongue, kissing her into the bed.

Kissing her into oblivion.

Claudia was finally able to grab a breath when he freed her mouth from his onslaught, but it was only brief before he sucked it away again as he set about kissing a wet trail down her throat and into her cleavage. He swiped his hot tongue along the exposed swells of her breasts and Claudia moaned.

'Undo your top,' he said, his breath ragged. 'I need to look at you.'

Claudia's fingers shook from desire as she lifted her arms to do his bidding. She didn't think to protest his command—because it *had* been a command—she just did it. She wanted him to look too. Hell, she wanted him to do a lot more than that.

She needed him to.

Finally her fingers managed the task and she was pulling her top down, exposing herself to his gaze. His satisfied hiss went straight to her nipples, hardening them before his eyes, and then he was feasting on them, exactly as he'd told her he wanted to, and Claudia was reduced to a mass of cries and moans and pleas not to stop as he lashed the sensitive tips with his tongue and sucked them both in turn deep into his mouth, going from one to the other until she'd lost all powers of higher thinking and just lay there in a sexual bubble where the only thing that existed was his mouth on her breasts.

Not even his hand sliding down her body and back up under her dress registered above the sensations he was creating with his tongue. And then he slipped a hand inside her pants, slid his fingers right into all the slickness and went straight for her clitoris.

The bubble burst.

'Luke,' she cried out, grabbing his shoulders as her body bucked and she felt as if she were falling. Her eyes flashed open.

'Shh, shh,' he murmured against her mouth, kissing her

long and deep and wet again as his fingers stroked her. 'You taste so good,' he whispered before returning to her breasts to feast again.

Claudia's eyes practically rolled back in her head as his fingers circled and rubbed and his tongue swiped and flicked, both of them setting a rhythm that complemented the other, both of them rocking her, pushing her, dragging her, driving her closer and closer and closer to nirvana.

And she was powerless to resist. She wasn't even in her own body any more; she was floating above it somewhere watching herself as all the pieces of her started to come apart. As sensation swelled in her belly and something tore deep, deep, deep inside her, ripping her open, shredding her apart as it swelled further, growing and growing and growing until it was unbearable, a pleasure so painful her body was begging for it to take her, consume her.

And then it did.

'Luke!' she cried out as it claimed her, breaking over her in an almighty shock wave that arched her back, squeezed her buttocks and stiffened her limbs.

'It's too much,' she gasped as it bucked and writhed through her like some kind of possession, like the serpent itself. 'I can't,' she said, fearing she would die as it broke over her again and again, dragging her breath from her lungs, pounding her heart in her chest. But it went on and on shifting and changing, stroking her body with a thousand carnal caresses.

And it *wasn't* too much and she *could*.

And as it started to ebb she reached for it again, crying out for more. She didn't want it to stop. She *never* wanted it to stop. She wanted Luke, his mouth at her breasts, his fingers *exactly where they were*, like this *for ever*.

And he didn't falter, he didn't lift his head or shift his hand, chasing the tail of the orgasm as she moaned and whimpered, quivering through the dying vestiges, wringing out every drop of pleasure.

They were both breathing hard when Claudia finally stilled, Luke collapsing against her, his forehead on her chest, his lips grazing the skin that lay over her heart.

'Are you okay?' he asked, his voice drunk on a sexual high.

Claudia shook her head. No. She was never going to be okay ever again. She felt as if she'd been picked up and shaken and all the cells in her body had fallen out and been put back together in a completely new way. Her heart beat like a drum and her blood surged through her head in painful intensity.

'Oh, my God,' she said, 'I think I just blew a blood vessel in my brain.'

Luke chuckled. His head pounded pretty hard too. He kissed her chest, then all the way up her throat to her mouth where he kissed her gently, reverently, and she sighed against his mouth and he kissed her more just to hear it again.

'I hope you can replicate that,' she said when he finally pulled away.

Luke chuckled. 'Repeat performances are my speciality.'

Claudia's fingers caressed his nape, brushing against his collar. 'God, I'm sorry, you're still fully clothed.' She cringed thinking about how she'd just lain there and let him *do* stuff to her. 'I'm not usually a starfish, I promise. I just…I think you put me into some kind of…stupor.'

'Good.' Luke kissed her brief and hard. 'That was the objective. Besides, you're not exactly naked either.'

Claudia looked down at herself. Her top hiked down, her skirt hitched up. 'I think we should do something about that, don't you?'

Luke grinned. 'Absolutely,' he said as he kissed her nose then eased off her, swinging his legs over the side of the bed and pushing to his feet. 'Take that dress off,' he said as his fingers made short work of his buttons.

Claudia didn't have to be told twice. It wasn't exactly an easy task lying on the bed trying to wriggle out of a dress that was already a twisted, hot mess, especially when she couldn't drag her eyes off Luke's mad scramble to lose his clothes. In fact she stopped altogether when he got down to his undies that were stretched to their limit by a very impressive erection.

Captain Sexypants indeed.

Luke glanced at Claudia as he hooked his thumbs into the waistband of his underwear. The dress still covered her legs.

'I swear if you don't take that thing off soon I'm going to rip it off.'

Claudia shivered at the silky undercurrent in his voice. Her gaze dropped to the hard ridge of his erection. 'I'm sorry,' she said, her belly twisting as she eyed if off, already knowing it was going to hurt *so damn good.* 'I got distracted.'

Luke grinned as he pulled the waistband out slightly and looked down at what was causing Claudia's distraction. He let it snap back into place. 'None of this until I see more of that.'

He nodded his head in the direction of her semi-nudity. Her dress was skew-whiff, her hair was a blonde mess and there were faint red marks on her breasts where he had sucked with a little too much enthusiasm, but she'd never looked more beautiful.

Claudia kicked free of the dress and reclined against the mattress, her arms above her head, arching her back slightly—he wasn't the only one who could tease. She smiled when he growled at her and said, 'Those too,' pointing to the scrap of red lace, the only thing between her and complete nudity.

A strange moment of modesty besieged her and she hesitated. This was the final frontier.

Oh, for goodness' sake, the Devil hissed, *he had his hands all up inside them less than two minutes ago.*

Claudia had to admit, the devil made a good point.

She held his gaze as she lifted her hips and stripped them

down off her legs. When she was completely bared to his view he dropped his gaze and looked his fill. A flush of heat swamped Claudia's body, head to toe, and took up residence between her legs in the exact spot he had found with his fingers to devastating effect.

'Your turn now,' Claudia said, her voice husky, loaded with anticipation.

Luke was out of his underwear in two seconds flat and it was Claudia's turn to look her fill. And she did. Oh, how she did. He jutted out so thick and proud, she understood why women in times gone by would swoon at the sight of a naked man.

If she weren't a strong modern woman she'd just about swoon right off the bed.

Instead her pulse fluttered, her mouth watered, her belly lurched.

Captain Sexy-no-pants!

Luke watched as Claudia licked her lips and his erection grew harder, tighter and he thanked the hotel gods for mini-bar condoms. He snagged the three-pack off the nearby bench and strode the two paces to the bed. Claudia opened her arms and her legs and he went to her, settling between them, his hardness nudging all her slick heat.

He looked at her for long moments, his hands either side of her face, wanting to tuck this memory away for ever. His eyes roved over her features, mapping every one. Blue eyes, cute snub nose, pointy little chin.

'Hi,' he said after a while.

'Hey.'

And then he kissed her and it was deep and slow and sweet, not urgent and hurried like last time. The kind of kiss that melted from the inside, delivering a long, slow burn. Lethal and sexy all at once. And when she moaned against his mouth and twined her arms around his neck to drag him closer the flame burned brighter.

Luke pulled away slightly, moved his mouth to her cheek,

her neck, kissing his way down, aiming to go much further south than he had last time with his mouth.

But then Claudia was pulling on his shoulders and when he looked up at her she said, 'No. I need you in me. Now.'

Luke grinned. He liked her impatience. 'Soon,' he said, returning to his ministrations.

'No,' Claudia said and Luke glanced up again. *'Now.'*

He smiled as he dropped a kiss to her sternum. 'Claude… I don't think I'm going to last too long.'

That was the whole point of dragging out her pleasure, making it good, making it memorable because he doubted his performance was going to be robust after several years of abstinence and sperm tubules that were about to rupture under the pressure.

Claudia cocked an eyebrow at him. 'And you think I'm going to?'

He grinned at her as he reached for the condoms. 'Hurry,' she whispered and he did, quickly donning one over his still-rampant erection.

And then he was back between her thighs, their hips aligned, and she was wrapping her legs around his waist and saying, 'Now, now,' and it was so easy to slide into all her heat, so easy and good and right, easy to pull out and go in again, easy to make her gasp and moan and beg him to not stop, *never stop*, easy to drive them towards the pleasure just a handful of strokes away.

Then they were coming together, gasping and calling out each other's names, rising and rising, holding on tight then letting go and falling, falling, falling.

CHAPTER FIFTEEN

THEY LAY IN silence long after they'd both bumped back
to earth. Luke had bundled her close, Claudia's head on
his shoulder, her breasts squashed against his ribs, her leg
draped across his thighs. And for the longest time they didn't
say anything, just drifted along in a delicious post-coital
haze.

Claudia supposed she should be feeling some kind of guilt
or remorse or mortification but she didn't—not tonight anyway. There would be time enough for recriminations in the
days and weeks ahead but for now she was just too damned
chilled out. Instead she absently circled a finger around his
nearest nipple, enjoying the tickle of the hair.

'You should stop shaving,' she said.

Luke's eyes drifted open. 'No.'

Claudia smiled. 'I like stubble.'

'Then you grow some,' he murmured.

Claudia turned to face him, propping her chin on his
chest. 'I remember when you used to look very unshaven
and shaggy.'

She lifted her hand and stroked his smooth jawline. God,
as a teenager she'd drooled watching him come home from
uni all shaggy-haired and scruffy as he headed straight for
the beach.

Luke let his eyes drift shut again, enjoying her light caress. 'I lived at the beach, I had to look the part. But I'm a
professional working man now and I need to look that part.
Shaving *is* London. Stubble is Crescent Cove.'

Claudia sighed, not too far gone to get the message. But

mellow enough to accept it. Accept that, for him, the length of his whiskers defined the type of man he was. 'Whatever,' she murmured. 'You'd still look sexy with stubble.'

Luke smiled. 'I'm sexy enough.'

Claudia smiled too. Arrogant but true. Not that she was going to let him get away with such a cocky statement. 'There's always room for improvement,' she murmured.

Luke opened his eyes and looked directly into hers. 'I know it's trendy these days to look a little ungroomed but a lot of my clients are old school. They respect men who take the time to present well.'

Claudia screwed up her nose. 'Sound like a bunch of old fuddy-duddies to me,' she said, snuggling her head back into his shoulder again.

Luke chuckled at her disdain. Yeah, some of them were but they were also wealthy fuddy-duddies who could afford multimillion-dollar ad campaigns.

They were his fuddy-duddies.

He stroked her hair as his eyelids grew heavy again, enjoying the low-level buzz still undulating through his pleasure receptors and vibrating against his skin.

He was almost asleep when Claudia's quiet, 'So, what did happen between you and Philippa?' drifted his eyelids open. Maybe it was a measure of how relaxed, how ironed out he was that the question didn't particularly alarm him. Earlier he'd told her it wasn't any of her business but now, he wanted her to know.

Maybe it would help her to understand him a little better. Why he was so driven to succeed. Why he'd not had time for the Tropicana. Why he had to go back.

But where to begin?

Claudia waited. He didn't tense as she'd expected him to but it was a long time before he answered and she wondered if he'd gone to sleep.

'She'd gone to Paris for a work conference,' Luke said into the stillness of the night. The pale red light from the clock glowed in Claudia's hair, highlighting the blonde strands, and he played with them absently, sifting through them as he sifted through the memories. 'I was joining her for the weekend. But an opportunity came up and I was able to join her a day early. I thought I'd surprise her. She'd left my key at the desk so I grabbed it and let myself into the room. She was in bed with another man.'

Claudia, who had been distracted by the low sexy rumble of his voice as it vibrated through his ribcage, took a few seconds to process what he'd said. She turned quickly when the implications filtered in, flipping onto her stomach and using her elbow to drag herself closer to him, raising her head and chest above him, looking down into hooded eyes.

'Oh, Luke,' she whispered, stroking her free hand down the side of his impossibly smooth face. 'That's awful...I'm so, so sorry.' She kissed him then, a light press to his lips, to his cheek, to each eyelid in turn. 'I can't even begin to imagine how awful that must have been.'

Luke grimaced as he short-circuited the ugly scene before it played in slow-mo through his head yet again. 'I was... gutted.'

'You had no idea?'

Luke shook his head. 'He was an old lover of hers. Her first boss in advertising at a *very* prestigious, old-school firm. It had apparently been a long-standing arrangement,' he said and even after three years he could still taste the bitterness in his mouth. 'She said it never occurred to her to give him up.'

Claudia could feel his hurt and betrayal, could tell it was still a gaping wound for him. 'I'm so sorry,' she said again, dropping a kiss on his chest because what else could she say?

The angel nodded sagely and reminded her it *was* none of her business. The devil wanted to demand Philippa's address so they could go and scratch the unfaithful bitch's eyes out.

'Oh, it gets worse,' he said. 'Philippa and I were setting up a business on our own. It was all legally binding and set to go. When I dared to express my outrage at her infidelity, when I deigned to separate from her and back out of the partnership, she stole my biggest client, the *firm's* biggest client, right out from under me. Not only could I not go out on my own but the company lost money and took a blow to its reputation. I've spent the last three years trying to repair the mess.'

Claudia thought back to all the uncharitable thoughts she'd had about Luke the last few years and felt ashamed. No wonder he hadn't had any time for her and the Tropicana. No wonder he was looking to hightail it back to London as soon as possible.

'It wasn't your fault, Luke.'

Luke saw the compassion in her eyes; it glittered in the red light that played in her baby blues. 'Maybe not,' he said. 'But I'll always blame myself to a certain degree.'

Claudia couldn't bear the thought of it. 'Why?' she demanded quietly, cupping both of his cheeks in her hands. 'Because you loved someone and trusted them?'

'Yes,' he said, looking directly into her eyes. 'And I'll never be so foolish again.'

Claudia wanted to weep then. Not only had Philippa destroyed his faith in himself and his reputation at work but she'd also ruined him for love.

Ruined him for her.

She didn't know what to do or say to make it better or convince him that one stupid woman did not represent all women. That people did love and it was true and deep and honest. That it could be abiding and faithful. Because he knew that anyway.

He only had to look at his parents, or hers, to truly know that.

But one look at him now, his brown eyes practically glowing with indignation in the red light, she knew he didn't think it applied to him. That he'd shut himself off from the possibility altogether.

And her heart broke into a thousand pieces. Because *she* wanted to be the one to show him what kind of a woman he needed. Show him what love could be.

Because, God help her, she loved him.

She loved a man who could never love or trust again.

The words trembled on her lips but she lacked the courage to say them. Their relationship had taken a huge U-turn tonight and she didn't know where it was going to go from here—nowhere, she suspected—but it certainly wasn't the time to declare her love.

Especially to a man who had just told her he wasn't going there again.

Maybe it had even been a warning.

So she did the only thing she could think of—she rolled up on top of him, straddled his hips and kissed him. Long and deep and slow. He groaned as she pushed her tongue inside his mouth and she moaned back when he grabbed her naked butt and held her firm against his burgeoning erection.

Her pulse sped up, her breathing roughened.

So did his.

Then she kissed his face and his neck and his chest. She swirled her tongue around his nipples before drifting it down to his abs and then his belly button. His hardness pressed into her breasts and she rubbed them against him as she swirled her tongue lower.

The gasp he gasped when she fitted her mouth around him went straight to the hot tingle between her legs. He was as big and thick in her mouth as he had felt inside her and she took as much of him as she could.

'Claude!' he cried out as he buried his hands in her hair.

She let her tongue move all over him, up and down, round and round, finding his sensitive spots and then torturing them ruthlessly with the kind of tongue lashing he'd given her breasts earlier.

He groaned again, his hands leaving her hair to fist in

the sheets. 'If you keep doing that,' he panted, 'it's going to end real soon.'

Claudia could feel the tension in his thighs, his buttocks, see the whites of his knuckles. A sense of power washed through her as the tingling between her legs intensified to an excruciating level and she knew there was only one way to relieve it.

Her mouth released him and he groaned. Whether it was in protest or relief she wasn't sure. She just knew she had to feel all that wonderful hardness deep inside her, to the hilt, right up where that damn tingle had a stranglehold.

She dragged her way back up his body, grabbing handfuls of his flesh to assist her. When she reached her destination she straddled him again then leaned over, reaching for a condom from the bedside table. He tried to curl up, take a nipple into his mouth but she swatted him back down.

'No,' she said, because she knew how that went and before she knew it she'd be a drooling, boneless starfish all over again when what she needed was to dominate.

Not be passive.

Relieve the unbearable tension and show him with her body, if not with her words, that she was his.

'Keep your hands exactly where they are, mister.'

'Ooh, bossy.' He grinned, planting his hands firmly on her hips.

Claudia didn't bother to answer, she just tore the foil wrapper with her teeth, reached for him and rolled it on as if she'd worked in a condom factory all her life. And then she was positioning herself over him and then, slowly, sinking down.

'Oh, God.' Luke's groan matched her own as his fingers dug into her hips.

Claudia shut her eyes and threw her head back as she seated herself on him, completely impaled, the tingles obliterated. She was right—it *did* hurt so damned good.

When she opened her eyes again he was watching her,

his hands still firmly planted on her hips. 'What now?' he murmured.

'This,' she said, circling her hips, once, twice, three times, panting with the stretch and fullness of it. 'And this,' she said, leaning forward, placing her hands on his shoulders and slowly, very slowly easing herself off him all the way then sinking back down again.

Luke groaned as his groin leapt and his mouth watered. Her breasts were glorious, pert and swaying enticingly before him. 'Again,' he said, their gazes locking.

She did it again. And again. And again. He groaned all three times but his eyes didn't leave her face.

'You know,' she said as she lifted off all the way for the fourth time, 'not all women are like…' she pushed back onto him again, sinking to the hilt again '…her.'

Claudia almost said her name but she didn't want the ugliness of what she'd done to intrude on this moment.

She didn't want Philippa in *their* moment.

Luke nodded. 'I know,' he panted as his body fought to contain the gathering storm seething in his groin.

'Do you?' she whispered as she slid up again, fighting to keep her eyes from rolling back in her head. To keep them open. To keep them on him.

'Yes,' he hissed as he thrust up hard to meet her this time, holding her hips tight. The violent jiggle of her breasts and her gasp, deeply satisfying.

Claudia shut her eyes briefly as the friction turned to something else, something pulsatile. She opened them and looked straight at him as she lifted her hips one more time. 'I would never do that to you.'

Even though they could never be, she needed to know that he knew that.

Luke thrust. 'I know.'

She lifted. 'Do you?'

He thrust. 'Yes.'

Claudia groaned as the tingling returned and the pulses

grew and expanded, spreading from her belly button to her hips, her thighs, her buttocks, and she moved quicker, more urgently, trying to ease the glorious burn, not able to talk any more, only able to move up and down, up and down, up and down.

If she talked she might just say too much in this state of sexual insanity.

Luke sensed her urgency, felt it echo deep inside himself. He met her stroke for stroke, her lovely breasts taunting him with each one, giving her what she didn't even know she wanted, as his own orgasm pulled at his self-control, pulsing up from the root of his erection, fraying the world around him and when he couldn't take it any more he curled up, sliding his hands to the small of her back and sucking a nipple deep into his mouth.

'Luke!' she cried out, spearing her fingers into his hair, adjusting to their new position easily, riding him without missing a beat.

'Yes,' she said, 'yes, yes, yes.'

And then they both shattered together.

CHAPTER SIXTEEN

THE TELEPHONE JANGLED right near her ear the next morning dragging Claudia out of the deepest depth of slumber with all the finesse of a jackhammer. She reached for it automatically.

'Hello?' she mumbled, her heart racing.

'Claude?'

Avery? 'Yes.'

'What are you doing in Luke's room at six in the morning?'

Claudia's heart raced a little more as her surroundings filtered in. Same-looking hotel room as hers but this one had the addition of a large naked man spooned around her, his hand low down on her belly, his mouth pressed to her shoulder blade.

Last night. Luke's apology. A bottle of wine.

The Love Boat.

The love*making*.

Crap.

'Oh…er…we were just…having another…planning meeting…' Claudia winced at the obvious lie.

'You sound like I've just woken you up,' Avery said, her voice laced with scepticism.

'No, just tired,' Claudia assured and faked a yawn. 'Didn't really sleep much last night.'

And that *was* the truth. They'd been awake long enough to use the third condom before falling into an exhausted heap together.

'Well, you're supposed to be down here with us having breakfast, remember? We have to leave at seven-thirty.'

Claudia stifled a groan. She remembered. She'd only agreed to come away if they got back as early as possible on Sunday morning so they could have everything shipshape for the reopening of their doors on Monday.

But that was before her and Luke's wild, three-condom sexual spree. 'Sorry. Give us ten minutes. We'll be straight down.'

Claudia hung up. 'Let me guess,' Luke said in his deep voice, all sexy and rumbly from sleep. 'Avery.'

'Yes.' His hand moved from her belly to her breast, his lips buzzed her neck and Claudia shut her eyes briefly as her body flowered beneath his touch. His thumb grazed a nipple and it felt so damn good.

But they didn't have time for this.

'No, stop,' Claudia said, scrambling out of bed, far away from his magical mouth and his sinful hands. 'We have ten minutes to get down to the dining room,' she said, hunting around for her clothes.

Luke watched the view as she bent over to pluck her discarded clothes off the floor. Predictably, his body stirred.

'Don't just lie there,' she said as she threw her dress over her head, not bothering with her underwear, and his stirrings turned to a full-blown erection at the thought of her being completely commando. 'We have eight minutes to get to the dining room and I need to go and get changed.'

'Can't,' he said. 'Not yet. I have this swelling problem.' He peeled back the sheet to show her.

Claudia swallowed as her gaze zeroed in on him. *Dear God.* He was magnificent. Thick and large. His erection dominated the flatness of his belly with its potency.

Luke hardened further at her frank appreciation. 'Maybe you could help me with it?'

Claudia almost groaned out loud. If only she hadn't been so bloody gung-ho about getting back to Crescent Cove,

Avery wouldn't have rung trying to find her and she could have all that magnificent male hardness inside her right now.

Claudia shut her eyes to block out both the mental and *actual* picture. 'I doubt it's terminal,' she said as she turned her back on him, stuffing her feet into her shoes. 'Seven minutes.' She grabbed her key off the nearby bench. 'See you down there.'

And she didn't look back no matter how tempted she was. And she was very, very tempted.

How she got through the remainder of the day, Claudia didn't know. She felt as if she had a huge, flashing, neon sign above her head saying 'look at me, look at me, I had hot dirty sex last night with someone I shouldn't have'. So she was brighter, chirpier, she worked harder, she walked faster, she knocked herself out playing the best, brightest version of herself she could muster after a night of head-banging sex and only two hours' sleep.

In fact she might have overdone it slightly if people's concerned faces were anything to go by. 'Are you okay?' Avery had finally asked her around mid-afternoon. 'You seem kind of...wired.'

Claudia had nodded vigorously. 'Fine and dandy,' she'd chirped, 'Just excited about tomorrow,' and she had buzzed off to attend to something else.

But by the time night rocked around again and she finally retired to her room about nine o'clock she was utterly exhausted and ready to drop. She collapsed back on her bed and lay there for a few moments like a starfish.

But then that got her thinking about Luke. About lying passively, while he turned her into a drooling mess, bringing her to orgasm with his hand and his mouth. A familiar tingle started up again and she rolled on her side, stuffing a fist between her legs to ease the ache.

Maybe her body knew somehow, could sense that he was just in the next room, or maybe it was the delicious waft of

Luke, of their sex, washing over her. With no time to shower this morning she'd been smelling Luke on her all day—earthy and male and very hard to ignore.

She'd been semi turned on all day.

Of course she could have had a shower when she'd ducked up to her room to change into her uniform when they'd first arrived back but, perversely, she hadn't wanted to wash him away.

She'd wanted to savour it, savour him, for a bit longer.

The way she'd savoured the smiles he gave her whenever she caught him looking at her. Those dirty smiles. The kind of smile that said, I know what you look like naked and screaming my name.

She wanted to savour every moment because if getting the Tropicana opening-ready today while he spent half the day talking into his Bluetooth had taught her anything, it was that she belonged here and his life was on the other side of the world.

Whatever had happened between them she couldn't forget that.

So, she loved him. That was both a revelation and not. She'd always loved him. It was just the first time she'd admitted it to herself. But it didn't change things. She wasn't going to go halfway around the world for a guy who didn't love her back. A workaholic divorcee whose career was his number one priority. A guy who was determined to never be so *foolish* again.

And if he loved her back, if he asked her to go with him…?

Best not to build those kinds of castles in the sky. They hadn't yet talked about what had happened or said anything, for that matter, of a personal nature to each other all day. It would have to come, she knew, but for now she was just going to savour the memory.

The knock on the interconnecting door a minute later surprised the hell out of her and she sprang off the mattress, her heart racing. The last thing she needed was to be horizontal around Luke again.

'Come in,' she called as she stood awkwardly at the foot of the bed, self-consciously checking her hair was still up in its ponytail.

The door opened and she smiled at Luke, who entered very hesitantly. 'Hi,' he said.

'Hey.'

They both smiled as they remembered the last time they'd done this routine—naked and plastered together in a Cairns hotel room. Then, as if they'd both realised it wasn't an appropriate thought to have, their smiles faded simultaneously.

'I thought we should probably talk,' Luke said.

Claudia nodded. 'Yes...I guess.'

'You don't sound too sure.'

She shrugged. 'At the moment denial is looking pretty good.'

Luke chuckled. 'That's an option.'

Claudia laughed too, grateful for the easing of tension. 'You want a beer?' she asked.

'Sure,' Luke said. 'Thanks.'

Claudia was grateful for something to do with her hands other than option A, which was to put them all over him. He was wearing boardies and a T-shirt again and Claudia couldn't help but be aware of what easy access that was. She reached into the mini-bar and pulled out a frosty bottle and handed it to him, then poured herself a glass of wine from the half-empty bottle sitting in the door of the fridge.

One of the advantages to being the boss—free mini-bar.

Normally she'd have clinked her glass to his bottle but keeping a distance between them seemed wise. Taking a sip, she leaned back against the bench, the fridge door cool on her calves.

'So where *do* we go from here?' she asked.

Luke shrugged. 'A part of me wants to suggest that we

accept it happened and move on. Never mention it again. Never…go there again.'

Claudia swallowed as his words cut her to the quick. His eagerness to move on hurt. Despite telling herself not to she *had* been spinning castles in the air. Fantasising about him saying, 'I'm giving up London for you.' But she knew it was the only thing that made sense for two people with very different life goals.

'That's probably the wisest thing,' she said.

Luke nodded. 'Wise, yes.'

But Claudia didn't think his heart sounded in it and a tiny spark of hope flared to life. 'What about the other part of you?' she asked.

Luke took a swig of his beer. She so *did not* want to know about *that* part of him. 'I tend not to listen to that side,' he dismissed.

Which was a lie of course. That was his maverick side, his throw-caution-to-the-wind side. The creative part, the part that made him a gifted advertising executive, that formed new and innovative ideas that clients went nuts over.

He indulged that side all the time. Just *not* this time.

Claudia scrunched her nose. She wasn't a fan of the first option so she was willing to take anything on board. 'I still think it should get a vote.'

'Oh, no.' Luke shook his head. 'It definitely should not get a vote.'

'Oh, really? Why not?'

'Because that part wants to rip that awful uniform off you and spend all night making you come.'

Claudia stilled. How could a statement so blatantly dirty sound so posh? 'Oh.'

Luke took another swig of his beer. 'Yes. Oh.'

Claudia's hand trembled a little as her insides tied themselves into a massive knot. She placed her glass on the bench beside her, not trusting herself to keep hold of it as she slowly lost her grip on the real world.

'I could be…' she cleared her throat '…amenable…to that.'

Luke did not need another invitation. On a muffled expletive he closed the distance between them, sliding his beer onto the bench beside her wine before grabbing her around the waist, yanking her in close to him and slamming his mouth down onto hers.

And it didn't disappoint. 'God,' he groaned as his mouth lifted to kiss her cheek, her eye, her ear. 'I've been fantasising about this all day.'

Claudia went up on her tippy toes, clutching him around the shoulders, hanging on as his lips ravaged her neck, bending her back for better access as he swirled his tongue down into her cleavage. 'Luke,' she gasped as his hand yanked her blouse out of her skirt then glided up underneath, up, up, up to claim a breast, squeezing and kneading, rubbing across the aching tip with devastating effect.

'We could keep doing this,' Claudia said as Luke's mouth trailed a wet trail along a collarbone.

'Right,' Luke panted as his mouth trekked back down her chest. He yanked her bra cup aside and her long low moan was like music to his ears. 'We're mature adults—we can handle a temporary…thing.'

Claudia nodded then gasped as Luke's mouth found her nipple. 'Oh, God.'

'I don't want to stop this,' he murmured in between wet swirls around her nipples. 'Do you want me to?'

Claudia shook her head. 'No,' she said, her denial husky but no less forceful. She really didn't. Even if it was going to leave her crushed into the ground at the end, she'd take whatever he could give her here and now, because if she couldn't have all of him then she'd have this time and tuck it inside her for ever knowing at least she had loved once upon a time.

Luke smiled and swirled his way back up to her neck, her mouth. 'Good.' He grinned, cupping her cheeks, his mouth on hers. 'So good.'

And then he kissed her again, long and slow, savouring every delicious second, revelling in the knowledge that her kisses were going to be part of his life for the foreseeable future. Before coming back to Cairns the thought of giving one woman such power again would have scared the bejesus out of him but Claudia was right—all women weren't the same and she was no Philippa.

He pulled back slightly, breathing hard. 'Why aren't we horizontal?' he murmured.

She grinned. 'I have no idea. We should do something about that.' And she kissed him again, clinging to his neck as he slowly walked them backwards towards the bed.

But they hadn't gone very far when Claudia's room door opened and Gloria and Lena walked in. Claudia and Luke sprang apart as if they'd been hit by a taser. Gloria and Lena's conversation stopped abruptly as they stared open-mouthed at their respective children.

'Oh, Lena,' Gloria gasped, turning to Claudia's mother. 'It's finally happened.'

Lena grabbed Gloria's hand. 'I know,' she said. 'Finally.'

Gloria moved into the room, making a beeline for her son. 'We'd always hoped, didn't we, Lena?' she said. Lena nodded. 'But you went off to London and then you got married and you didn't want to manage the resort with Claude and we thought…well, it looked like it was never going to happen and now…'

Luke watched, horrified, as the two women approached with huge beaming smiles. He glanced at Claudia, who was thankfully covered and looking just as stunned by the events of the last minute. *What a freaking disaster.* Why the hell was her door open? If their mothers had been a minute later God only knew what kind of a state he and Claudia would have been in.

It certainly wouldn't have been vertical.

He cringed thinking about it. It was bad enough standing here at thirty-two, caught with his hands all over Claudia and a raging hard-on in front of his glowing mother; he didn't need to think about how much worse it could have been.

At least kissing was more easily explained. *Hopefully.*

Claudia glanced at Luke as their mothers kept raving about what a wonderful couple they'd always known she and Luke would make. Luke looked as if he was about to throw up.

She knew how he felt.

This was bad. Very bad. Exactly what they'd wanted to avoid—involving two people who wouldn't understand it when Luke left to go back to London.

She had to do something, say something—quick.

'This is not what it seems,' Claudia said.

CHAPTER SEVENTEEN

GLORIA AND LENA stopped talking abruptly and a spike of guilt at bursting their bubble poked Claudia right in the centre of her chest.

'Okay,' her mother said although clearly she didn't believe Claudia. 'What is it, then?'

Good question Luke thought as he glanced down at Claudia. How on earth could either of them explain away what their mothers had seen? *Convincingly.*

'Luke and I were just sharing a good-luck-for-opening-day kiss,' she said.

'That didn't look like a good-luck kiss to me,' Gloria said and winked at Lena.

'It got a little out of hand,' Claudia admitted, 'but we're both exhausted from working so hard and nervous about tomorrow… It was…pure reaction…just one of those strange *isolated* moments that sometimes happen when people work closely together on something and the stakes are high. That's all.'

'That's all?' her mother repeated, clearly unconvinced.

'It happens all the time in advertising, doesn't it, Luke?' she said, nudging Captain *Silent-pants* for help.

Luke nodded. It sounded crazy but maybe they could convince their mothers if they stuck to her ridiculous isolated-reactionary-incident-brought-about-by-exhaustion story. 'That's right.'

'Oh? Kissed a lot of your colleagues, have you?' his mother asked.

Luke cleared his throat. 'Some,' he said lamely. Lying to

his mother was more difficult as a grown man than it had been as a teenager.

'There is absolutely *nothing* between us,' Claudia said. '*Nothing.* Just old friends who let something go too far because we were exhausted and…overwhelmed and it won't happen again, right, Luke?' she asked him.

Luke nodded vigorously. 'It won't.'

Gloria and Lena glanced at each other and grinned a little. 'Okay, sure,' Gloria said. 'That makes sense. A one-off.'

'Won't happen again.' Lena nodded.

Luke narrowed his gaze. 'It won't.'

'Okay, sure,' Gloria said, and Lena nodded her agreement.

Claudia sighed. They both looked suspiciously bright-eyed and Claudia's dismay grew. She and Luke didn't need the pressure of their parental expectations. They both knew nothing short of the royalesque wedding their mothers had *apparently* been planning for the last twenty years would satisfy Gloria and Lena.

Their *thing* was over before it had even begun.

Dead in the water.

'Was there a reason why you barged in without knocking?' she asked her mother.

Lena tutted at her daughter's sass. 'The door was unlocked.'

'I haven't been locking it with the hotel empty.'

'We just wanted to let you both know that if everything goes smoothly the next two days we'll be setting off on Wednesday.'

Luke wanted to say, *And you couldn't use the phone?* but that would be rude and ungrateful and they spent the next few minutes talking over their parents' travel plans as if their mothers hadn't just caught them making out like horny teenagers.

It felt awkward and unnatural and Luke was relieved when Gloria and Lena took their leave. 'Be good,' Lena said as they both walked to the door, springs in their step.

'And if you can't be good, be careful,' Gloria threw over her shoulder as the door slowly closed.

Claudia and Luke stared at the door as it clicked shut on a burst of raucous female laughter and excited chatter they could hear despite the thick wooden barrier. 'Oh, God,' Luke said. 'They're already picking out china patterns, aren't they?'

Claudia nodded miserably. She wondered if her mother or Gloria had any idea that their unintentional interruption had actually had the opposite effect to what they'd clearly been plotting all these years.

'You and I can never just have a…fling, can we?' he murmured.

'No.' Claudia shook her head. 'Not with our parents knowing anyway. If we're in any kind of a relationship, they're going to be sending out invitations and humming the wedding march. But we always knew that…'

'Yes.' Luke rubbed a hand along his neck. *They had.* They'd just let their hormones get in the way.

Stupid!

Look what had happened the last time he'd let them take over—an ex-wife and a torpedoed career. Did he learn nothing?

'We can't do this, can we?'

Claudia looked at him. A quarter of an hour ago she'd been minutes away from having him naked and inside her. Now she knew she'd never know that feeling again and she thanked her lucky stars for last night. To have known Luke in the carnal sense.

'No. We'll break their hearts when you go back to London, back to your other life. I don't want that to be a source of friction between them.'

She waited for him to say he wasn't going to go back. That he'd decided to stay.

Luke shoved his hands on his hips. 'Yes.'

He looked frustrated and weary and Claudia knew exactly how he felt. Their kissing had revved her up and now she was standing here, her engine running, with nowhere to go. 'We'll always have last night.' She shrugged.

Luke gave her a half-smile. 'Yeah,' he murmured, his gaze dropping to her mouth briefly, the muscles in his corded forearms flexing and for a second she thought he was going to leap the distance between them and kiss her anyway.

But he didn't.

Instead he looked away, dropped his hands to his sides and headed for his room. 'See you in the morning,' he said, pulling the door closed after him.

Claudia stared at the door.

Morning.

One long, sleepless night away.

Opening day was a success. Everything went off without a hitch and their guests were all lovely, very aware of the hardship that had recently befallen the Tropicana and extra accommodating with the limited activities available. Mostly they were family groups, grateful for the lower-key atmosphere, happy to hang out at the pool and play on the beach.

On Wednesday their parents left to much fanfare and relief as far as Claudia was concerned. Even just the disappointment she'd glimpsed on her mother's face as she'd realised she and Luke had been serious about their non-relationship had been hard to take.

She couldn't begin to imagine how much worse it would be if they had gone ahead and had a fling, built up their mothers' hopes and dreams only to dash them all when Luke left to go back home again.

Because he *was* going back to London—he'd made that very clear.

Thankfully over the following days and weeks they were much too busy to dwell on it. Between running the hotel and moving things along with the spa complex, not to mention Luke working all hours of the night as well as working with Jonah on a new advertising campaign, they didn't have time to be social.

They didn't have time to be lovers.

Make time, that pesky little devil that seemed to have taken up permanent residence on her shoulder, urged her every night as she lay in bed trying *not* to think about Luke lying in his bed. Right next door. Completely naked.

Sure, she could make the time if she wanted to throw caution to the wind, set up something clandestine with him, but the outcome wouldn't change. He was still leaving and all nights and nights of endless sex and passion would ultimately get her was even more exhausted than she was now.

There was a lot to do and she had to be on her game—not yawning and constantly distracted by whatever acrobatic sex they'd had the night before. Her guests deserved bright, chipper Claudia of old and that was what they were getting. The Tropicana had been dealt a huge blow both physically and financially and turning that around took hard work and focus.

And that was what she chose to concentrate on. Getting the Tropicana back. Salvaging the old reputation at the same time she forged ahead with establishing another—a first-class spa facility with luxury tent accommodation.

Who needed nights and nights of endless sex and passion?

She put Luke and what could have been in a special place to pull out and look at again another day in the future.

Maybe when it had stopped hurting so damn much.

The weeks blended into months and the resort exceeded Claudia's expectations, achieving a seventy per cent occupancy over the winter season. Everyone was busy and it was good to have a cash flow again. They were able to re-establish a lot of activities—lei threading, bush-tucker tours, beachcomber collaging, shell jewellery and ballroom dancing were all added to the programme along with the Saturday night luau. Several regular themed nights—pirate, medieval and mermaids—were held in the dining room with food and entertainment to match, and proved popular with the families.

But the biggest change was the building of the day spa, which they'd decided to call Tropicana Retreat. Thanks to government and tourist-industry pressure on banks, councils and insurance companies, everything had gone through without a hitch and they were able to get the build started within two months.

Claudia had hired a local building company who were surprisingly available given how much of the area needed rebuilding. But so much couldn't be done yet, not until insurance money had come through, so the company had jumped at the chance to create something special at the Tropicana.

Once the work started it took hardly any time to build. It was just a simple rectangular plan with a large open reception area that flowed into a salon area where manicures, pedicures and facials were done. Beyond that were four rooms for massage treatments and another room where a state-of-the-art Vichy shower was installed allowing them to do scrubs and all kinds of body wraps.

The fit-out took longer with Avery and Claudia poring over every single tile, pedicure chair, paint colour and blind-fabric swatch. Claudia was pleased to have Avery and her eye for the exquisite and happy to leave her to it once the big decisions had been made, freeing her up to tackle the hiring of staff.

Luke took on the task of managing the luxury tent accommodation, which, again, wasn't a huge construction job. The wooden platforms were simple and sourcing the right fabric for the tent-like shelter wasn't as difficult as he'd thought. The largest part of the build was the attached luxury bathroom facilities.

Nobody paid a few hundred dollars a night to sleep in a tent to have to go walkabout for a bathroom in the middle of the dark so it was important that they catered for that.

The biggest issue and the one that caused the most debate

was deciding where each of the six tents would ultimately be located on the grounds. They had an enlarged aerial photograph of the grounds as they were now, post cyclone, that Jonah had taken from the chopper, and they used monopoly houses for the tent sites, which they moved around and around trying to choose the best positions.

It was exciting to watch *everything* come together. Claudia felt a renewed sense of pride and vigour in the Tropicana as her dreams slowly became reality.

And if there were times where things were a little tense between her and Luke or she caught him looking at her with such abject hunger she wanted to rip all his clothes off, then knowing they were creating something amazing together, that they were reshaping this wonderful legacy of theirs, helped to temper those times.

They were both doing the right thing with a relationship that was never going to go anywhere so pouring all their sexual energy into the Tropicana made sense.

Indulging would be easy. But the consequences would be hard.

It was better this way.

Two weeks out from the official launch of the Tropicana Retreat, Luke sat at his desk at eleven o'clock at night staring at the email recalling him, in no uncertain terms, to London. The multimillion-dollar account he'd been working on for months was ready to go and the company CEO in question wanted Luke there to do the presentation.

Only Luke.

It was his chance to redeem himself and restore his reputation. And he wanted it.

He *needed* it.

It wasn't as if he were needed here any more with the bulk of the new project complete. Claudia could handle it from now on in. Hell, she'd always been able to handle it.

Damn their interfering parents.

What *he* couldn't handle for too much longer was keeping his hands off her.

Another good reason to get the hell out of Dodge.

She swanned around in that awful uniform that was fast becoming the sexiest piece of polyester in the world, being all chirpy and pleasant and efficient, and all he wanted to do was drag her down behind that reception desk, demand that she open her legs and say, 'Yes sir,' to him, the way she said it to guests.

God, the number of times she'd leaned over that damn map moving a stupid little green plastic house around while giving him a full view of whatever bra she was wearing for the day…

He deserved a medal for not ripping that awful shirt off her and dragging her onto his lap.

At every turn she'd tempted him. Not deliberately, he knew that, but his body just would not listen to reason. He'd taken to running on the beach every morning just to run off his morning erection.

It was that or open the connecting door to their rooms and the consequences be damned.

Even the thought was making him hard, frustration biting deep into his groin. Irritated at himself, at his erection, at the continual sexual fantasies of Claudia, he tapped Qantas into the computer's search engine and looked for a flight leaving asap.

Fifteen minutes later he was booked out at lunchtime tomorrow. And his erection was gone.

Now he just had to break the news to Claudia.

CHAPTER EIGHTEEN

CLAUDIA WAS SITTING cross-legged on her bed cradling a frosty glass of Milo looking at some designs for a new range of Tropicana uniforms that Avery had selected for her to vet. Avery, who had declared the current uniform an unnatural disaster, had been working on Claudia for months now about the need for an update. She'd insisted on a different uniform for the spa—there was no way she was wearing polyester!—and Claudia had agreed.

But changing the Tropicana uniform wasn't such an easy thing for Claudia. She looked down at the shirt she was wearing and at the trousers she'd discarded on the chair by the bed earlier. All she'd ever wanted to do as a girl was wear this uniform and she'd always been proud of it. It was difficult to let go.

But, she had to admit, Avery's choices were quite stunning, remarkably similar in style to the current range of uniform, just some funkier patterns and nicer fabrics.

It was time, she knew, for the Tropicana—and her—to move on.

As she flicked through the catalogue, going from one diligently marked colour-coded tab to the next, she tried not to think about what Luke might be doing next door. She was aware, with the grand opening nearing, that their time was coming to an end.

That there would be nothing to hold him here soon.

The thought was depressing as hell. And what did that say about her? That she'd rather he be here making her miserable every day because she loved him and she couldn't tell him and she couldn't touch him, instead of on the opposite side of the world, which would at least give her aching heart a chance to recover.

Love really was cruel.

She dug a spoon around in the glass, which was more Milo than milk, and stirred it listlessly. Her ultimate comfort drink. Some people chose vodka—she chose a kids' chocolate milk drink. She reached over to the open tin she'd taken from the kitchen earlier and tipped two more spoonfuls into the glass and stirred, watching it as it mixed in, the glass mainly just a thick chocolaty sludge now.

She loaded a spoonful into her mouth and shut her eyes as the sweet crunch appeased her hormones.

She'd been drinking a lot of Milo lately. If she didn't watch it she'd be fat as a house. She looked down at her bare thighs. Was it just her funk or did she have more cellulite lately?

When a knock on the connecting door thundered a moment later she nearly upended the whole glass in her lap from fright. Some of it splashed out and landed on her shirt and flicked onto her neck as the door opened abruptly to reveal a rather brooding-looking Luke.

'I thought we were waiting for *permission* to enter *before* we entered?' Claudia griped as she wiped at the milky chocolate sludge on her neck.

It had been a long time since he'd been in her room and, conscious of her state of undress—and her bare, Milocellulitic legs—it was hard not to think about the kiss that had happened last time he'd been here.

The kiss that had almost become so much more.

Luke's breath seized in his chest for a moment. He couldn't believe what she was wearing. Or wasn't wearing, to be more precise. His gaze automatically drifted to her legs, his memory automatically drifting to how good it felt to have them wrapped around his waist.

And not forgetting that sexy awful blue and yellow palm-tree shirt that he'd fantasised about tearing off almost every night for three months.

She had to be wearing that.

'Sorry,' he apologised. 'I didn't think.' And he hadn't. He'd just wanted to come in and tell her he was leaving and get the hell out again.

But here she was. Not dressed to kill, not dressed to seduce, not dressed to attract.

But doing all three anyway.

For God's sake, she had a *milk moustache*. A milk moustache *should not,* in any way, shape or form, be sexy. But, God help him, he wanted to lick it right off her mouth.

'Well? What do you want, Luke?' she asked and he could hear the exasperation and wondered if it was born from the same well of frustration as his was.

He dragged his gaze off her mouth. 'I've booked a flight out lunchtime tomorrow.'

Something resembling a hammer blow hit Claudia fair in the chest at the unexpected news. Her heart beat painfully behind her ribs; a massive lump lodged itself in her throat making it hard to swallow, hard to breathe. She'd known it was happening soon but not this soon.

Not tomorrow.

She gripped the glass and handle of the spoon tight. 'I see.'

'I have to go back for this presentation, for that client I told you about. He only wants me.'

Claudia knew how the mysterious client felt. 'Okay.'

Luke had been prepared for tears and anger but not this quiet, calm acceptance. 'I wouldn't skip out if I didn't have to.' More quiet, more calmness from Claudia. 'It's my career,' he added.

'I said okay.'

The response was snappier and Luke was grateful to see some spark. 'You don't need me here, Claude,' he said gently.

Claudia looked at him, her heart really breaking now. Sure. But what about what she *wanted*?

This was it. He was really going.

'You don't know what I need.'

Luke sighed. She was right—he didn't. And he sure as hell didn't want to go there. It was dangerous territory for them both. 'I'll be back for the launch, I promise.'

Yeah, but then you'll be gone again. Claudia shrugged as she looked at him. 'Don't bother yourself.'

'I want to.'

'Really, there's no need. We've always known where your priorities lay.'

Luke felt lousy. 'Come on, Claude…I don't deserve that.'

Claudia shrugged. 'Just calling it like I see it.'

The unfairness of her statement stung but he chose to plough on. 'I'll be back for the opening,' he reiterated.

'Fine.'

Luke looked at her. He didn't like this cool and collected Claudia. He couldn't decide if he wanted to kiss her or shake her—anything to get some kind of reaction other than just sitting on the bed looking like his leaving was no big deal.

Saying okay and fine as if it were just another day.

'Hell, Claude.' He shook his head. 'You're hard on a man's ego.'

'Yeah, well, newsflash…I'm not here for your ego. I'm sure they'll appreciate it back in *London* though.'

Luke shoved his hands on his hips, deciding that shaking was looking like a good option. 'Fine,' he snapped. 'Have it your way.'

And he turned on his heel and stormed out of the room, slamming the door behind him.

A well of anger lashed Luke's insides as he strode into his room and began to pace up and down his floor. He knew what he was feeling was irrational. He'd made it clear all along that he was leaving and she was telling him it was fine. Telling him to go.

Making it easy for him.

But he knew all about words like *fine* and how women used them. If she wasn't fine with it, why didn't she just bloody well say so? And would it have killed her to show some kind of disappointment? He hadn't expected her to throw herself at his feet and beg him not to go; he hadn't wanted her to cry or cling.

But they'd made a good team, achieved a lot, dragged the Tropicana into the twenty-first century. Yes, there'd been tensions but they'd laughed and joked a lot too, reaffirmed a friendship that had fallen by the wayside.

Some emotion might have been nice. Instead of sitting all calm and cross-legged like some sexy, half-dressed, milk-moustached freaking…yogi!

His stomach took a tumble as his head filled with that vision and Luke clenched his fists. How was it possible to be so angry and want her so much at the same time? How was it possible to be so close to hating her and yet have a massive hard-on for her?

Goddamn it!

He stormed back into her room, not knocking at all this time. The spoon was halfway to her mouth and her eyes flew to his face. He braced his hands on his hips.

'I can't stand this any longer.'

She didn't say anything, just put the spoon back in the glass and waited. And in two strides he was at the bed, he was whisking the glass away and shoving it onto the bedside table, he was pushing her back against the pillows, reaching for the bottom of her awful shirt and in one quick move he'd grabbed both the edges and ripped.

'Luke,' Claudia gasped as buttons flew everywhere and her buttercup-yellow bra was exposed to his view.

'I've been wanting to do that for three damn months,' he growled.

Claudia knew she should be shocked, she should be scandalised, she should be outraged.

She *should* be trying to cover herself.

But the truth was he was eating her up with his eyes, burning up everything he touched with his gaze, and she was so turned on she could barely think straight.

'In about ten seconds I'm going to kiss you and then I'm going to go down on you and make you scream so loudly when you come, the whole hotel will be calling the cops, and if you don't want that then you better tell me to leave now.'

Claudia knew she did not have it in her power to tell him to leave. Yes, she should have more self-respect. He was leaving tomorrow and for him this was nothing more than slaking a thirst that had built and built and built over the months.

But she was pretty damn thirsty too and right now she'd take whatever she could get of him.

She didn't answer him; she simply reached down and unclipped the front opening of her bra.

Luke watched her breasts fall free and groaned. He didn't need any more encouragement. He fell on her, covering her with his body and kissing her into oblivion. Kisses that pulled at his groin and sank talons into the muscles of his belly. Kisses that called to a primal rhythm somewhere inside him. Kisses that wrapped a silken fist around his heart.

Kisses that tasted of pent-up desire and chocolate milk. 'You taste amazing,' he panted against her mouth, moving to kiss her neck. 'God,' he groaned, 'here too,' as his tongue found another sweet spot.

Claudia slid her hands up under his shirt, filling her palms with warm male flesh as she angled her neck to give him greater access. 'Milo...spilt...' she murmured, too far gone to string a coherent sentence together.

Luke groaned, wanting more of that. Wanting more Milo-flavoured Claudia. He pulled away slightly, reaching for the discarded glass on the side table. Claudia mewed in protest as he levered himself up and straddled her body.

'Shh,' he said as he settled on the tops of her thighs,

scooping up a spoonful of chocolate sludge. 'I want to eat chocolate milk off you.' And before she could protest he lowered the spoon to the hollow at the base of her throat and upended it.

Claudia gasped, her back arching, not because it was cold or even particularly runny, but because her nipples beaded instantly into tight, almost painful points. And he went there next, scooping more Milo sludge from the glass and painting it on her nipples, stopping to suck it off thoroughly, reducing her to a whimpering mess before repainting them again, licking it off again and then trailing the spoon down lower. To her belly button, where he played over and over, dousing the hard little button in thick chocolaty sludge, then licking it off, dousing, then licking, dousing then licking and all the while his fingers taunting the stiff points of her nipples until she was almost crazy with it.

He pasted her in Milo right to the edge of her matching yellow underwear and then he was stripping her out of it and she heard the spoon tink against the glass one last time and then she felt the warm sticky ooze of it join the other slickness between her legs.

Somewhere she heard the dull thud of the glass being discarded and then Luke was settling between her thighs, using his big shoulders to push her legs wider and she opened for him shamelessly, bucking when his tongue touched her.

'Luke,' she gasped.

Luke held her fast as he licked every last morsel of salty, chocolaty goodness from between her legs, circling and thrusting, teasing as he went. She was so close, panting and begging him for release, but this was going to be their last time and he wanted to savour every last drop of her. He wanted to feast here as he'd done that first time with her breasts.

He wanted her to remember this for as long as she lived. *He* wanted to remember it as long as *he* lived.

So he refused to give into her wild urgings, staying

right where he was until even he couldn't wait for her to come a second longer. And pushing her over the edge was so, so easy. A few quick flicks in the right place and she screamed—exactly as he'd predicted—her release, holding his head to her and he didn't stop, not even when she begged him to, he just held onto her hips harder and kept going until every last drop of pleasure had been wrung from her.

But even then he didn't stop.

When he was satisfied she was thoroughly spent he was determined to give her more, revive the fire that he knew still flickered. Crawling back up her body, he reefed down his track pants and underwear, his hardness nudging all her soft heat.

Claudia's eyes flew open and she gasped as all his delicious thickness pushed against her. Even though she was limp and exhausted, her body recognised this need on a primal level. Her back arched and she reached for his buttocks, holding him there.

'Yes,' she said, wanting him inside her with a sudden ferocity. Wanting him to stay in her for ever. Loving the loom of him. Loving the bulge of his biceps, loving the proximity of his chest, loving the closeness of his mouth.

Just plain old loving him.

She linked her arms around his neck. 'God, yes, please.'

And when he thrust inside her in one easy move she cried out, knowing she'd never want another man like this.

That only Luke would ever do.

And when he thrust again and again, groaning deep and slow in perfect time, building her quickly, she fought it off, pushed it away, hanging in there with him, desperate to be there with him at the end.

'Damn it, Claude,' he gasped in her ear, 'let go.'

'No,' she panted. 'Not without you.' If this was to be their last time then they were going out together.

Luke grimaced and on one last thrust and a primal groan that sounded as if it had come from the depths of the earth beneath the Tropicana itself, he came, over and over, calling out her name.

Then and only then did she follow him into the light.

Claudia stirred when Luke rolled off her onto his back a few minutes later. His breathing was still irregular, as was hers. They didn't move or say anything for long moments. Then Luke rolled on his side, slid his arm across her belly and pulled her close.

But Claudia resisted. She couldn't do that. She could make love with him one last time, give her something to exist on in the long lonely nights to follow, but she couldn't snuggle with him afterwards as if there were love between them.

As if he weren't leaving tomorrow.

That *would* break her heart and she just couldn't do it.

Luke frowned. 'Claude?'

She rolled on her side, away from him. 'Just go, Luke.'

He slid his hand onto her shoulder. 'Claudia.'

'I'm okay,' she assured, shrugging his hand away. 'I'm fine. But let's not pretend this is something it's not.'

Luke wanted to protest but ultimately he could see her point. They weren't in a relationship. Staying the night with her would just make it harder in the morning. At least this way, they both knew where they stood.

He rolled to his side of the bed and pushed to his feet, adjusting his clothing. A sudden thought struck him. 'You could be pregnant—we didn't use a condom.' Protection had been the last thing on his mind. He'd just needed to be inside her.

'I've been on the pill since I was nineteen, Luke. I'm not pregnant.'

He shoved a hand through his hair. 'I *have* to go, Claude.'

'I know.'

'I told you it was only temporary, that I'd have to go back eventually.'

'I know.'

Luke looked down at her, her back stubbornly turned away. He hated the distance even though he'd been the one to implement it. He felt a sudden urge to explain. 'My divorce…it was…hard. I can't go there again.'

'I'm not asking you to.'

Luke nodded. He knew that. But a part of him couldn't help wish that she had. 'Will I see you tomorrow?'

'I'll be round,' she murmured.

He stared at her back, torn between leaving and climbing back into bed with her—consequences be damned. But he'd learned too much from bitter experience to know the perils of disregarding consequences. 'Goodnight.'

Whether or not she answered he didn't hear as he walked back to his room and shut the interconnecting door with a soft click.

CHAPTER NINETEEN

'ARE YOU OKAY, dear?' her mother asked as Claudia dashed past the reception desk on her way to the kitchen to check the hors d'oeuvres were on track to be served in half an hour.

'Fine and dandy,' she chirped, before disappearing into Tony's domain.

Lena looked at Gloria. Avery and Jonah looked at each other. They were all poised to join the cocktail party down on the beach. 'Oh, dear. I see what you mean.'

'Yup,' Avery murmured. 'She's all *fine and dandy* again.'

'And she's been like that since Luke left?' Gloria asked.

Jonah, looking resplendent in a tux, grimaced. 'Oh, yes. Two whole weeks of her fine and dandiness.'

Gloria tutted as she shook her head. 'My son is an idiot.'

'Yes,' Lena agreed tersely. 'He is.'

Gloria turned distressed eyes onto Jonah. 'Can you talk some sense into him? He'll listen to you.'

Jonah shrugged. 'Unfortunately, Gloria, some things a man just has to figure out for himself.'

'When was he supposed to arrive?' Lena asked.

'Six hours ago,' Gloria confirmed. 'His flight was delayed out of Singapore. Which is why I told him he should have booked an earlier flight, that he was cutting it fine if anything happened.' Disapproval and anxiety laced her voice. 'I think he should have landed by now though.'

Claudia strode from the kitchen, her red gown fluttering around her ankles, 'Okay, are we all ready?' she asked.

'You guys go ahead. I'll wait for Luke,' Gloria said.

'All right,' Claudia said, smiling brightly, refusing to let his looming presence upset her equilibrium.

She'd held it together for the last two weeks just fine; she wasn't going to let his imminent arrival take the gloss off the night they'd all worked so hard towards. Even if she did feel as if she was about to throw up as the nerves in her stomach knotted ever tighter.

Where was he?

She'd been strung tight as a bow all day as the full gamut of emotions had run riot through her body and she wished he'd just get here already. Get the awkward, stilted greetings out of the way so she could enjoy this night she and Avery had been planning for a month.

Instead of waiting for Prince Charming—*à la Captain Sexypants*—like some lovelorn teenager.

'Let's go have some fun,' she said to the people who meant the most to her in the whole world.

The people who *did* love her.

Avery, who was looking as ethereally gorgeous as ever in a smoky silver frock, smiled and looped her arm through Claudia's. 'Let's party,' she said.

Luke glanced at the dash clock in his rented car. Damn it— he was an hour late. He cursed the state of the roads and the interminable stops for roadworks. He cursed the airline. He cursed the rental company that had mixed up his booking.

It seemed everything had conspired against him getting to the Tropicana Nights on time.

His mother, who was fanatically punctual, would not be impressed. And Claudia? No two ways about it—she'd be really pissed at him.

So what else was new?

His heart beat a little faster at the mere thought of seeing her again, angry or not. He'd thought about her obsessively for two weeks. Reruns of their last night together had played over and over in his head.

He hadn't missed the tension; he hadn't missed the temptation. But he *had* missed *her*.

God, how he'd missed her!

A decade in the UK and she'd barely crossed his mind. Three months back in Crescent Cove with her and he could barely think of anything else.

He felt as nervous as a teenager on his first date.

He didn't know what to expect, what he was going to say, how he would feel. How *she* would feel. He just knew coming back, seeing her again, had been the one bright spot in these last two weeks, getting him through interminably long days at the office, days that he'd once thrived on and had now lost their lustre.

He knew it was just jet lag and readjusting to the crappy London weather and having to wear a suit and tie again instead of boardies and a T-shirt. He'd fallen out of the groove and was having a hard time getting back into it. But he hadn't been able to explain how scoring the firm's biggest account to date—an enormous coup—had left him feeling so…underwhelmed.

How working on Jonah's low-budget ad campaign had been more satisfying and stimulating than the slick multi-million-dollar one that had taken up months of his life.

Coming back to Crescent Cove, with an office that looked out over the mighty Pacific and was less than a minute's walk to a beach of the finest powdery white sand, had somehow tripped a switch in his brain that refused to be reset.

A few months ago the only powder he'd cared about was the type that covered the ski fields of St Moritz. Now, he found himself yearning for the sun and the surf.

Another road worker with a stop sign loomed ahead and he raked a frustrated hand through his hair, bringing it down to rub at his smooth jaw as he decelerated. It made him think of Claudia. Of the conversation—the *naked* conversation— he'd had with her about stubble. He'd shaved on the plane.

He didn't know why—years of conditioning, he supposed—but suddenly even that annoyed him.

Shaving twice a day? What the hell for?

The bored-looking road worker stood aside, flipping the sign around and, ignoring the slow sign, Luke accelerated quickly away.

'It's going great, don't you think?' Avery said as she threw her arm around Claudia, who was watching everything from the sidelines.

Claudia nodded. 'It looks amazing!'

And it did. Avery and her vision had transformed the foreshore, where the avenue of palms met the beach, into a fairyland of lights strung through the trees and the nearby foliage.

A jazz band played on a temporary wooden platform that had been erected on the beach. It was large enough for people to dance and some had already taken advantage. The whole atmosphere was magical, the snazzy couples dancing to smooth saxophone notes against the backdrop of a russet ocean sunset were just the icing on the cake.

A roll of red carpet bordered and lit by flaming tiki torches formed a pathway from the foreshore to the spa where guests came and went exclaiming over the wonders of the posh new facility. Another red-carpeted, tiki-lit pathway led to the nearest luxury tent, drawing more appreciative buzz.

With travel agents and influential tourism representatives here both Claudia and Avery were confident they'd be filling the new luxury accommodation before too much longer.

But it wasn't just the business community who were kicking up their heels. Avery's brilliant idea to combine the black-tie launch with a fundraiser for the cyclone-ravaged area had ensured that plenty of locals were also out in force. Prizes of prestigious spa and accommodation packages had been offered and the locals of Crescent Cove had glammed up and brought their wallets.

And all this serenaded by something that no amount of money could buy. The swish of a calm ocean and the kiss of a gentle breeze. The weather had been the one wild card but even it had bowed to Avery's superior organisational skills. It was a gorgeous, crisp, starry North Queensland winter night. The quarter moon was on the rise, the horizon glowed with orange and pinks and the first stars in the velvety evening dazzled like diamonds.

After the destruction of a few months ago, the weather gods were smiling.

The only thing that was missing was Luke.

'I wouldn't have done half as good a job by myself,' Claudia said, dragging her thoughts back from the one topic that could cast a pall over her entire evening. 'Your eye for detail is awesome.'

Avery hugged her harder and they both just watched the spectacle for a few moments. 'Are you sure you're okay, Claude?' Avery ventured after a while. 'You seem really tense. Are you worried about seeing Luke again?'

'I'm fine,' Claudia hastily assured, not wanting her focus derailed. The party was here and now and Luke…

Luke was late.

'And dandy?'

Claudia glanced at her friend. 'Avery.'

'Claude, I love you, you're my best friend. I *hate* seeing you miserable.'

Claudia frowned—miserable? But she'd been killing herself to be chipper and chatty and chirpy. Just good old Claude. *Business as usual.* She glanced at Avery, looked into eyes that knew her way too well.

And she couldn't deal with it now.

'When does Raoul's studio perform?' she asked, looking back to the beach stage as she, not so deftly, changed the subject.

Avery sighed and checked her watch. 'During the hors d'oeuvres. So…soon.'

'Good,' she said. 'I'm starving.'

Even though she knew food was never going to sit well inside her squalling belly.

Luke followed his mother and the jazzy music towards the beach, straightening the bow tie his mother had hastily thrown together for him. The urge to stop in and see the finished spa and the accommodation was strong but he was already late enough. He pulled up short when he entered the clearing on the foreshore.

'Wow,' he said as myriad fairy lights dazzled his eyes and the party atmosphere instantly embraced him.

'It's spectacular, isn't it?' His mother beamed.

'Amazing,' he agreed.

'Claude and Avery have worked so hard,' she said.

Luke nodded. He'd not been involved in too much of the launch preparations, knowing it was in good hands with Avery. But this...this was utterly breathtaking.

His gaze roamed the classy crowd as his mother chatted about the set-up and the number of local dignitaries that were attending. Luke couldn't give a rat's arse that the state minister for tourism was here—he only cared about one person.

One woman.

A procession of waiters filed past him carrying trays laden with finger food, the aromas of garlic and basil lingering in their wake. They dispersed throughout the guests offering a range of gastronomic delights. Jonah spotted him and strode over to greet him, bringing somebody with him.

'You don't scrub up so bad, old friend.' Luke grinned, shaking Jonah's hand after he'd been introduced to the local tourism council chair.

He shrugged. 'Avery likes me in a tux.'

Luke felt a pang in his chest at the goofy smile Jonah had plastered to his face. As if he already knew how lucky he was going to get later.

The three of them made small talk about the resort and

the long-term recovery of the area as the waiters came around and entertainment took to the stage but Luke was too distracted to eat or be entertained. Too distracted for local politics as he surreptitiously searched the crowd for one particular person. He finally spotted her standing to one side with Avery and, damn, if she wasn't wearing *that* dress.

Everything lurched inside him.

For some reason he'd expected to see her in her usual travesty of polyester—ridiculous really, given that they were both at a black-tie cocktail party. Not that it would have mattered had she been in her uniform. She looked equally good in both, not to mention the fact that he'd helped her out of both in varying degrees of urgency.

She had her hair swept up as it had been that night in Cairns, a frangipani tucked behind her ear.

Do not think about that night in Cairns.

But it was hard not to. There wasn't one part of him that didn't rejoice in seeing her. That didn't want to wrap her up in his arms. That didn't want to drag her away from this party and have his wicked way with her.

Two weeks had felt like two decades and he was gripped by a fierce yearning to be deep inside her again.

Relief flowed through him at his strong physical reaction. He'd been confused by his feelings, unsure of how he felt about somebody he shouldn't be feeling those kinds of things for. Somebody who didn't want to feel them either. But sex he understood. Sex he could pigeonhole. Sex was biology and natural urges.

It wasn't emotional; it was physical.

He'd been lusting after her. And that was an easy fix.

He was just about to stop making polite conversation and excuse himself when a familiar guy in a tuxedo approached Claudia.

Raoul.

A surge of pure possession filled him as Raoul said something to her and both she and Avery laughed.

His heart thudded in his chest as the Spanish charmer flirted easily. Suddenly Luke wasn't feeling so sure of himself.

Suddenly this was a whole new ballgame. Biology, natural urges, lust—they all felt frivolous.

What he was feeling now, watching Raoul with Claudia, was much more primal.

Much deeper. Much more profound.

He watched as Raoul took Claudia's hand and led her to the dance floor and he had to suppress a roar of outrage that rose in his chest.

No!

It was like Cairns all over again. Except a thousand times worse because Claudia was the woman he loved—yes, he *loved* her! —and he wasn't into sharing.

'Excuse me,' he said, interrupting the conversation he hadn't really been listening to anyway. 'I'm sorry,' he apologised. 'There's somebody I really have to see.'

Jonah glanced across to where Luke was looking and nodded. He held out his hand and shook Luke's. 'Go get her, man.'

Unfortunately Luke was waylaid a couple of times but he managed to get to the stage just as the song was ending.

Perfect timing.

'Claude.'

Claudia stilled in the circle of Raoul's arms as a very familiar accent turned her legs to jelly. She leaned in to Raoul for a moment for support and, bless him, he ignored the thunder on Luke's face and let her.

'Mi querida. Are you okay?'

Claudia nodded as she pulled away from him. 'Thanks, Raoul. I'm fine.'

For a moment Claudia thought Raoul was going to challenge Luke, but she gave his arm a squeeze. 'I'll see you later,' she said.

Raoul, ever the gentleman, bowed slightly and took his

leave. Claudia watched him weave through the dancers, collecting herself for a moment before turning to face Luke.

Luke in a tux.

Her stomach dropped at the mere sight of him, her heart rattling along like the lid on a steaming kettle. But she was determined to play it cool.

'You made it,' she said as he held out his arms and she slid into a polite waltz stance and started moving, careful to keep her distance, hoping he couldn't feel the flutter of her pulse at her wrist. 'I thought you must have changed your mind.'

She felt him tense for a moment. 'I said I would be here. I'm here.'

'Why, Luke?'

Claudia was proud of the steadiness of her voice, considering she wanted to stamp her foot and beat her hands against his chest like a spoilt princess or a toddler having a tantrum.

'What's the point when you're just going to turn around and go back to London? It's a long way to come for three lousy days.'

It had been two weeks since Luke had wanted to shake her but only a minute back in her company and the urge returned with a vengeance. 'Because I love you, you irritating woman,' he said, then promptly dipped her and pashed her in front of everyone.

CHAPTER TWENTY

DESPITE HER SHOCK, it didn't take Claudia's heart—or hormones—long to betray her. Her senses filled up with him and she clung to his lapels, kissing him back, two weeks of sexual frustration bubbling up inside her.

It wasn't until the racket of applause finally penetrated their passionate bubble that sense returned and Claudia pushed against his chest, struggling for release. He yanked her up and let her go to more applause from the crowd.

She smiled awkwardly for a moment, then glared at him before muttering, 'Follow me.'

She marched ahead, furious with him and herself. She kicked her stilettos off as she hit the beach, leaving them where they were as she gathered the hem of her dress and made a beeline for the shoreline, conscious of him following more sedately behind.

'How dare you?' she said, turning on him when she was close enough to the water to drown him in it should the urge take over.

Luke held up his hands. 'Claude.'

'Don't you Claude me,' she snapped. 'Don't you come here acting all he-man. All…' she took in his particular brand of delicious in his tuxedo and nearly swooned at his feet '…Captain Sexypants and act like a Neanderthal and expect me to drop at your feet.'

Captain Sexypants? 'Okay.'

'And don't you okay me either,' she seethed, completely oblivious to the romance of the stars overhead and the lapping waves. 'You expect me to believe that you suddenly love me? That this isn't about you being a horny, jealous, possessive jerk?'

Luke had to admit she made a good point. 'Oh, no, it's about all of those things as well,' he admitted candidly. 'When I saw you across the avenue before, it was absolutely about getting you into bed in the fastest possible way. To be honest, it was a relief to feel such a strong physical connection because then I didn't have to think about anything deeper. And then Raoul showed...'

'And you decided you'd come over all territorial and stake your claim?'

Luke wasn't going to apologise for going after what he wanted. A decade in advertising had taught him to hold firm. 'No. I realised what I feel for you goes way beyond the physical.'

Claudia snorted. She refused to let his pretty words sway her. 'Really? Well, too bad. You can't just waltz in here, throw the L word around and use me for three days before you waltz out again. I'm not going to be your little Aussie bonk-buddy.'

'I'm not interested in something casual. I love you, Claudia Davis.'

Claudia shook her head, quashing the excited flutter in her chest. No. She wasn't falling for that. 'You told me two weeks ago that you *couldn't go there again* after your divorce. You expect me to believe that's all changed in just two weeks? That you're suddenly over the most emotionally devastating experience of your life and that you've fallen in love with me? In *two weeks*?'

Luke shook his head. 'Tonight, actually. I fell in love with you tonight.'

'Oh, *great*. That's *so* much better,' Claudia said, folding her arms across her chest.

'What happened with Philippa...the divorce...you're right, it was devastating and I've been clinging to that as an excuse to focus on my career. But I looked across at you tonight and suddenly, all the hurt and humiliation, none of it mattered any more. Yes, I loved Philippa but the truth is, I didn't *fall* in love with her. Not like just now.'

He took a step closer to Claudia because he needed her to hear him. 'We fell into a relationship, we were a convenient couple. We were always at work together, we had a lot in common but I didn't *know* her. Not like I know you. You've been part of the fabric of my life for ever. You're in my DNA, Claude.'

Claudia glared at him, not sure she liked the biological comparison. 'How romantic. I sound like a disease.'

Luke ignored her sarcasm. 'I guess you are,' he admitted. 'You infected me a long time ago and you've been lying dormant inside me until today and now you've totally overrun me. I can't believe it's taken me so long to see what was right in front of me.'

Claudia wanted nothing more than to throw herself into his arms. To take his words at face value and make a grab for her happiness while it was standing right in front of her. But it all just seemed too good to be true. Could love between old friends ever be that simple?

He lived on the other side of the world, for crying out loud!

'Oh, yeah, and how do you see it working between us?' she demanded. 'With you in London and me here?'

Luke shrugged, unfazed. It had taken him a long time to trust enough to love another woman—he wasn't going to do it by halves. 'I don't want to be anywhere you're not and if that means here then so be it.'

Claudia couldn't believe the words coming from his mouth. In just about every way possible it was exactly what she'd wanted to hear. Except *if that means here* was hardly a ringing endorsement. She'd loved Luke most of her life—he'd definitely been in *her* DNA. She knew how much he'd wanted London. How much he'd wanted to be at the forefront of the global advertising industry.

How long before he resented his choice? Before he resented her?

'Come on, Claude,' he murmured. 'I think you might love me too. Give me a chance.'

Claudia looked at him and shook her head, her heart breaking just a little bit more. Of course she loved him. She loved everything about him. Including his pride and his self-respect and how much his career was wrapped up in that.

'So what are you going to do?' she asked. 'Play hotel manager with me? Something you've already rejected?'

'No.' Luke shook his head. He loved the Tropicana but he needed something else. 'Start my own business here, I guess.'

Claudia snorted—it didn't sound as if he'd put a whole lot of thought into it. 'You *guess*?'

Luke raked a frustrated hand through his hair. 'I know it sounds like I'm making this up as I go along but I didn't realise how…over London I was until I came back here. I'd put my dissatisfaction down to work…to the divorce. It wasn't until I came here I realised… This place kind of got to me again. I took it for granted growing up—that was stupid. I really enjoyed working on Jonah's budget campaign. It felt…grass roots. I think I could make that into something.'

Luke surprised even himself with his words but it suddenly felt *right*. Like being here with Claudia did.

'I thought you needed the bright lights?'

'Yeah,' he admitted. 'I did. But I was eighteen, Claude. I've been there and done that. People are allowed to change their minds.'

'I didn't.'

Luke smiled. That was just one of the things he loved about her—ever since his mother had given her that clipboard for Christmas, she'd been so sure.

'People are allowed to stay the same as well.'

Claudia looked at his beautiful face, nicely delineated by the slither of moonlight emanating from the quarter moon.

Thanks to his close shave she could see every line and dip of his jaw and cheeks; she could even make out the remnant of his Crescent Cove tan not yet faded after two weeks in rainy London.

She loved it. Loved every plane and angle. She even loved the ruthless smoothness of his face. But it was a blaring reminder of who he really was. She took a couple of paces towards him, lifted her hand and ran her fingers over his face. He watched her as she caressed his cheek, his jaw, his chin. The top of his lip.

All perfectly smooth. Perfectly London.

Not Crescent Cove.

'You shaved on the plane?'

Luke nodded. 'Of course.'

Claudia dropped her hand. He thought he wanted to be here with her? She didn't think so. Initially maybe when there was lots of sex and sunshine, and then what, when his business didn't match up to his expectations and the bright lights called again? She couldn't risk it. Having him for a while only to lose him again?

Maybe he did love her—her breath caught at the thought, her heart tap-danced in her chest, but she quashed them instantly. She just didn't think he'd thought it through properly. He was acting on lust and desire and a screwed-up sense of possession and she needed more than his jealous bullshit.

'I have to get back,' she said.

Luke took a pace towards her, worried at the sadness, the finality in her tone. 'Claude.'

'Don't,' she said. 'Don't come here with half-arsed, on-the-fly plans.' She picked her hem up again. 'I have to get back,' she said, turning away.

Luke watched her go, frustrated by her stubbornness but encouraged. 'You never told me if you loved me,' he called after her.

She turned to face him, walking slowly backwards. 'I've

always loved you. Doesn't mean it's enough,' she said before turning her back on him again.

Luke knew that was true. But it was a start.

Claudia was in her office working on the housekeeping roster, or pretending to anyway, the next morning when her mother knocked on the door. 'Thought you might like a cuppa,' she said.

Claudia smiled. 'Thanks.' She often thought rosters should be done with a bottle of vodka but a cup of tea would suffice.

'Last night was a huge success,' her mother said as she sat in the chair on the other side of the desk. 'The phone's been running hot down at the retreat all morning.'

'Yes. And we raised fifty grand too. Not bad at all.'

They chatted for a while about the party and the Tropicana before her mother gave her *that* look.

'I saw you and Luke disappear down to the beach last night.'

Claudia almost told her to stop but she'd noticed things were a little tense between her and Gloria and she didn't want that. Maybe if they knew the truth they'd see there was never going to be anything between her and Luke.

'It's never going to happen, Mum. We want different things.'

Her mother put down her cup of tea. 'Claude…we didn't give you this place to tie you down, to act like some kind of anchor to keep you here. If you want to be with Luke and he's on the other side of the world then go and be with him. Do whatever you need to do. We can get managers in. I know you love the Tropicana but it's not worth losing someone you love over.'

Claudia blinked, mentally rejecting the suggestion outright. Leave the Tropicana? It had never occurred to her. She stared at her mother, who looked deadly serious.

'It is okay, you know.'

Claudia opened her mouth to tell her mother no, but her quiet words of acceptance hit like a truck. Was it okay?

Maybe she'd been waiting for permission all these years. For someone to say it *was* okay to leave.

The thought was foreign; she'd never wanted to do anything else, but hadn't Luke said last night that people were allowed to change their minds?

What would she do, who could she be if she stepped outside the security of the Tropicana?

The thought was terrifying but if she had Luke?

She put her cup of tea down, her heart racing a little as she stood. 'Thanks, Mum.'

She smiled back. 'He's down at the beach.'

Luke stood on the near-deserted beach, his ankles in the water, looking at the Tropicana glowing white and proud in the morning sun like the glorious old relic she was. He could see the new spa building through the foliage and a couple of the luxury tents. In a year's time the foliage regrowth would obscure most of it, hopefully.

A surge of satisfaction rose in his chest. He was looking forward to that.

Now he understood what Claudia had been rabbiting on about every time she mentioned their legacy. This place—the place of his childhood, the legacy of his heart—was in his DNA as surely as she was.

Sure, he'd thrived in London. Hell, he'd *needed* London. He'd had to go away to appreciate what he'd really had. What had been right under his nose.

Including Claudia.

But he got it now.

A movement in his peripheral vision caught his eye and he glanced over to find Claudia coming his way looking resplendent in polyester and a ponytail. Avery had shown him the new sample uniform last night and it was a vast improvement but in some ways he'd be sorry to see the old, ugly one go—it had some very hot memories.

She didn't bother greeting him, just stood in front of him with folded arms and said, 'You love me?'

Luke's heart pounded. Could this be…? 'Uh-huh.'

She looked at him a bit longer. 'I'll come to London with you,' she said and turned to go.

Luke frowned. Wait. *What?* 'No.'

Claudia whipped around. 'What do you mean, no? You love me, I love you. Let's just go to London already.'

Luke chuckled at her crankiness. 'No,' he said again.

'I swear to God, Luke, I'm trying to compromise here.'

'No, you're not. You're trying to sacrifice what you want for what you *think* I want.'

'London is where your career is. I'm not going to hold you back.'

'I don't care about London. Not any more. But you… *you* care about that…' he pointed to the Tropicana '…and here's a newsflash—I do too. I can do my job anywhere. I don't need a fancy office or a city skyline. But there's only one Tropicana.'

Claudia glared at him looking all cool and clean-shaven. Even in his boardies and T-shirt the man screamed London. 'You're being impossible.'

He chuckled again. 'I don't think I'm the only one.'

She shook her head and turned on her heel and marched away.

The following morning, after another long, restless night with her on the *other* side of the connecting door, Luke looked at himself in the bathroom mirror.

He knew women found him attractive. He knew Claudia found him *very* attractive. Hell—she loved him. She'd always loved him. That was what she'd told him. So why couldn't he get her to take the leap with him?

He rubbed his hands through his hair in frustration and then across his jaw. The slight rasp of his whiskers had him reaching automatically for his shaving cream and he opened his palm and squirted a dollop in, watching it foam up.

He slapped it on, remembering how Claudia had touched his face the other night and the conversation they'd had in bed when she'd suggested he grew some stubble. Shaving was London, he'd told her, stubble was Crescent Cove.

His hand stopped then as an idea slowly dawned and he smiled at his reflection before turning on the tap and ducking over the sink to wash it all away.

Claudia looked up from the reception desk a couple of hours later as Luke approached. He was in boardies and a T-shirt and no shoes and there was an overnight shadow on his jaw that did funny things to her equilibrium.

'Morning,' he said, acknowledging both her and Isis. 'Jonah and I are heading north to catch some waves,' he said. 'Be back in a couple of hours.'

Claudia couldn't tear her eyes off his jawline. 'Uh-huh,' she said.

She and Isis watched him walk away. 'Mmm. Captain Sexy-Stubble,' Isis murmured.

The next morning was the same. More surfing, more unshaven jaw. By the third morning he had a very definite three-day growth and it was all Claudia could do not to reach out and touch it.

'Not shaving these days?' Claudia said, trying to sound nonchalant.

'Nah, shaving's for city boys.' He grinned and winked at Isis before heading out of the door again.

'Oh, he's playing *dirty* now,' Isis said as they watched him walk away.

Claudia pursed her lips, refusing to say anything.

But *damn,* she'd known he'd look hot with stubble.

* * *

She was waiting for him when he returned in the afternoon, the connecting door wide open.

'I know what you're doing,' she said, entering his room as soon as she heard his door open. His boardies were damp and his hair was wet and the shaggy jawline was the cherry on top of his very delicious beach-bum look.

Luke suppressed a smile. 'Oh? What's that?'

She crossed her arms. 'The stubble.'

He stroked the back of his hand up his throat. 'You want to touch it, don't you?' He grinned.

Claudia glared. 'Luke.'

Luke sighed at the reprimand in her voice. 'Claude,' he said, moving towards her until he was just a hand's reach away. 'I've thrown my shaving foam in the bin. I'm not going back to London. I'm *done* with London.'

He reached for her then, tentatively at first, sliding a hand onto her waist. When she didn't push him away, he tugged her closer. He looked into her eyes, a kaleidoscope of conflict.

'*I love you.* I'm setting up business right here and I'm never shaving regularly again. Now how about you stop being all sacrificial and stoic and just kiss me already?'

Claudia wanted to. She wanted to very badly. She wanted to throw caution to the wind and let him ravage her with his stubbly kisses. 'The Tropicana has never been your dream. I can't…' She paused, searching for the right words. 'I wouldn't survive if you decided it wasn't enough for you some time down the track.'

Luke smiled at her gently. 'The Tropicana is big enough for both our dreams. And besides…the Tropicana *is* you and *you're* my dream. *I love you.* Nothing else matters. Nothing.'

He leaned into her neck and nuzzled it where her pulse beat frantically and was satisfied by her low, throaty moan.

'Tell me you love me,' he said, pulling away.

Claudia ran a finger along his jawline from ear to chin, loving the spikiness against her skin. 'You know I do.'

Luke went for her throat again, moving higher this time. 'Tell me.'

Claudia angled her neck and shut her eyes as a wave of goose bumps sounded a warning call to the rest of her body. 'I love you.'

And, *damn*, didn't it feel good to get it off her chest?

Luke nipped her triumphantly and she gasped, grabbing two handfuls of his shirt and pulling him closer. 'Don't stop,' she moaned. She'd been lying awake for nights thinking about him in the next room, grinding her heels into the bed to stop herself from going to him.

Luke smiled as he stroked his tongue where his teeth had just been. 'I'm never going to stop,' he said.

'I'm going to hold you to that,' she murmured.

Luke grinned against her neck, then, in one swift movement, picked her up and carried her over to the bed, dumping her in the middle.

His gaze roved over her looking all tousled and sexy despite the uniform. 'Unless you want me to rip that—' he pointed to the hideous polyester '—off you again, I suggest you take it off right now.'

Claudia grinned, grabbed the two edges of her shirt and ripped, buttons flying everywhere.

The new uniforms were arriving tomorrow.

'We are going to be *so* good together.' He grinned.

Claudia smiled up at him, her heart almost too big for her chest. 'Yes, we are.'

EPILOGUE

Six months later

THE STAGE WAS set for a far north Queensland double wedding in the way only Avery could orchestrate. The powdery sand was blindingly white, the ocean was as clear and flat as cut glass, the sky was a stunning blue dome that not one cloud was game enough to besmirch.

Mother Nature knew better than to ruin an Avery Shaw creation.

'It's perfect, Avery,' Claudia whispered, squeezing her best friend's hand as they stood with their fathers before the petal-strewn sandy aisle, waiting for the music to strike up.

'*They're* perfect,' Avery whispered back, looking at their men waiting at the other end.

Claudia nodded. 'Yes, they are,' she agreed as the first violin note rent the tropical air and the guests all turned in their beribboned chairs, then stood, smiling at the brides.

The two women couldn't have looked more different. Avery, dressed in designer squillions, looked all lean and long in her filmy white mermaid gown that brushed the sand, her shoulders bare, her hair falling in long, elegant, surfy waves down her back, a Swarovski crystal flower catching up one side of her locks in dramatic fashion.

Claudia, despite threatening to wear her uniform, looked stunning in a white, georgette slip dress with shoestring straps. It hugged her body close and fluttered around her ankles. She wore her hair swept up as she had that night she and Luke had first made love, a hibiscus flower tucked behind her ear.

The only things in common were their simple frangipani posies.

Luke held out his hand for her and smiled as she reached him and Claudia's heart felt as if it were bursting from her chest. He was looking his shaggy best, all suntanned and stubbly, his hair longer now and sunstreaked.

'You look beautiful,' he murmured.

'So do you.'

And he did, his mocha-coloured trousers and cream shirt showing off his tan and his muscles to perfection. He'd thrived on the challenge of setting up his own business and become honed and fit from his early morning beach runs.

'Are we ready?' the celebrant asked.

Claudia looked at Avery. Her father was murmuring something to her and Claudia was pleased that Avery's parents had set aside their differences and had both travelled from the US to be here for her today. Mr Shaw kissed his daughter on the cheek, then passed her hand to a scrummy-looking Jonah, clad in sand-coloured linen trousers and white linen shirt.

'We're ready,' Jonah said.

Hull, who was sitting beside him, a big white bow attached to his collar, barked in agreement much to everyone's amusement.

And with the mighty Pacific in front of them and their beloved Tropicana behind, the couples pledged their love and fidelity.

'You may kiss your brides,' the celebrant murmured, after the rings were exchanged and the ceremony came to an end.

Jonah whooped and dramatically dipped Avery to much applause. Claudia laughed and shook her head, enjoying their moment until Luke picked her up, her feet dangling well clear of the sand, and twirled her in his arms.

'You've made me happier than I ever knew I could be,' he said.

Claudia smiled, wrapping her arms around his neck. 'I love you,' she said, pulling him close, kissing him with greedy intent.

When they finally surfaced some time later her head was spinning and she grinned at him. 'I feel giddy.'

'Good.' Luke chuckled. 'Because you make *me* giddy.'

And then he twirled her around and around and around beneath the tropical sun.

* * * * *

ROAD TRIP WITH THE ELIGIBLE BACHELOR

MICHELLE DOUGLAS

At the age of eight **Michelle Douglas** was asked what she wanted to be when she grew up. She answered, 'A writer.' Years later she read an article about romance writing and thought, Ooh, that'll be fun. She was right. When she's not writing she can usually be found with her nose buried in a book. She is currently enrolled in an English Masters programme for the sole purpose of indulging her reading and writing habits further. She lives in a leafy suburb of Newcastle, on Australia's east coast, with her own romantic hero—husband Greg, who is the inspiration behind all her happy endings.

Michelle would love you to visit her at her website: www.michelle-douglas.com

CHAPTER ONE

'HELLO.' QUINN LAVERTY tried to find a smile for the customer service clerk on the other side of the counter. She raised her voice to be heard above the jostling crowd. 'I'm here to collect the car I booked.'

'Name, please?'

Quinn gave him her details and tried to slide her credit card free from its slot in her purse with one hand. Chase hung off her other hand, all of his six-year-old weight balanced on one leg and her arm as he stretched as far as he could reach along the counter with his toy car, making the requisite 'broom-broom' noises.

She made him straighten and stand on two legs and then grimaced at the customer beside her who'd been 'driven over' by said toy car. 'I'm sorry.'

'No problem at all.'

He flashed her a smile and she found herself smiling back. Nice smile. *Really* nice eyes. Actually...

She frowned. There was something faintly familiar about him. She stared and then shook herself and shrugged it off, turning back to the clerk. It might just be that he was the exact model of son her father had always wanted—clean-cut, professional and respectable. She did her best not to hold that against him.

Speaking of sons...

She glanced to her left. Robbie leaned with his back

against the counter and stared up at the ceiling, his face dreamy. Quinn tried to channel some of his calm. She hadn't expected this all to take so long.

Mind you, when she'd booked the car over a month ago she hadn't thought there'd be a national plane strike either.

'I'm afraid there's been a slight change to the model of car you booked.'

Her attention spun back to the clerk. 'What kind of change?'

'Ow!' Chase pulled his hand from hers and glared.

'Sorry, honey.' She smoothed down his hair and smiled at him, but a fist tightened in her chest. She glanced back at the clerk. 'What kind of change?' she repeated.

'We no longer have that model of car available.'

But she'd booked it a whole month ago especially!

The commotion in the car rental office didn't die down. Beside her she sensed her neighbour's frustration growing too. '*I have to leave Perth today!*' He didn't shout, but every word was clipped and strong.

He glanced at her and she suddenly realised she was staring. She sent him a buck-up smile and turned back to the clerk, doing her best to block out all the background noise. 'I'm driving across the Nullarbor Plain. I need a car that can go the distance.'

'I understand the reasons you booked a four-wheel drive, Mrs Laverty, but we just don't have any available.'

Brilliant.

She didn't bother correcting him on the *Mrs*. People made that assumption all the time.

She lifted her chin, preparing for a fight. 'I have a lot of luggage to fit into the car.' Another reason she'd chosen a four-wheel drive.

'Which is why we've upgraded you.'

Was that what they called it? She folded her arms. She'd chosen the car she had because of its safety and reliability rating. As far as fuel efficiency went it was one of the best too. It was the perfect car to take them across the country.

'We've upgraded you to a late model station wagon.'

'Does it have four-wheel drive?'

'No, ma'am.'

Quinn closed her eyes briefly, but all that did was underscore the scent of desperation and outrage in the air.

'I want to speak to the manager,' the man beside her clipped out.

'But, sir—'

'Now!'

She drew in a breath and opened her eyes. 'I need a four-wheel drive. The fuel consumption on that wagon will be outrageous and as I'll be travelling to New South Wales in it that's an awful lot of fuel.' She'd be driving the car for forty hours. Probably more. 'And, I might add, with none of the benefits the four-wheel drive offers.'

Driving suddenly seemed like the stupidest idea a woman had ever had. She lifted her chin another notch. 'Thank you, but I don't want an upgrade. I want the car I originally booked.'

The clerk scratched his nose and shuffled his feet, staring everywhere but at her. 'The thing is, ma'am, with the plane strike, you understand there just aren't any four-wheel drives currently available.'

'But I booked this over a month ago!'

'I understand and I do apologise. We won't be charging you for the upgrade. In fact, we'll be offering you a discount and a credit voucher.'

That was something at least. Quinn couldn't afford to stray too far from the budget she'd set herself.

'And the crux of the matter is…' the clerk leaned confidentially across the counter '…there isn't anything else available.' He gestured to the crowded room behind Quinn.

'If you don't want the station wagon we'll have plenty of other takers who will.'

She glanced back behind her too and grimaced.

'I can't guarantee when a four-wheel drive vehicle will become available.'

She bit back a sigh. 'We'll take it.' She didn't have any other option. They'd sold up practically everything they owned. The lease on their house had run out and new tenants were expected within the next few days. Their lives no longer belonged here in Perth. Besides, she'd made a booking at a caravan park in Merredin for this afternoon. She didn't want to lose her booking fee on that as well.

'Excellent. I just need you to sign here and here.'

Quinn signed and then followed the clerk out through a side door. She made sure both boys had their backpacks— they'd refused to leave them with the rest of the luggage back at the house.

'Keep the paperwork on you. You'll need it for the New-castle office. And if you'll just wait here the car will be brought around in a jiffy.'

'Thank you.'

The relative quiet out here after the cacophony in the office was bliss.

Robbie sat on a nearby bench and swung his feet. Chase immediately knelt on the ground beside the bench and 'broom-broomed' his toy car around.

'I'm sorry, Mr Fairhall, I wish I could help you. I have your card so if something comes up I'll let you know im-mediately.'

Fairhall? That was it! She'd known she'd seen him before. She turned to confirm it anyway. Uh huh, her neighbour at the service counter had been none other than Aidan Fairhall, up-and-coming politician. He'd been trav-elling the country canvassing for support. He had hers.

He had a nice on-air manner too. No doubt it was all

orchestrated as these things were, but he came across as intelligent and polite.

Polite shouldn't be overrated. In her opinion there should be more of it. Especially in politics.

She watched him slump onto a neighbouring bench as the man with the manager badge pinned to his shirt strode away. His shoulders drooped and he dropped his head to his hands. He raked his hands through his hair and then suddenly froze. He glanced up at her—a long sidelong look from beneath his hand—and she swallowed, realising she'd been caught out staring at him *twice* now.

He straightened. Her heart did a crazy little thump-thump. She swallowed and shrugged. 'I couldn't help over-hearing. I'm sorry.'

He smiled, but she sensed the strain behind it. 'It looks as if you've had more luck.'

Her lips twisted. 'Considering I booked this car over a month ago…'

He let out a breath, nodded. 'It'd be very poor form if they cancelled it on you at this late date.'

'But they're not giving us the car we wanted,' Robbie piped up.

She should've known he'd been listening. His dreamy expression lulled her every single time. 'But it's a better one,' she said, because she didn't want him to worry. Robbie had taken to worrying about everything.

'We're moving house,' Chase declared, glancing up from his car. 'All the way across the world!'

'Country,' she corrected.

Chase stared at her and then nodded. 'Country,' he repeated. 'Can we move to the moon?'

'Not this week.' She grinned. Robbie and Chase—her darling boys—they made it all worthwhile.

'It sounds exciting,' Mr Fairhall said. He glanced at

Robbie. 'And if you're in an even better car now that probably means your trip is going to be lucky too.'

She liked him then. Amid his own troubles he found the time to be nice to a couple of young boys—and not just nice but reassuring. If he hadn't already won her vote he'd have had it now.

'The plane strike seems to be turning the country on its head. I hope it ends soon so you can be where you need to be.'

He must have a crazy schedule. Actually—she rested one hand on a hip and surveyed him—maybe this would prove a blessing in disguise. He looked tired. A rest from the hurly-burly might do him the world of good.

His eyes darkened with some burden that would have to remain nameless because she had no intention of asking about it. 'Rumour has it that things on that front are going to take…' his shoulders sagged '…time.'

She winced.

'Mrs Laverty?' A man bounced out from behind the wheel of a white station wagon. 'Your car.'

She nodded as he handed her the keys with a cheery, 'Safe driving.'

'Thank you.'

Mr Fairhall rose. 'You boys have a great journey, okay?' And as he spoke he lifted their backpacks into the back of the wagon.

'Can I sit back here with the backpacks?' Chase asked, climbing in beside them.

'Most certainly not,' she countered, lifting him out again. 'Thank you,' she said to Mr Fairhall as he closed the wagon.

'Where are you going when the planes work again?' Chase asked as Quinn ushered him around to the back seat.

'Sydney.'

'That's near where we're going,' Robbie said. 'We looked

it up on the map.' He pulled out the map he'd been keeping in his shorts pocket.

The swift glance her polite politician sent her then had her stomach tightening.

'You're going to Sydney?'

She shifted her weight from one foot to the other. 'A couple of hours north of Sydney.'

'You wouldn't consider…?'

He broke off, no doubt in response to the rictus of a smile that had frozen to her face.

'No, of course not,' he said softly, as if to himself.

The boys glanced from her to him and back again.

Darn it! This was supposed to be a *family* trip. This road trip was about giving the boys a holiday…with the opportunity to ask her whatever questions they wanted about this new life they were embarking upon. In a relaxed atmosphere. Another person—a stranger—would throw those dynamics out completely.

She made herself brisk. 'C'mon, boys, in the car. Seat belts fastened, please.'

Aidan Fairhall nodded at her. 'Safe trip.'

'Thank you.'

Darn it. Darn it. Darn it.

He moved back to the bench. She stowed her handbag, made sure the kids had their seat belts fastened and then moved to the driver's seat. She glanced at Mr Fairhall and bit her lip.

'He wanted to come with us,' Chase said.

Why did children have to be so perceptive when you didn't want them to be and so obtuse when you did?

'You always tell us we should help people when they need it,' Robbie pointed out.

She turned in her seat and surveyed them both. 'You'd like to invite Mr Fairhall along on our journey?'

Robbie stared back. 'How'd you know his name?'

'I've seen him on the television. He's a politician.'

'Would he come all the way with us?'

'I'm not sure. As soon as the plane strike ends he might jump ship at any place that has an airport.'

'He's a nice man,' Chase said.

She had a feeling Chase was right.

Robbie studied the object of their conjecture and then turned back. 'He looks kinda sad.'

'Yeah.' She tried not to let those slumped shoulders pluck too hard at her. It was just… She knew exactly how that felt—the defeat, the worry and the helplessness.

'It might make our trip luckier,' Robbie said.

She couldn't mistake the hope in his eyes. She bit her lip to stop from saying something rash. Her eldest son ached for a male role model and the knowledge cut at her. Not that she expected Aidan Fairhall to fill that role. Still…

She blew out a breath and wound down the passenger side window. 'Mr Fairhall?'

He glanced up.

'We've just had a family conference.'

He stood. He wasn't terribly tall—he might be six feet—but he had a lean athletic body that moved with effortless grace. She watched him approach—stared as he approached—and her mouth started to dry and her heart started to pound. She tried to shake herself out from under the spell, only she found she'd frozen in position. She wished now she hadn't called him over. With a superhuman effort she cleared her throat. 'As we're…uh… all headed in the same direction we thought if you would like a lift all or part of the way…'

He blinked. Hope lit his face, making it truly beautiful, firing his brown eyes with a light that made her swallow. They weren't a boring brown, but a deep amber that brought to mind blazing hearth fires, fine brandies and rich caramel.

Then the light in those beautiful eyes faded and for some reason her heart sank too. Maybe it was the unspoken judgement she recognised in those deep amber depths. She sat back a little. She swallowed. 'I'm not given to recklessness, Mr Fairhall. I recognised you and I like your public persona. I like your education policies more.'

His lips twisted but the darkness faded from his eyes. His fingers drummed against the roof of the car.

'But, as I don't actually know you, and if you do take us up on our very kind offer, I'll be informing the manager of this car hire company that you'll be accompanying us. I'll also be ringing my aunt to tell her the same.' He didn't say anything. She shrugged and forced herself to add, 'But if we can help you out in any way then we'd be happy to.'

'Why would you do that?'

'People should help each other out always,' her earnest eldest son said.

'And you looked sad,' Chase added.

The light in those amazing eyes faded again, although the lips kept their smile.

Quinn rushed on. 'Also, it'd be nice to share some of the driving…not to mention the fuel costs. I'm afraid it wouldn't precisely be a free ride.' She'd sensed that would go against the grain with him.

There was a long silence. Quinn kicked herself. 'I'm sorry we have you at a disadvantage. I'm Quinn Laverty and these are my sons, Robbie and Chase.' She fished her licence out and handed it to him as proof of both her identity and the fact she could drive. 'If you decide to accompany us I'd want you to phone someone to let them know about your plans and who you're travelling with.'

He handed the licence back to her. 'I'm not given to recklessness either, Mrs Laverty.'

She didn't bother correcting the *Mrs*. 'Quinn,' she said instead. As she had no intention of becoming romantically involved with any man, let alone a politician—dear God!—the *Mrs* provided her with another level of protection.

Not that she needed protection from unwanted suitors. She could squash them flat as easily as swatting bugs. But correcting that Mrs might give the wrong impression.

Aidan Fairhall was from her parents' world and she had no intention of returning to that world. *Ever.*

She shuddered. Another long silence ensued. Eventually she cleared her throat. 'I'm sorry to hurry you, Mr Fairhall, but we'd really like to get going soon.'

Aidan's gaze snapped to Quinn Laverty's. 'If it was just work commitments I wouldn't dream of imposing on you like this.' His father would hit the roof if he ever heard Aidan utter that sentiment. 'But…' He hesitated.

'But?'

She had an unhurried way of speaking that was restful.

'I have a family commitment I have to meet.'

'Like I said, if we can help…'

She'd probably harangue him the entire way, pointing out all the flaws in his proposed policies, but… He had a sudden vision of his mother's worn eyes. He nodded. The alternative was worse. He made his lips curve upwards even though the heaviness in his heart made that nearly impossible. 'I will be forever in your debt. Thank you, I'd very much like to take you up on your very kind offer.' He pulled his cell phone from his pocket and gestured the manager back over.

Quinn spoke to the manager.

Aidan rang his mother.

As he expected, she fretted at the news. 'But you don't even know this woman, darling, and it's such a long way to drive. How do you know you'll be safe?'

He tried to allay her fears. Not very successfully. Eventually he said, 'If it will make you happier, I'll remain in

Perth until the plane strike is over.' He had to grit his teeth as he said it. He had to remind himself there were a lot of reasons for her anxieties and apprehensions.

'But you must be back in time for the party!'

Yes. He bit back a sigh. He must be back in time for the party. Still, it was a fortnight away.

'Harvey thinks the industrial action will be protracted. He's talking seven whole days. I can't get a train or bus ticket out of the place or hire a car for the next week. Everything is booked solid.'

'Oh, dear.'

He didn't need to see her to know the way her hands fluttered about her throat. 'This is my best option. As soon as the strike ends, I'll make my way to the nearest airport and be home as soon as I can.'

'Oh, dear.'

'I really don't think there's anything to worry about, Mother.' And movement of any kind beat kicking his heels in Perth.

There was a slight pause. 'Of course you must do what you think best, darling.'

And thereby she absolved herself of any responsibility and placed it all squarely on Aidan's shoulders. He tried not to bow under its weight. 'I'll call you this evening.'

He collected his overnight case and stowed it in the back. 'You travel light,' Quinn observed.

He slid into the passenger seat. 'I was only supposed to be in Perth for a single night.'

She started the car up and eased it out of the car park and onto the road. 'It's a long way to come for just a day.'

'Two days,' he corrected. 'And one night.'

He thought she might glance at him then, but she kept her eyes on the road. 'I see you're a man who knows how to make the most of his time.'

'That's me.'

Quinn Laverty had a blonde ponytail and wore a kind of crazy oversized tie-dyed dress that covered her to her ankles. She wasn't exactly a flower power child, but there was something of the hippy about her.

The longer he stared at her, the more he wanted to keep staring. Crazy. He loosened his tie a fraction and turned to the boys. 'Robbie and Chase, it's great to meet you. Thank you for letting me share your journey.'

'You're welcome, Mr Fairhall,' the elder, Robbie, said with perfect manners.

He could see the path set out for the boy now—school prefect, school captain, dux, university medal and then a high-powered job in the public service.

What a nightmare!

Only for you.

He pushed the thought away. 'If it's okay with your mother you can call me Aidan.'

Quinn glanced at him briefly. Her lips tilted up into an easy smile. 'That's okay with me.'

Ten minutes later they stopped at an unprepossessing house and loaded the back of the car with an assortment of boxes and suitcases. The backpacks moved onto the back seat with the boys. Aidan insisted on doing all the heavy lifting.

'See you, Perth,' Quinn said with a jaunty wave at the house.

Both boys waved too.

'Can we play our Gameboys now?' Chase asked.

'You can.'

Both boys whooped and dived into their backpacks. She glanced at Aidan and rolled her eyes. 'They were specially bought for the trip.'

Probably quite a financial outlay for a single mum. Not that he had any proof that she was single.

'And the deal was that they weren't allowed to play them until the trip itself started.'

Smart move. Those things would keep the boys occupied for hours, which, quite obviously, had been her plan. He settled back in his seat as the suburbs of Perth passed by one after the other. 'I know the clerk back at the store called you Mrs Laverty, but I also notice you're not wearing a wedding ring.' He kept his tone neutral. He didn't want her thinking he was judging her or condemning her in any way. 'Are you married or single or...'

Her brows lifted. 'Does it matter?'

He loosened his tie a tiny bit more. 'Not at all. But some people get fixated on titles so I always like to get them straight.'

'I prefer Ms.'

Which told him precisely nothing at all. When he met her gaze, she laughed. Sparkling green eyes momentarily dazzled him. 'You first,' she dared.

A question like that would normally have him sitting up straighter. Instead he found himself chuckling and relaxing back into his seat even more. 'Single. Most definitely single. Never been married; hence, never been divorced and not currently in a relationship.'

'Ditto,' she said.

'So, are you moving back home? Is Newcastle where you grew up?'

'No.'

Her face shuttered closed—not completely but in a half-fan—and he bit back a sigh. False start number one.

A moment's silence ensued and then she turned to him with a smile that was too bright. 'Is your campaign going well?'

He bit back a curse. Was that all people could think to converse with him about—his darn job? 'Yes.'

Another moment's silence. False start number two. For

pity's sake, he was good at small talk. He opened his mouth. He closed it again. The deep heaviness in his chest grew. Normally he could push it away, ignore it, but today it gave him no quarter. It was this stupid plane strike and the break in his routine. It had given him time to think.

Thinking wouldn't help anything!

She glanced at him, her face sober, and he knew then that she was going to bring up the subject he most dreaded. He wanted to beg her not to, but years of *good* breeding prevented him.

'How are you and your parents now, since your brother…?'

That was a different approach to most, but…The heaviness started to burn and ache. He rested his head back against his seat and tried to stop his lip from curling.

'I'm sorry. Don't answer that. It was a stupid thing to ask. Grieving in public must be harrowing. I just wanted to say I'm truly sorry for your loss, Aidan.'

The simple words with their innate sincerity touched him and the burn in his chest eased a fraction. 'Thank you, Quinn.'

Two beats passed. Quinn shuffled in her seat a little and her ponytail bounced. 'I'm moving to an olive farm.'

He straightened and turned to her. 'An olive farm?'

'Uh-huh.' She kept her eyes on the road, but she was grinning. 'I bet that's not a sentence you hear every day, is it?'

'It's not a sentence I have ever heard uttered in my life.'

'It's probably not as startling as saying I was moving to an alpaca farm or going to work on a ferret breeding programme. But it's only a degree or two behind.'

She'd made things good—or, at least, better—just like that. With one abrupt and startling admission. 'What do you know about olives?'

She lifted her nose in the air. 'I know that marinated olives on a cheese platter is one of life's little pleasures.'

He laughed. She glanced at him and her eyes danced. 'What about you; what do you know about olives?'

'That they grow on trees. That they make olive oil. And that marinated olives on a cheese platter is one of life's little pleasures.'

She laughed then too and he couldn't remember a sound he'd ever enjoyed more. He closed his eyes all the better to savour it. It was the last thing he remembered.

Aidan sat bolt upright and glanced around. He was alone in the car. He peered at his watch.

He closed his eyes and shook his right arm, but when he opened them again the time hadn't changed. He'd slept for two hours?

He pressed his palms to his eyes and dragged in a breath before stretching to the right and then the left to ease the cricks in his back and neck. Finally he took stock of his surroundings. Quinn had parked beneath a huge old gum tree to give him shade. At the moment she, Robbie and Chase kicked a ball around on a big oval in front of him. She'd hitched her dress up to mid-thigh into a pair of bike shorts.

His eyes widened. Man, she was…fit!

He shook his head and pressed fingers to his eyes again.

With bones that literally creaked, he pushed out of the car and stretched. Warm air caressed his skin and he slid his suit jacket off to lay it on the front seat. Quinn waved and then pointed behind him to an amenities block. 'They're clean and well maintained,' she called out.

He lifted a hand to let her know he'd heard.

When he returned he found her sitting cross-legged on a blanket at the edge of the oval beside an assortment of bags.

'Where are we?'

'Wundowie.'

He pulled out his smart phone and searched for it on the Internet. 'We've been travelling…'

'Nearly two and a half hours, though we're still only about an hour out of Perth. There was a lot of traffic,' she said in answer to his raised eyebrow. 'And there was some mini-marathon we had to be diverted around.' She shrugged. 'It all took time. Would you like a sandwich or an apple?' She opened a cooler bag and proffered its contents towards him. 'Or water? There's plenty here.'

He reached for a bottle of water. 'Thank you, I'm parched.'

'But well rested,' she said with a laugh.

His hand clenched about the water bottle, making the plastic crackle. 'You should've woken me.'

She turned from watching the boys as they continued with their game. 'Why?'

He opened his mouth. He closed it again and rubbed the nape of his neck. 'I, uh… It wasn't very polite.'

'It wasn't impolite. You were obviously tired and needed the sleep.'

She selected an apple and crunched into it. 'Please eat something. It'll only go to waste and I hate that.'

He took a sandwich. Ham and pickle. 'Thank you.' And tried to remember the last time he'd let his guard down so comprehensively as to fall asleep when he hadn't meant to.

It certainly hadn't happened since Daniel had died.

His appetite fled. Nevertheless he forced himself to eat the sandwich. He wouldn't be able to stand the fuss his mother would make if he became ill. And this woman beside him had gone to the trouble of making these sandwiches for her children and herself and had chosen to share them with him. The least he could do was appreciate it.

He and Quinn sat side by side on the grass with their legs stretched out in front of them. They didn't speak much. A million questions pounded through him, but they were all far too personal and he had no right to ask a single one of them.

But the inactivity grated on him. It didn't seem to have that effect on Quinn, though. She lifted her face to the sky and closed her eyes as if relishing the sun and the day and the air. Eventually she jumped up again. 'I'm going to have another run with the boys for a bit. Stretch my legs. Feel free to join in.'

He glanced down at himself. 'I'm not exactly dressed for it.'

She took in his tie, his tailored trousers and polished leather shoes. 'No,' she agreed and he couldn't remember the last time he'd felt so summarily dismissed. 'Oh, I meant to tell you earlier that we're only going as far as Merredin today,' she shot over her shoulder before racing off towards the boys.

He looked Merredin up on his smart phone. A quick calculation informed him it was only another two hours further on. Surely they could travel further than that in a day? He scowled and started answering email. He might as well do something useful. He made phone calls.

They stayed in Wundowie for another thirty minutes. He chafed to be away the entire time but was careful not to keep glancing at his watch. If they were only going as far as Merredin they'd be there mid-afternoon as it was. An additional half an hour in Wundowie either way wouldn't much matter.

Aidan would've liked to have kept working when they were back in the car, but he suspected Quinn would consider that bad manners.

He dragged a hand through his hair. What was he thinking? Of course it'd be bad manners. Besides, she and the boys had kept quiet so he could sleep and it hardly seemed fair to continue to expect such ongoing consideration. Especially when they were doing him a favour.

The fact his phone battery was running low decided it. He tucked it away and glanced around to the back seat. 'Do you boys play a sport?'

'Soccer,' said Robbie.

'Robbie is the best runner on his team,' Chase said.

Quinn glanced at him. 'He means fastest.'

Robbie's mouth turned down. 'I mightn't be in my new team.'

Quinn tensed. Aidan tried not to wince. He hadn't meant to tread into sensitive territory. 'Uh…' He searched for something to say.

'Do you play sport?' Robbie asked.

'Not any more.' And all of a sudden his heart felt heavy as a stone again.

'Why are you on the television?' Chase demanded to know. 'Mum said she'd seen you.'

'Because of my job. I'm a politician so I go on television to tell people how I'd run the country if they vote for me.'

Robbie frowned. 'Do you like your job?'

A bitter taste lined his mouth. 'Sure I do.'

'What do you do?'

'Well, I go into my office most days and I go to lots of meetings and…' Endless meetings. It took an effort of will to keep the tiredness out of his voice. 'I go on the television and talk on the radio and talk to newspaper reporters so they can tell all the people about the things I think would make our country run better. I have people who work for me and we draft up proposals for new policies.'

'Wouldn't being a fireman be more fun?'

'A fireman would be excellent fun,' he agreed. Lord, his mother would have a fit! He almost laughed.

'When you're finished being a politician maybe you could be a fireman,' Chase said.

'And then you could play soccer too,' added Robbie.

He didn't know how those two things were linked. He glanced at Quinn for direction. She merely smiled at him.

'Mum, can we play one of our CDs now?'

'I did promise the boys we'd play one of our CDs on this leg of our journey. We burned a few especially.'

'I don't mind.' It'd save him searching for topics of conversation.

'We sing pretty loud.'

'You don't need to apologise about that.'

For some reason that made her grin. 'You haven't heard our singing yet.'

He forced himself to smile.

She slipped a CD into the player. 'The Purple People-Eater' immediately blasted from the speakers and his three companions burst into loud accompaniment, the boys laughing throughout most of the song. That was followed by 'Llama Llama Duck' and then 'My Boomerang Won't Come Back'.

He stared at her. 'You have to be joking me?'

'Fun novelty songs are our favourite.' Her grin was so wide it almost split her face. 'If there's a doo-wop or chirpy-chirpy-cheep-cheep to be had then we love it.'

Hell, that was what this was. Absolute hell. He slunk down in his seat and stared straight out in front of him as the songs came at him in a relentless round. 'This isn't music!' He glared at the road. 'You could've warned me about this back in Perth.' No way would he have got into the car with her then.

Then he thought of his mother.

Quinn merely sang, 'I'm a yummy, tummy, funny, lucky gummy bear,' with extra gusto.

He closed his eyes, but this time sleep eluded him.

CHAPTER TWO

THEY REACHED MERREDIN ninety minutes later. It had felt like ninety hours. Aidan had endured forty minutes of the 'Monster Mash', 'Achy Breaky Heart' and many more novelty songs, which was enough to last him a lifetime. Twenty minutes of I Spy had followed and then a further thirty minutes of the number plate game. There was only one rule to the game, as far as he could tell, and that was who could make up the silliest phrase from the letters of a passing number plate.

PHH. Penguin haircuts here. Purple Hoovering hollyhocks. Pasta hates ham.

LSL. Larks sneeze loudly. Little snooty limpets. Lace scissored loquaciously.

CCC. Cream cake central. Can't clap cymbals. Cool cooler coolest.

And on and on and on it went, like some kind of slow Chinese water torture. His temples throbbed and an ache stretched behind his eyes. He didn't join in.

He sat up straighter though when Quinn eased the car down the town's main street. He glanced up at the sky. There was another four hours of daylight left yet. Another four hours of good driving time.

Manners prevented him from pointing this out. Biting back something less than charitable, he studied the few shops on offer. Maybe he'd be able to hire a car of his own out here?

Quinn parked the car in the main street and turned off the motor. 'The boys and I are staying at the caravan park, but I figured you'd be more comfortable at the motel.'

A caravan park? He suppressed a shudder. Again, he didn't say anything. Quinn was obviously on a tight budget.

She and the boys all but bounced out of the car. Aidan found his limbs heavy and lethargic. It took an effort of will to make them move. He wondered where Quinn found all her energy. Maybe she took vitamins. Unbidden, an image of her racing around the soccer oval in her bike shorts and dress rose up through him and for some reason his throat tightened.

He glanced up to find her watching him. He felt worn and weary, but her ponytail still bounced and her cheeks were pink and pretty. She waited, as if expecting him to say something, and then she merely shrugged. 'The motel is just across the road.' She pointed. 'We'll collect you at nine in the morning.'

He snapped to and retrieved his overnight bag from the back of the wagon. 'I'll be ready earlier. Say six or seven if you wanted to get an early start.'

'Nine o'clock,' she repeated, and he suddenly had the impression she was laughing at him.

She swung back to the boys. 'Right!' She clapped her hands. 'Chase, I need you to find me a packet of spaghetti and, Robbie, I need you to find me a tin of tomatoes.'

As they walked away he heard Chase ask, 'What are you looking for?'

'Minced meat and garlic bread.' And they all disappeared into the nearby supermarket.

He'd been summarily dismissed. Again.

From a grocery trip? He shook the thought off and headed across the road to the motel.

His room was adequate. Merredin might be the regional centre for Western Australia's wheat belt, but as far as he was concerned it wasn't much more than a two-horse town and his early enquiries about hiring a car proved less than encouraging.

He strode back to his motel room, set his phone to charge and then flipped open his laptop and searched Google Maps. He frowned. What the heck…? If they kept travelling at this pace it'd take them two weeks to drive across the country!

His hands clenched for a moment. Counting to three, he unclenched them and pulled a writing pad from his briefcase and started to plot a route across the continent. He spread out a map he'd grabbed from the motel's reception and marked logical break points where he and Quinn could swap driving duties.

That took all of twenty minutes. He closed his laptop and glanced about his room. There didn't seem to be much more to do. He wandered about the room, opening the wardrobe doors and the desk drawer. He made a coffee that he didn't drink. He reached for his cell phone to call his mother, stared at it for a moment and then shoved it back onto its charger.

Flopping back onto the bed, he stared at the ceiling for what seemed like an eon. When he glanced at his watch, though, he cursed. What on earth was he going to do for the rest of the afternoon, let alone the rest of the night?

He raised himself to his elbows. He could go and find Quinn and the boys.

Why would you do that?

He sat up and drummed his fingers against his thighs, before shooting to his feet. He tore the page from his writing pad and stalked from the room.

It didn't take him long to find the caravan park. And it didn't take him long to locate Robbie and Chase either. They played—somewhat rowdily—on a playground fort in primary colours so bright they hurt his eyes. And then he saw Quinn. She sat cross-legged on a blanket beside a nearby caravan, and something about her sitting in the afternoon light soothed his eyes.

'Hey, Aidan,' she called out when she saw him. 'Feeling at a loose end, huh?'

He rolled his shoulders. 'I'm just exploring. Thought I'd come see where you were camped.'

She lifted her face to the sun. 'This is a nice spot, isn't it?'

It was? He glanced around, searching for whatever it was that she found 'nice', but he came up blank.

'I thought you'd be busy catching up on all of your work.'

It hit him that in amongst all of his restlessness it hadn't occurred to him to ring back into the office. They knew he was delayed, but…

It didn't mean he had to stop working. There'd still be the usual endless round of email that needed answering. He could've set up meetings for this evening on Skype.

The thought of all that work made him feel as tired as the idea of ringing his mother. When Quinn gestured to the blanket he fell down onto it, grateful for the respite.

He had no right feeling so exhausted. He'd done next to nothing all day. He shook himself in an effort to keep the moroseness at bay, glanced around as if he were curious about his surroundings. If he pretended well enough, maybe he'd start to feel a flicker of interest and intent again. Maybe. 'Are you planning to stay in caravan parks for all of your journey?'

'You bet.'

He kept his face smooth, but somehow she saw through

him and threw her head back with a laugh. 'Not your idea of a good time, I see.'

'I wouldn't say that.' He wasn't a snob, but… Walking to an amenity block when he could have an en suite bathroom? No, thanks.

'Only because you're incredibly polite.'

She made that sound like an insult.

'Look about you, Aidan. This place caters to children far better than your motel does. Most caravan parks do. Look at all that open green space over there. The boys can kick a ball around to their hearts' content. And then there's that playground, which I might add is fenced.'

In those eye-gouging primary colours.

'Robbie is old enough not to wander off, but Chase is still easily distracted.'

He straightened when he realised this place gave her peace of mind. 'I hadn't thought of that.'

'And there're usually other children around for them to play with too.'

He watched another two children approach the playground.

'Most people here won't mind a bit of noise from the children, but I bet you're glad we're not staying in the room next to yours at the motel.'

He rolled his shoulders. 'It's not a bad noise. It's just a bit of laughing and shouting.'

She raised her eyebrows.

'But I take your point.'

'It'd be hard to get any work done with all that noise.'

There she was, talking about work again.

He promptly pulled the itinerary he'd plotted out for them from his pocket along with the map and smoothed them on the rug between them. 'I thought that tomorrow we could make it as far as Balladonia. If we wanted to take two-hour shifts driving, which is what all the driver reviver and driving safety courses recommend, then we could change here, here and here.' He pointed out the various locations on the map.

Quinn leaned back on her hands and laughed. 'I've seen this movie. In this particular scenario you're Sally and I'm Harry, right?'

He stared at her. What on earth was she talking about?

'*When Harry Met Sally*,' she said when he remained silent. 'The movie? You know? Sally who's a bit uptight and super-organised and Harry who's casual and laidback?'

He searched for something to say.

'There's a scene early in the movie when they're driving across America together and...' Her voice lost steam. 'You haven't seen the movie?'

He shook his head.

Her face fell. 'But it's one of the classic rom-coms of all time.'

For some reason he felt compelled to apologise. 'I'm sorry.'

And for some reason he couldn't fathom that made her smile again, only it wasn't the kind of smile that reached her eyes. She touched his map and shook her head. 'No.'

He blinked. 'No?' But...

She laughed and he could see it was partly in frustration with him, but she didn't do it in a mean way. She rested back on her hands again. 'Aidan, you really need to learn to relax and chill out a bit.'

And just like that she reminded him of Daniel.

It should've hurt him.

But it didn't.

'I...'

He stared at her as if he'd never seen her before. Or as if no one had ever told him to slow down and smell the roses. He stared at her as if that very concept was totally alien.

She bit back a sigh. This trip—spending time with her boys and doing all she could to make this transition in their lives exciting and easy—was important to her. Taking pity on Aidan and inviting him to join them had thrown the dynamic off more than she'd anticipated. She'd promised the boys a holiday and she wasn't going back on her word.

And eight hours a day driving wasn't a holiday in anybody's vocabulary.

'We probably should've compared notes about the kind of travelling we were expecting to do before we left Perth.' How could he know she meant to take it slow if she hadn't explained it to him? He was obviously in a hurry, but… 'It didn't occur to me at the time.' She moistened her lips. 'But we're obviously working on two different timetables here.'

Her stomach churned. He was probably used to everyone rushing around at a million miles an hour. That was what people from his world—her parents' world—did.

Don't hold that against him. It doesn't make him like your parents.

'I made enquiries in town to see if I could hire a car of my own.'

She swallowed. It'd be one solution to the problem. 'And?'

'No luck, I'm afraid.'

'I see.'

'You're regretting taking me on as a passenger.' He said it simply, without rancour, but there was such exhaustion stretching through his voice it was all she could do to not reach across and clasp his hand and to tell him he was mistaken. Only…

She glanced across at her boys, now happily playing with the newcomers to the playground. A fierce mixture of love and fear swirled through her. Pushing her shoulders back, she met his stare again. Pussyfooting around would only lead to more misunderstandings. 'Aidan, you've been unfailingly polite, but you haven't really been all that friendly.'

'I beg your pardon?'

He gritted his teeth so hard his mouth turned white. She hated being the reason for that expression, but she soldiered on all the same, hoping she wasn't punishing him for the reminders of the past that he'd unwittingly brought rushing back to her. 'You didn't join in on our singalong. You didn't play I Spy or the number plate game.'

He stared at her. For someone groomed to project and maintain a certain image, he looked all at sea. 'Please don't tell me you want to part company here in this two-horse town.'

'Of course not!' How could he think she'd abandon him like that?

'Once we reach Adelaide I'll make other arrangements.'

'Okay.' She bit her thumbnail for a moment, unable to look at him. Adelaide was still six or possibly seven days away yet. If she could make him see how important this trip was…well, then, he might make more of an effort to fit in. Maybe.

She stretched her legs out in front of her. 'You know what I think? I think we should break the ice a little. I think we should ask the questions that have been itching through us and get that all out of the way.'

He looked so utterly appalled she had to bite her lip to stop from laughing. This man took self-contained to a whole new level. 'Or, better yet, why don't we tell each other something we think the other wants to know?'

His expression didn't change but she ignored it to clap her hands. 'Yes, that'll be much more fun. I'll go first, shall I?' she rushed on before he could object. She crossed her legs again. 'I'm going to tell you why Robbie, Chase and I are on a road trip across the continent.'

He shifted, grew more alert. She could tell from the way

his eyes focused on her and his shoulders straightened. Oh, he was appalled still, of course, but she hoped his curiosity would eventually conquer his resistance.

'The olive farm is in the Hunter Valley wine district and it belongs to my aunt. She's the black sheep of the family.' She rolled her eyes. 'And I happen to take after her.'

'Your family consider you a black sheep?'

A question! She schooled her features to hide her triumph. 'Actually, in all honesty, I'd be very surprised if my parents thought about me at all these days. They're from Sydney. I became pregnant with Robbie when I was eighteen. They wanted me to go to university and carve out some mythically brilliant career. When I decided to have my baby instead, they cut me off.'

His jaw dropped. He mightn't be 'friendly' in a traditional sense, but he didn't strike her as the kind of man who'd walk away from his family when they needed him.

And you're basing that on what—his pretty smiles and earnest eyes in his television interviews?

Hmm, good point.

'Siblings?'

Another question! 'None. So, after my parents handed me their ultimatum, I packed my bags and moved to Perth.'

'Why Perth?'

'Because it was about as far away from Sydney as I could get while still remaining in the country.'

He stared at her for a long moment. She held her breath and crossed her fingers that he'd ask a fourth question.

'Did Robbie's father go with you?'

She wanted to beam at him for asking. 'Yes, he did.' But she didn't want to tell him that story. 'When I had Robbie my Aunt Mara—'

'Of black sheep fame?'

He was totally hooked, whether he knew it or not. 'The very one. Well, she came across to Perth to help me out for a couple of weeks. I was barely nineteen with a new baby. I appreciated every bit of help, advice and support she gave me.'

He plucked a nearby dandelion. 'That's nice.'

'She didn't have to. We'd had very little to do with each other when I was growing up.' Her parents had made sure of that. 'But those two weeks bonded us together in a way I will always cherish. We've been close ever since.'

'You're moving to be nearer to her?'

A little twist of fear burrowed into her gut. She shifted on the blanket. She was turning all of their lives upside down. What if she was making a mistake? They'd had a perfectly comfortable life in Perth.

You weren't happy.

Her happiness had nothing to do with it. She scratched her nose and stared across at Robbie and Chase.

'Quinn?'

She shook herself and pasted on a smile. 'Mara is only fifty-two but she's developed severe arthritis. She needs a hip replacement.' She needed help. 'My boys don't have any family in Perth. I think it'd be nice for them to know Mara better.'

Comprehension flashed across his face. 'You're moving there to look after her.'

'I expect we'll all look after each other. Like I said, she owns an olive farm and her second-in-command recently married and moved to the States.'

'And you're going to fill the position?'

He didn't ask with any judgement in his voice. She shouldn't feel as if she'd been found so...lacking. 'Yes.'

She tossed her head. Besides, she was looking forward to that challenge. Her admin job in the Department of Chemistry at the University of Western Australia had palled years ago. Not that it had ever had much shine.

Still, it had provided them with the security of a fortnightly pay packet. It had supported her and the boys for the last five years. It—

She slammed a halt on the doubts that tried to crowd her. If worse came to worse, if things didn't work out at Aunt Mara's, she'd be able to pick up an office job in no time at all. Somewhere.

She bit back a sigh and then straightened her spine. There was absolutely no reason why things wouldn't work out. She loved her aunt. So did the boys. The Hunter Valley was a beautiful place and the boys would thrive in all of that sunshine and the wide open spaces. They'd go to good schools and she'd get them a dog. They'd make friends fast. And so would she.

She crossed her fingers. The change might even help her overcome the ennui that had started to take her over. She'd learn new skills and maybe, eventually, she'd stop feeling so alone.

Win-win for everyone. Perfect!

She turned back to Aidan and pressed her hands together. 'This is such an exciting time for us.'

'And a scary one too, I imagine.'

She didn't want to admit that. Not out loud.

'I mean you're turning your whole life on its head.'

She sucked her bottom lip into her mouth and concentrated on keeping her breathing even.

He stared across at the playground. 'And it's not just your life that this decision impacts either so—'

'Are you trying to make me hyperventilate?' she demanded.

His jaw dropped. 'Heck, no! I just think it's amazing and courageous and...'

She gritted her teeth for a moment before pasting on another smile. She suspected it was more a grimace from the way Aidan eased back a fraction and kept his eyes trained on her. 'Which is why this road trip of ours is so important to me. I've promised the boys that we'll treat it as a holiday. I'm determined that we'll take our time and that everyone will be as relaxed as possible so I can answer any questions about this new life of ours, help ease any fears and apprehensions that might come to light, and to just…'

She reached out as if to grasp the words she sought from the air. 'To help us all look forward to this new beginning and be excited about it.' She turned to him, willing him to understand. 'It's the reason I've been chirpy-chirpy-cheeping with all of my might.'

Beneath his tan, he paled. 'And I'm screwing that up for you.'

'No you're not. Not exactly. But now that you know, maybe you can ease up a bit.'

'And part company with you at Adelaide.'

She slapped a hand down on the blanket between them and leaned in closer. He smelled of something spicy and sharp like eucalyptus oil or crushed pine needles. She breathed him in and the constriction about her lungs eased a fraction. 'By going with the flow and relaxing,' she corrected. 'You're obviously stressed about this plane strike and getting back home to Sydney, but…'

He latched onto that. 'But?'

'We're all stuck with each other for the six days or so, right?'

'Six days!' He swallowed. He nodded. 'Six days. Right.'

'So can't you stop chafing at the constraints and just… just look at this time as a bit of a gift? Embrace it as an unexpected holiday or a timeout from a hectic schedule?'

He stared at her. 'A holiday?' He said the words as if testing them out. Very slowly he started to nod. 'Fretting about the delay isn't going to change anything, is it?'

Precisely.

'In fact, it would be making things harder on you and the boys.'

'And on you.' She shook her head. 'I hate to think what your raised cortisol levels are doing to your overall heath.'

'Cortisol?'

'It's a hormone that's released into our bloodstreams during times of stress. It's not good for us in large constant doses.' It took an effort of will not to fidget under his stare. She waved a dismissive hand. 'I read about it in a book.'

This man would benefit from regular meditation too, but she didn't suggest it. She'd suggested enough for one day. She leant back on her hands and lifted her face to what was left of the sun and made herself laugh. 'We're certainly getting holiday weather.' Summer might be over officially, but nobody had informed the weather of that fact.

He glanced around and nodded.

'Look at how blue the sky is and the golden haze on the horizon. This is my absolute favourite time of day.'

His shoulders loosened.

'I love the way the shadows lengthen and how stands of trees almost turn purple in the shade, like those ones over there,' she murmured.

He pulled in an audible breath and let it out in one long exhalation.

'I just want to drink it all in.'

They were quiet for a few moments. She hoped he was savouring the afternoon as much as she was.

'You remind me of someone.'

It was the most relaxed she'd heard him sound. 'Who?'

He swivelled to face her. 'My turn.'

She blinked. 'For?'

'For sharing something I think you want to know.'

It took all her willpower to not lean forward, mouth agape. She hadn't expected him to actually take part in her 'you tell me yours, I'll tell you mine' strategy. She'd just wanted to impress upon him the importance of this trip. Not that she had any intention of telling him that now, though.

'Okay.' She forced her eyes back to the hazy horizon, careful to not make him feel self-conscious.

'Daniel's death has devastated my family.'

His brother had died in a car accident eight months ago now. It had made all the headlines. She gripped a fistful of blanket, her heart burning for Aidan and his family.

'He was the apple of my parents' eyes. His death shattered them.' He stared down at his hands. 'Hardly surprising as he was a great guy.'

He didn't have to say how much his brother's death had devastated him. She could see it in his face. A lump ballooned in her throat.

'Ever since Danny's accident my mother has lived in mortal fear of losing me too.'

The poor woman.

And then Quinn saw it, what Aidan wasn't saying. With an effort, she swallowed and the lump bruised her all the way down until it reached her stomach. 'So this plane strike and your road trip across the country, it's going to be a real…worry for her?'

And that was what had really been chafing at him. Not the interruption to his political campaigning or the fact he was missing important meetings.

'What did you call it? Cortisol?'

She nodded.

He pointed skyward. 'Hers will be through the roof.'

And Aidan wanted to do whatever he could to ease his mother's suffering. Her heart tore for him.

'My parents' thirtieth wedding anniversary is soon and—'

'When?' Good Lord! She had to make sure he got home in time for that.

'Not until the twenty-fourth of the month.'

She let out a breath. She was hoping to be at Mara's no later than the twenty-second. He'd get home in time.

'I should be there helping with all the preparations. There's a huge party planned. I encouraged them to have it. I thought it might help.'

That was when she started to wonder how much of his life he was putting on hold in an effort to allay his parents' grief. And what of his own grief?

She surveyed him for a long moment. When he turned to meet her gaze the rich brown of his eyes almost stole her breath. She swallowed, but she didn't look away. 'Aidan, I am truly sorry for your loss.'

He looked ragged for a moment. 'Thank you.'

The silence gathered about them and started to burn. 'May I say something about your mother?' she whispered.

He stilled. He turned back. 'Only if you say it gently.'

Gently? Her heart started to thump. She moistened her lips and stared across to the playground with its riot of happy laughter. 'I can't imagine how bad it would be to lose one of my boys.' Her voice wobbled. 'I can't actually imagine anything worse.'

He reached out and squeezed her hand.

'In fact, I can't actually comprehend it, and I'm utterly and probably somewhat selfishly grateful for that.'

'It's not selfish, Quinn,' he said quietly.

'Your poor, *poor* mother, Aidan.' She clasped his hand tightly. 'God forbid if I should ever lose Robbie, but…I can't help feeling that wrapping Chase up in cotton wool would not be a good thing to do. For him or for me.'

He met her gaze, his face sober. 'She can't help her grief.'

'No.' But tying Aidan down like this was hardly fair. 'You will get home safe and sound and in one piece.' It was probably a foolish thing to say because neither one of them could guarantee that. But she couldn't think of anything else to say.

'Of course I will.'

'And there's nothing you can do for your mother at the moment except to give her a daily phone call to let her know you're okay.'

'No,' he agreed.

'Can you live with that?'

'I guess I'll have to.'

'You know,' she started slowly, 'this might be a good thing.'

'How?'

'Maybe it'll force her to focus beyond her fear, especially if she has the party to turn her attention to. And once she does that she might realise how irrational her fear is.'

His face lit up. 'You think so?'

Oh, heavens, she'd raised his hopes. Um… 'Maybe.'

He stared at her for a long moment and then he smiled. 'That person you remind me of?'

Her heart started to thump. 'Uh-huh?'

'It's Daniel. Quinn, you remind me of my brother.'

CHAPTER THREE

AIDAN TOOK THE first driving shift the next day. He'd thought he might have an argument on his hands about that but, after subjecting him to a thorough scrutiny, Quinn merely handed him the keys and slid into the passenger seat.

He surveyed her the best he could without alerting her to that fact. She looked a little pale, a little wan.

'Okay, boys.' She turned to Robbie and Chase in the back. 'You have one hour of Gameboy time.'

Both boys whooped and dived into their backpacks. She shrugged when she caught Aidan's eye. 'I know it'd make things a whole lot easier and simpler, not to mention quieter, if I just let them play with their Gameboys all day, but I don't think that's good for them.'

'I don't either.'

Her brows shot up. 'It's something you've thought about?'

He might not have kids, he might not really know any kids, but it didn't make him totally ignorant. 'Only in the abstract.' Besides, he hoped to have kids one day. 'The rise in childhood obesity is worrying. I've been part of a government task force that's been looking at strategies to combat it.'

'That's good to know.' Yesterday she'd have asked him all sorts of questions about it. Today she stifled a yawn and stared out of the window with a mumbled, 'Glad our taxes are being put to good use.'

Aidan had set their course on the Great Eastern Highway and the scenery grew browner and drier by the kilometre. All that was visible from the windows was low scrub, brown grass and brown dirt. For mile upon endless mile.

He glanced across at her again. 'Rough night?'

She straightened and he wished he'd kept quiet and just let her drift off for a little while.

'The bed was hard as a rock.'

She smiled but it left him vaguely dissatisfied. Quinn might spout assurances that this move across the country was the greatest idea ever, but he sensed a certain ambivalence in her.

That she doesn't want to talk about.

Yesterday's disclosures didn't give him the right to pry.

'I'll sleep very well tonight, though.' She sent him one of her buck-up smiles. 'Whether the bed is made of rock or marshmallow.'

He determined in that moment to let her rest as much as he could. 'Mind if I turn on the radio? I'll keep the volume low.'

'Sounds nice.'

Although he willed her to, she didn't fall asleep. She merely stared out of the window and watched the unending scrub pass by. At the one hour mark she snapped to and turned to the boys. 'Time's up.'

There were groans and grumbles and 'let me just finish this bit' but within five minutes they'd tucked their Gameboys back into their bags. Quinn then asked them what games they'd been playing and received blow-by-blow accounts. She spoke her children's lingo. She connected with them on every level and he suddenly and deeply admired her.

She was a single working mother, but she'd evidently spent time building a solid relationship with her children. It couldn't have been easy, she'd have had to make sacrifices, but he suspected she hadn't minded that in the least.

Robbie stretched out his arms to touch the back of Aidan's seat. 'How long is Aunt Mara going to be in hospital for?'

'If all goes well, just a few days. But she'll have to take it easy for weeks and weeks. Don't forget, though, that her surgery isn't scheduled until later in the year.'

'I'll read to her.'

'She'll like that.'

'And I'll play cars with her,' Chase piped up, evidently not wanting to be left out.

'Heavens! She'll be back on her feet in no time with all of that attention.'

Robbie stretched to touch the roof. 'What are we going to do for a car if we have to give this one back?'

'We're going to share Aunt Mara's car for a while and there's a farm ute we can use too. But we'll buy a new one eventually. What do you guys think we should get?'

A lively discussion followed, mostly based on television ads that the boys liked. It made Aidan smile. And then he remembered Quinn's words of yesterday and how she'd thought him unfriendly and the smile slid straight off his face. He had to do more than just listen. 'What about a minivan?' he suggested. 'One of those bus things that can practically carry an entire football team.'

The boys thought that a brilliant idea. Quinn accused him of harbouring a secret desire for a shed on wheels, which made him laugh.

'So,' he asked when silence reigned again, 'are you boys looking forward to the move?'

'Yes,' said Chase without hesitation.

In the rear-view mirror he saw Robbie frown and chew

the side of his thumb. 'I'm going to miss my friends Luke and Jason.'

Quinn's hands clenched. He flicked a glance at them before turning his attention back to the road. 'I know it's not precisely the same, but you'll be able to Skype with them, won't you?'

Robbie frowned more fiercely. 'What's that?'

'It's like talking on the phone only on the computer, and you get to see each other.'

He stopped chewing his thumb. 'Really?' His face lit up. 'Can I, Mum? Huh, can I?'

Quinn's hands unclenched. 'Sure you can, honey.'

She sent Aidan such a smile he was tempted to simply sit back and bask in it. But then he remembered yesterday's impression. Unfriendly? He wasn't having a bit of it.

'And can I Skype with Daddy too?'

He swore every single muscle Quinn possessed bunched at that. 'I…' She cleared her throat. 'I don't see why not.' She flashed Robbie a smile. For some reason it made Aidan want to drop his head to the steering wheel. He kept both hands tight about it, though, and his eyes glued to the road ahead. 'You'll have to ask him the next time he rings.'

''Kay.'

'Look, kangaroos!' Aidan hollered, pointing to the right and blessing Providence for providing them with the perfect distraction.

Both boys strained in their seats, their mouths open and their faces eager as they watched four large grey kangaroos bounce through the scrub beside the car.

Quinn leant her head back against the seat and closed her eyes.

Aidan pulled in a breath. 'Okay, Robbie and Chase, I think it's time I taught you a song.'

'Is it a fun song?' Chase demanded, as if that was the only kind of song he was interested in.

He scrubbed a hand across his chin. 'It has a yellow submarine. Does that make it fun enough?'

'Yes!' the boys chorused.

Besides, it was a classic. If they were all so hell-bent on novelty songs they might as well learn the best. So he taught them the Beatles' 'Yellow Submarine'. By the time they'd finished they'd reached their first rest stop. While Quinn spread out the picnic blanket in the park area behind the lone roadhouse, Aidan grabbed his laptop and downloaded the song so the boys could listen to the original version. The three of them sang along at the tops of their voices.

When they'd finished, Aidan turned to find Quinn curled on the blanket, fast asleep. He thought of his exhaustion of the previous day. He thought about how she was turning her whole world on its head. He swung back to the boys. 'How about we kick a ball around and let your mum sleep?'

'I'm tired of kicking a ball around,' Chase grumbled. 'I wanna play hopscotch instead.'

Hopscotch?

Without a murmur, Robbie went to the boot of the car and pulled out a plastic mat which, when unfolded, formed a life-sized hopscotch…court, shape or whatever one called it.

'Uh, guys…' Aidan glanced at Quinn. He shook his head. 'Never mind.'

So they played hopscotch.

And darn if it wasn't fun!

'Are you guys worried about making friends in your new home town?'

Chase hopped. 'Mum said it'll be really easy to make friends in school.'

'I expect she's right.' Aiden patted Chase's back. 'Well done, buddy; that was a big hop to end with.'

Robbie took his turn. 'Mum said I can play Saturday morning soccer in Pokolbin, just like I did in Perth.'

'Sport is a great way to make friends.' He stepped back to give Robbie plenty of room to finish his turn. 'You're quick at this.'

'I know.' Robbie nodded, but as Aidan took his turn he could tell the boy was pleased with the praise.

'You'd be quicker if you had play clothes.'

Aidan puffed over the finish line. 'Ain't that the truth? I'll have to buy some when we get to Norseman this afternoon.'

Robbie squinted up at Aidan, chewing his lip. Aidan mightn't have a kid of his own, he mightn't have friends with kids, but it didn't take a rocket scientist to work out that Robbie had something he wanted to ask. 'Out with it, buddy,' he advised.

'You gotta promise to tell me the truth.'

Jeez! He rubbed a hand across his jaw. 'I'll do my best.'

'Is hopscotch a girls' game?'

Aidan automatically went to say no, that anyone was at liberty to play hopscotch, which wasn't really a lie, but… He closed his mouth. Kids could be cruel and, as far as he could tell, political correctness wasn't high on their radar, regardless of what their parents tried to teach them.

He squatted down in front of Robbie and Chase, a glance over his shoulder confirming that Quinn still slept. 'Okay, it shouldn't just be a girls' game, but it kinda is.' He didn't want these kids getting bullied. 'So I wouldn't play it at your new school.'

'Right.' Robbie nodded, evidently glad the question had been settled.

Chase leant against Aidan and the rush of the child's heat against his arm did something strange to Aidan's stomach. He had a sudden primeval impulse to take out anyone who tried to hurt these kids.

'But,' Chase whispered, 'I like playing hopscotch.'

And nobody should be allowed to prevent these kids from enjoying such an innocent diversion. 'That's why I think you should play it at home whenever you want. If anyone finds out about it and gives you a hard time, tell them your mum makes you play it with her. In fact—' a grin built through him '—when you have friends around, tee up with your mum beforehand to make you all play it.'

They'd all love it. He'd tell Quinn to make cake…or chocolate crackles. Kids would forgive any eccentricity for chocolate crackles. They might groan to their parents or other kids that Ms Laverty made them play hopscotch, but then they'd remember the chocolate crackles and still think she was great.

It'd be a win all round.

He beamed at the boys. They beamed back. 'C'mon, who's up next?'

Quinn woke to find Aidan playing hopscotch with Robbie and Chase. She blinked. She sat up and then had to blink again. He actually looked as if he was having fun!

She suddenly grinned, all trace of her thundering headache gone. The sun, the clear blue sky and the dry dusty smells of the rest area seemed filled with a promise they'd all lacked earlier.

She lifted her chin and pushed away the doubts that had spent the night harrying and hounding her. This new beginning should be savoured, not dreaded. Mindless worrying wouldn't help any of them.

Aidan glanced around as if he'd sensed her gaze. Her heart did a silly little flip-flop. Actually, maybe it wasn't so silly. Perhaps it was entirely understandable. Aidan looked a whole lot more…uh, personable without his jacket and tie…or his shoes and socks.

'You lot must be ready for a drink and a snack,' she

called out, but her voice came out a bit higher and threadier than it usually did. She blamed it on the dust in the air. The boys raced over, full of reports of their game, but she only heard every second word. Her eyes never left Aidan. He packed up the game and then ambled over—practically sauntering—and it highlighted the leanness of his hips and the power of his thighs.

And it made her throat as dry as a desert. An ancient hunger built through her. Ancient as in primeval. And ancient as in she hadn't experienced this kind of hunger in over five years. She dragged her gaze away, refused to let it dwell on a body that interested her far too much. Bodies were just bodies. Hormones were just hormones. And this was nothing more than a hormone-induced aberration. She handed out sliced apple, carrot sticks and bottled water and kept her eyes to herself as best she could.

Aidan fell down onto the blanket beside her, slugging her with his heat. The scent of his perspiration rose up, making her gulp. She tried telling herself she loathed man sweat. But it was clean sweat earned in the service of playing with her children and she couldn't hate it. Beneath it threaded that woodsy spice that she'd like to get to know a whole lot better.

'How are you feeling?'

His words rumbled against her. She grabbed an apple slice and crunched it, nodding her head all the while. 'Much better. Thank you for letting me sleep—' she glanced at her watch '—for a whole hour!' He'd taken care of the boys for a whole hour? 'Oh my word! What kind of irresponsible mother you must think me!' What kind of mother just fell asleep in a strange place and—?

'I think you're a brilliant mother, Quinn.'

She had to look at him then. Her mouth opened and closed but no sound came out.

'So do we,' Robbie said.

Chase nodded.

She had to swallow a lump. 'Thank you.' She cleared her throat. 'All of you.'

'I'm going to run now,' Robbie said gravely, and then proceeded to do precisely that. Chase followed at his heels.

She turned back to Aidan to find those molten amber eyes surveying her. 'Thank you for keeping them entertained.'

'It was no big deal.'

He lifted a shoulder, which only alerted her to the fact that while he might not have the physique of a bodybuilder, his shoulders had breadth and his chest didn't lack for depth.

Oh, stop it. She dug fingernails into her palms. A man let her sleep for an hour and she became a sex maniac? *I don't think so.*

'The boys and I had fun. You obviously didn't sleep well last night and I expect the last few weeks have been hectic with the preparations for the move. You're entitled to some downtime too.'

And for the first time in a long time she caught a glimpse of what it must be like to co-parent rather than having to do it all on her own. The vision was unbelievably beguiling.

A man let her sleep for an hour so she built family fantasies about him? She bit back a snort. *I don't think so.* Those fantasies were nothing but a big fat lie. In her experience, most men couldn't be trusted to stick to something as important as fatherhood and even if Aidan proved to be one of the exceptions he never would with her.

And she sure as heck wouldn't with him! Nothing—*nothing*—would ever induce her back into his world and that privileged circle again. She could see it already—the claims of his job would eventually take precedence over his wife and any children he might have. In effect, his wife would be a single parent. Mind you, she'd have the money to hire nannies, but what were nannies to a parent's love? Quinn refused to raise her children in a world where social status and professional prestige were more important than the warmth and intimacy of family ties.

She bit into another slice of apple and glared at a nearby stunted tree, grateful Aidan hadn't connected her with the Sydney Lavertys. It wasn't something she publicised and it certainly wasn't something she wanted to talk about.

But the memory of his world brought her back to herself. It reminded her of all of his responsibilities and duties. 'How was your mother when you rang her last night?'

He grimaced.

This was one of the many things she'd considered in the wee small hours when sleep had refused to come. 'I thought about her last night.'

He lifted a brow. 'And?'

'I think you need to give her a task, something concrete to do.'

'To take her mind off…other things?'

'It's hard to brood when you're busy.'

He considered her words and very slowly the line around his mouth eased. 'I could get her to double check the arrangements with the caterers and—'

'I was thinking—'

She broke off and flushed. 'Sorry, that was rude of me. I have no right stomping on your ideas with my big fat hypothetical work boots.'

'I'd like to hear your idea.'

He would? She glanced up to find him watching her closely and it occurred to her that he wouldn't have been nearly as open if he'd known her. But as they'd never clap eyes on each other again—well, she might see him on the television but that didn't count—after the next few days it was almost as if they were in a bubble. A bubble that had no impact or relevance on their real day-to-day lives. And when they returned to those real lives there'd be barely a ripple of this time to ruffle the surface.

It was unbelievably freeing. She understood that.

It was also unutterably sad, which she didn't understand at all.

She shrugged that off and dragged her attention back to the conversation. 'I just think you need to give your mother something to do that she can't shrug off as unimportant or that she can delegate to someone else.'

'You think she considers the party unimportant?'

Yikes! She'd need to tread carefully. Aidan had been through enough and she had no wish to hurt his feelings. Before she could roll out a tactful response, though, he said, 'You think the party is making me feel better, but not my mother.'

'I don't know your mother, Aidan, so I can't possibly comment on that.' He leaned away from her. Lines of strain fanned out from his mouth and it made her heart clench. 'I bet it's making your father feel better.'

His head snapped up, confirming her suspicions. She made herself smile. 'And that's no mean feat, surely?' The man had lost his child too.

Air rushed out of him. 'Dad and I concocted the party idea between us.' He lifted a hand as if to push it back through his hair, but he let it drop as if he didn't have the energy for it. 'It's given us something else to focus on.'

Her heart thumped. 'Aidan?'

He looked up.

'A party, no matter how ritzy and beautiful, or how well-meaning, won't…'

'Won't make up to my mother for losing a son,' he said, blunt and emotionless.

She tried not to flinch.

'You must think I'm an unbelievable idiot, and shallow to boot, to think a party would help.'

'I think you're worried about your mother and want to see her happy.'

He met her eyes.

'But I think you might be better served giving her something to do that *she* thinks is important. I mean as important as your desire to cheer her up is to you.'

He mulled her suggestion over for a moment. She could see his mind ticking over, but she had no idea what conclusion he came to. 'You make a good case.' The faintest of smiles touched his lips and something inside her unclenched a fraction. 'I take it you have had a thought or two on that head as well.'

'Well…yes.'

The smile grew a millimetre or two bigger. 'C'mon then, out with it.'

She pulled in a breath. 'I asked myself what your mother would consider important and I didn't have to go far to find it—you. She's invested in your happiness and your welfare, yes?'

His lips twisted. 'Yes.'

'Therefore, I expect your career is of prime importance to her.'

He closed his eyes and just like that any trace of a smile vanished. Her throat tightened as if a fist squeezed about it. She wasn't sure what she'd said wrong, but she had no intention of adding to her travelling companion's heartache. She straightened and eased back. 'I'm sorry. Like I said before, this is none of my business and I have no right—'

'I would like to hear what you have to say.'

She bit her lip but his gaze held hers so steadily that eventually she nodded. 'I was thinking that you should ask her to go into your office to oversee the daily operations of your campaign while you're not there.'

'I have staff to do that!'

'You could tell her that you respect your staff, but that you trust her rather than them to have your best interests at heart.' She rubbed her right hand back and forth across her left. 'You could tell her that you believe she was one of the reasons your father was elected when he ran for office back in the nineties. You could tell her that if she can find the time and has the heart for it, that it would mean the world to you if she would help you run your campaign.'

He'd gone grey. 'It's the one thing I've been avoiding.'

She bit her lip but the question slipped out anyway. 'Why?'

He stared up at the sky for a long moment. 'Selfish reasons.'

She bit her lip so hard then that nothing could slip out.

He straightened and pushed his shoulders back. 'You're right, though. That's precisely the kind of thing that would give her another focus. Dad and I have been wrapping her in cotton wool and that's the last thing she needs right now. What she needs is to be busy with some project close to her heart.'

'It's not selfish to want to protect the people we love. It's natural.'

He reached out to grip her shoulder, squeeze it, but his smile didn't reach his eyes. 'You're wise beyond your years. Thank you.'

She frowned. 'You're welcome.'

His hand remained on her shoulder and every nerve in her body sprang to life, making her breath hitch. He stilled and then his gaze speared to hers. He took in the expression on her face and that hot caramel gaze of his lowered to her lips. Something inside her started to tremble and gasp and her blood quickened in a sweet rush of need.

His eyes darkened. Hunger flared in their depths. His gaze locked to hers. 'Quinn?' He leaned towards her.

She tried to shake her head, to negate the question in his eyes, but her body refused to cooperate with her common sense. Her lips parted. If she leaned towards him...

A stream of childhood laughter reached her and it gave her just enough strength to close her eyes and lower her chin. Aidan removed his hand and eased back, but his scent—all spice and woods—wove around her, and she started to ache. She heard him climb to his feet. If she just whispered his name...

'Probably time for us to hit the road again.'

She snapped her eyes open and steeled her spine. She gave a swift nod of agreement. Excellent idea. She didn't say the words out loud, though. She didn't trust her voice not to betray her.

They reached Norseman at five o'clock.

Norseman had a population of sixteen hundred and was one of the few towns on the Nullarbor Plain with decent facilities. Quinn had called ahead to book her and the boys a caravan for the night. Tonight, regardless of how hard her bunk might prove to be, she'd be asleep by the time her head hit the pillow.

She and the boys had hamburgers for dinner. She allayed her guilt by telling herself they were on their holidays.

She didn't know where Aidan ate. Or when. Her efforts to avoid him had met with spectacular success. She suspected that was due to the fact that she had his full cooperation on that front.

She thought of that moment again—the moment when they might have kissed—and her breath jammed. How much she'd wanted to kiss him! But kissing Aidan was out of the question. The world he belonged to had betrayed her before. She wasn't giving it a chance to hurt her again.

Thank heavens for Robbie and Chase. They kept her

busy, claiming most of her attention and giving her little time to brood. However, they both fell asleep before seven o'clock. Quinn might be tired, but seven o'clock was far too early for a grown woman to go to bed.

She glanced around the caravan, rubbed her hands together a few times, picked up a magazine and then put it down again. She was too wired. With a glance at the sleeping boys, she eased the door to their caravan open and slipped outside. If the insects weren't too fierce she could sit out here at one of the picnic tables for a bit and lap up the quiet.

And the quiet was amazing. So was the dark. It had never been this dark in her suburb in Perth. She glanced up and her jaw dropped. She took a few steps forward. Stars, magnificent in their brightness and multitude, stretched across a navy dark sky and she wasn't sure she'd ever seen anything so spectacular in all her life.

'It takes your breath away, doesn't it?'

Aidan! She half turned but kept her gaze firmly fixed on the stars. *He* stole her breath. 'They're amazing.' And if her breath came out a tad husky she'd blame it on the night air and the majesty of the sky.

'I was hoping you'd be out here.'

That made her look at him.

He held a bottle of wine in one hand and two wine glasses in the other. Her mouth dried. 'Aidan,' she croaked. 'I—'

'It's just a glass of wine, Quinn. That's all, I promise.'

Without another word, she took a seat at the table he gestured to and accepted a glass of wine with a murmured, 'Thank you.' She couldn't help it. There was something about this man she trusted.

'Cheers.' He raised his glass. She raised hers back. They both sipped…and grimaced. 'Sorry,' he murmured. 'There wasn't a whole lot of choice at the hotel.'

'Don't apologise. This is nice.' She gestured to the bottle. 'Makes me feel like a grown-up.'

Which, perhaps, wasn't the message she should be broadcasting. 'I mean it's such a change from sitting holding a toy car or a super-soaker or someone's crayon that—'

'I knew what you meant.'

His words, soft and warm in the dark, skimmed the bare surface of her arms and neck and she had to suppress a shiver. A *sexy* shiver. For heaven's sake, she had to find a way to get over this stupid awareness. She glanced at Aidan. And this stupid awkwardness. She'd been fine before she'd started lusting after him. She'd been fine when they'd been talking about his mother.

Speaking of which…

'Have you spoken to your mother tonight?'

'Yes.'

He didn't elaborate. She bit the inside of her cheek and then took a hasty sip of wine. 'It improves on a second tasting,' she offered.

He suddenly laughed. 'You're minding your manners beautifully. To answer the question you refuse to ask, your little suggestion has worked a treat. My mother is racing into my office first thing tomorrow to make sure everything is shipshape. And heaven help my staff if it's not.'

'Have you warned them?'

'Oh, yes.'

'And your mother seemed…' Happy was too much to hope for. 'Engaged?'

'Yes,' he murmured. 'Yes, she did.'

'Well, that's good isn't it?' He sounded pleased and not pleased at the same time.

'Of course it's good.'

He didn't add anything else.

Okay. Um…

Quinn went back to staring at the stars until the silence

chafed too badly. She risked a glance at her travelling companion and found him staring into his wine glass with pursed lips.

'So…uh…are you staying at the caravan park too?'

'I'm staying in one of the cabins here.'

He didn't say anything else. It took all her willpower to stop from jiggling her legs. Tonight this silence with Aidan was too fraught. She wanted the distraction of conversation. 'So…' She decided against asking if his cabin was nice or not. It might be a step up from a caravan, but she expected it would still be fairly basic. 'Have you always wanted to be a politician?'

'No.' The word shot out of him. A moment later his head snapped up. 'I mean, I know that's what the Fairhalls do and what we're known for, but it was always Daniel's passion, not mine.'

A sliver of ice traced a path down her back. 'What were you doing before you made the move to politics?'

'I was a lawyer.'

'Oh?' She injected every ounce of curiosity and interest that she could into that single syllable.

'I worked for a big firm in Sydney that prided itself on its social conscience.' He named the firm.

'I've heard of them!'

'Yeah.' He grinned crookedly and it flipped her heart right over. 'We made the news a lot. We'd take on high profile cases and charge through the nose so we could afford to subsidise the cases we were really interested in.'

'You guys did great work.'

'We did.' He sobered. 'They still do.'

Without him. And that was the moment she realised what he wasn't saying. 'You're keeping the family tradition alive by giving all of that up and going into politics.'

He glanced up as if he'd heard the censure in her voice. 'I will do good work in politics too, Quinn.'

'I don't doubt it.' But at what cost to himself?

The silence between them stretched. Eventually she cleared her throat. 'You know what you said to me yesterday afternoon about who I reminded you of?'

He stilled.

'Is that a good thing or a bad thing?' Did it bring him pain to spend time in her company?

His lips lifted. It was as if she'd removed a weight from him. He met her gaze. 'A good thing.'

She didn't know what to say after that.

He went to top up her glass but she snatched it up and shook her head. 'I really should go to bed now.'

'It's not even eight o'clock.' He set the wine bottle down with an audible thump. 'What are you afraid of, Quinn? That I'm going to make a pass at you and pressure you to have sex with me?'

The thought filled her with a heat almost impossible to ignore, although she did her best to do precisely that. 'I don't want to give you the wrong impression.'

'You're not.'

She leaned towards him. 'I haven't done anything impulsive in a very long time. To be honest, me and impulsive are barely on speaking terms these days. But this trip, and you, it feels as if...'

'What?'

He'd stilled but she recognised the hunger burning deep in his eyes. 'This trip feels like a timeout from the real world, and it feels as if what happens now couldn't possibly affect the future.'

'And that scares you.'

'You're darn tootin' it scares me. I know it's an illusion, a lie. How on earth do you think I ended up single with two children?'

Even in the dark she could see the way he paled.

'Aidan, we're from two different worlds.' Which wasn't

precisely true. 'And we're on two different paths.' Which was. 'You're a politician who certainly doesn't want to blot his copybook by doing something reckless. And I'm a single mum who can't afford the luxury of recklessness.'

She stared down at her hands. 'I've turned my whole world upside down and there's a part of me that's screaming in panic. I like you, you're a very attractive man, but I don't want to go looking for comfort and reassurance where I shouldn't. Experience warns me it will only get me into trouble.'

'I don't want to cause you any trouble, Quinn.'

'I know that.' She rose. 'Which is why I'm going to bed. I'll see you in the morning. Thank you for the wine.'

He didn't say anything, but she could feel the weight of his gaze and it slowed her steps. But it didn't stop them.

CHAPTER FOUR

AIDAN MADE COFFEE—instant—from the complimentary jug and tiny sachets in his cabin. The cheap shorts and T-shirt he'd bought at a discount store in Norseman's surprisingly adequate shopping strip yesterday scraped against his skin with an unfamiliar stiffness. That said, they were strangely comfortable, even if they didn't fit as well as the closetful of designer clothes he had in his apartment in Sydney. He slid on his brand new tennis shoes and, mug in hand, headed outside.

The harsh Outback light bouncing off caravan windows made him blink and he had to squint until his eyes adjusted. He'd slept later than he'd meant to, but with the easy, unhurried hours Quinn kept he didn't think that'd be a problem. He glanced around and something tugged at him, something off-key that he couldn't identify. Stifling a yawn, he shrugged it off. This whole situation was strange and off-key.

He ambled up and down the line of cabins and caravans for a bit, reminding himself to get what exercise he could. Mind you, they were only going as far as Madura today—less than six hours of driving. He spent twice that long in his office chair most days.

For pity's sake, they were still only eight hours from Perth! They had another twenty to go before they reached Adelaide. That was what was off-key—this plodding, leisurely pace. He sipped coffee and then frowned. No, what was off-key was his easy acceptance of it.

He closed his eyes and shadows danced behind his eyelids as he acknowledged his utter disinterest in returning to Sydney and his wretched campaign.

But the way his mother's voice had quickened on the phone last night. He forced his eyes open again. Her immediate interest and concern had pulled her out from beneath a morass of apathy. Just like that.

It was why he'd bought the wine. It was why he'd sought out Quinn's company. He'd been searching for solace and reassurance.

Liar.

He blinked.

You wanted her. You still want her. You hoped—

No he didn't! His head reared back. He…

His brain synapses slowed to the consistency of cold treacle. Realisation spread like a toxic chill. He *did* find Quinn attractive. *Very* attractive. From the moment when he'd nearly kissed her yesterday he hadn't been able to get the thought of what she'd taste like out of his mind.

He scratched a hand through his hair and scowled at his feet. Why had he hidden his motives behind a barricade of petty justifications and oh-woe-is-me excuses?

His lungs suddenly cramped. Because of Danny? Because Danny was no longer around to pursue and woo a pretty woman?

For a moment he thought he might throw up.

And then, out of all the spinning chaos in his mind, one tiny shard of comprehension detached itself. That sense of wrongness when he'd stepped out of his cabin…

He spun, coffee flying out in an arc around him. Her car was gone. Quinn's car was gone. She'd left him. *Abandoned* him!

Air punched out of his lungs. He bent at the waist, resting a hand against his knee, while he fought to get oxygen back into his body. He'd screwed up. *Royally.* Quinn's every instinct last night had been spot on. He might've lied to himself, but she'd seen through him. He'd gone looking for temporary respite in its nearest available form—Quinn.

Why? Because he'd felt backed into a corner after that phone call with his mother? What on earth did that have to do with Quinn? *Nothing*!

He straightened. Taking, that was all he'd been interested in. He deserved this. Totally deserved it. But…

He braced an arm against the side of Quinn's caravan— Quinn's *empty* caravan—and rested his head against it.

'Aidan?'

He lifted his head.

'Aidan?'

He jerked around.

Quinn!

'What's wrong?' Her brows drew together.

He glanced beyond her to see the station wagon parked on the other side of the caravan. Robbie and Chase loitered nearby. 'I, uh…just waking up. Where have you been?' His voice came out on a croak.

'Just into town to grab some supplies. This is the last decent-sized town now until we reach Ceduna or Port Augusta.' She shrugged. 'On impulse we popped out to the Beacon Hill lookout.' She shifted her weight. 'I left a message for you at reception in case you were looking for us.'

Of course she had!

She frowned then and planted her hands on her hips. He didn't want her to question him too closely. 'What time do you want to set off?'

'Within the hour.'

'I'll…um…go get packed up.'

He stumbled back into his cabin and collapsed onto the sofa and dropped his head to his hands, his coffee mug still dangling from his fingers. He'd been given a second chance.

Don't mess it up!

Aidan intended on being the best darn travelling companion Quinn and her kids had ever had.

With his encouragement, the boys spent most of the first hour telling him about the Beacon Hill lookout. They'd seen salt lakes and giant mine tailing dumps. The view obviously hadn't been pretty, but it had certainly left an impression. He tried to squash the sense of having been left out. Instead he recalled his gratitude when he'd lifted his head to see Quinn standing in front of him this morning.

The talk moved from that lookout in particular to lookouts in general and Aidan found himself trying to describe the view from Corcovado in Rio de Janeiro.

And to then explaining that there weren't any tigers in South America, other than in zoos. Which in turn led to a discussion about zoos. The boys loved zoos—no surprises there. 'You should get your mum to take you to Taronga Park Zoo in Sydney once you've settled in. It'll only be a couple of hours in the car.'

'You live in Sydney,' Robbie said. 'You could come too.'

'If I'm free it's a date,' he promised.

Quinn glanced at her watch. 'Okay, you have an hour of Gameboy time if you want it.'

The boys were soon immersed in their games. She glanced at him, their eyes clashed for the merest fraction of a second before she whipped her gaze back to the road. Damn it! He didn't want her feeling tense around him. He wanted her relaxed and happy. Not because he wanted to seduce her, but because she was a nice woman who'd helped him out and she deserved good things in return.

He shifted on his seat, cleared his throat. 'I've gotta

say the variety and splendour of this scenery is something to behold.'

'Uh-huh. Dirt and scrub for as far as the eye can see. You could go a long way before seeing something so…'

'Appealing? Engaging? Captivating?' All words that could describe her. He cut off further musings in that direction. It wasn't going to happen.

'It's amazing, though, isn't it?' she said. 'It's so unvarying, so…unrelieved.'

'I think it's amazing anyone can eke a living out here.'

She puffed out a breath. 'I don't think I could live so far from civilisation.'

Polite chit-chat. Nothing threatening. He excelled at this stuff. He bit back a sigh.

From the corner of his eye he saw her glance at him again. He lifted his chin. 'Do you know we're now on the single longest piece of straight road in Australia?'

'A hundred and forty-six point six kilometres.'

She did know.

'Aidan, you're being great with the boys and I appreciate it, but I don't want you to feel as if you have to make promises to them.'

The change in topic threw him. 'I don't. I…' He stared at her. 'You mean the zoo?'

She nodded.

He rolled his shoulders and stared back out to the front. 'If you want the truth, I'd love to spend the day with you and the boys at the zoo.'

Her knuckles whitened around the steering wheel and he snatched back a curse. 'I've not had much to do with kids. I didn't know…'

She didn't look at him. 'What?'

'I didn't know how much fun they'd be or how much I'd enjoy their company.'

Her knuckles returned to their normal colour. 'Really?'

'I always figured I'd marry and have kids one day. I mean, it's what you do, isn't it?' He scraped a hand across his jaw. 'But… Now I *know* that's what I want.'

The softest of smiles touched her lips and an ache started up deep inside him. An ache that stretched and burned and settled in his groin. He shifted on the seat and did what he could to ignore it. 'I gotta tell you the conversation I had with the boys over hopscotch yesterday.'

He proceeded to tell her about Robbie's question and the plan they'd concocted between them, embellishing where he could until she was laughing so hard he had to reach out and help her steer for a moment.

'Oh, that's priceless.' She dabbed at her eyes—first with her left wrist and then with her right.

She had colour in her cheeks. She'd stopped biting her lip every other minute. He settled back into his seat and listened as she hummed along to a song on the radio. The view outside hadn't changed—still an unending expanse of sand and scrub—but it somehow looked brighter and more inviting than it had earlier.

They reached Madura late afternoon. They'd had what Chase quaintly phrased 'pit stops' at Balladonia and Caiguna. Settlements that were mere specks on the maps. Balladonia had a population of nine. Nine! That put the concept of isolation into perspective. The boys had a lot of fun choosing the nine people they'd most like to have in town…and the nine they'd least want.

Like the rest of the Nullarbor Plain, they were dry dusty places with that same endless low scrub. But they did have roadhouses and accommodation.

Madura was a little larger and some would say a little more scenic, situated as it was at the base of the Hampton Tablelands. As far as Aidan could tell, that just meant that the land undulated a bit more. They booked rooms at the motel and the boys were over the moon to discover it had a pool.

Which was how Aidan found himself wandering around outside the pool fence with Quinn while the boys splashed and whooped inside. Out of the corner of his eye he saw Robbie race from one end of the pool enclosure to the other as a run-up for a big jump into the water. It had been a long time since he could remember running for the sheer joy of it. He wouldn't mind running now.

He ran a finger around the collar of his T-shirt and reminded himself he was a grown man. 'Quinn, about last night…'

She tensed. She tensed so much she stopped walking.

He squinted at the sky. 'Last night I was feeling at a bit of a loss. I didn't know what to do with myself.'

She started a jerky forward motion again. 'Because of your conversation with your mother?'

'Do you think it's crazy of me to worry about her?'

'No.'

His collar stopped trying to strangle him.

She glanced at him. 'Do you read?'

'Sure I do. Not that I get much time for it.' When she raised an exaggerated eyebrow he had to nod. 'You're right, there's plenty of time for it at the moment.'

'If you're interested, I have a few books in the back of the car.'

Reading for pleasure had become a rare treat. He straightened. 'I'd love to borrow one.'

'C'mon, then.' She hitched her head in the direction of the car.

She moved with the grace of a gazelle, dainty and elegant, though neither of those things hid her supple strength. He had to force his gaze from the long length of her legs and back to his surroundings before he betrayed himself.

She shifted a couple of boxes in the wagon and then pointed. 'That box there, can you drag it out?'

He did. When he peered inside it his lip started to curl. 'Science textbooks?'

Her grin was sudden and swift and he thanked heaven he was leaning against the car or he might've fallen face first into the dirt. 'I worked in one of the science departments at the University of Western Australia and one of the professors had a clean-out of his bookshelves last week. I helped myself to a couple.'

Good Lord, why? He didn't ask, but she must've seen the question in his face. 'If you find such things dull and dry, they're guaranteed to put you to sleep in five minutes flat.'

She didn't find them dull or dry, though, did she? What had she meant to do with her life before fate had intervened in the shape of an unplanned pregnancy? He stared at the textbooks.

'Dig deeper.' She nodded at the box. 'There's quite a selection in there.'

He chose an autobiography of a famous actor. He turned it face out to show her. 'Do you mind? I've been wanting to read this for ages.'

'Help yourself.'

He packed the box back up and stacked it in its original position. When he finished he turned to find her leaning against the car with her eyes closed and her face lifted to the sun.

A breath eased out of him.

Her eyes sprang open. 'What?'

Stop staring! He shut the trunk. 'I was just thinking how much more relaxed you look today than you did yesterday or the day before.'

'Oh, that.' She blinked and then she smiled and it was such a beautiful smile the breath punched out of him all over again. There were moments when this woman smiled with her whole being, the way Daniel used to. It made him crave something he had no name for.

'When we set off from Perth I started having panic attacks wondering if I was doing the right thing or not.'

'And now?' His heart pounded though he couldn't have explained why.

'Now I've decided to embrace what's ahead of me—to enjoy it and make the absolute best of it.'

'Bravo!' No sooner had the word left his mouth than his mind started to whirl. Could he take a leaf out of her book, follow her example? Could he find a way to embrace the course set before his feet—the political life?

His legs and shoulders grew heavy. The day darkened, even though the sun remained high and warm above them.

They started walking again because their only two options were walking or sitting and they'd both had enough of sitting.

He supposed he could excuse himself and retire to his room with the book. He didn't want to, though. There'd be enough time for solitude later. He rolled his shoulders and tried to throw off his funk. 'What are you hoping to gain from your move, Quinn?' Considering her future—and the boys'—was a more promising option than trying to make sense of his. Still, he intended to retract the question if it made her look the least bit uncomfortable.

A breath eased out of him when it didn't.

She nodded towards the boys and he had to remind himself not to hold her gaze for too long. *Don't let her see how much you want to kiss her.*

He watched the two boys dive simultaneously into the pool. He clapped his hands and shouted praise.

He glanced from them and back to their mother. Steel flooded his spine. He was not going to mess with her. Him and her, they were on different courses and he had no intention of dragging her or her boys into his own private hell.

What are you hoping to gain from your move?

Aidan's words scored through her. Quinn twisted her hands together and watched her boys. They were so absorbed in their splashing and diving, and her heart filled with so much love it almost hurt.

She pointed a finger at Chase, who looked as if he was about to tear off down the other end of the enclosure. 'No running,' she said for the second time. 'Wet feet and wet concrete are not a good combination.' Her second son had a tendency to learn his lessons the hard way.

She glanced back to find Aidan watching her with a queer light in his eyes. She didn't know what it meant. Today he'd been so *friendly* that she'd started to think she'd been mistaken about the vibes she'd sensed last night.

He might not want you, but you still want him.

He must know lots of beautiful polished women. The idea of him being attracted to a single mother who wore next to no make-up and didn't give two hoots about designer outfits was laughable.

She tried to push that thought aside, tried to shake off the heaviness that threatened to descend and to concentrate on what really was important—her move across the country.

What are you hoping to gain from your move?

'Family,' she finally said. 'I'm hoping to give my boys, my aunt and myself a family.'

'Family,' he repeated, annunciating each syllable in a kind of slow homage to the word.

'You're close to your parents.' She wasn't sure if she was asking or stating.

'I guess.'

But he'd become guarded, wary, and her heart burned

for him. She refused to pry, though. He and his parents had suffered so much. She dredged up a smile and a shrug. 'I found myself watching my friends in Perth over the last year and seeing what a source of strength their families were to them. I'm talking about extended families—parents, grandparents, siblings, cousins, aunts and uncles—and I started to envy them.'

Somewhere along the line she'd stopped walking. She kicked herself back into action, forced one foot in front of the other. Aidan's long legs kept easy pace beside her. The sun had started to lower in the west and the scrub, low trees and sand all glowed orange and khaki. A sigh eased out of her. 'I know their families were occasionally—even often—a source of frustration, but they were a source of happiness too.' A source of belonging.

'And you want that?'

'Yes.' With all her heart and she wasn't ashamed to admit it. She knew her own strength. She knew she could continue to go it alone. But if she didn't have to…

'And as I only have one relation who is the slightest bit interested in wanting to know me…' She'd made her voice tongue-in-cheek, but Aidan didn't smile.

She reached out and pulled him to a halt. His arm flexed beneath her fingers and she sensed its latent strength. Reluctantly she released him. 'I'm tired of feeling alone, Aidan.'

She didn't know what it was about this man that made her so ready to confide in him. Maybe it was the innate 'ships passing in the night' nature of their association. It had broken down the usual barriers of reserve.

His face became gentle. He reached out as if to touch her cheek, but he drew his hand back at the last moment. The usual barriers hadn't broken down that much.

'Don't get me wrong.' She forced herself to start walking again. 'I'm not lonely. I have friends, colleagues, not to mention my boys. I'm not unhappy. It's just when I have to make a decision about one of the boys—should I go up to the school and make an issue about Chase's appalling handwriting or another child's constant use of a bad word, or should I let Robbie stay up late on the occasional Saturday night so he can watch a rugby test match, or any number of things like that. To be able to talk it over with someone who's also invested would be such a comfort. Even if we didn't agree.'

'Wow,' he eventually breathed.

She immediately cringed. 'Sorry, that was probably way more information than you wanted and—'

'Mum!'

Chase's scream and Robbie's shout had her spinning around, adrenaline flooding her every cell. Heart pounding, she raced for the gate, all instinct and fear.

Blood.

Blood in the water.

Chase in the water.

She tugged and tugged on the safety latch on the gate, but her fingers kept slipping and finding no purchase, as if she'd forgotten how to use an opposable thumb. Her breath came hard and short in little sobs. *Please, gate. Please open.*

It wouldn't open!

In one easy vault, Aidan cleared the fence and, without breaking stride, dived into the water and pulled Chase into his arms. 'He's okay,' he called to her.

Okay meant he wasn't drowned. It didn't mean he was *okay*.

Magically the gate opened and she flew to Aidan as he emerged with a howling Chase from the shallow end. There was so much blood!

She reached for him and Chase reached for her, but Aidan pushed her down onto the banana lounge that held the boys' towels and shirts before setting Chase onto her lap.

She held him close and rocked him, murmuring nonsense in an effort to quiet him, while Aidan tried to stem the blood from the cut above Chase's eye. She handed him one of the shirts she half sat on. They could replace a shirt, but she would never be able to replace one of her beautiful boys.

Her heart thunderstormed in her chest as she watched Aidan's face, trying to gauge the extent of the damage by his expression, but he kept his face carefully schooled and she couldn't read it at all.

Fear gripped her by the throat. If Chase were badly hurt…way out here in the back of beyond, it'd be her fault. *Please God. Please God. Please God.*

She glanced up to find Robbie staring at her with fear in his eyes. She did what she could to swallow her own. 'What happened, honey?'

Robbie scuffed a toe against the cement. 'He, um… slipped and hit his head on the side of the pool before falling in.'

They'd been running! She should've been keeping a closer eye on them! She should've been watching them properly, not pouring her heart out to the first man who'd shown a modicum of interest in her in months!

Aidan straightened and her gaze flew back to him. 'What?' She couldn't push anything else out.

'He's going to have a heck of a lump and a shiner tomorrow, and probably a corker of a headache tonight, but the cut's not deep and it won't need stitches.'

She closed her eyes and sent up a prayer of thanks. 'There was so much blood,' she whispered.

'Head wounds bleed a lot.' He sat back on his heels, a smile touching his lips. 'With two young sons, I'd have thought you'd have known that.'

Crazily, she found herself almost smiling back.

Chase's sobs had eased and Aidan gestured to him. 'I'd like to check him for concussion.'

'Hey, baby,' she crooned. 'Can you look at Mummy?'

Chase sat up a bit and touched his head. 'It hurts,' he hiccupped.

'I bet it does. That was a heck of a tumble,' she soothed, smoothing his hair back.

'There was blood.' His lip wobbled.

'You're not wrong about that, buddy.' Aidan crouched down in front of them. 'We're going to play a quick game.' He hurried on before Chase could refuse and bury his head in her shoulder again. 'How many fingers am I holding up?'

'Three.'

'What's my name?'

'Aidan.'

'And what comes after D in the alphabet?'

Chase started reciting the alphabet under his breath. 'E.'

'Excellent, Chase, you got a perfect score.'

Chase snuggled into her and started to shiver. Aidan grabbed a towel and wrapped it around the child. 'We need to get him warm and dry.'

'How do you know so much about this?' Aidan seemed so calm and professional—utterly unfazed, unlike her. Besides, talking kept the demons at bay.

'I did a St John's Ambulance course six months ago.'

She struggled to her feet. In another year Chase would be too big for her to carry. But she could still manage it at the moment. 'What made you decide to do that? Not that I'm not grateful, of course, but—'

She broke off. Daniel. The car accident.

Right.

In his grief, Aidan had chosen to do something positive rather than negative. Good for him.

'Thank you,' she murmured when he opened the gate for her.

'You're welcome.'

And then he draped a towel around the shoulders of a too quiet Robbie and rested his arm across her eldest son's shoulders in a gesture of comfort and companionship and walked them back to their room.

It didn't make her knees weak. It didn't make her pulse quicken. But it did make her heart tremble.

Aidan was sitting to one side of her door in a camp chair when she slipped out of her room that night. He rose and set another chair out for her.

And then he handed her a can of beer.

And a chocolate bar.

Tears pricked her eyes. A big lump lodged in her throat, making it impossible to squeeze out so much as a thank you. She sat.

'Thought you could do with a pick-me-up.'

She nodded, sniffled and pulled in a breath that made her entire frame shudder. And then she opened her beer and took a gulp. She tore open the wrapper of her chocolate bar and took a big bite.

She closed her eyes, sat back and let the tension drain out of her. She drank more beer. She ate more chocolate. It was a disgusting combination and she relished every single mouthful.

Aidan sat with his legs stretched out and eyes to the front, quietly surveying the night. No rush or impatience or expectation. His stillness slowly eased into her. She finished both the beer and the chocolate bar. 'That's exactly what I needed.'

'Good.'

'Thank you.'

'You're welcome.'

She turned to him as much as her tired limbs would allow. 'I want to thank you for springing into action so quickly today.'

'It was no big deal.'

'It was a huge deal to me. I couldn't even get the rotten gate open.'

'You would've eventually.'

She shuddered. 'Chase could've drowned by then.'

'Stop exaggerating,' he chided. 'He was holding his head out of the water when I got to him.'

He had been? A little more of the residual fear eased out of her.

'He was just a bit dazed and in pain. How is he now?'

'Asleep, thankfully. They were both exhausted.'

'And how are you?'

She sent him a wan smile. 'Well, I've slowed down on the blame game and I'm slowly recovering from the fright.' She stared out towards the scrub beyond the circle of light cast from the motel, but she couldn't see a thing. It was all deep blackness. 'I never knew I could feel so afraid until I had children.'

'Did I really say earlier that I wanted them?'

She laughed. 'It's worth it.' But not if you worked in excess of eighty hours a week. She glanced at him. She opened her mouth. She closed it again. *None of your business.*

They were both silent for a while. 'Funny, isn't it?' she eventually said. 'How love and pain can be so closely linked. Not just romantic love, but love for one's children and parents and friends.'

Though this man knew more about that than most. 'Still—' she pulled in a breath '—life's not worth living without it.'

'Which makes the human race either incredibly stupid or incredibly brave.'

'I'll go with brave if they're the only two options on offer.'

She was rewarded with a lopsided grin and a shake of his head.

'I thought you were very brave today. I'm in your debt, Aidan. I doubt I'll ever be able to repay you, but if there's anything I can do…ever…'

He turned to her and behind the tempting brightness of his eyes she sensed his mind racing. 'There might be one thing you could do…'

The look on his face made her breath catch and her stomach do slow loop the loops.

He wouldn't!

He rose. 'I'll give it some thought and let you know in the morning. Goodnight, Quinn.'

She could only stare after him, wondering what on earth he was playing at. Or if he was playing at anything at all.

CHAPTER FIVE

THE NEXT MORNING Quinn and the boys enjoyed a picnic breakfast at a table near the pool. It wasn't fancy—cereal and toast. Quinn had lugged cereal and long-life milk with her from Perth. She'd bought fresh bread from the road-house that morning.

While it might not be fancy, the warm morning and the novelty filled the boys with glee and took their minds off eating in the roadhouse restaurant. It wasn't that she needed to count every penny, but she did want to be careful. Besides, she wanted them to eat as healthily as she could manage whilst on the road.

She was blowing on her coffee when Aidan sauntered into view. The steam floated up into her face, haloing him in a smoky soft focus. He looked like a mirage, like a man walking out of the desert. A sigh breathed out of her and more steam drifted upwards.

She shook herself and then blew on her coffee until the steam blinded her. When he reached the table, she smiled in his direction, but took a moment to hand Robbie a paper napkin so she didn't have to address him. Of course, that didn't block his scent when he sat beside her. She breathed him in, and the knot in her chest unwound.

'Morning, troops.'

The boys sing-songed their greetings back to him through mouthfuls of Vegemite toast.

'Have you eaten?' She sort of half glanced at him. His hair was damp as if he'd just showered and he wore a different T-shirt than he had yesterday. The T-shirt had obviously come in a packet and two creases bisected his chest and another his stomach. He looked utterly different from the man who'd begged her for a ride. Her father wouldn't have approved. She did, wholeheartedly.

'Help yourself.' She gestured to the cereal boxes and pile of toast. 'There's another cereal bowl in our room if you'd like it.'

He nodded behind him to the roadhouse. 'I've already eaten.'

She hoped his breakfast had been healthy. She opened her mouth. She closed it again. *None of your business.*

He glanced at their table. 'But this looks nice.'

She couldn't mistake his wistfulness, though it was harder to explain the burn in her heart. 'Well, you're absolutely welcome to join us for soggy cereal and cold toast tomorrow.'

He laughed as she'd meant him to, but the burn in her heart only intensified.

He glanced at Chase. 'How's the head, buster?'

'It's better.' He glowered at Quinn. 'I keep telling Mum I'm all better and that I can go swimming in the pool again, but she won't listen.'

She had to bite back a smile. Both of her children would need to be seriously under the weather to resist the lure of a swim.

'Your mum is probably right. A quiet day could be just the thing.'

Chase heaved a sigh, evidently exasperated with clueless adults.

'Which is why I want to run a proposal by you all.'

Aidan ran a hand down his shirt as if to smooth out the

creases and she suddenly realised she'd been staring. She shook herself. 'Proposal?'

His look told her he was thinking of last night and her 'returning the favour' remark. The boys glanced to her and she sat up a little straighter. 'We're all ears.'

'I was thinking we could all do with a day off from driving.'

She'd been working on the theory that it'd take them ten days to reach Aunt Mara's, longer if they decided to tarry somewhere. With the NSW school holidays currently operating, the boys weren't missing any school. This was only day four of their great 'across the country' expedition, so they weren't even halfway through their journey yet, but she didn't say anything. She was too curious to see what Aidan meant to propose.

In the morning sunshine his eyes twinkled. It could've been the reflection cast up from the pool, but she didn't think so. She had a feeling it came from within. She hadn't seen him fired up with enthusiasm before, except for that moment when he'd talked about his law firm. Now, though, he smiled and twinkled and she could barely drag her gaze away. An answering enthusiasm built through her. 'A day off?'

He leaned in towards her, his smile growing and she pulled in a great breath of him. 'I know you don't want to drive longer than five hours a day if you can help it…'

They'd had to drive five and a half yesterday. It made the boys restless. And look at what had happened at the pool afterwards.

'But if we drove to Penong today—'

'How long?'

'A bit over six hours.'

She grimaced and gestured for him to continue. 'The thing is, Penong is close to a place called Cactus Beach.'

'A beach!' Robbie and Chase gazed at her as if pleading for her to accept any proposal that included a beach.

'Cactus Beach is well known in surfing circles.'

Aidan was a surfer? Really?

'If we drive to Penong today, we could spend all of tomorrow at the beach.'

'So…we'd spend two nights at Penong before heading for Port Augusta?'

'That's right.'

The lure of not having to pack up everything for a whole day spoke to her. Loudly.

The boys started shouting out their excited endorsements of Aidan's plan, interspersed with lots of pleading and assurances that Chase was better and that they'd be extra good.

A whole day at the beach? It sounded wonderful. This was exactly the kind of adventure she'd hoped for on their journey. Her boys' excited faces almost sealed the deal, but she forced herself to pull back. It was harder than it should've been. 'What about your burning need to get to Adelaide asap?'

Robbie scowled at Aidan. 'Why you wanna do that? Aren't you having fun with us?'

'I'm having the best time,' Aidan assured him. 'And I have another song to teach you later.'

Robbie's scowl vanished.

Aidan ran his hand down the crease in his T-shirt again. She tried not to follow his hand's progress. 'I think my absence in the office for another couple of days could be a…' The happy light in his eyes faded a little. 'A good thing.'

Why should that leach the happiness from him?

She glanced down at her toast. She'd had a thought or two on that head, but… *It's none of your business.* Then she recalled the way he'd vaulted the pool fence and the way he'd lifted Chase into his arms.

She could make it her business.

At the beach.

'It sounds like the best idea ever.' She crossed her fingers. Aidan grinned. The boys cheered.

She turned to Robbie and Chase. 'It does mean a long time in the car today.'

'We promise to be good.' Robbie nudged Chase, who nodded enthusiastically. 'If we get grumpy we'll just think of the beach and we'll be happy again. It'll make it all worth it.'

Oh, how she wished she could've given them more fun, more outings and holidays in their short lives. She swallowed a lump. 'Okay, then. Let's get this mess cleaned up and start packing.'

They reached Cactus Beach at the end of a long dirt road. The landscape surrounding them amazed Quinn. Nullarbor translated from the Latin to mean no trees and today it definitely lived up to its reputation. Rocks, low scrub and amazing sand dunes stretched out on all sides. When the beach came into view, nobody uttered a word.

A crescent of white sand with rocky outcrops at either end and a sea of jewelled blues and greens spread out before them like an ancient Mecca. It was utterly deserted. And it was utterly beautiful.

The boys just stared at it with their mouths agape. Aidan folded his arms and grinned. She let out a long, low, pent-up breath.

Aidan swung to them, his grin widening. 'Cactus Beach has three perfect surfing breaks—Castles and Cactus which are both left-handers and Caves which is a powerful right hand break.'

'And that's good?'

'It's epic!'

Right. 'I hate to rain on your parade, but you, uh, don't have a surfboard with you.'

He shook his head. 'Doesn't matter. I can now say I've been here.'

Robbie and Chase broke free from their enthralment long enough to tug at her, their excitement palpable. 'Can we, Mum? Huh, can we?'

She'd already slathered them both in sunblock back at their on-site van in Penong. It might be late March, but the sun shone with all of its usual enthusiasm and the faint breeze was warm with the memory of summer. 'Okay, give me your shirts and off you go.'

Both boys raced straight for the water.

She could tell Aidan itched to hit the waves as much as her children did. Still, he waited for her to choose the perfect patch of sand before setting down the cooler bag that practically burst with their supplies for the day. She'd packed sodas, water, sandwiches and fruit. She'd even splurged on cheese and crackers.

'Go on.' She gave him a playful push. 'I can tell you're as eager to be out there as Robbie and Chase.'

She glanced at the boys. For all of his talk of big breaks, the surf was remarkably gentle today.

He flashed a grin that made her heart stutter before dragging his shirt over his head and revealing a perfectly toned torso. Wind instantly rushed in her ears, filling her head with noise. She stared, pressing hands to cheeks that had grown red-hot. With a start she pulled them away and pushed them into the small of her back instead and pretended to stretch, praying he hadn't noticed her heat and confusion...her desire.

She sent up a prayer of thanks when she finally managed to make her eyes focus. He just stood there as if relishing the feel of the sun against his bare skin. She glanced away, having to fight the urge to reach out and touch him.

For all his talk of castles and caves and whatnot, he wasn't what she'd call tanned for this time of year. Exactly how many hours was he putting in at that office of his?

Her lips twisted. At the moment she'd bet eighty-hour weeks were a conservative guess. The thought made her shudder. It eased the burn threatening to consume her too. He might have a hot body—the hottest she'd seen in a very long time—and he might be a nice man—the nicest she'd come across in a very long time—but his lifestyle was repugnant to her. Why would someone embark on a relationship with a man like him? You'd never see him long enough to enjoy the hot body or to indulge in long, intimate conversations.

Why? Her lips twisted. Status, standing and prestige, not to mention wealth. That was why. And none of that could tempt her.

He took a step towards the water. 'I hope you're wearing sunscreen.' As soon as the words left her mouth, she realised how ludicrous they were. The man had been trying to get a flight out of Perth. One thing he hadn't been doing was planning a beach holiday.

He turned back and his grin when it came was low and wicked. She wanted to respond. She wanted to take the bottle of lotion from her bag, amble over to him with a sinuous swing of her hips and slowly rub lotion into his shoulders, his back and his chest. She'd like to—

She snapped herself out of her fantasy—reminded herself about eighty-hour working weeks—seized the bottle of sunscreen and tossed it to him.

'Are you coming in?' he asked when he was done, handing the bottle back to her.

He hadn't been able to reach all of his back. *Not your problem.*

With a sigh she took the bottle from him and poured lotion into her hand. She didn't need a travelling companion with a serious case of sunburn. Or sunstroke. She slathered it on his back with as much cool efficiency as she could muster. Reciting the periodic table in her mind helped.

'Would you like me to return the favour?'

She recapped the bottle a little too vigorously. 'Uh, no thank you. Robbie and Chase took care of it earlier.'

'So, are you coming in?'

That was when she realised she'd been biting her lip the entire time. She released it. 'Sure I am. In a bit.' She couldn't explain why, but she didn't want to pull her sundress over her head to stand in front of him in nothing but her birthday suit.

Bathing suit! Lord, talk about a Freudian slip.

She was a mother. She had responsibilities. Ignoring Aidan, she walked down to the shore to paddle and keep an eye on the boys. She was no longer that impulsive girl who'd let passion rule her head. Even if a remnant of that girl remained in the woman she'd become.

Eventually, though, the lure of the water became too much and she tossed her dress to the sand. She splashed with the boys. She laughed and relaxed and forgot to worry about anything for a while.

Chase didn't have Robbie's confidence in the surf, but he begged her to take him out to the deeper water. Robbie wanted to go out too. He was a good swimmer, but if either one of them got into trouble she'd be hard pressed to deal with the both of them. She was about to suggest she take them out one at a time, but suddenly Aidan was there with a summer grin and holiday eyes.

'Hey, Robbie, you wanna learn how to body surf?'

'Yes!'

So they all moved into the deeper water beyond the break of the waves. The gentle rolling of the swell rocked them and it eased the frenetic craziness of the last few weeks. She gave Chase a swimming lesson, and then they both floated for a while. She turned her head to watch Aidan and Robbie.

A laugh spurted out of her oldest son and then he looked up at Aidan as if…

She straightened. Her heart caught and then vibrated with sudden pain. Aidan was all kindness and attention and her eldest son was blossoming under that influence. In fact, Robbie lapped up every scrap of Aidan's attention like a starving dog.

Her eyes stung. She knew he hungered for this kind of male bonding. If only Phillip would spend more time with his sons!

'Ow, Mum, you're hurting my hand!'

She immediately relaxed her grip on Chase's hand. 'Sorry, honey.'

'Can we go in so I can jump over the waves again?'

'Sure we can.'

She and Chase jumped waves, but the entire time she could see her eldest son's hero worship growing—it was reflected in the way he laughed too loudly, the way he gazed up at Aidan, and in his absolute lack of self-consciousness as he came out of his usual reserved shell.

Damn it! Why couldn't she be everything her sons needed? Why couldn't she be both mother and father to them? She didn't want them to lack for anything and it wasn't right that they should.

She re-tied her ponytail. She only had one set of arms and one set of legs, though, and there were two of them and some days she was spread too thin as it was.

'Are you okay?'

She jumped to find Aidan beside her, staring down at her with narrowed eyes. She spun and located both Robbie and Chase. 'Yes, I'm perfect.'

'I'll second that.' He grinned down at her and it snapped her out of her funk in an instant. The remnant of the reckless girl she'd once been gave a long, low stretch. Her common sense raised an eyebrow. She had to bite back a groan. If she weren't careful she'd end up with a serious case of hero worship too.

Robbie insisted on sitting next to Aidan when they had lunch. He argued about putting his shirt and hat back on, until Aidan put his shirt on too.

She liked Aidan. She liked him a lot, but it would do Robbie no good to become too attached to him. They'd see neither hide nor hair of Aidan once this adventure was over.

Aidan would return to his relentless workload and his social position and his prominence on the political landscape and he'd have no time for surfing with young boys.

She rested back on one hand and bit into an apple. 'I guess we'd best make the most of your company while we have it, Aidan. I mean in another two days we'll be in Adelaide.'

Robbie stared from Aidan to her. 'What happens in Adelaide?'

'The plane strike ended today so I guess Aidan will catch a plane back to Sydney.'

'But we could drop him off in Sydney in the car.'

'We could,' she agreed. It took an effort to keep the smile on her face and her voice breezy. 'But it'll take a few days longer and Aidan can't afford any more time off work.'

Aidan looked as if she'd slapped him. *Oh, Aidan…* She ached to reach out and hug him.

'Aidan could come visit us at Aunt Mara's.'

''Course he can,' she agreed. 'Just as soon as he has some free time.'

Robbie's face fell and she knew he was thinking of his father's endless litany of excuses for why he couldn't visit.

Oh, Robbie… She wanted to hug him and never let him go. But that wouldn't help him either, not in the long term.

'Hey, who wants to go and explore the rock pools over there?'

That distracted both of the boys. She packed up the remnants of their lunch before grabbing the can of soda she hadn't finished yet. The boys raced ahead.

'Are you looking forward to getting rid of me?'

The bluntness of Aidan's question shattered her carefully constructed veneer. 'Oh, Aidan, no.' She reached out to grip his arm. 'I don't know if you realise this or not, but Robbie is developing a serious case of hero worship where you're concerned.'

'I…' He blinked.

'You're being great with him. I don't want you to change the way you are…'

'But?'

She realised she still held him. She let him go. 'These aren't waters I've had to navigate before.' Adelaide loomed ahead like a dark cloud. 'I just want him to be prepared for when we do part company, that's all. I wasn't trying to make you feel unwanted.'

He grimaced and scratched a hand through his hair. 'Sorry, I'm not usually so touchy.'

But they'd been having the most perfect day and her words had obviously taken him off guard.

'I'm clueless—' he waved towards Robbie '—about the whole kid thing.'

'So am I some days.'

'What about their father? Where's he?'

'In London at the moment. When he's in Australia he's mostly in Sydney. His contact with the boys is erratic.' It was the politest way she could put it.

Aidan called Phillip such a rude name she snorted soda

out of her nose. Not that she disagreed with him. 'That's one way of putting it.'

'Sorry.'

'You are not.' But she didn't mind in the least. 'He claims that our living in Perth makes it difficult for him to visit. But now surely a two-hour drive north isn't too much of an effort when he is in the country. I'm hoping this move means Phillip will start spending more time with Robbie and Chase. God knows they crave it.'

He stopped and fixed her with those fiery amber eyes. 'That's the real reason you're moving, isn't it?'

He said it as if it were the most amazing thing. She wrinkled her nose and rolled her shoulders.

'It is, isn't it?'

It was part of it. So what? 'There are a whole host of reasons.'

He caught her hand, pulled her to a halt, turning her to face him. 'It is, isn't it?'

The warmth and sympathy in his eyes had a lump wedging in her throat. She wanted to fling herself into his arms and soak up some of his strength and goodness. But that way lay ruin, as her mother would so quaintly put it.

Instead she very gently disengaged her hand from his. She swallowed. When she was sure her voice would emerge normally she said, 'You know what I hate? That a vast section of our society still looks down on single mothers, thinking they're only out for what they can get. Phillip pays child support, yes. When he first left a part of me wanted no contact and no links, but that's not my decision to make. I have no right putting my pride before my children's welfare.'

Shading her eyes, she turned to survey the boys, who were both clambering over the rocks, safe and occupied. She swung back. 'Another woman once told me she thought it a form of child abuse for a woman to refuse child support from her child's father. She said it'd be depriving the child of a better financial future. And she's right.'

'And now you feel you owe Phillip?'

'No! I owe Robbie and Chase. I owe them a good future. It's my responsibility to ensure they have all the things they need.' And at the moment they ached for their father. At least, Robbie did, and in a couple of years so would Chase.

'But it seems to me that society doesn't commend women for making those kinds of sacrifices. And it seems to me that in the vast majority of cases it's women who do actually make the real sacrifices.'

He stared down at her, his eyes soft. Aidan would never abandon a child. She didn't know what made her so sure, only that she was.

'I think you're amazing. I think you're wonderful.'

She had no hope of hiding how much his words touched her. 'Thank you.'

'I—'

'No,' she warned, keeping her voice crisp. 'Don't lay the compliments on too thick or you'll spoil the effect.'

He laughed. It was a good sound.

'C'mon, let's see what the boys are up to.'

They'd walked five steps when he asked, 'What happened between you and Phillip?'

A sidelong glance told her he wasn't looking at her. In fact he was looking suspiciously nonchalant. Her pulse leapt. She tried to stamp on it. 'That's a story for another day when the boys are in bed.' And while she didn't mean them to, the words emerged as a pledge.

The rest of the day lived up to its perfect promise. They explored the beach. There was more swimming and eating. The boys built sandcastles and as the tide came in the surf built up into the perfect breaks that Aidan had spoken about earlier.

His eyes lit up. 'I'm going to come back here one day with a surfboard.'

The afternoon waned and the sun had started to sink into the sea to the west when she and Aidan drove two very tired boys back to Penong.

After showers and a makeshift dinner of beans on toast, Aidan built a campfire in the pit in front of their on-site vans—he'd chosen to hire the one beside hers rather than stay at the motel—and then produced a bag of marshmallows.

They sat around the fire and toasted marshmallows as if they were a real family. Her heart wanted to spring free to dance and twirl but she wouldn't let it.

'It's been the best day in the world,' Chase said, leaning against her.

'The very best,' Robbie said, leaning into her other side.

They both grew heavy with sleep. 'Bedtime, I think,' she murmured to Aidan.

Without asking, without even apparently thinking about it, he rose and lifted Robbie into his arms, waited until she'd lifted Chase into hers, before following her into the van and helping her put them to bed. Both boys were asleep before she and Aidan left the caravan.

It made the task so much easier with someone to help. If only... She shook her head. She shook her whole body. 'Soda?'

'I bought a bottle of wine.' He rubbed the back of his neck. 'I thought...'

He looked delightfully nonplussed. She shifted from one foot to the other and then finally nodded. 'A glass of wine would be lovely.'

They sat beside the dying embers of the fire and sipped wine, staring up into the majesty of a glittering sky. She knew he was still curious about her and her history, but he'd be too polite to ask again. Well, she had questions of her own, and if she talked first maybe he'd open up to her too.

She crossed her fingers.

'I discovered I was pregnant in the time between graduating high school and the start of the university academic year.' Though he didn't move, she sensed she had his full attention. 'To say it was a shock is an understatement. For everyone.'

'You didn't consider an abortion?'

'Sure I did. I was only eighteen. I was supposed to have my whole life in front of me. I had plans. Plans a baby would interfere with.'

'But?'

With his non-judgemental attitude, Aidan would make a very good politician. She wondered if he realised that. 'But my parents and Phillip's parents insisted I have an abortion.'

'And that got your back up?'

'Oh, yes. I sometimes wonder if I only went ahead with the pregnancy just to spite them.' She glanced at him. 'That's not a very edifying thought, is it?'

'And not something I believe for a minute.'

She smiled at the fire. Maybe not. There'd been a part of her that had started loving the child inside her the minute she'd found out she was carrying it. A part of her she hadn't been able to ignore.

'Did Phillip want you to have an abortion too?'

She sipped her wine and then leaned back on one hand. 'Actually, he was really good. He didn't pressure me at all. He was a reasonable human being back then.' She had hopes he'd become one again. 'He said he'd stick by me whatever my decision. I didn't find out for another three years that he'd hoped I'd choose the abortion.' That had been the same night he'd accused her of ruining his life.

'As I believe I mentioned before, my parents cut me off

completely when I refused to obey their ultimatum. They thought it'd bring me to heel, but it didn't. Phillip's parents weren't quite so harsh, but they counselled him to go to university as planned and to have minimal contact with me and the baby.'

'Nice.'

His sarcasm wrung a smile from her. 'They didn't cut him off, but they refused to acknowledge me and I wasn't welcome in their home.'

She crossed her legs. 'So we moved to Perth. He got a job in a bank as a teller. I did a short office admin course and picked up some temp work until the baby came. Robbie was three months old when I picked up some part-time work as an administrative assistant at the university and we put him into childcare two days a week.'

'It sounds tough.'

'Thousands of people do it every year.' She shot him a smile. 'It was a challenge to make ends meet, but we were young and…I loved him.'

Aidan didn't say anything. She glanced at him. 'Have you been in love?'

He shook his head.

'It's wonderful. It gives you wings. It gives you hope. And it can make you very determined. It makes the tough times worthwhile.' She sipped her wine—a cool, crisp Sauvignon Blanc that slipped down her throat smoothly. 'But when love goes bad it's terrible.'

'I'm sorry it went bad for you, Quinn.'

He earned a big fat Brownie point for not asking why it had gone bad. Her fingers tightened about her glass. If she shared that with him, though, maybe he would share with her. She could only try. 'Things were going fine until I fell pregnant with Chase. It sounds dreadfully irresponsible, doesn't it, but we'd used birth control both times I fell pregnant. I'm obviously disgustingly fertile.'

A low rumble left Aidan's throat. It eased the heaviness that threatened to settle over her.

'It was too soon for us to have another child.' And yet she'd felt the same love for it as she had for Robbie.

'Much too soon for us to have another baby,' she whispered again, almost to herself.

'What happened?'

'Phillip panicked.' She shrugged. 'He panicked throughout my pregnancy about how we'd make ends meet. He asked me to have an abortion. I refused. I wanted Robbie to have what I'd never had—a sibling.' A friend. 'Phillip kept right on panicking after Chase was born and he never connected with him the way he had with Robbie. I cut back on our expenses as much as I could, but...'

The fire blurred for a moment. Aidan reached over and took her hand. And bless him. He just waited. He didn't try to hurry her.

'I discovered his secret bank account. He told me it was his university fund. He hadn't been panicking about how we'd make ends meet at all. He was panicking that he might have to dip into his university fund.'

Air hissed from between Aidan's teeth.

'And then his parents pounced when Phillip was at his weakest.' She pulled her hand from his. 'They offered to pay for him to study in London.'

The night wasn't really silent—there were the chirrups of night birds and insects, and the occasional crackle from the dying embers, but the night pressed in hard around them. Aidan stared at Quinn and ached for her.

'So when Chase was four months old, Phillip left.'

Phillip had left her with two small children? One of them just a baby? The jerk had turned his back on his own flesh and blood? 'The low-life rat scum!'

She gave a small laugh, but the thread of tiredness that stretched through it caught at his heart.

'So there you have it, Aidan, my sordid little story.'

His chin jerked up. 'I don't think it's sordid.' Not on her part at least. Phillip was another matter. And so were her parents. The people who were supposed to love her had all let her down, abandoned her. He made a vow to himself then to check out her Aunt Mara. He wasn't letting anyone else take advantage of Quinn.

That's not your decision to make.

He ground his teeth together. She was his friend. He'd make it his business.

He started when he realised her glass was empty. He lifted the bottle towards her in a silent question.

She hesitated and then held it out. 'Half a glass would be lovely.'

'I think you've done a great job with Robbie and Chase, Quinn. They're great kids. You should be proud of yourself.'

'Thank you.'

When she smiled at him he had to fight the urge to reach across and place his lips on hers. He closed his eyes and hauled in a breath. Kissing her wouldn't help. He forced his eyes open again. 'Do you ever regret the path you chose?'

'No, I don't. And I'm sure that's made things easier.' She turned to him more fully on the blanket. 'Remember how I said love makes everything easier?'

He nodded.

'Well, that goes for all love, not just romantic love. I love the boys with everything I have. They make it all worthwhile.'

Had she had to sacrifice all her dreams, though? 'What were you going to study at university?'

'Science. I was a major science geek.'

He recalled the science texts in her car. 'Is that why you chose to work in a science department at the university?'

'You bet. It meant I got to live vicariously through the research going on there. It was fun.'

His heart ached at the fierceness of her smile.

'But enough about me.' She dusted off her hands. 'I have a couple of questions of my own.'

He swallowed and shrugged. 'Ask away. After everything you've just shared, the least I can do is answer a couple of questions.'

She laughed and it flowed through him like some kind of energy drink. 'Careful, you might regret that impulse.'

What was it about her that could lift his spirits so instantly and comprehensively? 'Do your worst,' he dared on a laugh.

Slowly she sobered. She leaned in towards him. 'Aidan, why are you standing for office if you don't want to be a politician?'

CHAPTER SIX

AIDAN STARED AT Quinn and reminded himself to keep breathing.

How did she know?

His heart thumped. Perspiration prickled his scalp. He forced himself to sit up straighter and to lean away from her and the temptation of warm lips...of warm woman. 'Of course I want to be a politician.'

The sparkle in her eyes faded. 'Uh-huh.' She set her half glass of wine to one side and started to rise. 'It's been a lovely day, but a long one.'

She was going to leave? But she hadn't finished her wine! He didn't want the day to end, but he had no intention of talking about this.

'I hadn't thought it through properly, but of course you'd be worried I'd take such a story to the papers.'

'I think no such thing!'

Her face was a study in scepticism. 'Goodnight, Aidan, sleep tight.'

He scowled. He'd given her and her children a lovely day. Why did she have to push this?

Oh, so this day was more for their benefit than yours, was it?

He scowled harder, but Quinn didn't see. She was half-way back to her van by now.

And he didn't want her to go.

'When my brother died...'

She didn't turn, but she stopped. She didn't come back. She waited. He swallowed and tried to match his voice to the quiet of the night. 'I already told you that Danny's death devastated my parents.' A beat passed. 'Everything changed!'

She came back and sat on the blanket. She didn't pick up her wine glass. She didn't touch him. She didn't say a word.

He wanted her to say something—needed her to—because a lump had lodged in his throat and he couldn't push past it.

'What about you, Aidan? You must've been devastated too. You obviously loved your brother.'

The warm cadence of her voice helped him to relax, eased his throat muscles. 'I...' He ignored his wine to seize a bottle of water. He knocked back a generous swig. 'You have to understand that Danny was full of life, full of fun. If you were feeling low you could rely on Danny to cheer you up. You always found yourself laughing around him. He was the life of the party without being a party animal.' He capped the water bottle. 'When he died it felt like the light had gone out of the world.'

He hadn't said that out loud before. It wasn't something designed to cheer his mother or father, or anyone else for that matter. Quinn shuffled closer until their arms and shoulders touched. She took his hand. Strangely, her warmth did give him a measure of comfort.

'I always wanted a brother or sister. I can't imagine what it would be like to lose one I loved.'

Lost? They hadn't lost him. He'd been taken from them. Stolen. But it occurred to him then that he had memories Quinn would never have. Memories he could hold tight for the rest of his life. Something inside him shifted and changed focus by several degrees. He wanted to put his arm around her and hug her. He'd lost a brother, but he'd never been alone the way she had been.

'I was at a loss how to console my parents. Daniel wouldn't have been.'

She pulled herself up to her full sitting height. He'd slumped so the top of her shoulder almost came to the top of his. Although he should be focusing on other things, he couldn't help but enjoy the warm slide of her against him.

'Aidan Fairhall, you can't know that! You cannot possibly know how much Danny would've been affected if circumstances had been reversed. He might've gone completely to pieces.'

He shook his head. Danny would've known exactly how to comfort their parents. Besides, although none of them had said it out loud, they all knew his parents wouldn't have needed as much consoling if his and Danny's positions had been reversed.

That fact could still make him flinch.

Quinn's hold on his hand hauled him back. 'What does Danny's death have to do with you giving up a career you love and becoming a politician?'

He'd been foolish to think this woman had been fully preoccupied with her cross-country move and her two energetic sons. She'd picked up on a lot. Probably too much. 'Danny was always going to be the politician.' He moistened his lips. 'As you probably realise, Fairhalls always stand for office.'

'Your father, his father and his father before him, yes, but nobody could've foreseen what happened to Danny.'

He met her gaze. The light of the fire glimmered in her eyes. 'The only thing that brought my parents a moment of respite and consolation was my promise to stand for office in Danny's place.'

Her lips parted. Her eyes and their sympathy burned

through him. 'Oh, Aidan,' she whispered. 'Would it have been such a bad thing if it skipped a generation?'

He set his jaw. 'It might not be my first career choice, and I realise I'm probably going to make a dreadful politician, but—'

'No you won't! You'll be very good at it.'

He closed his eyes.

'But it'll be such a tough job if your heart isn't in it.'

He opened his eyes again. 'So I'm left with a choice that's really no choice at all. Either quit politics and break my parents' hearts all over again or reconcile myself to a job I have no real passion for.'

She swore. It was low and soft, but he caught it all the same and it made him swing towards her, his eyebrows lifting.

'Sorry,' she murmured. 'I just realised I'd made things ten times worse when I suggested you drag your mother into the office to help out with your campaign.'

That had sealed the deal. Not that there'd been much hope of pulling back now anyway. None of that was Quinn's fault.

'I think you're making a big mistake, Aidan.'

He shrugged. When a person got right down to it, what did his happiness count in the greater scheme of things? Besides, he wouldn't be miserable. He just wouldn't be following the path he'd choose for himself. It was no biggie.

His shoulders slumped.

'It wouldn't all go to hell in a hand basket if you were to retire from the campaign,' she argued, squeezing his hand. 'There are people who could step into your shoes, like your second in command.'

He appreciated her efforts, but she didn't understand how fragile his parents were.

'And you're not being fair to Daniel.'

Every muscle he possessed stiffened. He swung to her,

a snarl rising up inside him. 'Not fair to Daniel? When I'm keeping his memory alive?'

She stared at him with wide eyes. She dropped his hand and it left him feeling strangely adrift. 'We keep our loved one's memory alive by remembering them and talking about them. Not by making a mockery of what they held dear.'

He bared his teeth. 'A mockery?'

'Well, what would you call it?' Her eyes flashed. 'He loved politics, yes? While you…you're just going to grit your teeth and force yourself to go through the motions. How do you think he'd feel about that, huh?'

Bile rose up through him.

'On a personal level, if he was any kind of brother at all, I bet he'd tell you to do whatever made you happy. On a professional level he would kick your butt for using the job he loved to make yourself and two other people feel marginally better.'

His jaw dropped. His stomach churned.

'Because he'd know politics is more important than that. Or, at least, that it should be. And he'd also know that you stepping into his shoes wouldn't bring him back.'

His head rocked back. Wind roared in his ears. His every last defence had been ripped away in one scalding wrench. He struggled to his feet, but he didn't know what to do once he'd reached them.

Flee?

Stand and fight?

Won't bring him back.

What he wanted to do was punch something and then hide in the dark and bawl his goddamn eyes out!

He backed up to lean against a nearby boulder outside the circle of light cast by the dying embers of the fire. Bracing his hands against his knees, he tried to pull air into lungs that didn't want to work.

He didn't hear her move, but suddenly she was there, insinuating herself between his legs, her arms going about his shoulders.

He couldn't help it. His arms went about her and he pulled her against him tight, his face buried in her shoulder.

Won't bring him back. But he wanted Danny back. He wanted it with his every aching atom, with every single, secret part of himself.

'You don't know what it's like, Quinn.' His voice came out raw and ragged. 'The pain…it tears at you from the inside out and you make deals with a God you don't believe in any more just to make it stop for five minutes. You'll do anything to try and get it to stop, to ease it a little bit, but…' Nothing worked. Not for long.

'I know, baby,' she crooned, cradling his head against her as she would if he were Chase or Robbie.

Won't bring him back.

He started to shake. A great hulking sob tore at his throat. Claws, cruel and vicious, raked at the parts of him he'd tried to protect, savage jaws closing about tender flesh as teeth, keen and sadistic, bit at him. A black pit opened up. A great scream roared in his ears. And all he could do was groan in grief and denial as night enclosed him, inside and out.

He didn't think he would ever be able to find his way out of it—out of the darkness—but faintly, ever so faintly, he heard Quinn's voice and he tried to focus on it, tried to move towards it. And eventually the shaking eased and the pain moved back a fraction and he could breathe again.

Slowly, the warmth of Quinn, the comfort of holding someone close, of having them hold him close, seeped through, pushing the darkness back further and further.

Finally he lifted his head. He wiped his eyes and said

the rudest word he knew. Quinn didn't flinch. Beyond her, in the sky, he could see a thousand stars.

He swore again. 'I just bawled like a great big baby, didn't I?'

'Oh, for heaven's sake.' She moved to sit beside him. He missed her warmth but he realised then that he'd been the first to let go. 'You're not going to come over all macho and tell me real men don't cry, are you?'

He blinked.

'For heaven's sake, how outdated are you? That is one message I won't be passing onto Chase and Robbie. You're human, right? Men feel just as deeply about things as women. Or are you going to tell me all men are shallow brutes?'

Nope. They weren't. Well, not most of them anyway, though he had serious doubts about Phillip.

'Bottling up grief like that makes everything bad. It doesn't let us keep hold of the stuff that's good.'

'What's good to be had from crying like that?' he muttered.

Even in the dark he could tell she'd fixed him with a 'look'. He found himself having to fight a smile.

She jumped up, refilled their glasses and handed him one. 'You told me Danny was full of life, the life of the party and all that. Give me a specific example.'

He blinked. He opened his mouth and closed it again. He took a sip of wine and found it soothed his throat. A sigh sneaked out of him. One example of Danny's funness, huh?

The first memory hit him. Then a second. And then they flooded him, one after the other. Nights at the local with their mates. Fishing trips. Surfing. Lots of laughing. Fights that had ended in laughter too. Barbecues. Late night talks sitting over a nice bottle of single malt.

He glanced at Quinn. She smiled and he found he could

smile back without any effort at all. He knew then that he didn't have to relay a single one of those memories—she knew. How? He thought about all she'd been through and promptly stopped wondering.

'You must be tired.'

Her words were a caress in the night. 'You'd think so.' She'd barely touched her wine. He suspected she wasn't used to drinking. 'But I'm not.' He felt oddly invigorated. Besides, it couldn't be much more than nine-thirty. 'Danny and I used to have these late night talks. We'd discuss how we were going to save the world—him the politician and me the human rights lawyer.'

The human rights lawyer.

'Sounds nice.'

His chest clenched. So did his hand. 'You're right, you know? He wouldn't want me living his dream.' Danny had possessed a heart as big as the Great Australian Bight. 'He'd have wanted me to follow my own dreams.' Danny had always cheered him from the sidelines.

'I wish I'd known him. He sounds like a great guy.'

It was the perfect thing to say. They stared at the stars for a while. 'My parents won't see it that way, though.'

'No.'

It was half-question, half-statement.

She leant against him, shoulder to shoulder. 'Are you going to try?'

'I think I have to.' But how? His mother's pale, haggard face and haunted eyes rose in his mind. Who did he most owe his allegiance to—his parents or Danny?

'You owe it to yourself,' Quinn said quietly, and he realised he'd spoken his thought out loud.

He didn't trust that, though. Following his dream, doing what he wanted seemed wrong and selfish in the circumstances. Yet it was the path Danny would have urged him to take.

'I take it your mother has been depressed, lethargic, hard to rouse?'

He nodded, his heart heavy again. Helping out on his campaign had certainly roused her, though.

'Have you ever considered the idea that behaving badly might rouse her more effectively than toeing the line?'

His glass halted halfway to his mouth. He slanted her a sidelong look. 'What are you talking about?'

She lifted one shoulder. 'If your mother thought that in your grief you were going off the rails…'

'It'd only add to her worries.' Surely?

'Or it might give her something different to worry about—something she could actually act on and make a difference to.'

She couldn't do anything about Danny's death, she couldn't bring him back, but she could certainly pull Aidan back into line.

'There's a thread of deviousness in you, isn't there?'

'I know.'

She puffed out her chest and it made him laugh. 'What did you have in mind?'

'Well, I was thinking that maybe when you reach Adelaide, rather than catch the first available flight back to Sydney, what if you were seen out on the town, gambling and drinking? I'm not saying to actually do those things, but if it appeared as if you were…'

Quinn watched the implication of her idea ripple behind the smooth dark amber of Aidan's eyes.

'She'd be livid.'

'Livid could be good,' she offered. 'It's better than apathy.'

'If I could somehow help her remember the good stuff too…'

He turned to her and his face was so vulnerable in the

starlight she wanted to hug him. He was such a good man. 'She won't forget her grief, Aidan. Just like you won't forget yours.' They'd carry it always and there'd still be bad days. She hoped he knew that. 'But hopefully she'll learn to live with it.'

'You helped me get rid of something dark and heavy inside me, Quinn, that I didn't even realise I was carrying around.'

'You'd been pushing your grief back to focus on your parents' needs instead.' No wonder he'd been ready to explode. Who'd been looking after his needs?

'And you think if I force my mother to focus on me instead of her grief, that it might help her?'

'I don't know. I don't know your mother, but I thought it might be worth a try. What do you think?'

He stared at the fire. 'I think it might be worth a try too.' He cocked an eyebrow at her. 'Going off the rails, huh?'

He grinned. It made her heart chug. She set down her glass. The wine was obviously going to her head.

'You left out one important element in your little "going off the rails" scenario, Quinn.'

'What's that?'

'An inappropriate woman draped on my arm.'

His grin deepened and she knew she was in trouble. She did what she could to swallow back a knot of excitement. 'Do you really think that's necessary?'

'Absolutely! Drinking, gambling and carousing with wild women won't do my campaign any good.'

She stared at him.

'What?' he eventually said.

'You seem to think your mother will only be worried about your campaign and the damage you might do to it.'

He glanced away.

Didn't he think his mother would be worried about him on a personal level? She understood that some people found it hard to separate the personal and professional, but what did a job matter when it came to a loved one's mental and emotional health and their—?

She broke off, remembering the world he came from—a world where duty and position and prominence were more important than loving your family.

'If I'm going to do this, Quinn, I mean to do it big.'

So he couldn't turn back? She understood that—way down deep inside her in a place she didn't want to look at too closely. He wanted to give his mother an almighty jolt *and* he wanted to sabotage his campaign at the same time. Two birds. One stone. She felt suddenly uneasy, though she couldn't explain why.

'Will you help me?'

'You want me to be that wild woman on your arm?'

'Yes.'

She wasn't opposed to helping him. She and the boys had plenty of time to dilly-dally. 'Tell me what it would entail.'

He drummed his fingers against his thigh. 'It'd mean spending a couple of nights carousing on the town. So… three nights all up in Adelaide.'

'Okay.' That was manageable. 'What about the boys? I don't want them in the papers.' She and Aidan wouldn't make front-page headlines, but they'd make the social pages.

'We can shield them. And we can do fun stuff with them through the day too,' he added, unprompted. It turned her heart to jelly. 'There's a zoo. And I bet they'd love the Adelaide Gaol Museum, not to mention the Haigh's Chocolate visitor centre. And there's this fabulous aquatic centre with slides and caves and all sorts of things.'

He cared about making her boys happy. She knew then that she wouldn't be able to refuse him.

Not that you ever intended to.

'We'll stay somewhere upmarket that has a babysitting service.' He straightened and pinned her with his gaze. 'And I'll be covering all the expenses in Adelaide. That's non-negotiable.'

She rolled her eyes. 'I'm not exactly penniless, you know? I have enough to cover it.'

'You might not be penniless, but you're understandably careful with your money. Besides, given the choice, you wouldn't stay in an upmarket motel. Also, you're doing this as a favour to me so I'm paying.'

She planted her hands on her hips. 'On one condition.'

'Shoot.'

'That you don't pay for my car rental.' He'd paid for all of their fuel so far and she'd figured that was a good enough deal.

He'd started to turn away but he swung back. 'How'd you know I was going to do that?'

'Oh, Aidan Fairhall, you are as see-through as glass.'

He thrust his jaw out. 'I am not!'

She just laughed.

His jaw lowered. 'All right then, *you* might see through me but most people don't.'

She'd give him that. Most people, she suspected, only saw what they wanted where Aidan was concerned.

'Okay,' he grumbled. 'You have yourself a deal.'

He held out his hand. She placed hers in it and they shook on it. He didn't release her. 'Thank you, Quinn. I can't begin to tell you how much I appreciate it.'

She opened her mouth to tell him to try, but realised that might be construed as flirting. Her reckless self lifted its head and stretched. She cleared her throat. 'You're welcome.'

One side of his mouth hooked up in a slow, slightly wicked smile. He still held her hand. 'I'm looking forward to hitting the town with you.'

She should pull her hand free. 'Why?'

He tugged her a little closer and her reckless side shimmied. 'Do you dance?'

Her breath caught in her chest, making her heart thud. 'Like you wouldn't believe.'

'I'm better,' he promised.

'We'll see about that.'

'What's your favourite cocktail?'

'A Margarita. Yours?'

'A whiskey sour.'

His thumb caressed the soft skin at her wrist. 'Can you play blackjack?'

'With the best of them.' The nearest she'd come to gambling was the odd flutter on the Melbourne Cup. 'Although I prefer roulette.'

'I'm going to take you out dancing and gambling and drinking.'

'And I'm going to hang off your arm and gaze up at you adoringly. And I'm going to laugh and tease you and be every kind of a temptress I can think of.' His mother would have a fit.

'And I'm going to kiss you.'

And then his mouth came down on hers in the dark of the night, hot and demanding, and it stole her breath. His kiss wasn't polite or quiet. It was dark and thrilling and she threw all sense of caution to the wind, winding her arms about his neck and kissing him back.

He pulled her in closer, trapping her between lean, powerful thighs, and deepened the kiss. She didn't resist. His hands curved about her hips and explored them completely, boldly and oh-so-impolitely. She moved against him restlessly as the thrill became a dark throb in her blood. Thrusting her hands into his hair, she held him still to thoroughly explore a mouth that set her on fire, inciting him to further bold explorations of her body with hands that seemed to know exactly what she craved.

Aidan's kiss made her feel impulsive and young.

It made her feel beautiful.

It made her feel like a woman.

She wanted him, fiercely and deeply, as if his lovemaking would be an antidote to some secret hidden pain she carried inside her.

She broke off to gulp air into starved lungs. His lips found her throat—no butterfly whispers here, just hot, wet grazes and suckles that built the inferno growing inside her. His hands were beneath her dress. They were beneath her panties, cupping her bare buttocks, kneading and pleasing and building that inferno. Her hands went to the waistband of his shorts—

Wait.

No, no, she didn't want to wait. She wanted to lose herself in sheer sensation. She wanted to forget her troubles and soar away in mindless and delirious pleasure. Oh, please let her...

Ask the question.

She froze. Aidan's clever, heat-inducing, pleasure-seeking fingers started to move and she knew that in a moment she would be lost. Totally and completely.

With a groan of pure frustration, she slapped her hands over the top of his, the fabric of her dress between them.

He stared up at her. 'Oh, God, Quinn. Please don't pull back now.'

'I have to ask a question.'

'Ask away.' His breathing was as ragged and uneven as hers.

'Not of you, of me.'

She pulled his hands out from beneath her dress. She stumbled back over to the blanket and lowered herself to it, drawing up her knees and wrapping her arms around them. Aidan didn't move. She could still taste him on her tongue. She needed a drink of water, but she didn't want to wash the taste of him away.

'What's the question, Quinn?'

The question scared the beejeebies out of her. 'Would I be prepared to fall pregnant to you?'

Although the fire was now completely out, she saw the way he rocked back at her words. She didn't blame him.

'You see, twice now I've fallen pregnant without meaning to. When precautions had been taken. So I've had to make this my default position.' It played havoc with her sex life.

Her non-existent sex life.

He came to sit on the blanket too. But not too close. 'Wow.'

'You should ask it of yourself too—would you be prepared to make love with me if it would result in me getting pregnant?'

She couldn't read his eyes. She suddenly laughed. 'Boy, wouldn't that throw a spanner in your campaign?'

He didn't laugh.

'But I don't think we want to scare your mother that much.'

'Quinn...'

When he didn't go on she pulled in a breath. 'I like babies and I like you, Aidan, but I'm not prepared to get pregnant to you.' She would never again give a man the chance to accuse her of ruining his life.

He moved in closer. 'We wouldn't have to...you know. We could improvise, set boundaries and rules.'

She edged back. 'No, we couldn't. That kind of passion—' she gestured over towards the boulder '—is dangerous. Boundaries get crossed and rules get broken. And in the heat of the moment neither one of us would care.'

And she'd woken up before to the cold, hard light of day.

'Maybe I'd risk it if I'd been on the Pill for three months and had a diaphragm and spermicide cream with me and you used a condom, but…'

'I don't even have a condom!' He sat back with a curse. She didn't blame him.

'Aidan, if you want me to play the role of wild woman in Adelaide then you have to promise me that won't happen again.'

Even in the darkness she could see the way his eyes narrowed. 'Why not?'

She could almost see his mind ticking over—there were condoms and diaphragms and spermicide creams and any number of things available in the city.

'Because we're from different worlds, that's why not. We—us—are not going to happen. It can't go anywhere.'

'What the hell are you talking about?'

'You're all corporate meetings and flash hotel suites. I'm P & C committees and bedtime stories.'

'Lawyers and politicians have kids.'

'Not with me, they don't.' Not when they worked eighty-hour weeks. 'What would your parents say?'

That shut him up. She twisted her hands together. 'I mean after Adelaide we won't even see each other again.'

'So we're not even friends?'

Friends? She swallowed. 'We're just ships in the night.'

'Without the benefits,' he bit out and she had to close her eyes and give her reckless self a stern talking to.

'Adelaide,' she croaked. 'Are we on the same page?'

He didn't say anything for a long moment. Finally he nodded. 'Publicly affectionate but hands off in private.'

A quick kiss dropped to the lips or pressed to the cheek was very different to—

Don't think about it!

'I'm glad that's settled.' But she had to force the words out from between gritted teeth.

CHAPTER SEVEN

TWO DAYS LATER, Quinn stretched out on the five-star comfort of a queen bed and let out a low satisfied groan. She, the boys and Aidan had spent the majority of the day at the aquatic park. The boys had had a blast on the water slides. So had Aidan.

And so had she, though she didn't doubt for a single moment that she deserved a mid-afternoon rest. Somehow she'd managed to keep her hands to herself and her mind mostly on the boys rather than with fantasies filled with Aidan, which was no small feat considering he'd been parading around in his board shorts for most of the day.

Robbie abandoned his Gameboy to climb up onto the bed beside her. The door to the boys' adjoining twin room stood wide open. Rather than watch television in their own room, however, they'd chosen to settle in her room to play their Gameboys.

'It's been the funnest day,' he said, nestling in beside her.

'It has, hasn't it?'

'Is there a water park in Pokolbin?'

She shook her head and watched carefully to see if his face fell. It did a bit.

Chase climbed up onto the bed too. 'I love holidays! What are we going to do tomorrow?'

She opened her free arm so he could snuggle in against

her too. 'Well, now, if you two let me have a sleep-in, maybe we could see our way to visiting the zoo.'

Both boys started to bounce.

A knock sounded on the door. Before she could move, a voice on the other side called out, 'It's Aidan.'

'Come on in,' she called back. Reclining on her bed probably wasn't the best place to receive visitors—especially one as alluring as Aidan—but she did have the safeguard of two young boys tucked in at her sides and they'd banish anything loaded from the situation.

When he saw them, Aidan's grin hooked up one side of his mouth. 'That rest you said you were going to take...' He glanced at the bouncing, wide-awake boys. 'It looks... uh...successful.'

She forced her eyes wide. 'Oh, yes.'

They both laughed.

Chase launched himself off the bed and across to Aidan. 'Mum said we might go to the zoo tomorrow.'

Aidan lounged in the doorway, all hot, relaxed male, and it made her stomach tighten and her breath shorten.

'But only if we let her have a sleep-in first.' Robbie joined them in the doorway.

'That sounds like a fair exchange.' Aidan glanced at her and she suddenly realised she was alone, adrift on this enormous bed. He sucked his bottom lip into his mouth and his eyes darkened.

She hitched herself up higher against the headboard and made sure her dress covered her legs to below her knees. She avoided direct eye contact, but couldn't stop herself from looking in his direction. He bent down to whisper something to the boys. They glanced at her with barely contained excitement and raced off to their room.

And then Quinn found herself alone in all of this five-star luxury with Aidan, and she couldn't move a muscle.

It took all of her strength to wrestle the fantasies rising through her to the ground.

'I hope you're not going to be upset by what I've just organised.'

She had to get off this bed!

She swung her legs over the side, forced steel to watery knees and moved across the room to one of a pair of tub chairs. She motioned for Aidan to take the other but he remained lounging in the doorway and she suddenly realised he didn't trust himself to come any further into the room.

Heat scorched her cheeks. A whimper rose inside her. She cleared her throat. 'What have you organised?'

'An afternoon of pampering for you while I take the boys to the movies.'

'Oh! Oh, that sounds divine, but...'

'Please don't refuse. You put everyone else's needs before your own and...' He folded his arms. 'I wanted to thank you. I really appreciate what you're doing for me.'

'You've repaid me tenfold by helping me give the boys a holiday they'll never forget.'

'I'm enjoying it as much as they are.'

So was she.

'So...?'

There was something in his eyes, something hopeful and happy that she didn't want to wound. *Pampering*? She smoothed her dress down over her knees and lifted one shoulder, glancing at him sideways over it. 'What exactly have you organised?' What kind of *pampering* were they talking about here?

'A massage, a facial, a manicure, a pedicure and a stylist for your hair and make-up.'

Her eyes widened. She did her best not to drool.

'And someone from the hotel boutique will be up with a variety of outfits for you to choose from for tonight.'

'Oh, that's too much!'

'It's not half of what you deserve.'

'But…'

'Look, Quinn, I suspect you'd rather just stay in and watch a DVD with the boys than hit the town tonight.'

Then he thought wrong.

'So I'm trying to make this as pleasant for you as possible.'

She really should say no.

'I suspect you don't have anything appropriate in your suitcase to wear for this evening—it wasn't the kind of trip you had planned—and I don't want to put you to unnecessary expense and the bother of having to go out at short notice to buy something.'

It was true. She didn't have a single thing in her suitcase that would do. She'd been hoping to dash out to buy something. And there was still time, but…

She should've known he'd have taken all of this into account. The allure of a few hours all to herself circled around her, warm with promise. She hadn't had the kind of pampering Aidan was proposing since the afternoon of her eighteenth birthday party. 'I should refuse.'

'There are no strings.'

She smiled. She already knew that. 'I really should refuse, but I'm afraid your offer is far too tempting. It sounds heavenly, Aidan. Thank you for thinking of it.'

He grinned at her. Her heart started to thump. She moistened her lips. 'I'll just make sure the boys are ready to go to the movies.'

She started to rise, but a hand on her shoulder kept her in her seat. 'Leave the boys to me. I'll collect you for dinner at seven-thirty.'

And then he was through the adjoining door into the boys' room with the door between them firmly closed, as if he'd been afraid to linger.

She hugged herself. He was taking her hands-off

policy seriously and it touched her, made her feel safe. Even as it left her body clamouring with frustration.

Quinn swung from surveying herself in the full-length mirror to answer the knock from the adjoining door. The boys' babysitter stood on the other side—a fresh-faced eighteen-year-old with a wide smile and a winning manner.

'Robbie and Chase want to say goodnight.'

'I'll come through.' She went to step into the room but Holly didn't move. She just stared at Quinn. Quinn swallowed and ran a hand across the electric-blue knit of her dress. 'What do you think?'

'I think you look hot!' Holly straightened. 'Oh, I mean—'

'No, no.' Quinn laughed. 'That was perfect.'

Both boys' eyes widened when she walked into their room. 'You look beautiful,' Robbie breathed.

'Beautifuller than beautiful,' Chase whispered.

She kissed them both, told them to be good for Holly, double-checked that the sitter had her mobile number, and then moved back into her own room to pace. That was three votes in the pro camp so far, but Aidan's was the vote that counted.

Would he think she looked 'hot' and 'beautiful'?

She sank down to the bed and lifted a leg out to admire her strappy black sandals. A bow studded with diamantés sat high at each ankle. These were definitely wild woman shoes.

A glance at the clock told her she still had five minutes before Aidan would arrive. She checked her hair in the mirror. It had been swept up into a loose French roll. A couple of tendrils curled by her ears to brush her shoulders and neck. It was an elegant style to counter the sexiness of her dress and shoes and the glitter of dangling diamantés in her ears. She hoped Aidan would approve.

She stepped back to survey her overall image again. Oh, Lord! What if she'd gone too far and—?

A knock sounded.

She swung to stare at the closed door. Her fingers curved around her stomach to try and counter its crazy churning. She suddenly wished herself next door with the boys, watching whatever movie it was that they'd chosen.

There was another knock.

Oh, get over yourself!

She kicked herself forward and opened the door. Aidan stood there in black trousers and a white shirt with a black jacket casually tossed over one shoulder. Her mouth dried. He looked…

Divine. Scrumptious. Sexy.

And like a stranger.

She held her breath and waited for him to smile.

His gaze swept her from the top of her French roll to the tips of her ruby-coloured toenails, and back again. Her blood thundered in her ears.

His eyes flashed and his lips pressed into a thin, hard line. Her heart slithered to her knees. She wanted to close the door and hide behind it, but she forced her chin sky-ward.

'We'd best go if we don't want to be late.' Clipped and short, the words shot out of him like arrows, barbed and flinty.

'I'll just get my purse.'

She turned, blinking hard against the stinging in her eyes.

Aidan punched the elevator button and kept his eyes firmly fixed straight ahead.

Damn it! He should've arranged to meet Quinn in the foyer. It would've been a heck of a lot safer. What had he been thinking? He tried to slow the tempo of the blood in his veins. He tried to remember to keep breathing. In out. In out. He gritted his teeth. It wasn't hard.

The elevator doors slid open on a silent whoosh. He motioned Quinn ahead of him, careful not to touch her. He caught a glimpse of long tanned thigh and swallowed a groan.

Pull yourself together. He'd seen more of her body at the aquatic centre earlier in the day. He slammed a finger to the button for the ground floor. *Hurry up*! He didn't need a confined space at this point in time. He'd made her a promise—a promise he wouldn't break. His hands clenched. But all he could see from the corner of his eyes was a vibrant tempting blue.

Her swimsuit had been a simple one-piece designed for modesty. The dress she wore now was anything but. It was flamboyant and provocative. And those heels! She was wearing take-me-to-bed shoes. What he wouldn't give to do exactly that and—

Nostrils flaring, he forced his gaze straight ahead to the polished metal of the elevator doors. He stared at them, willed them to open onto the ground floor asap and deposit them into a crowd and safety.

'I'm sorry, Aidan.' Quinn pushed the button to halt the elevator's progress. 'But I can't do this. I can't go out if what I'm wearing is inappropriate.'

He turned. She'd caught her bottom lip between her teeth, but not before he'd seen its betraying wobble. He closed his eyes and tried to collect himself, resisting the urge to run a finger around his collar. 'Quinn, what you're wearing is perfect for this evening and—'

'You hate it.'

He'd hurt her feelings? *Careless brute!* 'I love it!'

'No, you—'

'But I'm in danger of forgetting my promise to you so I'm trying to get us out of the danger zone as quickly as I can.'

She blinked. Not an ounce of comprehension dawned in her eyes. He leaned in closer. 'At the moment all I want to do is haul you back to your room, toss you onto your bed like some darn caveman and to slowly and very thoroughly explore every—'

Her hand clapped over his mouth. 'I get the picture.' Her voice came out hoarse and she pressed the button to set the elevator in motion again. 'Sorry, I thought...'

She brought her hand back. 'I've never worn anything this risqué before and I thought maybe I'd taken the whole wild woman thing too far. I mean, look how short this hem is! Not to mention that this material hugs every curve, leaving next to nothing to the imagination.'

He closed his eyes again.

'And now I'm rambling. Sorry. Nerves. I have to try to get your suggestion out of my head or...'

He bit back a groan.

'Not that what you suggested would work in practice.'

He opened his eyes and raised an eyebrow.

'I mean, the minute the boys heard we were back they'd be straight into my room and I expect that would be something of a mood killer.'

He laughed then. He couldn't help it. The door whooshed open and he took her hand to stride out into the foyer. He said now what he should've said at her door. 'Sweetheart, you look absolutely ravishing. I am going to be the envy of every man that claps eyes on you tonight.'

She beamed back at him. 'We're going to have so much fun this evening.'

They would. Just as long as he remembered the promise he'd made. And kept reminding himself that he was a man of his word.

Quinn was right. Dinner was fun.

She recounted the pampering she'd received that afternoon, and her sheer enjoyment of it touched him. Life had been unkind to Quinn, but she didn't waste time feeling sorry for herself. She took full responsibility for her own happiness. Still, it felt good to have given her a treat.

'Have dessert,' he urged. 'I mean to.'

She shook her head. 'I couldn't possibly fit it in. But I'd love a coffee.'

That made him grin. 'Not used to late nights, Ms Laverty?'

Her eyes danced. 'Not ones that don't involve earaches or tummy upsets.' She glanced around. 'I have to say, Aidan, this is a really lovely restaurant.'

They sat at a window table that overlooked Adelaide's streetscape. The lights of the city twinkled beneath them with an effervescence he found infectious.

He ordered coffee for Quinn and chocolate mousse cake for himself. When the waiter had gone, Quinn turned from the view to survey him. 'So…how will the press know that you're out on the town tonight?'

'They've been tipped off.'

'Right.'

'When we leave here there'll be a photographer somewhere. He could be hidden or he could be brash and in our faces.'

'If it's the latter, how should I act? Natural or furtive?'

He considered that. 'It won't matter.' Either would garner his mother's full attention. 'And there'll be more of the same at the nightclub we're going to.' He'd arranged for a photographer to get in and take photos of him and Quinn dancing. He didn't tell her that, though. He didn't want her feeling self-conscious the entire evening.

She stared out of the window with pursed lips and he frowned. 'What's the matter?'

'I'm feeling a little uneasy…'

'You don't need to. I promise to look after you and—'

'About doing all this to sabotage your campaign.'

He was prevented from answering when the waiter arrived with dessert and coffee.

'But that's the whole point of the exercise,' he said when the waiter was gone.

'The point is to rouse your mother from her depression and make her look beyond her grief.' She reached out and touched his hand. 'Why can't you just tell your parents the truth—that you don't want to be a politician?'

How could he tell Quinn that her plan was a losing game? His parents loved him, sure, but it had never been on the same scale as they'd loved Danny. Besides, he didn't want to have that particular conversation with his mother. It wouldn't be a conversation but an argument. It would end in her tears and his guilt. Lose-lose. This way…

'Aidan?'

The lights of the city were reflected in her eyes and it made something inside him start to pound. He swallowed and tried to ignore it. 'If I tell my parents I don't want to embark on a political career they'll be mortally offended.'

She frowned.

'What they'd hear is not that I love my job as a human rights lawyer, but me criticizing their entire way of life and value system. What they'd hear is me *spurning* their way of life and all they hold dear. And most of all, Quinn, what they'd see is me refusing to bring Danny's dream to fruition.' He stared down at the chocolate cake, his appetite all used up. 'They'd see it as a betrayal.'

Her lips parted a fraction and her eyes almost seemed to throb. 'Oh, Aidan,' she whispered.

He ached to reach out and touch her.

'So instead you're going to let them devalue all you hold dear, to belittle the life you want to lead?'

'I can live with that. My losing the campaign will be a blow to them, a major disappointment, but it's always been on the cards. That's the nature of politics. But me walking away from it all, they would find that unforgivable.'

'What if you're wrong?'

A weight settled on his shoulders. What if they didn't forgive him for 'going off the rails' and *inadvertently* sabotaging his political career?

'What if you're short-changing them? It's possible that they'd understand your position, you know. They don't sound like ogres. You're not narrow-minded. Danny doesn't sound as if he was narrow-minded, which makes me think they're not either. You're not giving them a chance to support you.'

'Danny has only been gone for eight months. I might not be prepared to sacrifice myself to a career in politics, but I'm not prepared to cause them any more pain than necessary. Not at this point in time.'

They stared at each other for several long moments and he clocked the exact instant she decided to leave it be. He should've been relieved, but he wasn't. Which didn't make any sense.

She reached across with her teaspoon and snared a spoonful of his cake. 'Oh, that is really good. I mean *seriously* good.' He went to push it towards her but she shook her head. 'The last thing you need is to be seen on the dance floor with a woman who has a distended stomach.'

Her wryness made him laugh. 'Quinn, when all of this is over, I'd like to keep seeing you.' Pokolbin was only two hours north of Sydney, maybe two and a half. It wasn't that far.

She snagged another spoonful of his cake and shook her head. 'Not going to happen.'

He forced himself to have a spoonful of cake too. Forced himself to hide how much her easy rejection cut at him. 'Why not?'

'Because I refuse to be a part of your strategy to ruin

your political career. And we both know a woman like me—a single, unmarried mother with a low-paying job and few qualifications—is not the kind of woman to stand at an aspiring politician's side.'

'That's not why I want to see you!'

'Maybe not.' She ate more cake and she looked utterly in control but the spoon trembled in her hand. 'But I remind you of Danny. I remind you of better times and I wonder how much of the real me you see.'

He flinched and abandoned all pretence of eating. 'You're just grasping after any excuse. You want to deny what's happening between us.'

She set her teaspoon to her saucer. 'There's an element of truth in that.'

Her simple statement made his jaw drop.

'You're a nice man, Aidan. I like you a lot, but...' She glanced up and met his gaze. 'Honesty is important to me.'

A chill slid beneath his ribs.

'Phillip lied to me about what he really wanted because he thought that was the right thing to do. The same way that you're lying to your parents.'

Her words couldn't hurt him. His heart had numbed and frozen over. 'You're saying you don't trust me.'

'Are you saying you'd never lie to me?'

Of course he wouldn't! He could say that till he was blue in the face, though. She'd never believe it. Phillip had done a right royal job on her.

'Your actions speak louder, I'm afraid.'

His parents and his relationship with her were two different issues!

'I'm not some child that needs protecting and I refuse to ever be treated like that again.'

He sat back. He scowled at his cake. Quinn drained her coffee. 'Stop being so glum,' she chided. 'We're supposed to be having fun, remember? You promised me dancing.'

Quinn was running scared. That was what all this was about. He scrubbed a hand down his face. He had the rest of tonight, all day tomorrow and tomorrow night to work on her.

If he dared.

Aidan woke to the piercing ringtone of his mobile phone. He fumbled for it. 'Hello?' he mumbled.

'Aidan Carter Fairhall, have you seen the papers today?'

His eyes sprang open. 'Mum!' He sat bolt upright in bed. He dragged in a breath. Right. 'Hold on.'

He padded to the door of his room and opened it. As requested, copies of all the national newspapers awaited him. He scooped them up and moved back to the bed. 'I have them all here. Which one in particular were you referring to?'

'All of them!'

He flicked through to the society pages and then grinned. Perfect. 'Ah…' He hemmed and hawed, injecting what he desperately hoped were notes of equivocation and vagueness into his voice.

'What on earth did you think you were doing?'

'I was just having a bit of…fun.'

'You're practically pawing that woman in public!'

'She's a very nice woman.'

His mother snorted.

'Look, what's the big deal? I went out. I had fun.' The irritation that edged into his voice wasn't feigned.

'The big deal is that photographs like this—where you look drunk, not to mention *lewd*—will do untold damage to your political image! What on earth do you think you were doing?' she repeated as if she couldn't believe his stupidity.

He scrubbed a hand across his chin.

'Aidan?'

'Do you know how far it is across the Nullarbor, Mum?' Silence greeted him. 'And it's all just endless sand and scrub for mile upon weary mile. It gives a man time to think.'

'What do you mean?'

The wobble in his mother's voice made his gut clench. He wished he could've spared her all the pain she'd suffered in the last eight months. 'Ever since Danny...' He couldn't finish that sentence. 'For the last eight months I've thrown myself into work to try and forget, but it doesn't work like that, does it? I need a holiday. I'm *taking* a holiday.'

'You don't have time for a holiday! You can have a holiday once you've been elected to office. You listen to me, Aidan. You are going to haul your backside out of whatever seedy hotel it's currently residing in, you will say goodbye to your slutty little friend, and you will get yourself to the airport. *Now!* We have work to do if we're to minimise the damage you've already done.'

Slutty?

'Do you hear me?'

He thrust out his jaw. 'No.'

An indrawn breath reached him down the end of the phone. 'I beg your pardon?'

That tone had made him quail as a kid. A part of him was glad to hear it now. He hadn't heard his mother this riled in a long time. But Quinn *slutty*? 'No can do, Mum. I'm not ready to come home. I'll call you in a couple of days to let you know my plans.' And he cut the line.

They spent the day at the zoo.

Aidan took every opportunity that presented itself to touch Quinn—a hand in the small of her back at the turnstile and again in the queue for the canteen, a brushing of fingers when he handed her a drink, the touch of arms and shoulders as they sat on a bench for a rest, a hand at her elbow when they ascended some steps. The startled glitter in her eyes and the flush that developed high on her cheekbones had him biting back a groan, along with the urge to rush her off somewhere private.

He wanted her mind filled with the sight, smell and feel of him. He wanted it to plague her with the same insistence it gnawed at him. He wanted the frustration of unassuaged hunger to batter down all her defences until not a single one was left.

He didn't know how far he and Quinn could cultivate their relationship but, presented with the stark fact of parting company with her tomorrow, he knew he had to try something.

She's a single mother. Leave her alone. This is just lust. Scratch that itch elsewhere.

He thrust out his chin. It went deeper than mere chemistry and it deserved to be explored.

Aren't you hurting your mother enough?

A fist clenched in his chest. This had nothing to do with his mother!

What would Danny tell you to do?

Everything stilled. His mind went blank.

'Will we get to see them eat?' Robbie asked as they moved towards the big cat area.

It had just been dinner time at the seal and dolphin enclosures. The boys had been fascinated.

'Not today,' Quinn said, reading a nearby sign.

Robbie pouted. 'Why not?'

'Because lions and tigers don't get fed every day. The zoo tries to mimic how they'd feed in the wild. It keeps them healthy.'

Aidan nudged her arm. She started. He bit back a grin. 'How'd you know that?'

'You'll be sorry you asked,' she warned.

He folded his arms. 'Go on.'

She shrugged. 'I've been reading up on some of the latest research into human health and nutrition.' He raised an eyebrow and she shrugged. 'It appears that just as it's healthier for wild animals to intermittently fast, the same might be true for humans.'

His mind flicked back to those textbooks in her car.

'There are links that suggest fasting can decrease both the incidence and growth of some cancers, reduce the risk of developing diabetes, and perhaps even Alzheimer's. It appears that fasting could promote cell renewal. I mean, the research is only in its infancy, but it is fascinating.'

He listened in astonishment and then awe as she rattled off facts and figures with an ease that spoke of close scholarship. She eventually petered off with a shrug and an abashed grin that speared into his heart. 'I told you you'd be sorry.'

'It's amazing and interesting,' he countered. He thought of the way she'd just spoken, of the fire in her voice, of those darn textbooks and the lecture she'd given him that first day about his probable cortisol levels. He pulled her to a halt. 'Quinn, why are you wasting all of this passion and talent? Why aren't you at university, conducting your own research?'

She stared at him for a moment and then pointed—to Robbie and Chase.

Ah.

In the next instant he rallied. 'But there's nothing to stop you from going to university now.'

She glanced pointedly to Robbie and Chase again and then raised an eyebrow.

'You could study part-time. You'd get government assistance while you were studying and—'

'You mean I'd end up with a big fat student debt.'

'And a bright and shiny qualification.'

'Look, Aidan, I made my decision nine years ago when I found out I was pregnant. I have to work full-time to make ends meet, that's non-negotiable, and I'm also a full-time mum. Studying even part-time would mean spreading myself too thin. Robbie and Chase deserve more than my part-time distracted attention. They deserve at least one fully involved parent.'

He opened his mouth, but she held up a hand. 'Maybe I'll rethink that when the boys are in high school and a bit more self-sufficient.'

By which time he didn't doubt she'd have come up with a whole new set of excuses. Her shuttered expression, though, told him the subject was closed.

That evening they went to Adelaide's night races.

Quinn instantly fell in love with the pageantry, the colour and the sheer excitement.

'Which one do you fancy?' Aidan asked her as the horses paraded in front of them.

'Number four,' she said, selecting a giant chestnut. The jockey wore the exact same shade as Aidan's shirt.

'Come on.' He took her hand and led her to one of the betting windows and handed her an obscene amount of cash. 'Put it all on the nose.'

'All?' she breathed.

He just grinned and it made her heart hammer. Heaven's, how on earth was she going to adjust to reality again tomorrow? When Aidan would be gone. For good.

She pushed the thought away. Tonight was for fun. There'd be time enough to miss all of this, to miss him, tomorrow.

She watched the race with her heart in her mouth, gripping Aidan's arm. As the horses hit the home straight she started jumping up and down and shouting along with the rest of the crowd, cheering on her horse with all her might.

When number four crossed the finish line a nose ahead of the rest of the field, she flung her arms around Aidan's neck. 'We won! We won!'

He swung her around before setting her back on her feet and grinning down at her. She eased away, the hard imprint of his body burnt on her brain. Did she really mean to let this man go? 'I'm having the best time,' she breathed.

You don't have any choice.

'Me too.'

Live for today. Tomorrow will take care of itself. It wasn't a view she tended to subscribe to, but she threw herself into it wholeheartedly now.

Despite the heat that flared between them and its insidious insistence that throbbed deep in her blood, Quinn found herself laughing when she and Aidan entered the foyer of their hotel later that evening. Even the knowledge lurking at the corners of her consciousness that their fun was at an end couldn't prevent her from holding tight to these last precious moments.

The foyer was empty except for the concierge and a receptionist, and an elegant woman sitting stiffly in one of the easy chairs. Aidan froze when he saw her. Quinn frowned up at him, completely attuned to his mood. 'What is it?'

The woman rose, her chin tilted at a haughty angle. 'Hello, Aidan.'

Aidan turned to Quinn, his smile stiff. 'Quinn, this is my mother, Vera Fairhall.'

CHAPTER EIGHT

AIDAN'S MOTHER!

Quinn's eyes widened and her jaw slackened. One glance at the other woman and she decided not to offer her hand. She swallowed and did her best to push her shoulders back. 'How do you do?' she said. She didn't say, 'pleased to meet you'. She doubted she'd be able to pull that lie off.

Mrs Fairhall didn't reply. Beneath her chilly gaze, Quinn's flirty red skirt seemed too short and her cream silk singlet top too skimpy. Which, of course, was true on both counts. She wore her strappy black sandals again, the ones with the bows, and the look they received basically said, 'woman of the night shoes'.

She choked back a giggle. Oh, Lord, they were in the middle of a farce!

'And who is this, Aidan?'

Tension vibrated through him and Quinn's desire to giggle promptly fled. His eyes flashed and his hands clenched. All of his easy politeness had disappeared, leaving a deep, burning anger she found hard to associate with him. She curled her hand around his arm and squeezed, tried to silently transmit that he not do or say anything he'd regret later.

Eight months might've passed but he and his mother were still both in deep mourning. People did and said things they didn't mean when operating under such stress. And Aidan mightn't be drunk, but they had been drinking.

He stared down at her for a moment and his face relaxed, and then a gleam she didn't trust lit his eyes. He slipped his arm about her waist and pulled her in close to his side. 'Mum, I'd like you to meet Quinn Laverty, the woman I mean to marry.'

The foyer spun. Quinn sagged against Aidan's side. She kept her eyes firmly fixed on the floor, knowing if she didn't they'd betray her. She closed them. What did he think he was doing? She should bring this lie to a close. It wouldn't do any of them any good, not in the long run.

'You expect me to congratulate you?'

He coiled up as if he were ready to spring. She leaned against him harder to keep him where he stood.

'Just once it'd be nice to hear you congratulate me on something that actually mattered to me.'

The words might've been drawled, but she sensed the very real pain beneath them. An innate loyalty for this man shot to the fore. 'Aidan,' she chided. 'We weren't going to tell anybody about this just yet.'

She lifted her chin and met his mother's gaze squarely. She didn't want to add to this woman's pain, but she'd do what she could to prevent her from adding to Aidan's. 'It's getting late.'

The dismissal was unmistakable and Vera Fairhall's eyes widened, and then they just as quickly narrowed. 'I will leave the two of you to say your goodnights. Aidan, I expect you in my room—' she gave her room number '—in ten minutes.'

'I really think you ought to leave that till the morning,' Quinn ventured.

The other woman spun to her. 'Don't you dare presume to tell me how to deal with my son!' And then she turned on her eminently respectable court shoe heels and stalked away.

Once she'd disappeared from view, Quinn pulled out of Aidan's grip, lifted both hands and let them drop. 'What on earth did you tell her we were engaged for?'

'I didn't say we were engaged. I said you were the woman I mean to marry.'

'You knew it's what she'd think!'

He scowled. 'She said you were slutty.'

Quinn went back over the conversation. 'No, she didn't.'

'Not just then.' He slashed a hand through the air. 'This morning, when I spoke to her on the phone. She called you my slutty friend.'

Quinn planted her hands on her hips. 'What's wrong with that? It was the look we were aiming for, remember? I'm *supposed* to be the wildly inappropriate woman.'

He stabbed a finger at her. 'She had no right to say it. It seriously cheesed me off.'

That was more than obvious.

'And just now she looked as if you were something unpleasant she'd stepped in.'

'It doesn't matter what she thinks of me.'

'Yes it does!'

Her heart started to pound. She pressed a hand against it. She was *not* going to travel this road with Aidan. 'You're going to have to tell her we're not engaged.'

He thrust out his chin and glowered at her. 'Or you will?'

Not on her life! 'I'll leave that particular joy to you.'

He didn't say anything. Tension crawled in all the spaces and silences between them. 'I'm sorry if this hasn't turned out the way you wanted,' she whispered. She tried to find a smile. 'But you've certainly galvanised your mother to action.' She wanted to reach out and touch him, but the fire burning between them was too fierce and she was afraid of getting burned. 'I just didn't know that it would create so much upheaval in you too.'

He dragged a hand down his face. 'Quinn...?'

She pulled herself up and glanced at her watch. She was *not* inviting him back to her room. 'Please don't lose your temper with her tonight. Try to get out of there as quickly as you can and sleep on it. See how you feel in the morning.'

'Will I see you in the morning?'

'Of course you will.' To say goodbye. She turned and made for the nearest elevator. Aidan didn't follow her and she didn't look back.

Quinn hadn't been in her room fifteen minutes when the phone rang. She grimaced and picked it up. 'Hello?'

'I suspect my mother is on her way to your room.'

Oh, great. Just great. 'You gave her my room number?'

'No, but I know how she operates. She'll have rung down to Reception to get it. Do you want me to come by to intervene?'

Aidan and all of his sexy male temptation in her room? No way! 'I'll deal with it.'

'Are you going to tell her we're not engaged?'

She let out a sigh and she didn't care if he heard it. 'No, but you're going to have to.'

A knock sounded on her door.

'Goodnight, Aidan.'

'A moment of your time, if I may?' Mrs Fairhall said when Quinn opened the door.

She'd have swept into Quinn's room if Quinn hadn't blocked the way. 'On one condition—that you keep your voice down. My boys are sleeping next door and I don't want them disturbed.'

The other woman's eyes flashed, but she nodded and Quinn let her pass.

'You have children?'

'Two boys—eight and six.'

Vera's gaze went to Quinn's left hand.

'And, yes, I'm unmarried. I've also been working in a low-level admin position and I have no tertiary qualifications worth speaking of.'

'That's none of my business.'

'But it's what you came down here to find out.'

She suddenly realised she stood in front of Aidan's mother in an oversized powder-blue T-shirt nightie with the words 'Super Sleep Champion' plastered on the front in big glittery letters. She pulled on the complimentary towelling robe provided for guests and tried not to feel at a disadvantage.

'That's not the reason I came down here, Ms Laverty.'

Quinn gestured to a chair. 'Would you like to sit?'

'I won't be here long enough to bother.'

Quinn sat. She did so in the hope it would help ease the acid burn in her stomach. 'You're here to offer me money to leave Aidan alone.'

'I see you've played this little game before.'

Just the once.

Vera whipped out a chequebook. 'How much will it take?'

And Quinn said now what she'd said back then. 'I don't want your money. I won't accept your money.'

'But—'

'Spare me the arguments. I already know the things I could do with the ludicrous amount of money you'd be prepared to offer me and, yes, I know the advantages my boys could gain from it, but I have too much self-respect. It's more important for me to be able to look my sons in the eye.'

Vera opened her mouth again, but Quinn kept talking right over the top of her. 'I have too much respect for

Aidan too. Do you have any idea how furious he'd be if he found out about this?'

Vera fell into the other chair as if she couldn't help it.

'I don't care about the insult offered to me. After all, what are we to each other? But the insult offered to Aidan…' Her hands clenched about the arms of her chair. 'How can you show him such little respect?'

'You will ruin him!' The older woman's face twisted. 'You will ruin everything good that he stands for.'

'How can you give him so little credit?' She sat back, her stomach churning harder and faster. The people from Aidan's world, though, would agree with Vera, would believe what she said with every conceited, supercilious bone in their bodies. They'd believe that a woman like her would blight Aidan's life.

Aidan was from that world, just as Phillip had been, and eventually he'd believe it too. She pulled in a breath. She and Aidan were *not* going to travel down the same path she and Phillip had. She'd make sure of it.

Not that Vera Fairhall knew that. She thought she was fighting for her son's reputation. The only son she had left.

Quinn reached across and squeezed Vera's hand. 'I know of your recent troubles and I'm very sorry for your loss. More sorry than I can say.'

'You know nothing!' Vera pulled her hand away, but she looked as if she might cry.

'You're right. I've never suffered a loss like that. The very thought of it makes me feel ill.'

Vera turned back.

'Aidan has talked to me about it a little. I know he and his father have been very worried about you and that they've been searching for ways to try and help you in your grief.'

'This is none of your business!'

'But in amongst all of this awfulness, who's been looking out for Aidan?'

'Don't you dare!'

Why not? Somebody had to. She leaned towards Vera. 'He's lost a brother he loved more than he's ever loved himself.'

'And you're taking advantage of his grief!'

Vera's pain was almost tangible. Quinn's eyes burned. 'No,' she said as gently as she could. 'I'm not the one who's taking advantage of him.'

Air hissed out from between Vera's teeth.

'If you continue trying to turn him into Danny, Mrs Fairhall, you'll have not only lost one son—you'll have lost the both of them.'

Vera rose and left Quinn's room without another word.

'That went well,' she whispered to the ceiling. And then she flung herself face down on her bed and burst into tears.

Quinn mightn't have slept much, but nevertheless she was up before either Robbie or Chase the next morning. The knock on her door, when it came, didn't surprise her.

Vera or Aidan?

She opened it.

Aidan.

She stood back to let him in and then went to the window and pushed the curtains even wider, flooding every inch of the room with as much sunlight as she could. It didn't erase the seductive appeal of the queen-sized bed, but it helped. A bit.

'The boys?'

'Still asleep.'

'Right. Okay.' He adjusted his stance. 'There's been a change of plan.'

Her stomach started to pitch and her heart grew heavy. 'Oh?'

'I'm going to accompany you as far as Sydney now.'

She gripped her hands together and shook her head. 'No.'

He frowned. He started to open his mouth.

'You're not invited,' she said before he could speak. 'This was always where we were going to part ways and we're sticking to that original plan.'

He turned grey then and she ached for him. It took all of her strength to remain where she was rather than racing across and flinging her arms around him.

He strode across and thrust a finger beneath her nose. 'We are more than ships in the night, regardless of what you think.' His voice was low and it shook, but there was no mistaking his sincerity.

Maybe. Maybe not. But one thing was certain. 'I will not be used as some kind of distraction or delaying tactic. You need to sort your life out, Aidan. Not tomorrow or next week or after you've lost the campaign, but now. And if you think putting it off is helping anyone then think again.'

He glared. She glared back, but she couldn't maintain it. 'I want to tell you something.' She sat in one of the tub chairs, though fell might've been a more accurate description.

He folded himself into the other. 'Go on.' His voice was so chilly it raised gooseflesh on her arms.

She met his gaze. 'Children don't owe their parents diddly-squat.'

His head rocked back. 'Steady on!'

'If parents inspire respect and love, that's great, but it doesn't mean children owe their parents a damn thing. It's the parents who owe their children.' She leaned towards him to try and drive her point home. 'It's the parents—or parent—who made the decision to bring a child into the world. It's therefore the parents' responsibility to keep that child safe and healthy. It's therefore the parents' responsibility to give that child as good a life as they can.'

'And the good schools and the extracurricular sporting activities and music lessons and the overseas trips, they all count for nothing?'

'Be grateful for them, by all means, but it doesn't mean you owe your mother and father for having provided them for you. And it definitely doesn't mean you have to lead the life they'd like to lock you into. Parents, if they've actually been successful at parenting, should've instilled in their children the strength to choose their own paths.'

'You're calling me weak?'

'I am not! But I think your grief and your worry for your mother has clouded your judgement.'

He leaned towards her and her throat tightened. 'You know what I think? I think this reasoning of yours is flawed, coloured by your experience with your own family.'

She tried not to flinch.

'Do you really think complete self-abnegation and self-sacrifice is a healthy example to give your kids? Do you want them to grow up thinking that finding a job they don't like but that will pay the bills is the best they can hope for out of life?'

Her jaw dropped.

'I don't know what you're scared of, Quinn, by refusing to go to university. Maybe you're afraid that you'll turn into your parents.'

She shot to her feet, shaking. 'That will *never* happen.'

He leapt up too. 'Or maybe it's the fact that some of what they said nine years ago was the truth.'

'They said we'd ruin our lives. I don't consider my life ruined.' Regardless of what Phillip thought to the contrary.

'But it's been no bed of roses.'

Her chin shot up. 'Do you hear me complaining?'

He stared at her for a long moment and then swore softly. 'I'm sorry. I shouldn't have said any of that.'

She rubbed her nose. 'I'm not going to apologise for what I said. I meant every word of it. And I think it needed to be said.'

Aidan tried to tamp down on the fear that rolled through him. This couldn't be goodbye. It *couldn't!*

He shoved his shoulders back. Quinn was running scared and who could blame her? For pity's sake, she was a single mother with more than one life to consider. *And* she'd met his mother.

The world they'd been living in for the last…eight… nine days? It had been a strange, contained and intense time—time out of time was what she'd called it—but that didn't make it any less real.

Everything had changed.

It occurred to him, with a wisdom he'd totally lacked these last few months, that a little time apart could be good for both of them. He needed to think. Hard.

But he wasn't letting her leave without extracting a promise that he could see her again. 'Can I come see you and the boys once you're settled?'

He could see the refusal forming on her lips when Chase burst into the room. He flung his arms around his mother's middle and beamed at Aidan. 'We had fun with Holly last night. Can we stay another day? I love Adelaide!'

Quinn chuckled, a rich warm sound he knew he'd miss. 'I'm sure you do, but today we hit the road again, buster.'

Chase pouted, but his heart wasn't really in it. And then his face changed completely from fun and mischief to something sombre and glum. 'Are you really not coming with us, Aidan?'

Aidan swore that every muscle Quinn possessed tightened until she practically hummed with tension. Chase had just handed him the perfect tool to worm his way back into their car for the rest of the journey. A glance at Quinn told him it wouldn't win him any Brownie points, though.

He crouched down in front of Chase. 'I'm afraid I have to get back to work, but I've had the best fun hanging out with you guys.'

Chase's bottom lip wobbled. Aidan whipped a business card from his wallet. 'See that number there?' He pointed. 'How about you ring it this evening to tell me where you are and what you did for the day?'

Chase's eyes widened and he was all smiles again. 'Okay!'

Quinn smiled her thanks. A guarded thanks, admittedly, but at the moment he'd take any kind of smile from her that he could get.

He rose to find Robbie surveying them from the doorway—*scowling* from the doorway. 'Hey, buddy.' How long had he been standing there, watching and listening?

Robbie didn't answer. Aidan had learned that Robbie, unlike his brother, wasn't precisely a morning person, but he sensed this was more than a case of the just-out-of-bed grumps.

Robbie glared at his mother.

Aidan pushed his shoulders back. He wasn't having Robbie blaming Quinn for this situation. 'I'm really sorry to abandon ship on you guys, but I have to be back in Sydney today.'

Robbie blinked and he looked so suddenly vulnerable an ache started up in Aidan's chest. 'I know, mate, I'm really going to miss you guys too.'

When Robbie started to cry, he couldn't help himself. He strode across, picked the young boy up and moved across to Quinn's bed. A glance at Quinn and her too-shiny eyes told him she was close to tears too. Chase pressed his face into her side.

'Boys aren't supposed to cry, are they?' Robbie eventually hiccupped, his storm over.

'Of course they are.' Aidan shifted, except… He glanced at Quinn. She wouldn't like it if he told the boys otherwise.

He glanced at each of the boys again. Darn it all! 'Chase, come up here too and I'll let you both in on a little secret.'

Chase raced over and climbed up beside him. Quinn folded her arms. Her eyes narrowed.

'It's always okay to cry with your mum. She's probably the absolute best person in the world to cry with. And I bet your Aunt Mara will be a good person to cry with too.'

'She is,' Robbie confided. 'And so are you.'

It was the strangest compliment he'd ever received, but a stupid smile spread across his face and his chest puffed out.

Chase nudged him. 'What's the secret?'

He sobered. 'It's not fair,' he warned, 'but life will be much easier if you don't cry in front of your friends at school. It's okay for girls, but not so much for boys.'

Chase looked across to Robbie. 'Is that true?'

Robbie bit his lip. 'I think it is, even though everyone says it's not.'

'Aidan!'

Quinn stood with her hands on her hips and her eyes flashing.

He lifted a shoulder. 'Look, I know it's not fair, but it's true. And I want the boys to have an easy time of it at school.'

Her lovely lips parted and a wave of desire washed over him. He gritted his teeth and searched for a way to soothe ruffled maternal feathers. 'Boys, I think if someone should cry, though, that's okay and that he shouldn't be teased for it.'

Robbie stared up at him.

'So if that ever does happen—' Aidan met Robbie's gaze square on '—I don't think you should join in the teasing. What's more, I think you should stick up for him.'

Robbie scratched his nose. 'That could be hard sometimes,' he finally ventured.

'I know.' Aidan pulled in a breath. 'Doing the right thing often is.'

And so, he was discovering, was parenting. It sure as heck wasn't for the faint-hearted. It wasn't all days at the beach and trips to the zoo. Which reminded him...

He met Quinn's gaze. He hadn't used the opening Chase had given him earlier as leverage, but... Her eyes narrowed, as if sensing he was up to something. Man, she wouldn't like this.

But he wasn't letting her go without a fight.

'Robbie and Chase, remember how I said we should all go to Taronga Park Zoo in Sydney?'

They both nodded vigorously.

'How about we do exactly that this Saturday?' It was Monday today. It'd give Quinn plenty of time to get to Pokolbin—she'd probably be there by Thursday.

Both boys leapt off the bed to jump and cheer. Quinn gaped at them, and at him. 'But...but we just spent a day at a zoo.'

He rose with a grin. 'Boys can never have too much of a zoo, Quinn.'

She pointed a finger at him, her brows darkening. 'You—'

He caught her finger and brought it to his lips. The pulse at the base of her throat throbbed and a deep ravaging hunger shook him. He had to get out of here. 'That evening is my parents' anniversary party. Please say you'll accompany me.'

Her jaw dropped. She hauled it back in place and nibbled at her lip. 'I...'

'We'll hire a couple of motel rooms in the city, just like we have here, and maybe we could do something on the Sunday before you have to head back to Pokolbin.'

'Say yes, Mum,' Robbie breathed.

She tried to tug her hand free, but Aidan refused to release it until he had her answer. She shifted her weight from one foot to the other. 'You were very good with the boys just then.'

He could be very good for her too, if she'd let him.

As if she'd read that thought in his face, her cheeks flamed. Finally she nodded. 'The zoo sounds like fun.'

'The party will be too,' he assured her. Maybe by then he'd have worked out which was the wiser course—to leave Quinn alone or to pursue her with everything he had.

'What do you mean, you don't want a political career after all? You were the one who decided to step into Daniel's shoes!'

This was not going to be an easy conversation, but Quinn had been right—trying to live Danny's life was never going to work. Not for anyone. Not in the long run.

'I will not allow you to let him down like this!' Every perfectly coiffed hair on his mother's head rippled in outrage.

'But it's okay with you if I let myself down?'

She stiffened. She stared and his heart ached and ached for her. He loved his mother. He loved both of his parents. He'd loved Danny too.

And Quinn?

He swallowed. Quinn understood him, she'd fought for him, she was strong and full of laughter and she'd made the sun shine in his miserable life again. He wasn't sure what any of that meant.

Maybe they were only ships in the night, but everything inside him rebelled at that thought.

'Aidan!'

His mother's words snapped him to. He pulled in a breath. First he had to fight for his life—for the life he wanted to lead. He wouldn't deserve Quinn otherwise. 'Dad asked me to take Danny's place.'

She sat, slowly, as if her bones hurt. 'Why?'

Her voice came out hoarse and he had to close his eyes for a moment. 'He thought it would give you a reason to… to keep going.'

Her eyes filled and his chest cramped. 'And I agreed to do it because I love you both and I wanted to do whatever I could to make you feel better and to fill the void Danny had left behind. But I'm not Danny. I'm never going to be Danny. And nothing is ever going to fill that void.'

'So on the strength of that you're going to let Danny's legacy die?'

His head came up. 'Danny's legacy wasn't his political career.' He stared at her for a long moment and then said, 'Do you know how long it's been since I went surfing?'

She waved an impatient hand. 'Grow up, Aidan. We all put away childish things.'

'Danny didn't.'

'Of course he did! He—'

'He attended every single home game the Swans had last year,' he said, naming one of the premier football teams in the country. 'He had a box.' Aidan found himself grinning. 'He told you and Dad it was for networking and hobnobbing, but it was really because he loved his footy.'

His mother gaped at him. He lowered himself down to the seat beside her. 'Danny's legacy wasn't his career, Mum. It was his love of life and how he managed to instil that into everyone he came into contact with. It was his support of my surfing, Dad's golf and your book club. Danny wouldn't want you sitting inside four walls constantly grieving. He'd want you out and about, doing the things you love and sharing that love with others, just as he did.'

She leapt up and wheeled away. 'You think it's easy to move on? You think a person—a mother—can do it just like that?' She snapped her fingers.

'I know it's not easy.' He rested his forehead against his palm and drew in a breath that made him shudder. If he continued to pursue Quinn it would cause his mother yet more grief. Could he really do that to her at the present time? 'I realise I'm not your firstborn, and I know I'm not your favourite son, but—'

She spun around. 'Your father and I didn't have favourites!'

Aidan lifted his chin. 'Danny was everything you wanted in a son. He was your golden boy. Mum, I don't mean to sound harsh, I loved Danny, but his life is not worth more than mine.'

She sat as if in a dream. She reached out as if to touch him, but drew back at the last moment. 'I didn't realise that's how you felt. Why have you never told me this before?'

He shrugged.

Her eyes flashed. Her hair quivered. 'You stupid boy! You should've said something!'

He blinked.

'That rotten reserve of yours, Aidan! Danny was always effusive and affectionate. It was very easy to show him affection in return and to be demonstrative with him. It was always much harder to break through your reserve.'

His jaw dropped.

'I can see why you might think we favoured Danny, but, son, that just wasn't the case.'

It wasn't? He'd spent all this time thinking he was the second son in every sense and yet...

'Come along, Aidan, it's time for us to catch a plane and head into this brave new world of ours.'

He caught hold of her hand. 'I've had a thought about our brave new world. Mum, you're as passionate about politics as Dad and Danny ever were. Why don't you stand for office?'

'Me? But that's nonsense!'

'Why? You're only fifty-three, and an energetic fifty-three at that. You know the ropes. You know how to play the game. You'd be an absolute asset to the party.'

Her jaw dropped but he could see her mind ticking over as his idea took hold.

'I'll go and pack.' Aidan rose, and he left with a lighter heart than he could've thought possible.

CHAPTER NINE

THE MOMENT THE knock sounded on Quinn's motel room door the following Saturday evening, a tempest burst to life in her stomach. The knock wasn't loud—a firm unhurried rat-tat—but it was clear and distinct. It *wasn't* enough to send a stampede of a thousand thrashing wings thumping through her.

At least, it shouldn't have been.

She pressed a hand to her stomach, moistened her lips and eased the door open, fighting the urge to fling it wide to feast her eyes on the man who stood on its other side. She'd already feasted her eyes on him earlier in the day when she'd found him waiting for her and the boys at the entrance to Taronga Park Zoo.

He'd feasted his eyes on her then too—just as hungrily, just as intensely, and with an intent that had made her stomach tighten.

The boys hadn't considered hiding their excitement. They'd hurled themselves at him, talking ten to the dozen. She'd envied them their lack of restraint. She'd have loved to have hugged him, but she hadn't. She'd merely nodded. He'd given her a quick peck on the cheek and his scent had filled her with so much longing it was all she'd been able to do to not run away.

Robbie and Chase had had the most brilliant day.

She hadn't. And she hadn't been able to tell if Aidan

had or not either. She'd tried to take pleasure in the boys' joy, in the gorgeous views of Sydney Harbour and in the antics of the meerkats, but her awareness of Aidan drove everything else out of her. That awareness had grown as the day progressed—a deep prickling burn that wore away at her. Conversation didn't ease it. At least, not the kind of polite surface chit-chat they'd maintained.

She gritted her teeth. They'd maintain it this evening too if it killed her. And then they'd never see each other again and she'd be free to get on with her life. Whatever sense of obligation had prompted Aidan would be allayed.

The thought made her want to throw up.

It also made her want to heave a sigh of relief.

He frowned. 'Are you feeling all right?'

She snapped a smile to her face. 'Of course.'

He stared at her. She stared back. Okay, polite chit-chat *but* with a little drop of honesty thrown in. 'Are you sure you'd still like me to accompany you this evening?'

'Why would you ask me that?'

His voice came out deceptively soft. It raised goose-flesh on her arms. She tried to rub it away. 'Aidan, this is a party to honour your parents. I imagine your mother, and probably your father too, will be far from thrilled that I'm attending as your date.'

'You leave my parents to me.'

Gladly, but would they return the favour? Or would she be trotted off to some quiet alcove and offered some other sweetie to disappear into the night and never return?

'I won't be offended if you've changed your mind.'

The aggressive tilt to his chin made her mouth water. 'I will be if you've changed yours.'

She bit back a sigh. 'Fine, okay. So be it.' She collected her wrap and purse. 'I guess we'd best set off. We don't want to be late.'

'Are you determined to treat this entire evening like an unpleasant chore?'

That pulled her up short. 'Of course not!' But it was true. She expected this evening to be an ordeal. Which was hardly fair to Aidan. 'I'm just concerned that...' She'd ruin everything for him.

'Well, don't be.' He took her wrap—a shot silk stole that matched her dress—and settled it around her shoulders. 'By the way, you look lovely.'

His breath disturbed the hair by her ear and sent a shiver arrowing down to pulse at a spot below her belly button. 'Thank you.' Her voice wobbled, betraying her.

His grip on her shoulders tightened and he pulled her back against him to show her how much she affected him too. Her breath caught. She closed her eyes, but rather than help her regain her balance it only highlighted the hardness pressing against her.

'If this were any other night I would do my best to seduce you here and now.'

She wasn't sure she'd have the strength to resist him if he did. With a superhuman effort she moved out of his grasp. 'But it isn't any other night. Besides, you look very debonair in your dinner jacket and black tie and it would be a shame to wrinkle you.' She could just imagine his mother's face!

She turned. 'I left the vamp behind tonight to dress as a lady. It's how I expect to be treated.'

He stared back at her, his eyes darker than she'd ever seen them. The very air throbbed. 'Have I ever treated you as anything else?'

'No.' He hadn't.

'C'mon, let's go.'

He took her elbow. She had to grit her teeth and lecture herself long and hard to keep her inner vamp under wraps.

* * *

The party was held in the ballroom of one of the city's grand hotels. It had glorious views of the Harbour and the Opera House. Lights twinkled on the Harbour and fairy lights winked on the two hundred guests—the elite of Sydney society—who mingled in all of their glamorous finery, and Quinn wished herself back into the isolation of the Nullarbor Plain and a night sky filled with an entirely different kind of light show.

She'd known Aidan would have hosting duties this evening. She'd known he would have to leave her for long periods of time. She hadn't minded. He'd introduced her to nice people. She'd made pleasant conversation. And it had given her a chance to observe him without his knowing.

'I understand you and my son had quite the adventure.'

Quinn swung from surveying the Harbour to find Aidan's father holding out a glass of champagne to her. She took it—without a single shake or quiver and all while maintaining a smile. Well done her! 'Happy anniversary, Mr Fairhall.' She touched her glass lightly to his. They both sipped. 'An adventure?' she finally said. 'Yes, I guess it was.'

Mr Fairhall opened his mouth, but his wife chose that moment to glide up between them. 'You look lovely this evening, Quinn. That dress is quite charming.'

She and her aunt had spent an entire day searching for this dress. She'd told Mara everything, of course. Mara had chuckled and decreed that Quinn needed a dress fit for a lady—a dress fit for Audrey Hepburn. And they'd found it. Pink silk shot through with the merest shimmer of black. Cocktail length with a scalloped hem, embroidered in black and with matching embroidery on the bodice. It was pretty, demure and very, *very* chic.

Quinn, however, caught the underlying meaning to Vera Fairhall's words. 'Thank you, Mrs Fairhall. The dress cost a bomb, but it was worth every penny.' She named the designer and had the satisfaction of seeing Vera's eyes widen. 'But we both know clothes don't make the woman.'

'That is very true, my dear.' She raised an eyebrow. 'I hear you've had quite the day of it.'

Had Aidan told her about their trip to the zoo? Or did she have spies? And, either way, did it matter? 'Yes, indeed.'

'I certainly understand if you're feeling tired and would like to sneak away early to go and check on your children. I mean we can't spare Aidan, of course, but we'd be more than happy to cover a taxi for you.'

'I'm sure you would,' Quinn said drily. 'Your reputation for hospitality precedes you.'

Tom Fairhall chuckled. Vera drew back. 'I'm only trying to be polite, Quinn. I'd understand if you felt slightly out of place here this evening.'

'Vera,' Tom chided softly.

'Not in the least,' Quinn sent back with all the fake sincerity she could muster. 'I see you even invited my parents. I do hope you didn't do that on my account.'

She gestured across the room. Vera swung to stare and her jaw dropped. 'You're *that* Laverty girl?'

Quinn raised an eyebrow, but her stomach sank. 'You don't need to concern yourself with me, Mrs Fairhall. I won't be troubling you for a taxi. I have a strong constitution and I don't tire easily.'

Vera stalked off. Tom patted Quinn's shoulder. 'Don't mind my wife, my dear. She's always been far too protective of Aidan. It's just become worse since…'

She glanced up uncertainly. 'I understand that. I…' She bit her lip. 'I did say to Aidan it might be best if I didn't come this evening.'

'My son, however, can be very persuasive.'

She smiled at that. 'Still, I don't want to ruin your or

your wife's enjoyment of the evening and if you think it's best I leave, I will.'

He stared down at her. He had eyes disarmingly like his son's. 'That's very generous of you, Quinn, but no. While Vera can't see it yet, we owe you a huge debt of gratitude. I'd unknowingly pushed Aidan into a course of action that was wrong for him and I didn't know how to reverse it. You helped him do that instead.'

So Aidan had stood up for himself? He'd turned his back on a political career? Her heart lifted. 'I'm not sure I can take too much credit.'

'I'm sure you're being far too modest.'

She recognised the guilt behind the dark amber of his eyes. 'I don't think you should feel guilty about pointing Aidan towards politics. Grief is a process. I think it helped Aidan more than hindered him.'

He smiled then. 'Thank you, my dear.'

Her parents glanced in her direction, pushed their shoulders back and she read the resolution in their faces. 'Now, off with you,' she shooed, not wanting him to witness whatever was about to transpire. 'You've neglected your guests for long enough.'

With a chuckle he strolled off.

She'd noticed her parents the moment they'd walked into the party—her father in an impeccable suit and her mother in sensible shoes. She wasn't sure how long it had taken them to recognise her. She suspected a percentage of the room was abuzz with news of Aidan's unsuitable girlfriend. Her name would've been passed from group to group and her parents would've heard it.

Not that she was Aidan's girlfriend.

You'd like to be.

It'd never work.

'If you have any sense of shame whatsoever,' her father said without preamble, 'you will leave this party at once.'

She and shame, at least her father's version of it, had never been close acquaintances. She pasted a big fake smile to her face. 'Hello, Daddy, lovely to see you too! You and Mummy look well. I'm sure you'll be delighted to hear that your grandchildren are healthy and happy.'

'Don't embarrass us in front of all these people, Quinn,' her mother snapped.

Quinn stared at them and shook her head. She hadn't seen them in nine years. It seemed strange to feel so removed from two people who had once been so important to her. But it was a relief too. She couldn't believe that once upon a time she'd wanted to be just like them.

'So you have your sights set on the Fairhall boy now, taking advantage of a family's grief, determined to ruin yet another man?'

She lifted her chin. 'The two of you lost any right to have a say in my life when you disowned me nine years ago. You are horrible people who lead sterile lives and I really don't want anything to do with either one of you.'

She'd have told them to go away, but Aidan chose that moment to return to her side. He glanced from her to her parents and back again. 'Quinn?'

'Aidan, these are my parents, Ryan and Wendy Laverty.'

She didn't say 'I'd like you to meet my parents', because that would've been a lie.

She recognised the shock deep in his eyes. Perhaps she should've been a bit more forthcoming about her background on that long drive from Perth, but it had all seemed so separate from her. 'My father is a vice chancellor at a nearby university and my mother is a leading researcher at another.' She gestured to Aidan. 'I expect you both recognise Aidan Fairhall.'

They all shook hands, but nobody smiled. It didn't surprise her when her father was the first to break the silence.

'Young man, I hope you'll take my advice and steer clear of this woman.'

Beside her, Aidan stiffened.

'I assure you that she is nothing but trouble and will only bring you grief.'

'I'm afraid, sir, that I have to disagree with you. Quinn is a remarkable woman with more integrity and true kindness than anyone I've ever met.'

Man, he was good. Smooth, unflappable and unfailingly pleasant.

'And if you say one more disagreeable thing about her I will have to ask you to leave.'

He managed to maintain his smile the entire time. She wanted to applaud.

He turned to Quinn, effectively dismissing her parents. 'Your drink is warm. Let's go get you a fresh one.'

And, with that, he took her elbow and whisked her off to the bar. She slid onto a stool as Aidan ordered their drinks, and when he handed her a mineral water she started to laugh. 'That was masterfully handled.'

'Jeez.' He settled on the stool beside her. 'And I thought my mother was a nightmare.'

Quinn grinned. 'She is.'

He choked on his drink.

She nudged his shoulder. 'I want more for you than a woman who has been around the blocks a few times.'

He winced. 'You heard that?'

'Uh-huh.' As she'd no doubt been meant to. It had been said much earlier in the evening. There'd been some mention of all the baggage Quinn carried too. She'd taken that to refer to Robbie and Chase. When Aidan had turned back to her she'd pretended to be absorbed in studying the table decorations to save him from embarrassment.

But he'd just witnessed her embarrassment.

Was an embarrassment shared an embarrassment

halved? She grimaced and sipped her drink. She suspected it might in fact be an embarrassment doubled.

'I'm sorry, Quinn. My mother—'

'Aidan, we put on one heck of a show in Adelaide. Your mother has every right to her reservations. She only has your best interests at heart.'

'Your parents don't, though.' He reached out to squeeze her hand. 'I didn't know they'd be here this evening.'

She squeezed it back before releasing it on the pretext of lifting her drink. The less she and Aidan touched the better. 'Neither did I. I'm sorry if they came as a shock to you. I probably should've been more candid about my background, but...' She glanced up at him. 'It all feels so remote from who I am now.'

Something burned in the backs of his eyes. 'We can leave if you want to.'

'Absolutely not.'

'I'm not buying into this casual nonchalance for a moment, sweetheart.'

Tears burned the backs of her eyes. She forced her chin up. 'But I do have my pride. I have absolutely no intention of giving either your mother or my parents that kind of satisfaction.'

He swore so softly she hardly heard it.

She sent him a smile. 'Besides, I promised your father I'd be one of the last to leave.'

He smiled then too. 'Wanna dance?'

She slid off her stool. 'I thought you'd never ask.'

Aidan walked Quinn to her hotel room. Neither one of them spoke. He didn't touch fingers to her elbow on the pretext of guiding her. He didn't take her hand. He didn't touch the small of her back. He kept his hands firmly—and deeply—in his pockets, did what he could to control the rapid pounding of his heart and reminded himself to keep breathing.

One foot after the other

One breath after the other.

He could do this. His hands clenched. *He could do this.*

They reached her door. They both stared at it for two beats rather than at each other. Finally Quinn seemed to give herself a mental kick and fumbled in her purse for the plastic key card.

He took it from her, inserted it into its slot and pushed the door open a crack. Quinn stared up at him, her eyes wide and uncertain, her lips a tempting promise in the dimly lit corridor.

You can do this!

He didn't step any closer. He would lose all pretence of control if he did that, if all of her sweetness pressed up warm and inviting against him.

Still, he couldn't resist dipping his head to kiss her.

Her lips met his, hesitant perhaps, but undeniably awake to the consequences that could ensue.

She kissed him back as if inviting those consequences. More than anything, he wanted to back her into her room and kiss her until they were both mindless with need. He ached to peel her clothes from her body and explore every inch of her to find what would make her gasp, what would make her moan, what would make her call out his name. He wanted to make love with her, frantic and fast. He wanted to make love with her painstakingly slow. He wanted to lose himself in the mindless pleasure they could find with each other.

But he couldn't let that happen.

He wanted more than one night with this woman. That had come to him swift and sure as he'd watched her make polite conversation with perfect strangers tonight. Quinn mightn't have wanted to attend the party, but not a soul would've guessed it. Meeting her parents had sealed the deal. Despite the pain it would cause his mother, he wanted to keep Quinn in his life.

Although she didn't know it, she held his heart in her hands. One misstep from him and she would drop it cold. And instinct warned him his heart wouldn't bounce. It would take a long time to get over her and he didn't want to have to try.

He deepened the kiss, wanting her aching so hard for him that she couldn't turn and just walk away. She tasted of champagne and coffee. She fizzed in his blood until he felt as if he were riding the biggest, most perfect wave of his life. Bracing one hand against the wall, he sucked her bottom lip into his mouth, nibbled it, laved it with his tongue. Her hands flattened against his chest and started to inch up towards his shoulders. Her tongue tangled with his and she made a mewling noise that angled straight down to his groin.

He broke free. 'Thank you for coming to the party with me this evening.' He didn't try to hide the hoarseness of his voice.

'Aidan?' Her hands slid against his chest and she made no move to hide the glitter in her eyes or the need in her face.

He backed up a step. Her hands fell to her sides. Her eyes dimmed. Disappointment flared in their depths… and relief. The relief kept him strong. Until she wanted him as unreservedly and unashamedly as he wanted her, he wouldn't let things go any further.

He could do this!

'I'll collect you and the boys at ten in the morning.'

'But…' She opened the door wider in silent invitation.

He shook his head. 'Goodnight, Quinn.'

He turned and walked away. He shoved his hands into his pockets and clenched them. He gritted his teeth and placed one foot in front of the other, pulled in one breath after the other.

* * *

They spent the following day on the Harbour. Aidan had booked a lunch cruise—family friendly—and he couldn't have ordered more perfect weather. The sun shone, but not too fiercely. A fresh breeze played through their hair, caressing their skin in a way that made it hard for him to think of anything but Quinn naked and his fingers trailing across her flesh. And hers trailing across his.

A burst of laughter from the children on the deck below snapped him back to himself. The colour on Quinn's cheekbones had grown high and he knew she'd read the direction his thoughts had taken. And if the pulse pounding at the base of her throat was any indication, she might have in fact added her own embellishments to the fantasy. His groin started to throb in time to the beat of her pulse.

'Why didn't you stay last night?' The words shot out of her as if some resistance had been breached. They sat alone at a table overlooking the foredeck, but she kept her voice low.

He leaned towards her and he didn't try to temper his intensity. 'Because I want you to want me with the same fire I want you.'

Her lips parted. She swallowed and her tongue snaked out to moisten them. 'Do you doubt it?'

He forced himself back in his seat. 'Are you telling me you didn't feel a thread of relief when I walked away last night?'

She glanced away. It was all the answer he needed.

'Aidan, neither one of us needs this kind of complication in our lives at the moment.'

He took a sip of his soda, but his eyes never left hers. 'Here's a newsflash for you, Quinn, but I don't consider you a complication.'

Her arched eyebrows told him what she thought about that. It might've made him smile a week ago.

'I like your father.'

He let her change the subject. 'I do too.' She laughed, as he'd hoped she would. He wanted to banish those lines of strain around her mouth forever. 'He likes you too.'

She glanced at him and quickly glanced away again. She tucked her hair behind her ears. 'He said you're making the break from politics.'

Thanks to her, he'd found the courage to be honest—to himself and to his family. 'Yes.'

'How's that working out for you all?'

'Very well so far. I'm taking some time off to sort out where I want to go from here, while my mother is still going into the office to sort out everyone else. My father watches us both indulgently from the sidelines and tries to fit in as many games of golf as he can.'

She grinned—one of those loving life grins that could transport him to a better place. 'That's excellent news.'

He reached out and ran a finger across the back of her hand. 'Can we talk about your parents for a moment?'

Her hand clenched and then she moved it out of his reach. 'If you want.' Her words came out reluctantly and his heart burned for her. 'But if you're thinking there's a chance for any kind of reconciliation, I'd counsel you to think again.'

He ached to hug her. 'Unfortunately, sweetheart, I agree with you.'

She blinked. Though whether at his words or the endearment, he had no way of knowing.

'Until they realise they're the ones who should be asking your forgiveness rather than the other way around, they're lost causes as far as I'm concerned.'

Her eyes filled and something snagged deep in his chest. This woman deserved so much more. She deserved to be loved and cherished.

And occasionally challenged.

'That's not going to happen. They have very rigid views about life and how it should be lived and anyone living outside of that box is given a wide berth. It's as if they're afraid it will pollute their ambition.' She drew a smiley face in the condensation of her glass. 'Their status at their universities and within their research communities is what matters to them. It's how they measure their success and happiness. They love their jobs and their institutions.' She scrubbed out the smiley face. 'What they haven't realised yet is that jobs and institutions can't love you back.'

Her parents lived in a rigid, narrow-minded world. The same world he'd been in danger of locking himself into.

'What was it like growing up with them?'

'Oh, I had all the privileges any girl could want.'

'It's not what I asked, Quinn.'

She glanced down at her hands. 'Lonely,' she finally said. 'It was lonely. My parents worked long, hard hours and when they were home their favourite thing to do in the evenings was work some more.'

He swallowed back the acid that burned his throat. When he'd been growing up his father had had to put in the hard yards, but it hadn't stopped either of his parents from finding time for him and Daniel. And he couldn't forget that for all of his childhood he'd had Danny as a playmate and companion too.

'So when Phillip and I started dating I fell hard. So did he.' She shrugged. 'For a while.'

He understood that completely, but...

'C'mon, out with it.'

He grimaced. It was lucky he had a poker face in the courtroom because it was obvious he didn't have one around Quinn. He drummed his fingers against the table. 'Look, I understand your resentment towards your parents.'

'Resentment?' She shifted. 'Oh, Aidan, so much of that

is just water under the bridge. All I want to do now is protect my kids from that kind of influence.'

'By turning your back on a whole way of life?'

She frowned.

'It's why you've shunned university, isn't it?'

Her eyes flashed. 'That was *their* dream, not mine. I'm living my dream.'

But she wasn't, was she? The childhood sweetheart was no longer at her side, helping her to negotiate parenthood's tricky waters or sharing love and laughter and all of those other things that made life worth living.

He wanted all those things for her. He wanted to share all of those things with her.

'And, quite frankly, I don't know why you have to keep rabbiting on about it.'

'Because, in a way, you're in danger of becoming just as narrow-minded as your parents.'

She gaped at him. 'I can't believe you just said that.'

Nor he. He had to be crazy. This was no way to woo a woman. But in his heart he knew he was right. Until Quinn fought to lead the life she wanted—the life she deserved—she'd never be truly free to love him. And he wanted her to love him. He wanted that with everything good he had inside him.

'Shunning university and a chance for a better life; is that a way of punishing your parents? Or do you believe that if you reject everything your parents value that you're giving validity to your current life?'

In a twisted way he could see how that might make sense.

'Oh, for heaven's sake!' she snapped. 'I'm not eighteen any more. I know that not everyone who has a degree is as inflexible or as detached as my parents...or as selfish as Phillip.'

She did? Then why wouldn't she even consider exploring her passion for science further?

She leaned towards him. 'You really want to know why I haven't considered furthering my education? It's because I don't want my children growing up lonely like I did.'

He saw then, in a light all too clear and blinding, the full effect her lonely childhood had had upon her. 'Oh, sweetheart.'

'Don't you *Oh, sweetheart,* me.' She batted his hand away. 'You don't understand how many hours I put into my schoolwork. It was something intelligent I could discuss with my parents.' She gave a harsh laugh. 'Oh, they trained me well. Those were the only times when I had their full attention and approval. And nobody could accuse me of being a slow learner. It got that I studied almost obsessively just so I could get a pat on the back from one or other of them.'

She'd learned to throw herself into her studies in the same way her parents had thrown themselves into their careers.

'My boys deserve to have a mother who is fully focused on them, not poring over some dusty old tomes in the library during their soccer games and forgetting parent and teacher evenings.'

He finally caught hold of the hand that had been making agitated circles in the air. 'Quinn, honey, you already have more life experience than either of your parents. You haven't been constrained by the narrowness of their world for nine years. You just told me you're not eighteen any more. And you're not. Nor are you going to turn into your parents. Ever. Regardless of whatever else you decide to do with your life.'

She stilled. Beneath his fingertips, her pulse pounded like wild surf.

'Quinn, these days your life is full and rich. It's better

than the kind of life you'd be leading if you'd followed your parents' path, yes?'

'Of course.'

'You no longer need to find something that will plug up the loneliness, do you?'

She shook her head.

'Then why don't you believe that you can reinvent your old dreams into the life you're living now? Why don't you trust yourself to make it work?'

She stared at him as if in a daze, as if what he was proposing had never occurred to her before.

'For some reason, your parents couldn't manage to be good scientists and good parents. Phillip hasn't been able to manage that leap either. But you're better than all of them. If you want to, you *can* make it work.'

Her chin came up. He wondered if she realised how tightly she gripped his hand. 'What makes you so sure?'

'Your love for your sons.'

She bit her lip.

He squeezed her hand and then he released it. 'You showed me I had to fight to live the life I was meant to be leading. You showed me I had the right to that life. Exactly the same goes for you.'

CHAPTER TEN

QUINN GLANCED UP from the kitchen table when she heard a car pull in behind the house. Aunt Mara's sturdy farmhouse was set well back from the lane, hidden in among the olive groves like a house in a fairy tale. The driveway was marked 'Private' so it was rare for tourists to accidentally wander down this way, though it did happen.

Mara had left for the shop over an hour ago. Quinn had manned the shop yesterday so today she and the boys were having a traditional lazy Sunday morning. She marked her spot in the university prospectus and moved to peer out of the door, ready to offer directions to whoever might be lost.

A man unfolded himself from the car. She blinked. What on earth…? Aidan!

Her heart hammered up into her throat, making her head whirl. She clung to the doorframe, unable to drag her gaze from the long clean lines of an athletic male body that filled her with a vigour and energy completely at odds with lazy Sundays.

After last weekend she hadn't thought she would see him again. She'd spent a ludicrous amount of time during this last week silently detailing all the reasons why that was a good thing. Absurdly, all she wanted to do now was jump up and down and clap her hands. Which was exactly what Robbie and Chase did when they caught sight of him from where they played in the side yard.

They bolted up to him and he hugged them both as if it were the most natural thing in the world. He grinned as if he were truly delighted to see them. And then he glanced to where she stood and he grinned as if he were truly delighted to see her too and her stomach twisted and turned like a purring cat weaving around its beloved owner's legs. Before she was even aware of it, she was across the veranda and down the back steps. 'Aidan, what a surprise.'

He bent to kiss her cheek. 'Not an unwelcome one, I hope.'

His scent and the touch of his lips woke her up more effectively than a strong shot of espresso. 'Of course not.'

'We can show Aidan everything!' Robbie said.

Aidan took them all in with one comprehensive glance…and that oh-so-beguiling smile of his. 'So you're all still enjoying your new home?'

He had a way of asking a question that made it seem as if he really cared about the answer. Both boys nodded vigorously.

'You can meet Auntie Mara and see the shop!' Chase said.

Chase had fallen under the spell of both, to Quinn's delight.

'And we'll take you down to the dam. We've got ducks!' Robbie added. 'And then we'll show you all the olive trees and—'

'Boys,' she hollered over the top of them when they both started to shout out their plans, 'let Aidan catch his breath first. You must've left at the crack of dawn to get here by ten.'

One shoulder lifted. A lean, broad shoulder that made her mouth water. 'I'm an early riser.'

She shook herself. 'Coffee?'

'Love one.'

It wasn't until they were seated with their coffees

that the urge to run hit Quinn. She couldn't explain it. It might've been the way those clear amber eyes surveyed her. It might've been the way they widened when they registered the university prospectus sitting on the table. It might've been the way his presence seemed to fill the kitchen. Whatever it was, it had her wanting to back up and run for the hills. Of course her inner vamp called her an idiot and dared her to sit on his lap instead. The idea left her squirming in her seat.

'Are you here for the whole day?' Robbie demanded.

'If that's okay with your mother.'

Three sets of eyes swung to her. 'I…' She swallowed. Why was he here?

He sent her a winning smile. 'I've heard so much about the place that curiosity got the better of me. I had to see it with my own eyes.'

'We can show you our new school too,' Robbie said.

'And where my friend Andrew lives,' Chase said.

'And the olive presses!'

'And—'

'Boys!' She clapped her hands. 'You're going to give Aidan half an hour to catch his breath after his long drive, while I make him something to eat.'

'Aw, but—'

'No buts.' She shooed them outside. 'You can make up an itinerary for the day.'

Robbie's face lit up and he grabbed Chase's arm. 'Will we start with the dam or the shop?'

She turned back. 'Eggs on toast?'

'I couldn't possibly put you out like that.'

'It's not putting me out at all.' It'd give her something to do, other than sit at the table and stare at him. 'Scrambled okay?'

'Perfect.'

She busied herself with breaking eggs into a bowl.

'It's not that far, you know?'

She glanced across at him. 'What isn't?'

'The drive from Sydney. It's two hours of mostly good road.'

'Oh.' She didn't know what else to say and the silence started to grow. She tried to focus on not burning anything—the eggs, the toast or herself. Eventually she slid a plate of scrambled egg and toast in front of him and hoped it'd ease the itch that had settled squarely between her shoulder blades.

The smile he sent her and his, 'This looks great,' only made her itch worse.

And the silence continued to grow.

'You were right,' she suddenly blurted out, slapping a hand down on the prospectus.

'I wasn't going to ask. I figured I'd hassled you enough. But I've been sitting here dying of curiosity.'

He grinned. She absolutely, positively couldn't help it. She had to grin back. He paused mid-bite to stare and those amber eyes of his darkened. Her heart stopped. Heat scorched her cheeks. She dragged the prospectus towards her and tried to focus beyond the buzz in her brain.

'Food technology is incredibly interesting,' she babbled. 'And can you believe it? Here I am, living on an *olive farm* and the processing of the olives is far more complicated than I ever thought it could be. Not only that, but there's the potential for us to expand our operations from providing just table olives. We could make our own olive oil too. And, I mean…' She knew she was jabbering, but couldn't help it. 'Obviously, that's down the track a bit, but…' She shrugged and forced herself to stop.

'It sounds fascinating.'

She glanced up to see if he was making fun of her, but sincerity radiated from him. 'You sound as if you've hit the ground running, Quinn, as if you've found your groove.'

'That's exactly what it feels like.'

'I'm happy for you. Really happy.'

She believed him.

He set his knife and fork down and patted his stomach. 'That hit the spot. Thank you.'

She collected up his plate and cutlery. 'I should be the one thanking you. If you hadn't kept hassling me about the possibility of going to uni I'd have continued to dismiss it. You made me shine a light on my own irrationality.' She grimaced, shrugged and tried to scratch the spot that itched. 'I felt that I'd lost my parents and Phillip to higher education. I mean that's utter rubbish, of course. I lost them to their own ambitions and prejudices. And you were right—in pursuing further study I won't become like them. I'll never be like them.'

'I'm glad you can see that now.'

She wouldn't have if it hadn't been for him. The sense of obligation weighed heavily on her, though, and she didn't know why. She rinsed his plate. 'I can't believe how many different study options there are. I have the choice of full-time, part-time, distance and all sorts of mixed mode delivery methods.' It made it very easy for people like her to fit study in around a busy timetable.

But enough about her. 'How are things in Sydney?'

'Excellent! I'm doing some freelance work for my old law firm.'

His grin told her how much he was enjoying it.

'And the big news is that my mother is running Derek Oxford's campaign.'

She did her best to pick her jaw up off the floor. 'Derek… your old second in command?'

'The very one.'

She sat. 'Wow! We've created a monster.'

'She's brilliant at it.'

'I don't doubt it for a moment.' She found herself laughing. 'I don't envy the opposition parties at all.'

'Mum, is it time yet?' Robbie and Chase stared from the doorway.

Aidan smiled, his eyes alive with fun. 'Are you up for a day of showing me around your new life, Quinn?'

A thrill shook through her. She leapt up. 'Just give me a few minutes to get ready.'

Quinn raced off to her bedroom with its tiny en-suite bathroom. It wasn't until she'd pulled on one of her prettiest blouses, though, that it suddenly hit her—she'd just put on a full face of make-up and pulled on her best jeans. A slow churning in her stomach had her dropping to the side of her bed. *What on earth do you think you're doing?*

She and Aidan, they weren't going anywhere. Things between them weren't going to progress beyond friendship.

They already have.

Then she had to put a stop to it before it was too late and someone got hurt.

She was not going to dress up for Aidan. She was not going to try and look pretty for him. She was not going to flirt with him. He might not consider her a complication yet, but he would eventually and she wasn't *ever* going to let that opportunity arise.

Slowly she stowed her pretty blouse back into the wardrobe and then went to scrub her face clean. She slipped on a long-sleeved button-down shirt that covered her from neck to mid-thigh. It was respectable, boring and asexual.

She glanced in the mirror and grimaced. Perfect.

Even though Quinn did her very best to maintain her guard, she had a day filled with laughter and fun. Aidan even taught them all a new fun novelty song.

'You've chosen a spectacularly beautiful place to live,' he said.

'I can't believe how beautiful it is here,' she admitted. Pokolbin was Hunter Valley wine country. Vineyards and grapevines spilled across gently rolling hills that spread out lazily in every direction. The vistas that greeted her whenever she topped a rise could still make her catch her breath. 'I never realised I was such a rural girl at heart.'

'Aidan, I have a problem,' Robbie suddenly said, his face serious and his eyes puckered.

They'd stopped for cake and coffee—milkshakes for the boys—and his young face looked so serious she straightened on her seat. He hadn't mentioned anything to her!

'What's up, buddy?'

Aidan took her son's words completely in his stride. She rolled her shoulders and forced herself to sit back in her chair.

'I don't like olives,' he whispered. 'And Chase doesn't either.'

She had to bite her lip to hide a smile, her heart filling with love for her serious elder son.

'We don't like olives, but Aunt Mara and...' he shot her a glance '...Mum love them. And I know that they're the reason we live out here and that we have money for food and other stuff. And we love living out here, but... they taste awful!'

'I see,' Aidan said, just as serious as her son.

Robbie crumbled off a piece of his cake. 'It makes me feel bad that I don't like them.'

She opened her mouth, but a swift glance from Aidan had her shutting it again.

'It's not that you don't like olives, guys. It's just that you don't like the taste of them. And, frankly, mostly it's adults who like to eat olives anyway so I don't think you should feel bad.' He leaned in closer. 'You know what you could say?'

Both boys stared at him. He had their complete attention and her eyes suddenly burned. They hungered for a male influence in their lives. Problem was, it was the one thing she couldn't give them.

'You can say that you love olives, but you just don't like to eat them. And by not eating any that leaves the farm all the more to sell.'

Robbie's face lit up. 'And that means more money for the farm!'

'Precisely.'

With both boys happy again, Aidan winked at her over the rim of his mug and she realised she had to put a stop to all of this as soon as she could. When she'd been worried, earlier, about someone getting hurt. She'd been thinking about him. She'd been thinking about herself. Not her boys. With each visit he won a little more of their trust and was given another piece of their hearts.

Her mouth dried. What had she been thinking? She couldn't risk their happiness like that.

She glanced down into her mug. She hadn't been thinking. That was the problem. She'd been too busy enjoying the ride, enjoying feeling like a desirable woman again, which just went to show what a fool she was.

'Are you okay?'

She glanced up to find those amber eyes focused on her. They narrowed to slits at whatever they saw in her face. He glanced at his watch and then slapped a hand to the table. 'Eat up, guys. It's almost time we were back at the shop like we promised your aunt.'

Mara had conscripted the boys into helping for the last hour this afternoon. It had been her way of tactfully ensuring that Quinn and Aidan had some time alone. Luckily, the boys loved helping in the shop. At the time Quinn had gritted her teeth at these machinations, but now she was grateful for them.

The sooner she brought a halt to all of this, the better.

Her heart slumped. So did her shoulders. There was nothing she could do about her heart, but she forced her shoulders back, forced a smile to her face. 'My cake was delicious. How was yours?'

It occurred to her then that it'd be a long time before she could face a piece of cake again with any equanimity.

'You want to tell me what's wrong?'

Quinn and Aidan strolled among the olive trees, back towards the house after having walked the boys to the on-site shop. The Olive Branch was a small but charming sandstone building stocked with olives picked from Mara's olive groves along with sourdough bread sourced from a local bakery, cheese from a local cheese maker and an assortment of recipe books.

Tourists found the place irresistible. To be perfectly frank, so did she and the boys. She and Aidan had stayed to watch the boys serve several customers and the way their chests had puffed out at Aidan's praise had made her heart burn.

'Quinn?'

Oh, how to do this gently?

She turned and swallowed. 'Aidan, I really like you. You're a lovely man.'

He closed his eyes and swore. Her heart clenched up harder and smaller than an olive stone.

'Give us some time, Quinn, please, before launching us into this kind of conversation.'

He opened his eyes and they flamed at her.

'Why?' she croaked. 'What would be the point?'

'The point?' He straightened. He shifted his stance, as if trying to hold back a torrent of angry words. Beyond him, the sun had started to lower behind the ridge of the ranges, turning the day smoky even as the edges of everything somehow retained their clarity. She glanced around at all the golden greenness and blue afternoon beauty and wondered how despair could eat away at her so completely.

This morning she'd been happy!

This morning you were still hiding your head in the sand.

He leaned towards her, his jaw set. 'The point is we have the chance to develop something not just good but spectacular if you give us a chance.'

Her heart pounded and her every muscle twitched. If she'd been a bird she'd have taken flight. Even thinking about what he proposed hurt. Hoping for what could never be hurt.

You ruined my life! She would never give Aidan the chance to hurl those words at her.

'You're wrong.' She might be crumbling inside but her voice emerged strong and sure. 'You have to stop coming around. The boys are coming to love you too dearly. They're starting to depend on you too heavily. This has to stop before someone gets hurt.'

His gaze held hers, fierce and strong. 'It's too late for that, Quinn. I'm already in too deep.'

A tremble shook her. She swayed. Whatever golden was left of the day leached out of it. 'Oh, Aidan.'

He stood straight and proud like a warrior and it occurred to her that he must cut a commanding figure in a courtroom. She might have just dealt his hopes a death-blow, but he was neither cowed nor vanquished.

His chin lifted. 'I can't believe you won't even consider the possibility of us.'

Scorn, closely held in check, rippled beneath his words. She flinched.

'Why?' he demanded. 'Why won't you even consider it?'

She flung an arm out. 'Let me count the ways!'

He widened his stance and folded his arms. 'Then let's have them.'

The amber of his eyes glowed and the longer she looked at him the more her mouth started to water. She clenched her hands to stop from doing anything stupid like reach for him.

'You don't want to make this easy, do you?'

'Not on your life.' And then it seemed as if he almost might smile. 'I have no intention of making it easy for you to walk away from me.'

She had to bend at the waist and draw in a breath, draw in her courage. She straightened. 'I know you don't think the distance between here and Sydney is prohibitive, but I do. I'm not into long distance relationships.'

'But if I set up a practice in either Newcastle or Maitland that problem won't exist. Did you know,' he said pleasantly as if they were talking about nothing more innocuous than the weather, 'that Maitland is one of the fastest growing regional centres in the state at the moment?'

He would relocate. For her?

No!

'Your mother doesn't like me and she's been through enough.'

'Once she gets to know you properly, my mother will love you.'

Her eyes suddenly narrowed. 'Is that why you hassled me so much about going to university? Because in my current "uneducated" state—at least in your and my family's estimation—I wouldn't be good enough for you all otherwise?'

'I'm not even going to dignify that with an answer.' He glared. 'I can see how this stupid inferiority complex of yours has been created by your parents and Phillip.'

'Stupid?' Her mouth worked but no other words emerged.

He stabbed a finger at her. 'I have never wanted anything for you but your happiness. A happiness you're pig-headedly determined to avoid.'

'Pig-headed?' She ground her teeth together. She told herself he had a right to his anger. She was dashing his hopes, hurting him. She tried to settle a mantle of rationality about her. 'We haven't known each other long enough to fall in love.'

He was quiet for a long moment. His eyes never left her face and it was all she could do not to fidget. 'I believe that's true of you,' he finally said, 'but it's not true for me.'

Her stomach gave a sickening lurch.

'It's why I've tried to take things slow.'

She flashed back to her hotel room last Saturday night.

'I fell in love with you the moment you ordered me to take a deep breath and relish the day.'

'Because I reminded you of Danny.' He was in love with a mirage!

'Because you reminded me that the world was good, that life could be good again and that it should be lived.'

The mirage vanished. He loved her? He truly loved her? She tried to gather her scattered thoughts, tried to seize hold of her common sense. 'Do you have an answer for everything?'

'Of course I do. I'm a lawyer.'

A laugh shot out of her, just like that. *This is no time for laughing!* She snapped her mouth shut.

Aidan's face gentled. The afternoon had started to cool, although they weren't far enough into autumn to need sweaters yet. A flock of sulphur-crested cockatoos wheeled around an ancient gum tree further up the hill, their raucous cries filling the air and masking the soft chirrup of a flock of rainbow lorikeets that swooped through the olive grove, heading for the bottlebrush trees on the opposite hill.

She tried to not let it all filter into her soul and relax her—or relax her guard.

'Quinn, what are you really afraid of?'

She moistened her lips. 'That you will eventually accuse me of ruining your life.'

'You'll only ruin it if you walk away.'

His eyes urged her to believe him. Her heart wavered, but she shook her head. They were just words and while she didn't doubt that Aidan meant them in the present moment she had no faith in their longevity.

She prayed for strength. 'You and your family, Aidan, you come from the same world as my parents, the same world as Phillip and his parents. Phillip's parents told him, and me, that I would ruin his life. Before he left, Phillip told me that was true—that I had wrecked his life. Your family believes the exact same thing. And eventually you will too.' She gripped her hands tightly in front of her. 'I'm sorry but I'm not prepared to go through all that again.'

He stared at her. And then his face changed, darkening until thunder practically rolled off his brow and lightning flashed from his eyes. A torrent of angry words shot out of him, most of them not repeatable.

'Of all the idiotic, cock-brained ideas!'

She blinked. Her shoulders started to hunch as he continued with a list of adjectives to describe her way of thinking. Her wrong-headed way of thinking, according to him. Aidan had never yelled at her before. Not really. And it was strange to discover that she hated it. Really, deep down in her gut hated it. She'd finally snapped his control. And she hated that too. Because...

She loved him.

She'd have laughed at the irony, only she didn't have the heart for it. She might love him, but that didn't change a damn thing. She already knew that love wasn't always enough.

He wheeled away from her, only to wheel back again. 'So, in essence, this all comes down to courage and the fact you have none?'

She stiffened at that. She might've lost her heart, but she still had her pride. 'I beg your pardon?' The way her voice shook, though, destroyed the effect of the iciness she'd tried to inject.

'You demanded courage from me when I was dealing with my mother.'

'That was completely different!'

'How?' he shot back. 'I wasn't leading the life I should've been leading. Just as you're not leading the life you should be leading.'

'Yes I am!' But, while they held vehemence, her words lacked conviction.

'You want to know your problem, Quinn?'

She folded her arms. 'What, I only have the one?' She knew she was being immature but she couldn't help it.

'You don't believe you're worth fighting for.'

Her mouth dried.

His eyes were hard, but strangely gentle too. 'I can slay all the other dragons for you. I can offer you all the assurances in the world. But this particular dragon is one you have to slay for yourself.'

He was going to walk away now, just as she'd wanted him to. And everything inside her wanted to sob.

His face twisted. 'Damn it, do you really think I'm like your parents? Do you really think I'm like Phillip?'

Her head rocked back. Of course not! But...

But what?

The ground lurched beneath her feet. She tried to steady herself against the branch of an olive tree, but it was thin and threatened to snap. She reeled over to a weathered fence post and leaned against it, careful not to catch herself on the barbed wire. She'd have to ask Mara why they had barbed wire on the property—an idle thought that filtered into her head and out again almost immediately.

She glanced across at Aidan. 'No.' The word croaked out of her. 'I don't think you're like Phillip.'

The hard light in his eyes died, replaced with an uncertainty that tore at her. 'And?'

She moistened her lips. That fact changed everything. If Aidan wasn't like the others—and she knew with everything inside her that he wasn't—then...

'Quinn?'

'It means something about my reasoning is wrong.' She slid down to the ground. 'I'm...I'm trying to work out just what that is.'

He lowered himself to the ground. Reaching out, he took her hand. 'I'm not rushing you, I swear I'm not, but... do you think there's even the slightest chance that you could ever love me?'

Her throat ached. 'Oh, I love you, Aidan, there's no doubt about that.' She held up a hand to keep him where he was when he made as if to gather her up in his arms. Tears burned behind her eyes but she refused to let them fall. 'The thing is, you see, I know that sometimes love isn't enough.'

He stared at her and she swore she saw the life drain out of his face inch by inch. The lump in her throat nearly choked her.

'So that's it, is it?' The words dropped out of him, flat and colourless.

Was it? Slowly she shook her head. 'You're not like Phillip. You're not like my parents. I...I need to think that through more thoroughly.' She had to work out what it meant for them—if it meant anything for them.

He continued to stare at her, but she couldn't tell what he was thinking.

'You said you wouldn't rush me!'

He dragged a hand down his face.

She chafed her arms against the rising tide of fear that threatened to swallow her. 'If you give me an ultimatum— make a decision now or else—I…I would have to tell you goodbye.' It almost killed her to say it, but she forced the words out all the same.

He shook his head as if it were a weight he could barely lift. 'I'm not going to give you an ultimatum, Quinn.'

But his face had gone grey and lines fanned out from his mouth and she had to close her eyes. 'Forgive me for dragging this out, Aidan,' she croaked. 'But I have to be sure.'

She set her back against the post and pushed upright. 'Not just for my sake, but for Robbie and Chase's too. And for yours.'

With that she turned and headed for the house.

'Quinn!'

It was a cry of raw pain. Tears scalded her eyes. 'I'll call you. I promise.' She didn't turn around. She didn't break stride. She kept her eyes fixed forward.

Quinn spent the next week missing Aidan so much her mind refused to answer a single question she needed it to. And those questions went around and around in an endless litany, denying her even a moment of peace. What if Vera never warmed to her or the boys? What if Aidan's friends refused to accept her, convinced she wasn't good enough for him? Would she be able to cope with seeing her parents at other society 'dos'? What if Aidan regretted setting up a practice locally? What if he found himself pining for his firm in Sydney? He'd blame her. What would she do if he broke her heart? It'd send her into the kind of spin she shied from even thinking about.

What if...? What if...? What if...?

She woke in the middle of the night, cheeks wet, and aching for him with everything she had. She stood on the brink of something amazing and exhilarating that could end in disaster. And she couldn't work out if it was worth it or not.

The following Saturday night she and Mara played Monopoly with the boys. Robbie turned to her. 'Mum, do you think I'll ever find a girl I'll want to marry and who'll want to marry me too?'

She handed Chase the dice for his turn. 'I'm sure you will, honey.'

'But Alison at school says I have to marry her!'

Mara chuckled. Quinn sucked her lip into her mouth and bit on it until she could school her features. 'I promise you don't have to marry anyone that you don't want to.'

He gazed at her gloomily. 'But she's nice. I like her. So why don't I want to marry her when she wants to marry me?'

Ah... 'That's the way it goes sometimes, honey. We can be friends with lots and lots of people and we can like them lots and lots, but it doesn't mean we want to marry them. You can't force someone to want to marry you. It doesn't work that way.'

He stared back and finally nodded. 'Okay.'

He seemed happy to take her word for it.

'Is Aidan going to visit us tomorrow?'

She didn't like the way the conversation moved from marriage to Aidan as if...as if it were some logical leap. She fought back a frown. 'I don't think so.'

'Doesn't he like us any more?'

'Sure he does,' Chase chimed in. 'He likes Mum and us best of all. He was sad in Perth. But he wasn't sad when he was with us.'

It took all her strength to choke back a sob. 'Bedtime,' she croaked.

She fell into her chair after putting the boys to bed. Mara pushed a mug of tea across to her. She tried to dredge up a smile. 'Some days they're exhausting.'

Mara merely raised an eyebrow.

Quinn burst into tears.

'Sorry,' she mumbled when she finally had control of them.

Mara sipped her tea. 'Would it be of any interest to you to know that Aidan is staying at the Ross's bed and breakfast at the end of the lane?'

Quinn shot to her feet. He was? Really? She half turned towards the door and then halted. She sat again and chafed her arms.

'Are you afraid of being happy, Quinn?'

She curled her hands around her mug. 'I'm afraid of making another mistake.' And then all those questions that had been plaguing her came pouring out—about his mother and his friends and his job and her parents and what ifs galore.

Mara sat back and surveyed her. 'Does what your parents think have any bearing on your decision to see Aidan again or not?'

'No, of course not.'

Mara didn't say anything, but she lifted that darn eyebrow again. 'Aidan is a grown man. And an intelligent one. He knows his own mind.'

She hunched over her mug. 'You're saying I should extend the same trust to him that I do to myself.'

Mara remained silent. Quinn stared into her tea. Suddenly, just like that, everything stilled. Her head snapped up. She'd been hiding behind all of those issues when… when it all came down to a simple question of trust.

Did she trust Aidan?

She shot to her feet. 'The B&B at the end of the lane?'

'That's right.'

Quinn grabbed a wrap from the hook by the door and set off down their lane at a run. She didn't even stop to catch her breath when she reached the B&B, but burst up to the front door and knocked.

She stared blankly at the man who answered. Oh! She kicked herself. Of course Aidan wouldn't answer the door. 'Hello, Mr Ross, it's Quinn Laverty from the olive farm. I understand that Aidan Fairhall is staying here and I wondered if I could have a word with him.'

'Sorry, love, but he's not here.'

He'd left? Her shoulders sagged. She backed up a step. 'I'm sorry to have bothered you.' The words almost choked her. 'Goodnight, Mr Ross.'

She turned away. The door closed behind her, shutting her out in the dark. Tears stung her eyes. She tossed her pashmina around her shoulders and held on tight. Of course Aidan had left. What hope had she given him?

'Quinn?'

She halted mid-sniffle. With a heart that barely dared to hope, she turned. 'Aidan? But…but Mr Ross said…'

He'd said that Aidan *wasn't there*. He hadn't said Aidan had decamped back to Sydney.

'I went out for a walk.'

She couldn't drag her gaze from him.

He shifted his weight. 'You wanted to see me?'

A smile built through her. He was here and it had to mean something. It had to mean he hadn't given up on her. Oh, how she loved him! 'Shall I be a hundred per cent honest?'

He folded his arms. 'It's the only way.'

She pulled in a breath, pulled her wrap about her more securely. 'I've spent all week wanting to see you, Aidan.'

'All you had to do was pick up the phone.'

She took a step closer, breathed him in. 'I've not just wanted it, but craved it with everything I am. It freaked me out.'

'I see.'

He stared at her. In the moonlight his face looked beautiful but grim and her heart caught. 'Yes, you probably do. You've seen everything much clearer than I have.'

Something quickened in his face. Suddenly she recognised what it was—hope. 'Oh! I'm not trying to drag this out and make it harder for you, Aidan! I love you. I want to be with you. I want there to be an *us*. If that's what you still—'

She didn't get any further. She found herself in Aidan's arms, caught up in a vortex of desire, relief, frustration and remembered pain as his mouth came down on hers and they kissed like wild things rather than the polite civilised people they pretended to be to the world. When they eventually broke apart they were both breathing heavily. Quinn rested her forehead against his jaw. 'Wow.'

He cupped her face and drew away to stare down at her. 'You mean it?'

'Yes.'

He smiled then and it held so much joy it swept all of the old pain away. 'I love you, Quinn.'

'I love you, Aidan.'

'I love your boys too. I'm going to be the best father I can be to them.'

Father?

He grinned at the way her eyes widened. 'When I ask you to marry me you are going to say yes, aren't you?'

She didn't even hesitate. 'Yes.'

'Excellent. Now that we have the important points out

of the way, you want to tell me how you *finally* came to the right conclusion—that we *could* work and that we *should* be together?'

She smiled up at him. 'I only realised it all a moment or two before I came hurtling up the lane to find you. All of those reasons I'd been giving you for why we couldn't be together, I realised they were just issues I'd been hiding behind. The question I should've been asking myself was—Do I trust you? When I finally asked the right question, it all fell into place.'

She sobered. 'I do trust you, Aidan. I asked myself what you'd do if you were unhappy in a relationship.' She shook her head. 'You wouldn't just walk away. You wouldn't seethe or fester in silence either. You'd work at making things better.' Communication was important to him. 'You don't have a shallow heart. You have a heart that is deep and true and will weather storms.'

His eyes darkened. 'I'll weather any storm with you, Quinn. But do you believe that you have a heart that is deep and true too?'

That was the risk Aidan took, she suddenly saw.

Her heart pounded. Ice touched her nape, but she refused to let the fear overcome her. She thought back over her life and how she'd dealt with her parents...with Phillip...and with her two gorgeous boys. Gradually a weight started to lift and the chill receded. 'Yes,' she breathed, beaming her love straight at him. 'Yes, I do.'

His hands went around her waist, drawing her closer. 'My lovely girl,' he whispered against her lips.

She cupped his face in her hands. 'I'm sorry it took me so long to realise the truth. Tell me you forgive me. I love you, Aidan. I love you with my whole heart.'

'Sweetheart—' he grinned down at her '—there's nothing to forgive. I needed you to be as sure about us as I was.'

She sobered. 'And are you?'

'I love you. I want to build a life with you. I have never been surer of anything in my life.'

His lips descended to hers and if she'd had any lingering doubts they'd have melted away. She flung her arms around his neck and kissed him back with all the love in her overflowing heart.

* * * * *

Join Britain's BIGGEST Romance Book Club

MILLS & BOON®

Why shop at millsandboon.co.uk?

Each year, thousands of romance readers find their perfect read at millsandboon.co.uk. That's because we're passionate about bringing you the very best romantic fiction. Here are some of the advantages of shopping at millsandboon.co.uk:

* **Get new books first**—you'll be able to buy your favourite books before they hit the shops

* **Get exclusive discounts**—you'll also be able to buy our specially created monthly collections, with up to 50% off the RRP

* **Find your favourite authors**—latest news, interviews and new releases for all your favourite authors and series on our website, plus ideas for what to try next

* **Join in**—once you've bought your favourite books, don't forget to register with us to rate, review and join in the discussions

Visit **www.millsandboon.co.uk**
for all this and more today!